BLOODLINES

By Karen Traviss

CITY OF PEARL
CROSSING THE LINE
THE WORLD BEFORE

STAR WARS: REPUBLIC COMMANDO: HARD CONTACT
STAR WARS: REPUBLIC COMMANDO: TRIPLE ZERO
STAR WARS: LEGACY OF THE FORCE: BLOODLINES

STAR WARS

LEGACY OF THE FORCE

BLOODLINES

KAREN TRAVISS

arrow books

Published in the United Kingdom by Arrow Books in 2006

1 3 5 7 9 10 8 6 4 2

First published in the United Kingdom in 2006 by Arrow

Arrow Books Limited
The Random House Group Limited
20 Vauxhall Bridge Road, London, SW1V 2SA

Random House Australia (Pty) Limited
20 Alfred Street, Milsons Point, Sydney,
New South Wales 2061, Australia

Random House New Zealand Limited
18 Poland Road, Glenfield
Auckland 10, New Zealand

Random House (Pty) Limited
Isle of Houghton, Corner of Boundary Road & Carse O'Gowrie,
Houghton 2198, South Africa

Random House Publishers India Private Limited
301 World Trade Tower, Hotel Intercontinental Grand Complex,
Barakhamba Lane, New Delhi 110 001, India

The Random House Group Limited Reg. No. 954009

www.randomhouse.co.uk

A CIP catalogue record for this book is available from the British Library

Papers used by Random House are
natural, recyclable products made from wood grown in
sustainable forests. The manufacturing processes conform to
the environmental regulations of the country of origin

ISBN 9780099492030 (from Jan 2007)
ISBN 0 09 9492032

Printed and bound in Great Britain by Bookmarque Ltd, Croydon, Surrey

For Bryan Boult

acknowledgments

My grateful thanks go to my editors, Shelly Shapiro (Del Rey) and Sue Rostoni (Lucasfilm), for their support and for letting me bring back Boba; my agent, Russ Galen, for handling all the small print; Ray Ramirez, for great Mando armor; Ryan Kaufman, for patient reading and generous encouragement; to Tom Hodges, for giving Vevut and Orade a face; and all the Fett fans and other Mando *fando'ade* who have indulged my Mandalorian habit without reservation. *Oya Manda!*

THE STAR WARS NOVELS TIMELINE

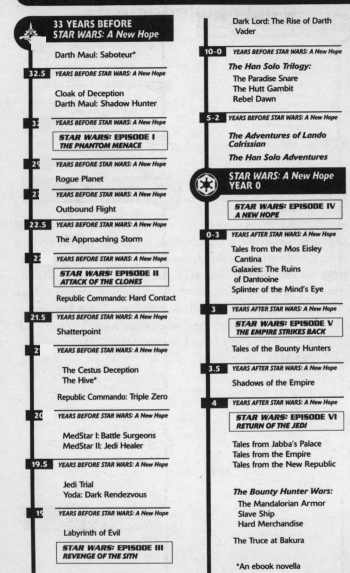

33 YEARS BEFORE STAR WARS: A New Hope

Darth Maul: Saboteur*

32.5 YEARS BEFORE STAR WARS: A New Hope

Cloak of Deception
Darth Maul: Shadow Hunter

32 YEARS BEFORE STAR WARS: A New Hope

**STAR WARS: EPISODE I
THE PHANTOM MENACE**

29 YEARS BEFORE STAR WARS: A New Hope

Rogue Planet

27 YEARS BEFORE STAR WARS: A New Hope

Outbound Flight

22.5 YEARS BEFORE STAR WARS: A New Hope

The Approaching Storm

22 YEARS BEFORE STAR WARS: A New Hope

**STAR WARS: EPISODE II
ATTACK OF THE CLONES**

Republic Commando: Hard Contact

21.5 YEARS BEFORE STAR WARS: A New Hope

Shatterpoint

21 YEARS BEFORE STAR WARS: A New Hope

The Cestus Deception
The Hive*

Republic Commando: Triple Zero

20 YEARS BEFORE STAR WARS: A New Hope

MedStar I: Battle Surgeons
MedStar II: Jedi Healer

19.5 YEARS BEFORE STAR WARS: A New Hope

Jedi Trial
Yoda: Dark Rendezvous

19 YEARS BEFORE STAR WARS: A New Hope

Labyrinth of Evil

**STAR WARS: EPISODE III
REVENGE OF THE SITH**

Dark Lord: The Rise of Darth Vader

10-0 YEARS BEFORE STAR WARS: A New Hope

The Han Solo Trilogy:
The Paradise Snare
The Hutt Gambit
Rebel Dawn

5-2 YEARS BEFORE STAR WARS: A New Hope

The Adventures of Lando Calrissian

The Han Solo Adventures

STAR WARS: A New Hope YEAR 0

**STAR WARS: EPISODE IV
A NEW HOPE**

0-3 YEARS AFTER STAR WARS: A New Hope

Tales from the Mos Eisley Cantina
Galaxies: The Ruins of Dantooine
Splinter of the Mind's Eye

3 YEARS AFTER STAR WARS: A New Hope

**STAR WARS: EPISODE V
THE EMPIRE STRIKES BACK**

Tales of the Bounty Hunters

3.5 YEARS AFTER STAR WARS: A New Hope

Shadows of the Empire

4 YEARS AFTER STAR WARS: A New Hope

**STAR WARS: EPISODE VI
RETURN OF THE JEDI**

Tales from Jabba's Palace
Tales from the Empire
Tales from the New Republic

The Bounty Hunter Wars:
The Mandalorian Armor
Slave Ship
Hard Merchandise

The Truce at Bakura

*An ebook novella

dramatis personae

Barit Saiy; (Corellian male)

Ben Skywalker; (human male)

Boba Fett; Mandalore and semi-retired bounty hunter (human male)

Cal Omas; Chief of State, Galactic Alliance (human male)

Cha Niathal; Admiral, Galactic Alliance (Mon Calamari female)

Goran Beviin; Mandalorian soldier (human male)

G'vli G'Sil; Coruscanti Senator, head of the Galactic Alliance Security Council (human male)

Han Solo; captain, *Millennium Falcon* (human male)

Heol Girdun; captain, Galactic Alliance Guard (human male)

Jacen Solo; Jedi Knight (human male)

Jaina Solo; Jedi Knight (human female)

Leia Organa Solo; Jedi Knight, copilot, *Millennium Falcon* (human female)

Jori Lekauf; corporal, Galactic Alliance Guard (human male)

Lon Shevu; captain, Galactic Alliance Guard (human male)

Luke Skywaker; Jedi Grand Master (human male)

Lumiya; Dark Jedi (human female)

Mara Jade Skywalker; Jedi Master (human female)

Mirta Gev; bounty hunter (human female)
Taun We; scientist (Kaminoan female)
Thrackan Sal-Solo; Corellian Head of State (human male)

prologue

Atzerri system, ten standard years after the Yuuzhan Vong war:
Slave I *in pursuit of prisoner H'buk. Boba Fett's private record.*

"Whatever he's paying you, Fett, I'll *double* it," says the voice on the comlink.

They say that a *lot*. They just don't understand the nature of a contract. This time it's an Atzerri glitterstim dealer called H'buk who's overstepped the mark with the Traders' Coalition to the tune of four hundred thousand credits. The coalition feels it's worth paying me five hundred thousand credits to teach him—and everyone else—a lesson about honoring debts.

I agree with the Traders' Coalition wholeheartedly.

"A contract's a contract," I tell him. *Slave I* is close enough on his trail for me to get a visual on him: I swear he's flying an old Z-95 Headhunter. No hyperdrive, or he'd have jumped for it by now. And no wonder he's surprised. An old, old Firespray like *Slave I* shouldn't be able to catch him on sublight drive alone.

But I've fitted a few more . . . *extras* recently. The only completely original part of *Slave I* now is the seat I'm in.

"My laser cannon's armed," says H'buk, breathless.

"Good for you." Why they *always* want a conversation, I'll never know. Look, shoot or shut up; I *know* you'll have to come about to target me with that cannon, and in that second or two I'll take out your drives anyway. "The galaxy's a dangerous place."

The Headhunter executes a neat turn to port with its aft maneuvering jets and the *Slave*'s laser locks on to the Headhunter's drive signature, matching its turns and loops with no need for guidance from me. His engine flares in a ball of white light. The fighter begins an uncontrolled roll and I have to gun it to get the tractor beam locked and haul H'buk in.

The grapple arms make a satisfying *chunk-unkkkk* against the Headhunter's airframe as I secure the fighter against the casing above *Slave*'s torpedo launcher. The sound of that reverberating through your hull, I'm told, is just like a cell door closing behind you: the point at which prisoners lose all hope.

Funny; that would only make me fight harder.

H'buk is making the noises of panic and pleading that I hardly notice these days. Some prisoners are defiant, but most give in to fear. He makes me offers all the way back to Atzerri, promising anything to survive.

"I can pay you millions."

The contract is to deliver him alive. It's *very* specific.

"And my stock holdings in Kuat Drive Yards."

I think it's the silent routine that gets to them in the end.

"Fett, I have a beautiful daughter . . ."

He shouldn't have said that. Now I'm angry, and I don't often get angry. "*Never* use your kids, scumbag. *Never.*"

My father put me first. *Any* father should. Not that I ever felt pity—or anything—for H'buk, but I'm satisfied now that he deserves everything that the Traders' Coalition is going to do to him. If I were the sympathetic kind, I'd kill him. I'm not. And the contract says *alive.*

"Want to negotiate a landing fee?" asks Atzerri Air Traffic Control.

"Want to negotiate an ion cannon?"

"Oh . . . apologies, Master Fett, sir . . ."

They always see my point.

Landing on Atzerri is a little tricky when you're hauling a crippled fighter on your upperworks. I set *Slave I* down on the landing strip, lowering gently on the thrusters, feeling the aft section vibrating under the load. And I have an audience.

The coalition wants to show they can afford to hire the best to hunt down *anyone* who crosses them. I oblige. A bit of theater, a little public relations: like Mandalorian armor, it makes the point without a shot needing to be fired. I walk along *Slave I*'s casing to clamber up onto the Headhunter's fuselage and crack open its canopy seal with the laser housed in my wrist gauntlet. So I hit H'buk harder than I need to, and haul him out of the cockpit to rappel down ten meters to the ground on the lanyard with him.

It hurts deep in my stomach. I don't let anyone see that.

Then I deposit the prisoner on the landing strip in front of the men he owes four hundred thousand credits. It makes the point. I *like* making points. Presentation is half the battle.

"Want to keep the starfighter, too?" asks my customer.

"Not my taste." The spaceport utility loader comes to remove it from *Slave I*. I hold out my palm: I want the rest of my fee.

He hands me the outstanding 250,000 creds on a verified chip. "Why do you still do this, Fett?"

"Because people still ask me."

It's a good question. I ponder it while I sit back in the cockpit and catch up with the financial headlines on the HoloNet news as *Slave I* heads for Kamino on autopilot. My doctor is meeting me there. He doesn't like the long journey but I don't pay him to be happy.

Now I find I'm thinking of a daughter—Ailyn—who I haven't seen in fifty years, wondering if she's still alive.

You see, I'm ill. I think I'm dying.

If I am, then there are things I've got to do. One of them is to find out what happened to Ailyn. Another is to decide who's going to be Mandalore when I'm gone.

And the third, of course, is to cheat death.

I've had a lot of practice at that.

chapter one

*How long are we going to have to bounce from one crisis to the
next? We're facing our third galactic war in under forty years—a
real civil war. It's just skirmishing now, but if Omas doesn't crack
down much harder on dissent this will spiral out of control. We
need a period of stability and I fear we're going to have to knock
heads together much harder to get it.*

—Admiral Cha Niathal,
in private conversation with Mon Calamari Senate delegates

CHIEF OF STATE'S RECEPTION SUITE, SENATE
BUILDING, CORUSCANT, SIXTEEN DAYS AFTER
THE RAID ON CENTERPOINT STATION.

The worst thing about being thirteen years old was that one
moment you were expected to be an adult, and the next
everyone treated you like a child again.

Ben Skywalker—thirteen and confused about what was
expected of him—sat trying to be patient in the reception
area of Chief Cal Omas's offices in the Senate Building, taking his lead from his cousin Jacen Solo. It was the kind of
office designed to make you feel like you didn't matter: a
whole apartment could have slipped into the space between
the outer doors and the wall of Omas's personal office. Ben
almost expected to see tangled balls of misura vine rolling
across the spotless pale blue carpet, driven by a distant wind.
He couldn't see the point of all that empty space.

But the Senate Building had been occupied and changed
out of all recognition by the Yuuzhan Vong, Jacen said. Architects, designers, and an army of construction droids had
taken years to wipe away all traces of the alien invasion
and restore the building to the way it had been. Ben tried to

listen in the Force for the echoes of the aliens and their weird living technology, and thought he heard unrecognizable sounds. He shuddered and tried to occupy himself with the holozines stacked on the low greelwood table.

The 'zines were all very dull and slightly outdated current affairs weeklies and political analyses, but one of them displayed an image of Jacen. Ben picked it up and activated it, smiling at the next image of a rotating Centerpoint Station, which didn't look quite so good in real life since he had helped sabotage it.

It's good to feel part of something important.

The holoreport featured clips of Corellian news reports of the raid on Centerpoint, but it didn't mention Ben, and he wasn't sure if that upset him or not. Some recognition would have been nice; but the Corellian sources that were quoted were pretty rude about Jacen, calling him a traitor and a terrorist. The reporter's voice seemed to fill the room even though the volume was set to minimum and the carpet and tapestries on the walls muffled the sound.

The report wasn't very kind about Uncle Han, either. A middle-aged man Ben didn't recognize was telling the reporter what he thought. "So he calls himself a Corellian. But forget that Bloodstripe on his uniform pants—it might as well be a big yellow streak down his back, because Han Solo is just a Galactic Alliance puppet. He's betrayed Corellia by sitting on his backside doing whatever his Alliance buddies tell him to. And his son's just the same."

Jacen seemed embarrassed. Maybe he was more upset for his dad. Ben would have been.

"You should use an earpiece to listen to those privately," said Jacen.

"But you're famous." Ben offered him the holozine. "Want to see?"

Jacen raised one eyebrow and seemed more worried about his meeting with Chief Omas. "Fine, but I could do without Thrackan Sal-Solo using me to humiliate my father in front of Corellia. You realize he gave all this information to the media, don't you?"

"Yeah, of course I do. But if we're not ashamed of it, why does it matter? We did the right thing for the Galactic Alliance. Centerpoint Station was a threat to everyone."

Jacen turned his head very slowly with that half smile that Ben had learned meant he was impressed. "But a lot of worlds are taking Corellia's side now. So do you think those stories do any harm or not?"

Ben could always spot a test now. He knew he had to say what he believed: there was no point trying to be too clever. He wanted to learn from Jacen so badly that it burned him up. "Some worlds will always go against the Alliance anyway. So we might as well let the people on our side know we're taking action. Makes them feel safer."

Jacen nodded approvingly and Ben felt a little Force-touch somewhere in his mind, as if Jacen were patting him on the head. "That's very perceptive. I think you're right."

"Everyone will know *you're* doing your best to stop a war, anyway." Ben put the holozine back on the table and glanced at the rest of the titles. "There seem to be more pictures of you than anyone."

Jacen's smile faded for a moment and he glanced toward the doors of Omas's office, looking as if he was willing the head of the Galactic Alliance to finish his meeting and come out. Ben began to pick up what had caught Jacen's attention: there was a definite sense of conflict, of people arguing, and it was almost as clear as hearing it if you knew how to listen in the Force. Ben did now. Jacen was a good teacher.

Ben concentrated on Jacen's face. He looked a lot older lately. Sometimes he looked almost as old as Dad. "What's happening?"

"Heavyweight politics," said Jacen, barely audible.

He put his fingers almost to his lips, a very discreet gesture; it wasn't obvious to anyone else—*anyone else* in this case being only the aide at the desk outside Omas's grand double doors—but Ben took the hint. *Be quiet.*

He was suddenly worried about letting Jacen down. Chief Omas wasn't a stranger; the man knew his father, and Ben had been brought to meet him at a state celebration. Pretty much all Ben remembered of that affair was feeling very small in a sea of tall people having conversations he didn't understand. But Ben wanted to be seen as Jacen's apprentice, not as Luke Skywalker's son, the *heir to the dynasty* as one of the guests had called him. It was hard being the son of two Jedi Masters whom everyone referred to as "legends." Ben had lost count of the times he had felt invisible.

"Chief Omas won't keep you, Jedi Solo," said the aide, tilting her head slightly toward the closed doors of Omas's office itself. "He's with Admiral Niathal at the moment."

I'm invisible again, thought Ben.

He composed himself and sat down with his hands folded in his lap, a mirror of Jacen's own posture. He tried to count the number of different species of animal depicted on the huge tapestry that covered part of the wall opposite. What he had first thought was just a mass of random color was actually thousands of overlapping images of every animal he could imagine from across the galaxy—across the whole Galactic Alliance.

Eventually the doors parted and Niathal strode out, radiating annoyance. Chief Omas appeared in the doorway behind her and forced a smile. "Ah, Jacen," he said. "I'm sorry to keep you. Won't you come in? And Ben. I'm glad you could make it, too."

Niathal glanced at Jacen as if she didn't recognize him. He acknowledged her with a slight bow of his head.

"Admiral," he said, smiling. "A pleasure to see you."

Niathal turned a little more to the side, the equivalent of

a very frank stare for a Mon Calamari, a species with side-set eyes, and scrutinized both of them. "You did a very fine job at Centerpoint Station, sir. And you, young man."

My name's Ben. But he had learned a little diplomacy now. "Thank you, ma'am."

Omas beckoned Jacen forward, and Ben followed meekly. Omas did *not* make the tired comment that Ben had grown since he'd last seen him; nor did he look past him when he was talking to Jacen. The Chief met his eyes. It was both unsettling and exciting to be treated as an adult. Ben concentrated hard on what was being said.

Omas sat behind his desk rather than in the chair opposite them, as if he were taking cover. "So what brings you here, Jacen?"

"I have a proposal."

"Go ahead."

"Crippling Centerpoint Station only bought us time with Corellia. We might have a few months at most before it's operational again, and then we're back where we began but with a much more aggrieved Corellia that's gathering more support."

"Is this an extrapolation from what you see in the Force, Jacen?"

"No, it's just obvious to the point of inevitability."

Ben felt Omas teeter on the edge of reacting. It was as if the two men were having an argument without any sign of it in their words or their voices.

"Go on," said Omas.

"Now is the only time we'll have for preemptive action, before any real opposition to the Galactic Alliance has a chance to organize. Corellia, Commenor, and Chasin need complete dissuasion, very *public* dissuasion to make a point to other governments about the need for unity—and a complete neutralization of their capacity to fight a war. The destruction of their shipyards."

Ben was glad Jacen had said *destruction*. It was the first clue he'd had of what *dissuasion* actually meant.

"This," said Omas slowly, "is not unlike another conversation I've just had."

The way he said *conversation* made it clear what he'd been arguing about with Niathal. So she wanted to take action, exactly as Jacen did. "We've slapped Corellia and made a martyr to a cause," said Jacen. "An *armed* martyr to an *armed* cause."

"But Corellia has seen what we're made of, and that'll make them think twice."

"And we've now seen what *they're* made of," said Jacen. "And *I* have thought twice. If you give me command of a battle group, I can destroy the main shipyards and put an end to this now. If Corellia can be brought to heel, it sends the message that no single planet is bigger than the Alliance."

"You're asking me to declare war, Jacen, and that's something I'd never get Senate backing to do. And I know where the Jedi council stands on this."

"War's coming anyway. If you draw a weapon on a Corellian, you'd better be prepared to use it. We drew it when we took out Centerpoint."

Omas was doing a good job of disguising his fear, but Ben could feel it. It didn't feel as if he was afraid of Jacen; it was more a vague and formless dread, as if events were drowning him.

"Talking of Corellians, would this attack not drive a huge wedge between you and your father?"

"It might well," said Jacen. "But I'm a Jedi, and it's precisely that kind of personal motivation we're trained to disregard."

"I'll take it under advisement."

"I'll take that as a *no*." Jacen seemed perfectly calm. "I can tell you, with the certainty of the Force, that failing to stamp out dissent completely now will result in the deaths of billions in the coming years. We stand on a tipping point where we can choose chaos or order."

Omas meshed his fingers, hands on the desk, and stared at them. "I agree we have a volatile situation here. Yes, this *is* a tipping point. But I think that escalating military action will be what tips us over into war, not what limits it. I *remember* the Empire, Jacen. I lived through it. And I dread seeing us become that kind of government."

Jacen just gave Omas a little nod and stood up to leave. "Thank you for listening to my concerns."

They took the long walk back to the Senate lobby, down a broad corridor lined with blue and honey-gold marble inlay, and traveled down to the ground floor in a turbolift with walls so highly polished they were almost an amber mirror.

"Is politics always like that?" said Ben. "Why don't you both say what you mean?"

Jacen laughed. "Then it wouldn't be politics, would it?"

"And why does everyone keep saying, 'Oh, I remember the Empire . . .'? Uncle Han says it was bad, and so does Chief Omas. If they're both afraid of the same thing, why are they on opposite sides?"

Jacen seemed to find it very funny. Ben was embarrassed.

"I was only asking, Jacen."

"I'm not laughing at you. It's just very refreshing to hear someone cut through the nonsense and ask real questions."

"So what are you going to do next?"

Jacen checked his comlink. "Dad's still not responding. I need to clear the air with him. He's angry about Centerpoint."

"I meant about Chief Omas."

"We'll be patient. The solution will become clear—to both of us."

"You and Omas."

"No, you and me."

Ben was delighted that Jacen seemed to take his opinions seriously. He was more determined than ever to conduct himself like a man and not a boy. He knew now that he would never play again.

They crossed through the forest of pillars of the Senate lobby and emerged into the hazy sunshine that bathed the plaza.

Strung out in a ragged line, a group of around two hundred people had gathered to protest in front of the Senate Building. Dozens of Coruscant Security Force officers had formed a loose line in front of the building, but it looked peaceful. The occasional shout of "Corellia's not your colony!" made it clear who the protesters were. Coruscant was home to beings from almost every planet in the galaxy, and even when war seemed to be coming, they stayed here. Ben found that . . . odd. Wars were about front lines and distant planets, not about people who looked a lot like him and who almost lived next door.

"Something tells me we'd better not stop and sign autographs," said Ben.

Jacen stopped to look back at the protest. "How many Corellians do you think live in Galactic City?" One of the protestors in the crowd had projected a huge holoimage onto the face of the Senate Building: it read CORELLIA HAS A RIGHT TO SELF-DEFENSE. "Five million? Five billion?"

"Do you think they're dangerous?"

"I'm simply thinking what a complicated war this will be for Coruscant because so many Corellians live here."

"But we're not at war. Yet."

"Not as far as governments are concerned," said Jacen. "But feel what's around you."

Ben's Force-senses were a fraction of Jacen's, trained in

not much more than physical skills and the beginnings of true meditation. He closed his eyes. He felt the vague tingling at the back of his throat, the hint of something dangerous but far away. The slight breeze across the plaza swept scents of foliage with it. The protest continued, now a little noisier, but still peaceful.

"I can feel a threat, but it's a long way away." Ben opened his eyes, worried that he had answered the wrong question. "Like a really bad storm coming. Nothing more."

"Exactly," said Jacen. "Billions of unsettled, unhappy people ready to fight. People who want things to be settled. People who need peace."

"And that's our job, right?"

"Yes," said Jacen. "That's our job."

"And I'll be working with you."

Ben wanted to make sure. He was learning his first lesson in what Jacen called *expedience*. A few weeks ago he had been a commando, a hero, a real soldier who had helped sabotage Centerpoint Station and enraged the Corellian government. Now he had to be quiet and speak when he was spoken to. He needed to know if Jacen would only treat him as an adult when it suited him, like his father did.

On some planets, you were a man at thirteen and that was that; no going back, and no worrying about what your parents would say. Mandalorian boys became warriors after trials at thirteen, supervised by their fathers. Jedi were trained from childhood, too, but trials took an awful lot longer than that. Ben knew he wouldn't be a Jedi Knight until he was well into his twenties.

It seemed like a lifetime away. Suddenly he envied Mandalorian boys he would never meet.

"Yes," said Jacen at last. "Of course you will. It's not always going to be easy, but you can handle it. I know you can. Some of the things we'll talk about have to be kept between us, but that's the way with military matters. Are you ready for that?"

As if he would discuss anything with his father. He wasn't even comfortable discussing some things with his mother these days. "Like Admiral Niathal?"

Jacen smiled. Ben had guessed right again. "Yes, like the admiral, who I think is going to be an ally of ours."

"I understand, Jacen. I know this is serious."

"Good. That's what I needed to hear."

Ben basked in Jacen's approval but knew that wasn't the right thing to feel when they were talking about war. He was now very clear about the huge gulf between practicing with his lightsaber—which was a game—and then having to fight for real. People had already died. More would die in the future. Once the excitement of battle had worn off, he had thought about that a lot.

Right then, he wanted to know what had really happened to Brisha, the strange woman he hadn't much liked on first sight, and the Jedi called Nelani, whom they had traveled with. Jacen would say only that they had been killed—no details, no explanation—but Ben recalled none of it even though he was certain that he had been somewhere with them.

Did Jacen tell Dad, and not me?

It was eating at him. He hated not remembering things that felt important, and this did feel serious and worth remembering.

"Something's bothering you," said Jacen as they walked away, leaving the Coruscanti protest behind them.

Yes: Brisha and Nelani. But Ben decided that part of growing up was knowing when to do as you were told, not like a child who didn't know any better, but as a *soldier* who understood that sometimes there were things you didn't *need* to know.

"Nothing important," he said. "Nothing at all."

MINISTER KOA NE'S OFFICE,
CLONING FACILITY, TIPOCA CITY, KAMINO,
TEN STANDARD YEARS AFTER
THE YUUZHAN VONG WAR.

"You're dying," said the physician.

Boba Fett could see the man's reflection in the wall-wide sheet of transparisteel as he stared out over the choppy seas. Light beige coat, white-blond hair, ashen face: he must have wondered why Fett had summoned him all this way to carry out more tests.

Because I think I need the Kaminoans' special medical expertise, not just yours. And I'm right.

Tipoca City was a sad ruin of the minimalist elegance that it had been in his father's day, but its few crippled towers were still more of a haven for Fett than Coruscant would ever be. He concentrated hard on the dark surface of the sea and waited a few moments to see if the aiwhas were gathering in pods again, then took in the doctor's words and digested them.

They tasted familiar, inevitable, and yet were a ball of ice in his stomach. He resisted all movement in his facial muscles and presented a mask to the doctor that was as impenetrable as his Mandalorian helmet.

Dr. Beluine was one of only a handful who had ever seen him without it. Doctors could handle disfigurement a great deal better than most.

"Of course I'm dying," said Fett. "I'm paying you to tell me what I can *do* about it."

Beluine paused and Fett watched him glance at Koa Ne, the Kaminoan scientist now in charge of a cloning facility that was a shadow of its former self. Perhaps Beluine feared telling a professional killer that he had a terminal illness, or perhaps it was the pause of a good doctor trying to tell his patient the bad news as kindly as he could. Fett turned from the huge window, thumbs hooked over his belt, and raised his scarred brows in a silent question.

Beluine took the cue. "Nothing."

You give up easy, Doctor. "How long?"

"You have a standard year or two, if you take it easy. Less if you don't."

"Don't guess. I deal in facts."

Beluine's eyelids fluttered in a spasm of nervous blinking. "There are *always* uncertainties in prognosis, sir. But the degeneration of your tissues is accelerating, even in your transplanted leg, you have recurring tumors, and the medication isn't controlling your liver function any longer. It might have something to do with the . . . unusual nature of your background."

"That I'm a clone, you mean."

"Yes."

"I'll take that as a *don't know.*"

Beluine—Coruscant-trained, very expensive, very *exclusive*—had the look of a man on the brink of making a run for the door. "It's understandable that you'd want a second opinion."

"I've got one," said Fett. "*Mine.* And my opinion is that I'll die when I'm good and ready."

"I'm sorry to give you bad news."

"I've had worse."

"If I had access to the original Kaminoan laboratory records, then perhaps—"

"I need to talk to Koa Ne about that. Show the doctor out."

The Kaminoan politician, all politely unfeeling gray grace, indicated the doors, and the doctor slipped between them before they had fully opened. He was *very* anxious to leave. The doors hissed shut behind him.

"So where's the data?" said Fett. "And Taun We?"

"Taun We has . . . left."

Well, *that* was a surprise. Fett knew Taun We as well as anyone could—any human, anyway—and she'd seemed solidly loyal to her own kind. She'd looked after him as a boy when his father was away. He'd even *liked* her. "When?"

"Three weeks ago."

"Any reason for the timing?"

"Perhaps the galaxy's current political instability."

"So she bolted in the end, just like Ko Sai."

"I admit that some of my colleagues have shown a willingness to accept employment elsewhere."

Kaminoans weren't exactly keen on travel. Fett couldn't imagine anywhere they'd find tolerable beyond their own closed world. "And they took your data with them."

Koa Ne seemed hesitant. "Yes. We have never located Ko Sai's original research."

"So what's Taun We taken?"

"Apart from her human developmental expertise? A great deal of minor data."

The Kaminoans had lost their reputation as the top cloning technologists of the galaxy more than fifty years earlier when their scientists defected, but nobody had ever equaled their quality since. Anyone who could assemble that knowledge again would make a fortune—enough to boost a whole planet's economy, not just a bank account.

If he hadn't been dying, Fett would have been sorely tempted to grab the opportunity.

"Are you not concerned that Beluine might talk?" asked Koa Ne.

"He won't talk any more than my armorer or accountant would." Fett was looking for aiwhas again, letting the distraction order his thoughts, instinctively prioritizing the actions he now had to take. "They get paid for silence. So what if he tells the galaxy that I'm dying? I've been a dead man before."

"It creates instability."

"For who?"

"Mandalorians."

"You don't care about *us*."

Koa Ne, like all Kaminoans, didn't care about anything except Kamino, whatever impression the polite façade created. Fett's ambivalent view of Kaminoans veered more toward dislike the older he became. They were for hire, just as he had been. He'd taken a fee for some dubious causes himself in his time. But there was still something less than admirable about a species that grew others to do their fighting for them.

"We have always had a special regard for you, Boba."

He didn't like Koa Ne using his first name. *Have you still got any of my dad's tissue samples? Still planning to make some use of him? No, you couldn't keep the material intact that long, could you?* "No point hunting Taun We. Even the leg she cloned for me is degenerating. Spare parts won't help."

"*We* have a use for that technology—"

"*I* don't."

"Taun We may yet be useful to you. She is most skilled."

"Maybe you should have hired me to hunt Ko Sai a few decades ago, rather than go after Taun We now."

"We have . . . reason to believe someone found Ko Sai. But we had sufficient expertise left to continue cloning without her, even if we had lost the original research on control of aging."

"If anyone found it, they never tried to sell it. Who would sit on merchandise worth that much? Nobody *I* know."

It was probably Ko Sai's research that Fett needed now, but that was a trail that had gone very cold more than fifty years ago. Even *he* would have a tough job tracking it down.

But someone had it. Ko Sai had defected *somewhere*. There was always an audit trail to follow, as his accountant called it. And Taun We might be a lead to it. Maybe she had

taken the same route out. Maybe she had the same pay-
masters; top-class cloners were rare.

"We both have reasons to recover as much data and as
many personnel as we can," said Koa Ne. If the minister
had been human, Fett suspected he would have been smirking. "Will you help?"

"Making the most of me while I'm still alive?"

"Mutual benefit."

"Benefit costs." Fett turned away from the window and
picked up his helmet. "I don't do *help*."

He wondered if Koa Ne ever thought of his father, Jango,
and knew that if he did that it was purely in terms of his
utility to the Kaminoan economy. He shouldn't have been
offended that another professional viewed life so dispas-
sionately: he did, after all. But this was his *father*, and that
wasn't a subject he reduced to credits or convenience. Using
clones of his own father to defend Kamino against the clone
army of the Empire had always stuck in his throat. It was
the ultimate exploitation. His father would have shrugged
it off as an inevitable part of the deal, he knew, but he suspected it would have angered him deep down.

One of Dad's friends used to call them aiwha bait. *I remember that.*

"We can pay."

"Okay. Dead or alive?"

"Alive, of course. A million to bring Taun We back alive,
with the data."

"Two million to recover her, and an *extra* million for the
data. Three million."

"Excessive. I do believe your father was paid only five
million for what amounted to creating and training an
army."

"That's inflation for you. Take it or leave it."

The thought left a staccato trail in his mind like skipping
a stone across water, joining up previously disjointed ideas.

When the Kaminoans had last given any thought to Jango Fett, there had been hundreds of thousands—no, *millions* of men like him, and now there were none.

Fett lowered his helmet over his head again and settled into the reassurance and identity of its confines as so many of them would have done, inhaling the deflected warmth and scent of his own breath in the brief moment before the seal closed and the environmental controls kicked in. Had the men been deployed for the good of Mandalorians, the galaxy might have been a very different place today.

But that wasn't his problem.

A year left. Time enough, if I concentrate everything on it.

He had no idea why he had started thinking so much about the long-distant war lately. Perhaps it was because he had known what news Beluine would break to him.

I'm really going to die this time.

"You need this technology as much as we do," said Koa Ne. "One million."

"I'll find it. And it's still three million if you want me to hand it back to you when I've taken the data that I need." The most satisfying part of negotiation was knowing your walkaway point. He'd reached it now. "A professional's worth his fee, Koa Ne. Take it or leave it. I'll find someone able to pay a lot more than you can—just to cover my expenses, of course."

"But what use is your wealth to you now?"

In a human, it would have been cruel mockery of a dying man. But Kaminoans didn't have enough emotion in them for mockery.

"I've *always* got a use for it."

Koa Ne was right. He didn't need any more credits, or any more power and influence, either: politics really didn't interest him. He'd served too many politicians, often in their machinations against each other, and he didn't even relish being the *Mand'alor,* leader of the scattered Mandalorian community.

So why do I care at all?

He was the head of a ragbag of scattered *Mando'ade.* There were farmers and metalworkers and families scraping a living back on Mandalore, and there were any number of mercenaries, bounty hunters, and small communities in diaspora across the rest of the galaxy. It was hard to call them a nation. He wasn't even a head of state, not in the way Corellians or Coruscanti understood it. In the wake of the Yuuzhan Vong war, he had just a hundred commandos to call on, but they were still doing what Mandalorians had done for generations: eking out a grim existence in the Mandalore sector, defending Mandalorian enclaves, or taking on the wars of others. He had no idea how many more people who thought of themselves as Mandalorians were spread across the galaxy.

A hundred *Mando* warriors was still a force to be reckoned with, though. And every Mandalorian was still a warrior at heart, man and woman, boy and girl. They all still trained from childhood to fight.

I'm going to be dead within two years. I'm seventy-one. I should have another thirty in me, at least.

"Fett . . ."

No.

"Three million."

I'm not finished yet.

"Two million credits, to find Taun We and bring her back. That is my best offer."

I'm my father's son. Death is a risk, not a certainty. Not if you use your fear for focus.

"I'm rebuilding your economy," Fett said. Kao Ne might have been offended: it was hard to tell with Kaminoans. "Don't insult me with small change."

"You talk as if you have no emotional attachment to Taun We at all."

"This is business. Even if I'm dying."

"Take the bounty, and we will give you all our intelligence on her."

And if you had enough of that, you wouldn't need me.
"Three million."

"Remember that even *you* cannot succeed alone."

"They always say that," said Fett. This was where he walked away for good. "When I find Taun We, I'll auction the data to cover my expenses. Start saving."

Fett expected Koa Ne to run after him onto the landing platform, like stubborn customers always did when they saw sense. But when he glanced back behind him, the platform was empty.

Maybe that's all he could afford. Too bad. This is either my last hunt, or it's the start of a new fortune.

He liked the odds. Yes, he felt he had a fighting chance. A year was a long time for a bounty hunter.

He slid into *Slave I*'s cockpit and lowered the canopy. He'd spent a fortune restoring her for the third time—and adding modifications his father Jango would never have dreamed of. Sitting in her pilot's seat looking out on an endless storm-locked ocean, he was a nine-year-old child again, delighted to be allowed to fly a mission with his father.

This had once been his home. He'd been at his happiest here. He'd never been that happy since.

They said your past flashed before you when you were dying. But then people said a lot of things, and he never took any notice of them unless it paid him to do so.

Fett started up the drive and lifted *Slave I* into a standard escape trajectory. He needed to get on Taun We's trail. But Koa Ne was right: what use would his wealth be to him now? Other men left empires: other men had families whose futures their wealth would protect.

He checked his highly illegal and very reliable comm scanner and set it to watch for unusual share trading in bioengineering companies. Taun We had something to sell, and she would sell it . . . and the ripples would spread far enough for him to detect them sooner or later.

You've only got sooner. *There won't be a* later *for you, not unless you find the data.*

Even his father had wanted more than credits from the Kaminoans. He'd wanted a son.

I had a wife and a daughter once. I should have taken better care of them.

He'd have nothing to show for his life except a professional reputation, and a Mandalorian needed more than that. Being the Mandalore—halfhearted or otherwise—didn't give you a *clan*.

It was time to look up old contacts. Fett leaned back in the seat, removed his helmet, and stared at his reflection in the viewscreen as *Slave I* followed the course he had laid in for Taris.

He hadn't realized how much he'd missed Kamino.

chapter two

Is it me?

Is it me?

Am I deluding myself, Jaina? Am I making the same mistake as Grandfather? I have days—most days—when I'm as certain of this as I've ever been certain of anything. And then I have sleepless nights when I wonder if the path of the Sith is a lasting solution for peace in the galaxy, or if that's my ego speaking for me. It terrifies me. But if I were motivated by ambition, then I wouldn't suffer this doubt, would I? Jaina, I can't tell you all this, not yet. You wouldn't see it. But when you do, remember that you're my sister, my heart, and that part of me will always love you, no matter what.

Good night, Jaina.

DELETE * DELETE * DELETE

Jacen Solo's private journal; entry deleted

AIR TRAFFIC CONTROL FREIGHT LANE, CORONET AIRSPACE, CORELLIA.

Han Solo would never get used to having to sneak into Corellian space like a criminal.

It was one thing outrunning real enemies, but to crawl back to his homeworld in the *Millennium Falcon* under cover of a bogus transponder signal really rankled. He didn't like the Galactic Alliance any better than the next Corellian; being howled down as a traitor and an Alliance stooge actually *hurt*. Now he understood what it felt like to be a double agent, always doomed to be seen as the bad guy, never free to boast what a bang-up heroic secret job you were doing for the home team.

He wasn't going to use Leia's diplomatic status as a cover for his return, either. This was his home: he had a right to walk in anytime he liked. No, he wasn't sneaking in. He was making a *covert entry*. It was all about discretion.

Who was he kidding? *Discretion*. He fumed silently and banked the *Falcon* a little more sharply than he planned.

"You need to learn to meditate," said Leia.

"I don't like the sound of the coolant systems."

She adjusted them manually without being asked. "Time for some maintenance, then." Han's rough handling of the ship left Leia making silent but pointed safety adjustments that were as eloquent as a retort. "Before she blows a coolant line. Or you burst a major blood vessel."

"That obvious, huh?"

"And Jacen's left *three* messages."

Han jerked the *Falcon* hard to starboard, a little too hard. The stabilizing drive groaned in complaint. "I'm not rational enough to talk to him right now."

"Really? Never stopped you before."

"Okay, maybe I'll relax by asking Zekk what his intentions are towards Jaina."

"That would help matters a lot . . ."

"I liked Kyp better. Whatever happened there?" Han asked. "And what about Jag?"

"I shot him down. You know perfectly well I did."

"Oh, yeah. I do recall. And *I* intimidate her boyfriends, do I?"

"You'd already shot down Jag long before I ever took a laser cannon to him, honey. I've got a list of intimidated exboyfriends somewhere. There's just Zekk left to put through the grinder and then you've got the whole set."

Han wanted to let Leia prod him into a better mood with some well-aimed sarcasm, but for once it wasn't working. Things had always been so clear before. He always knew who the enemies were, and they were good plain ones worth shooting: the Empire, the Yuuzhan Vong, and any number of aliens whose purpose and intent was obvious—to threaten him and all those he held dear.

Now he was in conflict with those very people he'd fought to protect—his oldest friend and his own son—and regarded as a Galactic Alliance crony by his own people. It wasn't so easy to be a hero now, even if he knew he was right. He'd never known what it felt like to be the bad guy before.

Hey, I'm not the one who's wrong here. It's the Alliance.

"Sorry, sweetheart." He hated himself when he took it out on her. "I just get mad when he won't see history repeating itself here. Y'know, big empire making decisions for the galaxy, whether it wants it to or not?"

"Now, is that about Luke or Jacen?"

"Okay. Both."

How could Luke *not* see it? Didn't he see the warning signals? Didn't he see how much like the old Empire the Alliance was becoming?

You got a short memory, kid.

"I'll keep talking to Luke," said Leia. "But you talk to Jacen, okay? I'm worried about him."

"Will do."

"Promise?"

"Would I argue with you, Princess?"

"Yes. You always do."

"So . . . promise *me* this will never come between us."

Leia laid her hand on his as he grasped the steering yoke, and squeezed harder than he thought she ever could. It almost hurt. "We've come through a lot worse than this."

"That's true."

"It's just a few more gray hairs." She grinned again. "And I like you *better* with gray hair, actually."

That was all he needed. She always put the galaxy back together for him. She was solid and certain, and she was usually right. He sometimes wondered what his life would be like today if he hadn't met her—if he hadn't met Luke. *A space bum, and an old, tired one at that.* Leia had given him a sense of purpose beyond himself and the energy that went with it.

She'd also given him three kids who were his heart and soul, and he had no intention of seeing his only surviving son sucked further into the Alliance's drive for galactic control.

Han took the *Falcon* on a high approach path over Coronet, looking down the green patchwork of parks, public gardens, and farmland beyond that made it so very different from the Coruscant landscape. He set the ship down on the civic landing strip, merging among a variety of vessels of all sizes and states of repair, and shut down the drives.

"Okay, time to be ordinary," he said.

They split up to walk the distance to the apartment they'd secretly rented a few days earlier, just two middle-aged people who weren't together and who were merely faces in the city crowd. No hidden passages or disguises were needed. It was all about looking casual: ordinary clothes, ordinary apartment, ordinary people just going about their business, and not the Solos in the middle of a war at all. They walked along the tree-lined street, idly glancing at shops like everyone else. Han stayed twenty meters behind Leia. She could sense where he was but he needed to keep his eyes on her, even though she was well able to look after herself if she was spotted by the wrong people.

But who are the wrong people? Apart from my own cousin, the biggest risk is political embarrassment to my in-laws. There's no real danger here.

He kept Leia in sight, sometimes losing her chestnut braid in the sea of people. It had come to Han as a surprise that the Solo family could be anonymous in public, but nobody seemed to recognize public figures unless they were holovid stars. Chief Omas could probably walk around here without anyone thinking he was more than just a vaguely familiar face they couldn't quite put a name to. Maybe he was the guy who read the evening holonews bulletin.

Han slipped into the lobby of the apartment building a little behind Leia and found her waiting at the turbolift. It was seedy compared with the apartment back on Coruscant. Seedy was just fine right now.

"Now, what's the first thing you're going to do when we get in?" she said.

"Call Jacen."

"Good. You catch on fast. Don't shout at him, okay?"

The lift doors opened onto the fifty-sixth floor and a dull beige-carpeted hall with a few stained patches. Leia took three strides toward their apartment door and paused, left hand held out to her side to stop Han in his tracks. The fact that her other hand slid into her tunic and emerged holding her lightsaber prompted him into drawing his blaster.

"Hear something?" he whispered, confused.

They approached the apartment door with slow, careful steps.

"*Felt* something," said Leia.

"Threat?"

"No, but something isn't *right*."

They stood to either side of the door and looked at each other, sharing a thought: *Who knows we're here?* Leia ran her palm down the door frame, not quite touching it, and shook her head.

"Nobody inside."

"Stand clear."

"But somebody's been here . . ."

"Booby trap?"

"I can't sense any immediate danger, just a feeling that someone was *very* nervous when they came here."

Han touched the entry pad, blaster ready. "Maybe they knew what a warm welcome we give uninvited visitors."

The doors slid open and they paused at the entrance, seeing only the apartment as they had left it days before, and hearing nothing except the faint sounds of the environment controls. Leia looked down and bent to pick up something from the carpet.

"That's nice," she said, examining it, and then handed it to Han. "Nothing like a happy family reunion."

It was a small sheet of flimsi. Someone must have slipped it through the gap under the doors, and that took some doing. A strange way to leave a message: but it was one that could never be traced electronically. Just a few words, scrawled on a surface that was rippled as if someone had struggled to force it through the gap.

Han stared at it.

SAL-SOLO HAS PUT OUT A CONTRACT ON YOU IN REPRISAL FOR YOUR SON'S ACTIONS AT CENTERPOINT. CALL ME. GEJJEN.

Leia raised an eyebrow. "Has your cousin threatened to kill you before? Formally, I mean. Random acts of violence don't count."

She always made light of things. Han knew that the cooler she became, the more worried she was. He joined in the mutual reassurance. His cousin was to be loathed and avoided, but he refused to fear him.

"Thrackan hasn't got what it takes, Princess. He's all talk." But Han's stomach still churned. It wasn't the prospect of assassination that worried him: he reckoned he could handle that. It was realizing that they were being watched by someone, and not knowing how and where. "And I don't know any *Gejjen*."

"So how does anyone know we're here?" Leia took the flimsi from his fingers and smoothed it out between her palms as if she was trying to sense echoes of whoever had written it. "Different names, new ID, no droids, no Noghri . . . are you sure you don't remember the name?"

"Should I?"

"Maybe not. I knew a man called Nov Gejjen who was very active against the Human League. He *loathed* Sal-Solo." She referred to Thrackan as she would a total stranger. It was touchingly diplomatic. "But he'd be long dead now."

"He had kids?"

"I don't know, but it's time I found out. Gejjen didn't bother to include his contact details, so he thinks one of us will know where to find him."

"Or *her*."

"Okay, or *her*. I'll see what I can find out while you call Jacen."

Life used to be so clear-cut. Han missed clarity. He opened his comlink, entered a code to conceal the origin of the signal—for all the good it had done—and waited for Jacen to answer.

Another contract out on me. I thought I was done with Thrackan but he just keeps popping back up.

Sometimes he almost missed Boba Fett. Fett, at least, had no family axes to grind. It was just business.

Thrackan would send Fett. Han just knew it.

CORUSCANT: THE SKYWALKERS' APARTMENT.

The shrouded man wouldn't leave Luke alone now.

The image of the man—cloaked, hooded, anonymous, intent on evil—intruded on his dreams more frequently, not in the way of normal nightmares but as a clear vision in the Force; and that was worse than any nightmare.

It had the potential to be real, if it wasn't already.

He couldn't see the man's face. In his dream, he was chasing him, trying to grab that hood from his face, but he always woke up at the point where he felt his fingers close on the fabric. It felt like lightweight bantha wool.

His fingers clutched again. Both the robe and the man dissolved, and Luke woke, heart pounding, fighting a feeling of overwhelming despair and anger at himself for not seeing what was close enough to touch.

He decided he wasn't going to get back to sleep and got up as quietly as he could to avoid waking Mara. With the light that spilled from Galactic City's twenty-four-hour activity and his own Force-sense, he didn't need to switch on the lights to pour himself a glass of water.

There were messages on the comm board—the routine fretting of C-3PO informing him that Mistress Leia and Master Han were well, and that the Noghri were becoming most agitated at the separation, and was it *really* necessary for the droids to remain at the Solos' Coruscant apartment when they might be needed . . . elsewhere?

Luke managed a smile, something he was finding increasingly hard to do lately. He had long suspected that droids had something in them far beyond their programming. C-3PO was as anxious and protective as any human relation would be of his family members, and it always gave him pause when anyone said, "just a droid."

"Yes, my friend," he said aloud. "Because the last thing they need is a big gold-plated droid advertising their presence . . . wherever that might be."

Nobody ever said *Corellia,* but it was very hard to misplace your sister and your best friend in the Force. Luke wished them some kind of peace. He knew how hard it was to find peace when the front line ran through the heart of his own family, even if his misgivings over Jacen's influence on Ben were a little way short of a full-scale feud.

Luke drank while he watched the constant movement of lights from the window. His discomfort over Jacen was definite in some ways—the lengths his nephew seemed prepared to go, the ways he used the Force—but vague in another way, a far deeper and more troubling one: he *feared* for Jacen. Maybe the hooded man was someone who would threaten Jacen or attempt to corrupt him. Whatever the man represented, he was a danger: not danger in the immediate sense, like someone wielding a weapon, but something far more general and all-pervading.

Luke didn't deal in words like *evil*, but that was the only word that felt as if it fit.

Maybe it's a vision of war. Well, I don't need a Force dream to warn me of that. Nobody does.

He felt Mara walk up behind him and give him a soothing touch from the doorway, just a brief warm reassurance at the back of his mind.

"You could have made us both a cup of caf," she said. "If we're going to give up sleeping, might as well do it right."

"You'd think I'd take times like this in my stride by now."

Mara tidied her hair with one hand as she fumbled with the caf dispenser. "Politics? I don't think that *ever* gets easier—not when your own family is tied up in it."

"It's Ben I'm most worried about."

"He gave a good account of himself at Centerpoint."

"But he's thirteen. Okay, I let him go, but he's still a child. *Our* child."

"How old were you when you dived headlong into the Rebellion? Not *that* much older . . ."

"I was eighteen."

"Whoa, veteran, huh?" She winked. He saw the grim, cold girl she'd been when he met her, and thought she looked lovelier now that life had been kinder to her for a few years. "Sweetheart, *Jacen* is taking care of him. He couldn't have a better teacher."

"Yeah . . ."

"Okay, I know we aren't going to agree on that."

"You know how I feel. Jacen makes me uneasy. I've never felt that way before. I can't ignore it."

Her smile faded. "I feel something a little different."

"I can't shake it."

Mara looked about to snap back, but she nodded to herself a few times as if rehearsing a more measured response. "I feel some worrying things in the Force, too, but I've got a theory."

"I'm all ears."

She paused again, looking down at the carpet. "I think he's in love and it's tearing him up."

"Jacen? *In love?* Come on . . ."

"Trust me. I felt something like it before with someone I was pursuing and I read it all wrong then, too. A messy, painful love affair can make people feel pretty dark—all that anger and desperate love."

"But he's a Jedi. He can control all that."

"We're Jedi. We married, so how much did we control *all that*?"

He wanted to believe her. Mara was as smart as they came: she would never have survived as the Emperor's Hand if she hadn't had a finely tuned sense of danger and the ability to put her own distracting emotions aside. She had to be able to see what was truly there, not what she wanted to see.

Her tone softened. "Shall I tell you what I see? I see Ben becoming someone who's comfortable with his Force powers and not resenting us for making him a Jedi. We couldn't put him straight, but Jacen could, and we should be grateful to him for that."

"Jacen plays fast and loose with his own powers. He projected himself into the future, and don't tell me *that* didn't worry you. I don't want Ben learning that kind of thing—and do we really know what skills Jacen learned while he was away? He's *changed*, Mara. I feel it."

She pressed a cup into his hand and stroked his hair, but all he could feel now was a distance that shouldn't have been there, as if she was becoming wary of him—or wary of upsetting him. "Jacen's grown up, too. He's taking a different path as a Jedi, that's all. We don't have all the answers."

"It's more than that. I'm having dreams and they're about a threat to us."

"You really believe Ben's at risk?"

"I feel *Jacen* is at risk. I don't want Ben sucked into this with him."

"The future isn't fixed."

"Oh, but it is when Jacen tampers with it."

"Whoa, let's not fight about this."

"I want us to find another mentor for Ben."

"Luke, did you happen to notice there's no line forming for the job?"

However strong her defense of Jacen, Luke didn't feel genuine certainty in Mara. He put the caf aside and pulled her to him, looking into her eyes. A few lines feathered from their corners, and there was a scattering of white in the mass of red hair framing her face, but she was still perfect as far as he was concerned, still his rock, still his heart.

And she was still *wrong*.

"Mara, I *can't* ignore this."

"Fine." He felt her shoulders tense. "Go ahead and alienate Ben just when he's starting to settle down. So what if Jacen's explored some strange philosophies and communed with bugs? We've *both* been into the dark side, and *we* came through it."

"So you *can* feel the dark side."

"No, I feel that Jacen's developing powers way beyond mine, and that he's good for Ben, and that he would never harm him." She stepped back from Luke and he sensed she was shutting him out now, perhaps to stop the conversation from degenerating into an argument that would have no winners. "That makes him a *good* influence. Without Jacen, we'd have a teenage son with strong Force powers who won't listen to us. Now that's *really* dangerous."

She had a point. It seemed a good moment to concede. "I can't argue with that."

"But . . ."

"I never said *but*."

"I heard *but* and I felt *but*."

". . . but I'd be neglecting my duty if I didn't put some effort into finding out who or what this is in my dreams."

Mara pursed her lips for a moment, looking to one side of him, and then managed a smile. She knew when she couldn't shift him from an idea. And he meant it. The dreams were too strong and insistent to ignore, even if it meant causing friction with Mara. She would come around in time; if he ignored his instincts, the consequences might be far worse than a few silent breakfasts and black looks.

Then the smile became broader, as if she knew that. "I'm going to get some sleep. And so should you."

"I'll finish my caf. Later."

Luke took a long time draining the cup. He sat staring out the window, focusing on the bright green light of a distant illuminated sign to be sure that he was meditating and not dreaming. He tried to reach for the hooded man to make him show his face. The green light wavered and filled his field of vision: there were shapes within it, a feeling of familiar things in different guises and somehow unrecognizable, but the figure in the hood remained elusive.

And it was getting light now. Coruscant's towers and spires were silhouetted against a pink-and-amber sunrise.

Of all the dreaded things that came to Luke in those dreams and visions, the one that plagued him most was the feeling of familiarity.

He had felt something like this before.
He just couldn't pin it down.

JACEN SOLO'S PRIVATE APARTMENT, CORUSCANT.

I wish you were here.

Jacen could reach out and touch Tenel Ka in the Force, and at that moment he would have given nearly anything to see her and his daughter, Allana, again. He closed his eyes and saw Tenel Ka—the same smile as when he had first left her, cradling the baby—and let his presence expand and merge gently with hers. He felt the warmth spread up from his stomach into his chest: she had felt him, and returned the touch.

Baby? Allana was four now; she was a little girl, walking and talking. Every time he sneaked a visit to see her, she'd grown a lot. Did she ask about her daddy? No, she was Hapan royalty, and even at that age she would have been schooled to remain silent about her parentage. How tall was she now? Was she aware of her Force powers yet? He had endless questions, the kind that a father who saw his daughter daily never had to ask.

I'm not there for her. I'm not seeing her grow up. I don't even have a holo of her.

It was much easier to reach out when he levitated like this, legs crossed, hands in his lap. Without the sensory distraction of a seat beneath him or the fabric of the chair against his hands, he could focus totally on the ebb and flow of the Force around and within him.

He let the warmth fade before it became a lasting beacon for . . . he wasn't sure yet. But Tenel Ka would understand that he had to be discreet even in the Force these days. He drew his touch back to the here and now. It felt like a final good-bye.

Jacen wasn't sure just how much Lumiya could detect, and his secret family had to be protected.

But the person he most wanted to have at his side then was his grandfather, Anakin Skywalker, a man he had never known but who had stood where Jacen stood now—on the threshold of becoming Sith.

Once crossed, there was no return. It wasn't one of his explorations of Aing-Tii flow-walking or some other arcane Force skill that he could dabble in and withdraw from when it suited him. It was everything he had been raised to reject; and yet what Lumiya had shown him was so true, so inevitable, and so *necessary* that he had no choice but to believe it.

But can I believe Lumiya?

Her skills were prodigious. He'd been taken aback by the Force illusion in her asteroid habitat. Lumiya might well have been a true Sith follower fighting to prove to Jacen that history was a one-sided story written by the Jedi; or she might have been a clever, manipulative, and infinitely patient woman with her own agenda, seeing Jacen as a useful stepping-stone along the way.

But the part about the Sith way being a force for order and peace if used selflessly . . . it's true. I feel it. I know it—and I wish I didn't.

But is it me?

Jacen still scoured his heart and soul for the slightest sign that his motivation was ambition. He could only feel fear and dread: he didn't want this burden.

That's why it's been given to you.

He lowered himself until he was sitting normally, and took deep breaths until he felt ready to reenter the everyday world. But given the choice right then between a chance to be with Tenel Ka and a moment to speak to Anakin Skywalker— yes, he would have opted for the latter. Just a few minutes, to ask this one question: *Did you feel the doubt and reluctance that I feel before you crossed that line?*

You had a secret love, too, didn't you?

Jacen's state of reluctant acceptance was punctured all too often now by wondering if he was falling into the same trap as his grandfather. He needed to know if it was different, because the outcome two generations ago had been disastrous for the galaxy. He just needed to be absolutely sure.

Many other beings in the galaxy's history had believed they were the Chosen One of their particular culture, born to create order, and all of them had clearly been *wrong*. Jacen never forgot that.

But while he was wondering, events weren't waiting for him and the war was coming closer. He needed to talk to Admiral Niathal. She was a hard-liner: ample proof that you couldn't judge every member of a species by its general reputation. For a peace-loving people, the Mon Calamari had produced an awful lot of tough naval officers.

But you couldn't maintain peace without the capacity for war. Everywhere he looked, Jacen saw the certain truth of Lumiya's words. The Sith way was neither evil nor dangerous in the hands of the sincere. He just wasn't sure about *her* sincerity.

And he had to be sure of his own.

Ben was still asleep in the suite next door. The boy had done a lot of growing up in the last few weeks, and Jacen saw the man he would become—strong, but measured and able to control his passions—but today's work was for Jacen alone. He summoned an air taxi and headed for the Senate Building.

The taxi dropped him in the plaza, where a few people were already entering and leaving the huge domed structure. Senate delegates kept odd hours. There was always activity in the building, always a debate or a select committee or some business in progress twenty-four hours a day. The

Mon Calamari started their day early, and Jacen wanted to simply run into Niathal without arranging a meeting and so attracting attention.

And he could do that.

He knew where Niathal was. When he had seen her the day before, he had formed a lasting Force impression of her as someone who wanted to talk to him very badly. She wanted Omas's job, although she was going to have to go through the office of Supreme Commander first. Admiral Pellaeon, new in the post but a veteran in the world of military politics, was not about to cede his office yet. *Of course* she wanted to talk to Jacen. Word of his willingness to solve problems decisively had obviously reached her.

So he could *feel* her now. And when he walked into the building and made his way along the marble public corridors and then along the carpeted ones accessible only to those with accredited identicards, he was tracking her.

Am I scheming? Jacen was ambushed by the thought. *No. I have to know who I can rely on, if I ever need them.*

He didn't need to influence her to get her to walk his way. He simply found the offices where she and other Mon Calamari had gathered, and found somewhere to sit where she would pass him sooner or later. He settled on a padded bench in the lobby and watched the doors.

A naval officer tied to a desk. No wonder she's frustrated. Jacen wondered how she would handle high office if she got her wish and took Omas's job. Politics were the ultimate frustration.

He thought of Lumiya while he waited. And Ben had asked if he was going to tell Luke about Brisha and Nelani. *Hello, Uncle, Lumiya's back. Thought you'd like to know— for old times' sake.* No, it wasn't news he felt he could break to him.

Jacen felt the ripple of disagreement and counterargument around Niathal and her resistance as she stood firm.

Sometimes he could almost see it, like a faint ghost image of color and shape and movement as the emotions ebbed and flowed. Niathal was all certainty. That was something he sought, too.

He heard doors part and the muffled sound of voices. Admiral Niathal appeared in the lobby in a white uniform, very formal, and had no choice but to spot him. He was facing the doors. She *had* to acknowledge him. Jacen stood.

No use of the Force. Let's see where this leads.

"Jedi Solo," she said, giving him that sideways stare. He felt her caution. "Are you here on business?"

"Just passing."

"I'd like to hear your account of the raid on Centerpoint. It would be very helpful."

Jacen bowed his head politely. "Would you like to continue the discussion outside this building?"

Niathal began walking toward the exit without answering. *That didn't take any persuasion at all.* They didn't speak until they were outside and crossing the plaza. Niathal was not one for small talk, and Jacen liked her forthright manner.

"How far back have we really set Centerpoint Station?" she asked. They headed for the public landing area and got into one of the waiting air taxis. "Cayan Club, driver."

That was a *very* exclusive officers' club that Jacen had never visited. *Useful.* He closed the partition that separated the passenger cabin from the cockpit to ensure privacy. "Six months," he said. "No more."

"Then," said Niathal, "that's how long we have until a full war breaks out."

She left the stark analysis hanging on the air, as if she was waiting for Jacen to fill the silence.

"I don't feel the galaxy can take another war so soon after the Yuuzhan Vong invasion," he said.

"It'll be the fourth major war in a century, yes. Poor odds."

"I'd like to be able to look forward to a century without war."

"And I'd like to be forced to look for another job, Jedi Solo."

Jacen thought for a moment that she was being brutally open about her political ambitions, but the way she rolled her head slightly and looked at the battle honor ribbons on her uniform made him realize she meant an end to any need for war.

Perhaps the two were the same thing. "My own family is divided over this."

"Most Jedi never have families," Niathal said.

"We've had an interesting relationship with what we call *attachment.*" Was she checking out his loyalties? "My duty as a Jedi is to consider trillions of other lives."

"If we continue to botch actions like the Corellian engagement, then we could be in for a long war."

"I've thought about how successful an attack on their shipyards might be," Jacen said.

"I doubt the political will could be bent to more than support for a blockade."

"Ties up a lot of resources."

"So do assaults on multiple fronts."

It was one of those conversations that was test and counter-test; but Jacen didn't blame Niathal for being wary of a Jedi's political will, given Luke's indecisive approach.

The taxi headed south from the Senate, through a city of people beginning the day and others returning after a night at work. They were in the heart of the restaurant district that served the Senate, its skylanes lined with smart places to eat and elegant hotels and private clubs where politicians and senior military officers could find rooms and discreet service.

"I prefer my club to having a home here," said Niathal, as if Jacen looked curious. He was just feeling distracted by something that began nagging at the back of his mind. "Now, perhaps we can give further thought to this block-ade, so—"

Jacen jerked his head around, suddenly seized by such a powerful sense of immediate danger that his instinct was to fling himself on Niathal and wrap the taxi tight in a Force shield. The vessel bucked hard as if it had been hit by a tidal wave. There was a second of silence before a deafening *whump* shook it like a box and they were caught in an instant blizzard of what seemed to be glittering snow. It hammered the hull as Jacen fought to hold the taxi steady, oblivious of the pilot's efforts.

Shattered transparisteel.

It seemed to go on for minutes. The pilot was shouting. Jacen straightened up, staring into the rapidly blinking eye of a shaken Niathal, and knew that they had caught the tail end of a huge explosion.

"Ohhh . . . just look at *that* . . . ," said the pilot. He seemed to be holding the taxi stationary now without Jacen's unseen assistance.

Niathal swallowed hard. "Well, this changes everything."

Jacen could feel what had happened, but it was still a shocking sight. Ahead of them, the skylanes seemed to be a gaping hole of nothing—as if a whole mass of speeders had fallen out of the sky, which they clearly had—and for a hundred meters the buildings on either side were like jagged, open mouths. Each transparisteel frontage had been blown out. The Force was torn with anger and fear and shock. The unnatural silence was broken by emergency klaxons and echoing shouts. Jacen realized the taxi's screens had collapsed into the cabin, although still in one piece.

And Jacen felt anger: real physical anger. This was mind-less, indiscriminate violence, and the galaxy might destroy itself in a billion more acts like this if order didn't prevail.

He abandoned his Jedi self-control for a moment and dared to savor his own outrage and his pity for the inevitable victims.

"Corellians," said the pilot. His voice was shaky. He'd reached an instant conclusion that didn't even allow for the possibility of an accidental explosion. So would many other Coruscanti. Like Niathal, his first thought was that a bomb had been detonated, and that the skirmishing had escalated into something that would harden everyone's stance.

Terrorism had returned to Coruscant.

Through the gaping rear window, Jacen saw airspeeders backed up behind them. He hardly dared think about what was happening hundreds of meters below, where debris and vessels caught in the blast had fallen. But he thought, and let anger fire him up and give him purpose again.

"Maybe not," Jacen said. "And maybe in the end it really doesn't matter who."

The driver looked at Jacen as if he were insane.

"Driver, take us back to the Senate Building any way you can," said Niathal. She'd composed herself fast: it probably took a lot to rattle an admiral who had seen action. She was already tapping codes into her comlink and calling aides to get information from the security forces. "Jedi Solo, I need to talk to our Senator."

The pilot managed to obey in that odd, quiet way that shocked people did, and spun the taxi around to lift into a higher skylane. Jacen assisted with a few well-timed Force pushes to gently part logjammed speeders.

Yes, Corellians.

I really wanted to be wrong about the war.

"This is going to get ugly very fast," he said.

"Going to take some strong reassuring action, then," said Niathal.

"What about the damage to my taxi?" said the pilot.

Neither of them answered.

Jacen's mind raced ahead. This was perfect timing for Lumiya's purposes—unnaturally so. The fact that he couldn't feel her hand in this meant nothing. She seemed to be capable of deceiving him.

But that almost didn't matter. Events had been unleashed that would have a life of their own. He was needed more than ever. *He* could avert total anarchy.

And that was a dangerous thought, but he thought it anyway.

Somebody had to. And somehow he needed to test Lumiya.

chapter three

Aliit ori'shya tal'din.
Family is more than bloodline.
—Mandalorian proverb

THE SKYWALKERS' APARTMENT,
CORUSCANT: 0800 HOURS.

Mara almost dropped her cup and steadied one hand on the table.

"What's wrong?" Luke caught her shoulder and leaned over her. She began mopping spilled caf with her napkin, distracted. "Honey, are you okay?"

"Jacen," she said.

Luke sought Ben in the Force immediately. He was there, with no hint of concern or danger. Jacen, though, was not. There was nothing of him to detect.

"He just blinked out," said Mara. She opened her comlink. "I know he can do that when he wants to, but this felt weird." She paused, eyes fixed in defocus at the far side of the room as she listened. "Ben? Ben, are you okay? . . . yes? . . . where's Jacen? . . . no, nothing important, don't worry. I'll call you later."

Luke didn't hear Ben's response, but he was clearly at Jacen's apartment as he was supposed to be, and unharmed. Mara stood up and pushed her hair back behind her ears, still looking distracted. She was far more attuned to Jacen than Luke was, and he wondered if she kept tabs on her nephew as a precaution. That reassured him. Her old assassin habits hadn't died; they were still very much a part of her, adapted, pragmatic, and *useful*.

"HoloNet," she mumbled, and switched on the screen, looking for a news channel. "I get the proverbial bad feeling about this. I just need to know what's going on."

She was right: Luke began to sense a welling anxiety and disturbance, a sense of something growing like a bank of storm clouds. While Mara made fresh caf, he wiped up the rest of the spill, watching her carefully. They were finishing breakfast when the HNE newsflash announced that there'd been an explosion in the hotel district south of the Senate. There was, said the holoanchor, speculation that it was a bomb.

Mara opened her comlink instantly, face set in blank concentration, and waited. "Jacen's not answering," she said.

It was easy to add two and two and reach a completely wrong total. Luke put his arm around her and squeezed.

"There'll be a simple explanation. It's a big planet and the chances of his being caught up in that are remote."

"I tend to plan for worst scenarios," she said, and returned the hug. "And right now I've got no idea whether we should be looking for him or not."

Like all people used to being in control and taking action, Mara had that instinct to do something in a crisis, even if there was nothing obvious for her to do. Luke shared it. *We can't stay out of it, even if we don't know what* it *is.* The Force didn't take a day off.

"If that really was a terrorist bomb," said Luke, "then we'd better head over to the Senate, because Omas is going to want to discuss the implications."

Mara's blink rate had slowed right down and she had gone quiet. He thought of it as her sniper mode: assessing, planning, coolly rational. He was always impressed that she could salvage the beneficial parts of her past life as an Imperial assassin and discard the darker aspects. But he was still glad they were on the same side.

She grabbed a jacket, not one of her usual fashionable ones but something gray and functional, as if preparing for combat. "I hope nobody jumps to conclusions too fast. It's one of those things that could tip people here into doing something rash."

Luke wasn't sure if she meant politicians or citizens. Perhaps it didn't matter: one would trigger the other either way. He gestured toward the landing platform. "I'll drive. You monitor the news."

HNE kept using the word *explosion* and managed to make it sound like *bomb* every time.

Luke tried to slip the airspeeder through the increasingly congested skylanes as traffic backed up from the scene of the explosion. It didn't take much to gridlock a crowded city that depended on tightly controlled transport.

He glanced at Mara. "What if it's *not* a bomb?"

"People jump to conclusions. If they want to believe it's a bomb, facts won't get in the way."

"I can't imagine Corellia resorting to planting bombs in civilian areas."

"Corellia," Mara said.

"See? We all do it. I thought of Corellia, too. We've got a thousand species on Coruscant and most of them have their dingbat element. It could be anybody."

"Perception usually overrides facts."

"You said it, sweetheart."

The speeder had slowed to a crawl in the traffic as skylanes above and below them backed up, too. Luke considered Force-pushing his way between vessels, but there was simply no longer the maneuvering room to do that safely. He found the next public landing area and set the speeder down to continue the journey on foot.

In theory, a pedestrian could cross the whole planet via walkways and streets. In reality, it was slow going. But it was useful to be close enough to people to get a sense of what they were feeling: and the overwhelming taste in the Force was mostly anger. It wasn't the political anger that emanated from Senate delegates—it was the personal, focused, fearful anger of people whose lives had been directly affected by a conflict on another planet.

Coruscanti had been used to feeling safe for millennia. They were just getting used to being safe again after the Yuuzhan Vong had been defeated, and now that fragile security had been shattered.

It felt like a volcanic fissure opening the dark side. The air seemed charged. The object of that anger—whom people hated, whom they blamed—would affect the course of the conflict with Corellia.

As Luke and Mara walked toward the Senate, the public holonews display screens were surrounded by people staring up at the unfolding news, grim-faced. The display showed which parts of Galactic City had now been sealed off, and harassed fire service officers explaining that they still hadn't reached the seat of the blast or assessed the total number of casualties.

Luke paused behind them; Mara carried on and disappeared into the crowd. Nobody recognized them. That might have been a blessing.

"Has anyone claimed responsibility yet?" he asked.

A young man in a delivery pilot's yellow coverall half-turned to him. "No, but they don't need to, do they?"

"They?"

The man's gaze darted back to the screen. "Corellia. Retaliation for Centerpoint, isn't it? Obvious."

Luke bit back a response and simply carried on walking. He caught up with Mara, who was waiting in a doorway and talking to someone on her comlink.

She looked up and shook her head at him. "One hundred and five dead so far, and rising; three hundred injured. I just called Omas's office. They've declared an emergency."

"Must have been a big device, judging by the damage."

"You don't need much to do a lot of damage in a crowded city made of towers."

Transparisteel blown out like a million blades, speeders falling thousands of meters, shock waves concentrated on buildings by the canyons—Luke could guess at the details. The Force around him felt in turmoil, but most of it seemed to be coming from the people nearby.

He took Mara's arm and pressed on through the crowds. It took them half an hour to reach the Senate, and Omas had already left the chamber to visit the emergency response command center deep below ground level.

Luke and Mara walked into a huge room that appeared to be one large holodisplay packed with uniformed officers. The sign above the doors simply said STRATEGIC CENTER. This was where joint Galactic City authorities managed the longer-term effects of an incident—planning for what was needed in the days that followed—while the minute-to-minute work went on at the tactical and operational command centers down the chain.

When Luke concentrated on what he had walked into, he realized that every branch of the city's emergency services had personnel there: he recognized Coruscant Security Force, Fire and Rescue, Air Traffic Control, medcenter managers, and the city authority. Omas stood talking to a young CSF captain in front of a data display. When Luke walked up behind them, he saw they were looking at a changing list of casualties. The entire wall was a mass of status boards, from lists of skylanes that had been rerouted to which medcenters were receiving the injured.

Omas turned to Luke and Mara and shook his head.

"We can rule out an accidental explosion," he said. "CSF picked up traces of commercial-grade detonite."

Mara maintained her detachment. Her gaze tilted up and down the casualty list—mostly unnamed, just descriptions, and Luke wondered if she was looking for Jacen among them.

"Where was it placed?" Luke asked.

"In one of the hotels," said the CSF officer. The ID tab on his tunic said SHEVU. "The Elite. There's no obvious motive for the location, but it looks as if it detonated in a guest room. Might have been an own goal."

"Own goal?"

"Blew up while the terrorist was handling it."

"So we have a room to go on. Then we ought to have an identity for the guest."

"We're checking that out."

"We can't afford to guess at this."

Captain Shevu looked down his nose at Luke, polite but clearly irritated by the suggestion. "I don't guess about anything, sir. We're working with hard information that's coming in from Tactical and Operational, and where there are gaps, they stay as gaps until we have data."

"And what will our response be if this turns out to be Corellians?"

Omas seemed to take exceptional interest in a status board showing the list of premises affected by the explosion with red points of light indicating whether they had been checked and secured yet. "If this isn't shown beyond doubt to be the responsibility of the Corellian government, then our response must be to treat it as any other crime."

"I think Master Skywalker means the less formal response," said a voice behind Luke.

He hadn't even felt Jacen enter the room. The fact that Jacen could startle him was disturbing. Mara turned, too, and even though Jacen was standing there in front of them,

Luke couldn't *feel* him, and—judging by her expression and her little flare of anxiety in the Force—Mara couldn't, either. Then, like scent suddenly wafting up from a blossom, Jacen's presence was *there,* all around them, magnified. *So he wants to show me how powerful he is.* Luke regretted the hostility in his thoughts. But it did nothing to reassure him.

"Sorry, Uncle," said Jacen. The tension was, of course, invisible to a roomful of non-Jedi. "I got caught up in the blast. I came to see what I could do."

"I'm glad you're okay." Luke picked up on his original question. "Yes, Captain, I mean the informal response. Retaliation, escalation."

"Victimization," Shevu suggested quietly, still watching the status boards. "That'll make life in the city very awkward. Latest tally from Immigration Control says we have nearly twenty million Corellians living here."

"Most of whom are harmless," said Luke.

"And not easy to identify except by ID docs," said Jacen. "They look just like us."

"They *are* just like us."

Omas put his hand on Jacen's shoulder and steered the conversation into calmer waters with the ease of a professional statesman. "Shall we continue this discussion elsewhere? We're getting in Captain Shevu's way. He has an incident to manage." He gestured to one of the dozen small rooms off the main chamber, each marked with a board above the doors: FIRE AND RESCUE CELL, CSF CELL, MED-SERVICE CELL. Omas ushered Mara, Luke, and Jacen toward a room marked INFORMATION CELL. "I'd like to discuss how we handle this with our public affairs people. Perception at times like this is everything. It's the difference between one hundred dead in a speeder bus crash and one hundred dead in a terrorist attack—one is a tragedy and the other is the beginning of a war."

Luke glanced at Mara, who met his eyes but showed no

outward sign of her anxiety. Most of the troubles they had faced in their lives had been big, *truly* big: invasions, alien armies, Dark Jedi, each of them well beyond the scope of tidy incident management by Coruscant's civil servants. This was a small event in global terms, but like a snakebite—small, painful, and with the potential to poison a whole planet.

Jacen walked ahead of them, his presence in the Force betraying nothing but calm determination.

UPPER CITY, TARIS.

Boba Fett didn't care if anyone recognized *Slave I* as his ship.

There wasn't much they could do about it: stealth was fine in its place, but he didn't have to hide. And the restored shell of once glorious Taris was so far off the beaten track these days, that there really was a chance that nobody here knew who he was.

It was a useful base for the time being. The galaxy seemed to have forgotten it existed, which was no bad thing seeing as it had been razed to the ground four millennia ago in the Jedi civil wars. Fett savored the irony: he'd come to think of most galactic wars as Jedi feuds, because they almost always came down to Jedi versus Sith. The Yuuzhan Vong had almost been a refreshing interlude.

Things never change, do they?

He also found it interesting that the total restoration of a ravaged planet resulted in pretty much the same social order as before, the world once again reflecting the huge gulf between its classes in literal architectural levels.

People never learn, either.

He set the defense shield on *Slave I* and walked along the promenade, drawing cautious glances from some of the smartly dressed residents out for their evening stroll. The

Upper City was again an echo of Coruscant, soaring towers inhabited by the solidly rich. The Lower City was a cesspit, and the subterranean levels—well, he vaguely recalled pursuing a bounty down there, years ago, and it had been very ugly even for a man who had seen the ugliest of the galaxy's faces.

Anyone who wants me to go down there again can pay triple.

The thought caught him off-guard. It was the sort of vague future plan that was beyond a dying man.

Goran Beviin was waiting for him at the plush Horizon Hotel. He sat at the bar with a large mug of Tarisian ale and a bowl of something that might have been deep-fried crustaceans of some kind. He had *almost* deferred to the bar's dress code—his helmet was placed on the bar beside him—but in his deep blue battle-scarred Mandalorian armor he still didn't fit in among the beautifully dressed patrons. Fett walked up behind him.

"You always sit with your back to the doors?"

Beviin turned, apparently not startled to hear the voice of his Mandalore, ruler of the clans, Commander of Supercommandos. Fett had never quite come to terms with his peacetime role.

"When I've assessed the risk, yes." He looked at Fett's helmet with slow deliberation. "Can I get you an ale and a drinking straw?"

"You're a riot. What are those?"

Beviin popped one of the fried things in his mouth and crunched with exaggerated relish. "Coin-crabs. Reminds me of those happy days we spent frying Yuuzhan Vong."

"Sentimentalist."

Beviin gestured around at polished wood and expensive upholstery. "This is pretty comfortable. I always think of Taris as a dead world."

"Maybe that's why I feel a kinship with it."

"What?"

"People often think I'm dead, too." The quip didn't seem quite as amusing now. There was no point telling anyone else about his condition, not yet—and maybe never. "So what have you got for me?"

Fett sat down on the stool next to Beviin, adjusting his holster carefully. The bartender—a middle-aged human male whose high-collared uniform looked as expensive as his customers' evening dress—had a question forming on nervous lips. Fett knew it was probably a reminder that *sir* should remove his helmet. He turned his head so that it was clear he was staring at the man through his visor and waited for him to change his mind. He did. Fett turned back to Beviin.

"Get on with it."

"Thrackan Sal-Solo approached me with a contract on the whole Solo family."

You know, I'd really like an ale now. Relax. Never done that. Not like ordinary people. "Direct?"

"Via an intermediary, but he forgets how good my com-link surveillance skills are. And my contacts, of course."

"Wonder why he didn't ask *me* to go after Solo," said Fett. He considered the coin-crabs and thought better of it. "Everyone else did."

"Maybe he thinks you'd be bored with it. And too expensive."

"Right on both counts." Han Solo was irrelevant now, *truly* irrelevant. Fett had never had a feud with him anyway: just a string of contracts, and contracts were never personal. "So?"

"So I hear he's had a few takers."

"Not you."

"I don't do families. I only *hunt* criminals. I don't want to *be* one."

"I'm still waiting."

"Okay. Word is that Ailyn's back and interested in the contract, too."

Fett was glad of the privacy of his helmet. He rarely registered surprise, because there was almost nothing left in the galaxy that could surprise him. But this felt suddenly raw even after decades.

His only child was *alive*. He'd heard nothing of her since the Yuuzhan Vong invasion, when billions had lost their lives. How old would she be now? Fifty-four? Fifty-five?

Somehow I knew she wasn't dead.

"It beats her taking a contract on *me*." His stomach chilled. *No, you don't mean that at all: you mean that she's your daughter, however much she hates you, however much she blames you for her mother's death, and you're dying, and you want to see her one last time. She's all you'll leave behind to prove that you ever existed.* "Who else knows?"

Beviin—late fifties, gray-haired, but with a grin that made him look like a mischievous kid—seemed to be staring into his eyes, concerned. Fett's helmet never appeared to be a barrier for Mandalorians: somehow they looked straight into the core of him. "I thought *nobody* did, because she's calling herself Ailyn Habuur."

Fett waited. Beviin took a pull of his ale and said nothing.

"So what makes you think she's Ailyn Vel?"

"My source tells me she's about fifty, has a Kiffar facial tattoo, and flies a KDY assault ship that I think you'd recognize. But I don't think that means much to anyone else these days."

His daughter had hated him enough to kill him and take his ship and armor—at least, that's what she'd thought had happened. Had she ever found out she'd killed a clone instead?

Fett had managed to shrug off the news at the time. It was more than twenty years ago. But it felt different now. He wanted to know where she had been, what she had done.

But it was stupid and irrelevant—and far too late. He put the impulse aside.

"I hope she's careful, then," he said.

Beviin was waiting for more reaction, eyebrows raised, but he wasn't going to get it. "Is that all?"

"Yes. I'm more interested in Kaminoans. What do you know about Ko Sai?"

"Apart from the rumors?"

"I'll take rumors right now."

"They said she was killed during the Battle of Kamino, but the general view was that she defected to the Separatists. Then there's a big black hole, and the next rumor is that someone sent her back to Kamino."

"I'd have known if—"

"A piece at a time."

"What?"

"Body parts. Well, some of them."

Only kidnappers did that kind of thing. They did it for credits—and that didn't fit a wartime defection at all. So *that* was how Koa Ne knew someone had located Ko Sai.

"Fingers?" That was the usual removable body part of choice if a kidnapper wanted to focus someone's mind. "Kaminoans don't have external ears."

"Not exactly. Parts she really needed, or so I hear."

Fett tried to imagine what the scientist could have done to end up dead and dissected. Maybe she'd tried to withhold her data. But why send the parts back to Kamino unless whoever held her wanted to pressure her government, or teach them a lesson?

And the data had never been sold. It would have been in use by now if it had. And as far as he could tell, the Kaminoans had never been asked to surrender anything—credits or data—in exchange.

That sounded like revenge. And that didn't help him find what he was looking for.

"Why are you interested in a disappearance that long ago?" Beviin asked. "If anyone wants you to find the rest of her, it's a bit late."

This was where things became uncertain for Fett. He had trusted only his father, who had put every scrap of his energy into making his son totally self-reliant. Boba Fett hunted alone. But from time to time he was reminded that he was also the Mandalore; he had a responsibility to a hundred warriors, and—this was the aspect that gave him the problem—a nation that wasn't only geographic but a nomadic culture, too, except that it had a homeworld, and a sector, and . . . no, it wasn't clear at all. He wasn't sure what being Mandalore meant anymore.

And he wondered if he thought of himself as Mandalorian first and bounty hunter second.

He didn't.

"*Verd ori'shya beskar'gam.*" Beviin took a pull at his ale. "A warrior is more than one's armor."

Fett rounded on him. "What?"

"Ailyn. Wearing your armor, flying your ship. No substitute for a fighting spirit." Beviin never appeared to fear him and never called him *sir*. A traditional Mandalorian never would, of course. "You still don't speak *Mando'a,* do you?"

"Basic and Huttese. That's what I do business in."

"Maybe we need a little less business and a little more Mandalore, *Bob'ika.*"

Bob'ika. Some of his father's associates had called him that as a kid. His father never had. But he ignored the over-familiar form of his name. "I'm busy right now."

"Nothing else you want done?"

"No."

"I'd better be going. Just call if you have orders for me." Beviin drained the last of his ale and scooped the uneaten coin-crabs into a napkin to fold them up and pocket them. "You're my *Mand'alor,* after all."

It might have been sarcasm. "You sound very tribal these days."

"Spirit of the times. Seems to be catching on."

Fett hadn't visited Mandalore or the surrounding sector for a couple of years. There was no reason why it should feel like home in the same way Kamino did.

We don't even know how many Mandalorians there are in the galaxy. You don't need an ID or a birth certificate to be one . . . of us.

Beviin replaced his helmet and walked out without a backward glance. Without a drink in front of him, Fett had no reason to sit there any longer, either. He slid off the stool, to the visible relief of the bar staff, and wandered back to *Slave I,* taking in the sights along the way.

There was a share-dealing shop on the walkway. Upper City was full of them, open all hours to catch trading on the thousands of trading floors throughout the galaxy that made up the Interstellar Stock Exchange. Share dealing had become an entertainment for the wealthy on this forgotten world. Fett paused and walked into the vividly lit lobby to stand in the constantly shifting interactive holodisplay of the various markets.

Coruscant's CSX—its domestic stock index—had taken a sudden dip since he'd last checked the markets on his inbound journey. The little red line was still edging down against the Top Million ISE index. Something must have spooked the traders: it didn't take much. A bantha could belch and wipe billions off stock prices if the market was nervous enough.

Fett stretched out a gloved finger and touched the index that read BIOTECH. A cascade of subindices tumbled out in a table and he ignored SELECT COMPANY to choose VOLUME SHARE MOVEMENT. That brought up the ranked list of companies where most shares had been traded over any given period. He chose ONE STANDARD MONTH.

Three companies topped the list: SanTech, Arkanian Micro, and AruMed. Arkanian Micro share prices hadn't shifted more than 10 percent, though, and they were always among the top-priced shares. It was AruMed that caught his eye; the green icon beside the name told him it was small and relatively new. But someone had bought a 25 percent block of its dirt-cheap shares in the last week.

Let's see what looked so appealing to them, then.

Fett checked the database that fed through to his helmet's internal display but found nothing remarkable at all about the company's activities. AruMed had been trading for a year and specialized in genetically tailored pharmaceuticals, and no dramatic new product seemed to be on the horizon to warrant speculative share buying.

Unless this is insider trading.

Unless someone knew the company had taken on a Kaminoan scientist recently, the shares wouldn't have been very appealing at all.

Fett noted the assistant watching him with discreet concern. He probably didn't get too many customers with jet packs and flamethrowers in the store.

The database located AruMed's headquarters on Roonadan. It seemed unusual for a small biotech company to be based in the Corporate Sector under the nose of the aggressively acquisitive Chiewab laboratories, so Fett recorded the details and went back to the holodisplay to browse general pharmaceutical companies. Only two more showed unusual share-dealing activity in the period since Taun We had gone on the run—and one of those was Rothana-based ConCare, which seemed to focus on drugs for older citizens.

Like me.

Kaminoans really didn't like being far from home. Rothana was within stone-throwing distance of Kamino in galactic terms. He made a special note to check that one out after AruMed.

"Care to invest, sir?" said the assistant.

Fett always did his share deals through his accountant, Puth, a Nimbanel who could launder and erase an audit trail almost as well as Fett himself. There was no point having an accountant who was smarter than you were, after all. But even a bounty hunter could be prone to impulse buys.

He took out a credit chip. "I'll take fifty thousand shares in SteriPac."

"They make battlefield dressings," said the assistant. His fixed stare told Fett he rarely sold a hundred thousand credits' worth of shares in one deal, and his hand folded around the chip as if he thought it would escape. "Expecting a war?"

"Always. And I'm never disappointed."

Fett made his way to the sparsely furnished apartment he'd bought a year before that would not, for once in his life, become an asset that made a quick profit. Taris wasn't a fast-moving property market, but it was worth paying for the relative privacy.

So someone sent Ko Sai home a piece at a time.

His helmet sensors told him a human was walking behind him, maintaining a constant distance.

Kaminoans could easily have done a little forensics work on that and figured out where the packages came from.

It was a young woman—eighteen, maybe—with dark curly hair cut close to her head. He could see the image in the HUD of his helmet, relayed from the range finder's rear view. And while she had a blaster holstered on one hip—who *didn't* go around armed these days?—she looked neither local nor hostile. She was wearing gray body armor, basic chest and back plates like a Mandalorian, but without colors or markings.

But she's following me. I know it.

So . . . if the Kaminoans knew who had grabbed Ko Sai, they had a very good reason for not going after them. And her research had never resurfaced.

Fett was troubled when he couldn't spot motives. *Everyone* had a motive.

Tomorrow, he'd set off for Roonadan and give Puth a call. He needed to get his fortune in order in case he lost his race against time.

What am I going to do with it?

He always thought he'd know one day, until that one day was overtaken by bad news. Behind him, the girl quickened her pace and caught up with him, close enough now to reach out, take two quick steps, and touch him.

He turned before she could do it, and stood blocking her path, irritated. She didn't seem startled. She stared into his visor much as Beviin had, which was unusual in itself.

"You're Boba Fett," she said.

"You passed your eyesight test."

"I need to talk to you."

"Whatever it is, you can't afford me."

"But can you afford *me*?"

Fett thought for a moment that he'd really read her *completely* wrong, but she held out her clenched fist, palm up, and parted her fingers to reveal a flat disc of opalescent stone, gold shot with red, blue, and violet. A leather strip was threaded through a hole drilled on one edge.

It was a heart-of-fire gemstone. He knew, because he had given one like it to Sintas Vel when they were married: it was from her home, from Kiffu. He'd been just sixteen, Sintas not much older.

No: he had given *this very stone* to her. This was the same gem. He could see the carved edge, like rope.

Four lines of a Mandalorian marriage vow that we didn't

understand. A stone that she said had some part of my spirit and hers held in it forever.

Forever amounted to three years. They'd split up before Ailyn was two. Sintas had gone bounty hunting when Ailyn was sixteen and never returned.

That's why my own daughter was ready to kill me.

"Where did you get this?" he asked as calmly as he could. It was clear that the girl knew he would recognize it. There was no point bluffing. He didn't need to.

"From the man who killed your wife," she said. "Your daughter owes me a bounty. And I know exactly where she is."

CARD'S TAPCAF,
BLUE SKY BOULEVARD, CORONET.

It was how you behaved that made the difference, Han decided.

He sat in the tapcaf facing the window and watched for Leia through the rain-streaked transparisteel. He'd thought he'd be recognized at last, but once he'd got used to *not* striding purposefully and drawing attention to himself, and started to move like a regular person—matching everyone else's pace, shoulders relaxed—nobody seemed to notice him.

He became just another Coronet citizen having a caf and whiling away the time on the boulevard. There was a holo-screen on the wall behind him, and NewsNet was running. Normally it washed over him as part of the background noise, but even over the hiss of steam from the caf machine at the bar, he heard very clearly the words *bomb* and *Corellian.*

So did everyone else in the tapcaf. Silence fell. The staff even shut down the hissing caf pressure filter, and everyone turned in their seats or on their stools to watch the bulletin.

The scenes from Coruscant were terrible: one hovercam shot tracked down from a shattered hotel frontage where the remnants of a sign, just the letters ELI, hung from a dangling section of permacrete clinging to the tower by a thin strand of durasteel reinforcing wire. The cam dropped level after level to the bottom of the urban canyon, showing less damage as it descended, but then settling on a shocking image of what had fallen finally to the ground level: speeders, masonry, and bodies. Han, a man used to war, looked away and shut his eyes.

The stunned silence gave way to debate among strangers brought together by common outrage.

"We didn't do that," said a woman.

"We fight clean."

"If we wanted to bomb Coruscant, we'd use the fleet."

"They're blaming us. Why? Don't they know us by now?"

No, terrorism wasn't Corellia's way of doing things. There was military sabotage, but Corellians tended to be pretty clear-cut about who was a legitimate target and who wasn't. Han wondered if the blast was a slick bit of black ops by Coruscant and the Alliance in general to polarize positions by bombing their own people.

I'm going crazy. This is Luke I'm talking about. The Jedi council wouldn't let the Senate get away with it.

But there were all kinds of murky agencies that the Senate probably bankrolled and didn't keep too close an eye on for pragmatic, plausibly deniable reasons. Luke wouldn't even know. He was just the same decent, idealistic kid at heart that he'd always been.

They're going to use this so-called bomb outrage to up the ante, to take a crack at us.

Han put his head in his hands and sat there for a moment, wondering what he could possibly do now to help Corellia

when he wasn't even welcome here. Eyes shut, he reached
for the cup, and it wasn't quite where he thought he'd left it.

Someone put a hand on his arm.

"Han . . ."

It was a man, and Han's instinct was to jerk his arm back
and draw a blaster; but he stopped dead, hand a split second from his holster. The man was about twenty-five: dark
skin, black hair cut almost military-short. A stranger.

"Do you know me?" Han was ready to drop him where
he stood. "Because I don't know *you,* pal."

"But your wife knew my father."

*Ah, Gejjen. No, play it cool. You have no idea who this
guy is at all.* "Prove it." Han saw familiar movement outside the window and Leia, the hood of her tunic pulled up
against light rain. "How did you find us?"

Gejjen—if that was who he was—dropped his voice almost to a whisper. "When you rented the apartment, you
paid in untrackable credits. That's a lot of hard currency—
unusual enough to draw attention right now."

"From who?"

"From our own security forces."

"So CorSec knows we're here and Thrackan doesn't?"
Han nearly spat out the name. Luckily it was a common
enough first name not to draw the same attention that snarl-
ing *Sal-Solo* would have done. "Right. Try again."

"You're assuming that everyone in CorSec would want to
tell Thrackan."

Han shook his head slowly. "Why do I get the feeling that
I don't want to know that?"

"Well, there's Corellia, and there's Thrackan, and they're
not the same thing in many people's eyes. People who'd like
to do something about it."

"Call me cynical, but I *think* you're talking about a
change of administration without an election. I'm trying to
remember the word for that."

Gejjen—he could be nobody else—sat down next to him.
As Leia came into the tapcaf, she stared at Han, and then at
Gejjen, and her lips parted as if she had realized something
that quite pleased her.

"You're the image of your father," she said.

"Dur Gejjen," said the young man very quietly. He held
out his hand for shaking, and their voices were lost in the
chatter that had swamped the tapcaf again. "At your service, ma'am."

"Hi, honey," said Han. "This nice young man is about to
ask me to take part in a coup." He smiled theatrically at
Gejjen. "Did I get the right word?"

"I asked him to meet us here," Leia said quietly. "But he's
early . . ."

"Apologies. It's a habit, just in case messages are ever intercepted. Shall we move on?" Gejjen indicated the door.
"You can choose the location. Just to reassure you in case
you think I'm setting you up."

"Good idea," said Leia. "I know just the place."

She beckoned to Han. He rolled his eyes, but gulped
down the remains of his caf and followed her out into the
rain, staying to one side of Gejjen so he could keep an eye
on him. Leia led them to a women's fashion store.

"There goes my tough-guy image," said Han, hesitating
at the ornately gilded doors.

"Turbolift," said Leia, gesturing both men inside with an
expression of narrow-eyed mock impatience. Under the circumstances, she seemed in a good mood. "There's a caf bar
on the top floor. Nice and public with several exits if anything happens that we're not expecting."

Gejjen took the suspicion aimed at him pretty well. "Sensible precaution," he said.

Han knew he'd never enjoy caf again in quite the same
way, because the taste was starting to become inextricably
linked in his subconscious with bad news. They huddled

around a table, surrounded by chattering shoppers and noisy children, and tried to look unremarkable. The ubiquitous holoscreen murmured away on one wall: Corellians were addicted to news. There was no getting away from that bomb blast.

"Okay, where were we?" said Han. "Ah, I remember. Removing the elected government. Go ahead and amaze me, kid." He offered Gejjen a small jug. "Cream? Sugar?"

"Han . . ." Leia fixed him with a stare.

"Sorry, honey." He leaned back and folded his arms. "Go on, Gejjen."

The young man was still totally unperturbed. "You're at risk, and so is Corellia. From the same source."

"Power-crazed galactic government?"

"Power-crazed individuals."

"That's half the galaxy on a good day"

"Sir, your cousin isn't doing *anybody* any favors."

"I didn't choose my family."

"Well, he's going to kill *yours,* because he's put out a contract on you, your wife, and your children. And if he carries on the way he's going, he's also going to get a lot of Corellians killed in a war we can't win."

Han still didn't know what use they were to Gejjen, but he took an instant dislike to phrases like *can't win.* "So you want us to do something? See, I have this hunch that you do."

"If Thrackan is removed, would you consider taking his place?"

Oh boy. "No."

Even Leia looked taken aback. "Absolutely not," she said.

"Yeah, I already said that, honey."

Gejjen managed a nervous smile. "I didn't mean to embarrass you, sir."

"I'll do anything for Corellia," said Han. "And I agree

that Thrackan's conducting his own war for his own ends, like he always does. But there's a real threat out there from the Alliance and it's going to take a united Corellia to stand up to it. Just give me a blaster. Not an office."

"You're not going to go back to Coruscant, then?"

"Why should I? We're not running from Thrackan." Han slipped his hand under the table and caught Leia's hand. She gave it a squeeze that threatened to numb his fingers. "And we're not going to live in hiding on Coruscant, either. Might as well be here."

"I understand."

"Fine."

"The good news is that Thrackan seems to think you're on Coruscant."

"Well, that's another good reason for staying put, isn't it?"

"When we find out who's taken the contract, we'll warn you." Gejjen stood up and shook their hands. He had a mature, solid air about him, an elder statesman in a young man's body. "If you'd like help to relocate, you know where to find me. If we could track you, so might others."

"I think I already know who'll find me." Han watched Gejjen leave. When he was sure the man had disappeared into the turbolift, he turned to Leia. "Well, you didn't say much for a hotshot diplomat . . ."

"It's not appropriate for a Jedi to discuss political coups."

"Yeah, I can understand how that might be a sensitive area. How did you trace him?"

"I looked up *Gejjen* in the comlink directories."

Han laughed out loud. A large woman in a bright orange suit that really didn't do her any favors turned to look at him for a second. "Funny, we always think this is cloak-and-dagger stuff."

"Gejjen doesn't need to hide. He's an elected representative of a legal political party, the Democratic Alliance. They have a lot of seats in the Corellian Assembly now. With the Corellian Liberal Front, they actually form the largest bloc of votes, but Thrackan's still hanging on."

"If that dirtbag comes anywhere near you or the kids, I'll kill him, I swear."

"You think he's got a chance, taking on three Jedi?"

"He won't. *Contract,* remember?"

"You think it's going to be Fett, don't you?"

"Yeah."

"No. Not *Fett.* Why would he? He saved us from the Vong."

"Because business is business, maybe." Han could feel something rising in his chest, and it wasn't the effect of way too much caf. It was something animal and irrational, something that was making his pulse pound in his temples. It was anger and fear; not for himself, though, but for Leia, Jaina, and Jacen. "Thrackan's done some dirty things, but he never went this far before. Not hiring hit men. That changes everything."

He had a thought, and it was one that almost made him recoil.

I'm going to kill the scumbag this time.

Nobody touches my family.

Leia reacted as if he'd said it aloud. "No . . . you're *not* going to contact Fett, and you're *not* going to hire him to hit your cousin."

"That never entered my mind," said Han, and it really *hadn't.* She could see that and she could feel it, too, he knew. Unfortunately, he knew he'd have a hard job concealing the fact that he still felt murderously protective. "Besides, I haven't had to deal with guys like that in a long time. Maybe you place a want ad in *Bounty Hunter Weekly* these days. Or call their agents."

"Yes, so remember we can take care of ourselves," said Leia. "I'll just warn Jacen and Jaina."

Jacen: Han kept missing him every time he called or returned a message. He really wanted to talk to him now, and not to remonstrate with him: he just wanted to hear Jacen's voice. Whatever insanity had put them on opposite sides of a divide, Jacen was his little boy and always would be, no matter how old or powerful or distant he might be.

Nobody touches my wife and kids.

Han Solo wasn't one of the galaxy's natural assassins. He would fight to defend himself, but he'd never gone after anyone with the intention of killing them. There was always a first time; this would be his.

Lost in his thoughts, Han stirred the remains of his caf with a spoon, wondering how they got the foam to last that long, and then was jerked out of his trance by the one thing guaranteed to get anyone's attention: his own name.

The words *Han Solo* cut through the hubbub of voices and children's squealing as if the tapcaf had fallen into total and complete silence for a moment.

"In a statement issued by the Office of the State, President Sal-Solo has declared Han Solo and his family to be enemies of Corellia following the attacks on Centerpoint and Rellidir, and he's ordered their arrest," said the HNE holoanchor.

Han tried not to swing around in his seat or curse at the screen. He raised his head very slowly, caught Leia's eye, and focused on the screen as if bored. No, he wasn't bored at all. He was furious, and a little scared. He wondered how good an actor he was; but nobody seemed to be looking at him.

It was probably because the image on the screen was of a younger Han, a man still with brown hair and relatively few lines. The picture of Leia was way out of date, too.

"I think we'd better be going," said Leia. "Some urgent laundry."

"Right behind you," said Han.

He didn't like running, and there was nowhere safer to run. Coruscant wasn't going to welcome him with open arms, either. Either way, they were fugitives. They split up as soon as they left the store and met up again back at the apartment.

"Have I changed that much?" said Leia.

"What?"

"The picture of me that they're running."

"I hope so," said Han. Maybe he should have assured her she looked as good as ever to him, but he thought that practical reassurance about her safety was more important than flattery right then. "And I'm going to grow a beard, just in case. How about you?"

Leia gave him a withering stare. "I didn't shave today. You didn't notice?"

"I meant change your hair or something."

"The Aurra Sing look? Yes, it's so me."

"I'm glad you've kept your sense of humor."

"You know what they say," said Leia, and took scissors from the kitchen. "If you can't take a joke, you shouldn't have joined."

chapter four

Vandals have desecrated the Corellian Sanctuary on Coruscant. The domed building, a resting place for Corellian dead, was daubed with paint during the night, and marble plaques were smashed. Inside, diamonds set in the dome—formed from the compressed carbon of cremated Corellians—were hacked out of the ceiling. Police are treating the attack as retaliation for yesterday's bombing of the Elite Hotel on skylane four-four-six-seven, which left six hundred and thirty-four dead and hundreds more injured. Nobody has yet claimed responsibility for the explosion, confirmed as caused by commercial-grade detonite.

HNE Morning News

UPPER CITY, TARIS.

"My name's Mirta Gev," said the girl.

Fett stared at the heart-of-fire necklace in the palm of his glove and wanted to clutch it in his bare hand, but he didn't know why. For the first time in many, many years, he felt *grief*.

None of that turmoil showed. He made sure of that and studied her: strongly built, heavy boots, practical armor, no jewelry, a battered shapeless bag over one shoulder, and no concessions to feminine fashion whatsoever. Passersby gave them a wide berth on the promenade. "So are you a bounty hunter, or do you just like armor?"

Mirta—if that was her real name—nodded twice, just little movements as if she was measuring what she was going to say rather than blurting out a smart answer. She seemed utterly unafraid of him, and that was *rare*.

"Yeah, I'm a bounty hunter," she said. "Object recovery more often than prisoners, but I've survived so far. Aren't you going to ask me who killed Sintas Vel?"

"No."

"Why?"

"Because we parted a long time ago."

Mirta shrugged and held out her hand for the necklace. "I know. You left your wife when your daughter was nearly two. Sintas left on a bounty hunt before Ailyn's sixteenth birthday and never came back. That's not common knowledge."

"Okay, that's proof you know Ailyn Vel."

"And I need to return that necklace. It's all she has left of her mother."

Fett hesitated and handed back the heart-of-fire. He wanted it very badly, but he didn't rob kids like her of their meager bounties.

So it's all Ailyn has left. Like all I had of my dad was his armor. And his ship.

"How is she?"

"What?"

Why am I doing this? "How's my daughter?"

"She's . . . okay, I suppose. Angry. But she's surviving."

"I think you know she tried to kill me."

"She did mention it . . ."

"Does she know I'm alive?"

"Of course she does."

Ailyn had chased him across the galaxy—or so she thought—and killed a clone she thought was him. If she knew he was alive now and hadn't tried again, then maybe she had changed her mind . . . no, that was stupid. *You left Sintas and your baby, and you never looked back. Is that how Dad treated you? No, he was always there for you. So what kind of man abandons his own kid?*

Every day of his life, Fett had thought of his father and missed him so much that he would have traded absolutely anything—sometimes even his life—for a few more minutes with him, for a chance to touch him and tell him he loved him. Right now it was unbearable. It was as raw as it had been on the day he saw him killed at Geonosis, perhaps more so, because the shock had worn off long ago and had been replaced by cold analysis and—sometimes—dull, gnawing hatred.

"Do you think I want to see her again? I wouldn't even recognize her. She was a baby when I last saw her."

"Why are you still talking to me, then?"

The girl was sharp. Not cocky, not insolent; just sharp.

I wouldn't recognize my own kid. I see my own dad every day in the mirror, and never my own kid. What a thought to die with.

"Why do you care if I find her?"

"Because you might pay me."

"Right answer."

"I'm just trying to get by in a tough galaxy."

"How much?"

She paused. It was the first time he'd seen her confidence waver. *She doesn't know how much to ask.* "Five thousand."

It was the cost of a repeating blaster. "Done. Payable when I see Ailyn Vel and proof of who she is." He didn't need her as a guide at all. All he had to do was find Han Solo, and he'd find Ailyn hunting him. But that necklace had seized his interest. "You got transport?"

"Well—"

"Just so you don't skip out on the deal, you come with me." *I can keep a good eye on you in* Slave I, *girl. I'm heading Ailyn's way anyway, so you're just ballast.* "Take it or leave it."

"Okay."

"Let's go."

Mirta never said a word. She just followed him. She didn't ask to go back and collect her things, or pose any questions.

She was either very cool or very naïve. And maybe her whole life was in that scruffy shoulder bag.

But she had his wife's necklace. And sooner or later he knew he'd ask how she came by it, and how Sintas died. He'd wait a little: he didn't want to look as if he cared. She could carry on believing that he needed her to locate Ailyn.

But you wouldn't recognize your own daughter. Just her ship—your old ship.

And here he was, a man who trusted no one, chancing himself on the word of a girl he didn't know, when he should have been concentrating on finding Taun We and Ko Sai's data.

But he could do that as well.

And if the girl turned out to be trouble, he could always shoot her.

SECURITY AND INTELLIGENCE COUNCIL MEETING ROOM, SENATE BUILDING.

"I think you could do this, Mara," said Chief Omas. "The enemies we face won't always be conventional armies, or even in a separate theater of war, so we feel we need a separate arm of the Defense Force concentrating on domestic security."

Domestic security. Sounds like a lock on the front doors and an intruder alarm. Jacen watched, still concerned by the speed at which events were unraveling.

Mara didn't move a muscle. She sat with her legs tightly crossed and arms folded, and Jacen felt her dismay from across the room without even wanting to. He tried not to look at Luke, who was standing by the window, staring out at the Coruscant skyline. There was something terrible about conflict with family that was even worse than with others. It felt much more savage and dangerous. You weren't supposed to have rifts with your loved ones, which was another good reason why Jedi weren't supposed to *have* loved ones—

But that's not Sith. Avoiding attachment is not the Sith way. Are you really wrong about all this?

Jacen shook himself mentally. The moments of indecision would pass. And . . . he wouldn't have doubts if he'd been driven by ambition. Reluctance was becoming his touchstone, his proof that he was doing this for the right reasons.

"Why me?" said Mara.

"You've been an intelligence agent," said Omas.

The head of the Security and Intelligence Council, Senator G'vli G'Sil, sat to one side of Omas in silence, scrutinizing Mara and then looking slowly toward Jacen and Luke as if he had never seen a Jedi before.

Mara's reluctance wasn't even disguised. "I'll do my duty for the Alliance," she said. "But I'm not sure I'm psychologically equipped to head up . . . well, a secret police force. There's no other word for it. Spying is one thing, and maybe even assassination, but this is new to me."

"We spent so much time dealing with the Yuuzhan Vong that we lost our focus on threats closer to home," said G'Sil. "But I'm old enough to remember that when terrorist activity starts, you need to move fast before it spreads and networks get established."

If they aren't already. The World Brain tells me they're on the move, gathering, meeting . . .

"Let me think about it," said Mara. But that was just words. Everything else about her was adding, . . . *and then say no.*

Luke turned slowly, hands deep in his pockets, and stared out the window, and for a moment Jacen wondered if he was going to volunteer instead. No, that kind of warfare simply wasn't Uncle Luke: he was head-on, lightsaber in hand, face-to-face with the enemy—the kind of enemy who came at you in open combat.

He was too decent and honest to think like a terrorist. He had rules. It was what made him strong.

"We'll be going, then, Chief," said Luke. He bowed his head slightly. "Let's see how the next few days pan out, and then revisit this."

He nodded politely to Jacen and left with Mara. She gave Jacen a glance over her shoulder and smiled anxiously. Omas waited for them to leave and then looked at Jacen.

"I can understand everyone's reluctance," he said. "It's not heroic work, spying on your neighbors."

G'Sil gave a little snort of amusement. "It's heroic until you're the person whose ID is being checked, and then it's an affront to your rights . . ."

"People are going to have to get used to that again. It won't be the first time," Omas said.

Jacen thought now was as good a time as any to ask again. "Have you had further thoughts on the matter I suggested the other day, sir?"

Omas's mind was clearly elsewhere. "Hitting the shipyards?"

"Yes."

"I'll discuss it with Admiral Pellaeon. If he thinks it has merit, I'll table it with the Defense Council."

"Thank you."

Jacen should have gone back to his apartment and used his time to teach Ben more of the subtle techniques of the Force, but he admitted to himself that he was as impatient as his young pupil. He had set Ben a study task to occupy him in his absence: to visit the sites of the bombing and the attack on the Corellian Sanctuary, and to sense what he could of the people and events surrounding them. It was a tough assignment. It would frustrate him—and keep him busy for at least a day.

And Jacen needed a day to himself to resolve his doubts over Lumiya.

She was still in her asteroid habitat near Bimmiel. He felt her there: when he concentrated, he could sense her emotions, which were an odd blend of relief and sincerity. *But if she can create the kind of Force illusions we experienced in her home, then she could fake anything.* She could have been anywhere, even on Coruscant. She might be able to project totally false emotions, too, because he could do much the same himself and fool even other Jedi Masters into believing them.

I'm not proud of that. But it's a necessary skill.

Jacen walked toward the restored Jedi Temple. It was there as it had been for millennia, albeit in a new, modern guise, and the destruction by the Yuuzhan Vong seemed no more than a brief absence, the guttering of a candle in a breeze. When the breeze dropped, the flame would reappear, as steady and unmoving as it had been before—and so had the Temple.

Jacen walked along the wide promenade to the entrance. The stepped base, cut from almost flesh-tinted stone, lifted the Temple complex a little above the buildings surrounding it. This wasn't a world of constructed canyons like the rest of Galactic City. This quadrant was low-rise, and from the transparisteel pyramid was a view that few in Coruscant ever saw—not the close gaze of another towering building opposite and a dense forest of others as far as the eye could see, but a wide vista. It was one of permacrete, stone, and transparisteel rather than grassy plains; but it was a rare open view of the horizon nonetheless.

The Temple's architecture and interior design were aggressively modern, but key parts of the layout, like the council chamber, had been retained; the marble floor was a replica of the original. It struck Jacen as obsessive rather than reverent, as if the Jedi order had never wanted change and challenge to interrupt its sense of permanence. Jacen paused, hands meshed, and saw something he had never seen before: he saw *ambition.*

He saw a love of power and status. He saw a statement of government, of inexorable permanence. *We're back. We're not going to be swept aside again.* The stone almost spoke to him.

This didn't feel like spirituality. He didn't like it. No wonder Luke had insisted that the new grand trappings in the council chamber be removed. Jacen shivered at the touch of mundane ambition.

And to think he'd been afraid that he was being lured to the Sith way by a lust for power.

He lowered his arms to his side and tried again to feel something that would explain the sense of a tightly grasped power that pervaded the building. It almost tingled in his fingers. It moved in his chest like a symbiont that had invaded his body.

It might be the ambition and pride of architects, craftspeople, builders. Don't judge so fast.

But construction droids had done most of the work.

He couldn't shake off the clear impression of the exercise of power—and the love of it—that felt as if it had built up like sediment in an ancient river over centuries. He hadn't felt it before.

Marble and pleekwood created an understated, cool interior interrupted occasionally by faithfully copied busts of great Jedi Masters, displayed in niches in exactly the same places as they had been before the Yuuzhan Vong, and before the Temple had burned in the purges following Palpatine's seizure of power.

Jacen paused again as he walked through the lobby.

There had been objections to the cost of the reconstruction of the Temple when so many urgent postwar restoration projects seemed more pressing. Some citizens couldn't see the point. The government insisted. The Jedi council said it wanted to restore *normality*.

Uncle Luke, this was never the way you saw the order, was it? How did they talk you into this?

Jacen knew exactly where he was now, and it scared him. He had a finely tuned sense of where he was in space. Had he rolled back time by fifty-nine years to this *exact* distance from the planet's core, this *exact* distance from the planet's north pole, this very point in three dimensions, he would have been walking with his grandfather Anakin Skywalker.

But I can *walk back in time.*

Jacen could time-drift. He was almost too afraid to. But he did, almost without thinking. As he projected himself into the past and merged with its reality, he saw a young blond Jedi with his lightsaber drawn, flanked by troops in white armor. Jacen was looking at him from behind. He could see the muscles in his jaw twitching as his head turned, seeking something: he could *feel* his dread and determination.

Nobody spoke. They were searching, all of them looking to one side then the other, aiming rifles and lowering them a little. Something terrible was happening.

Anakin.

Anakin Skywalker held his lightsaber two-handed, and for a moment Jacen was one with his grandfather's emotions. He was overwhelmed by a dread and reluctance—the same dread and reluctance he had felt himself when Lumiya told him his destiny. Jacen felt, too, a crushing sense of something terrible and deadly about to happen.

He hung back. He'd been spotted while time-drifting before and had been forced to withdraw. But he *had* to stay with this. He hardly dared think ahead.

I might be able to ask him. I might be able to ask Grandfather about his own fall to the Sith.

This would be his answer about his own path.

He touched Anakin's emotions again, comparing them with his own, and then he felt something that was not within him at all: it was desperate, terrified *loss*. For a second he couldn't identify it. Then it settled and became clear in the form of a tight sensation in his throat and the pressure of tears behind his eyes that stung and burned. It was very like the brief misery he had felt when he left Tenel Ka and his daughter. Anakin was facing separation from Padmé, and was terrified by it.

But it wasn't a moment's emotion for his grandfather: it was the *whole* of him. Anakin had been driven to the dark side by agonized love. The revelation stunned Jacen because it was so narrow and so . . . *selfish*. Relief flooded him.

This is different. That isn't what I feel, or what's driving me.

And right then he wanted to talk to his grandfather more than anything he could imagine. It was a burst of love for a man he had never known—a man who had helped bring balance to the Force.

You're insane. You're going too far. Don't even think about influencing the past—

But he had absolutely no idea what the past really was, right up to the point where he saw the younglings approach Anakin, scared but clutching their lightsabers, telling him there were too many soldiers for them to drive off. Anakin stared down at them. Then he drew his own saber and Jacen tasted absolute grief and shame and *duty*.

He was hunting Jedi. He was killing them somehow *for Padmé*'s sake. His reasoning was vivid and focused. Jacen knew that Anakin had done this, but seeing it—feeling it—living it—was agonizingly new and shocking because the emotion was so desperately animal in its intensity.

No, I'm not feeling this. It's one of Lumiya's vile tricks. I'm not seeing this.

Then one of the armored troopers appeared, raising his

rifle, and Jacen jerked himself out of time and back to the present, heart pounding.

Grandfather . . .

"Are you all right, Master?" said a very young apprentice. The girl had a bright, optimistic face like polished ebonite; she held a datapad in one hand. "Can I get you some water?"

"I'm fine, thank you," he lied. "Just a little giddy, that's all."

The girl bowed her head politely and walked off, eyes fixed on her datapad.

Jacen wanted to vomit. But he controlled his shock and revulsion: he now knew things he could never erase from his mind. It was Anakin's moment of madness, his surrender to slaughter even though he knew it was insane. That wasn't the man he had grown to understand through his mother and uncle.

Would *he* go *that* far for his own wife? Would *he* know where personal need outweighed his duty?

He centered himself with every scrap of effort he could muster and waited for the turbolift, eyes averted when anyone passed. He felt they could see the horror in his soul. But, of course, he was now adept at concealing even that from other Jedi.

I'm not Grandfather.

The lift seemed to take forever to arrive.

I was meant *to see how low he fell.*

He hit the control with the heel of his hand, fighting tears. "Come on. What's keeping you?" Two apprentices stared at him but hurried past.

That's my proof. That's my pain. I have to embrace it to understand that I am not *making my grandfather's mistake all over again.*

Jacen knew what it was to love, and he was older and far more experienced than Anakin Skywalker had been then.

He could *handle* what was happening to him now. He would never do another's bidding and he could become a Sith without fear of being sucked down into something evil. He still didn't relish the duty, but it *was* a duty, not a delusion: he *wasn't* repeating his grandfather's mistakes. He was absolutely certain of that now.

Relief, unbearable sorrow, and disbelief fought in him. He might have asked his grandfather for his reasons, but that was for his personal comfort and not for the purpose of peace, so it would have to wait. That was something for later, once he had become a full Sith Lord and brought peace and stability to the galaxy at last.

By then, he might be ready to deal with the truth of his grandfather's shame.

Finally—the turbolift doors opened. Jacen ascended to the re-created Room of a Thousand Fountains to sit among the plants and pools to meditate. He knew what he had to do now: he knew he had to test Lumiya to be sure she could help him achieve full Sith knowledge, as she promised, or if she was following her own agenda and planning to exploit *him*.

It should have been a terrifying thought, but a delicious sensation of complete stillness settled around him. He had found a precious piece of absolute *truth,* both about the universe and about himself.

Crossing his legs in a mediation position, he let his consciousness reach out across the Force, not as an open hand but as a commanding fist.

Lumiya. Come here, Lumiya.

Come to Coruscant and answer to me.

CORELLIAN SANCTUARY, CORUSCANT.

It was one of the saddest places that Ben had ever visited. He felt the loneliness the moment he got within fifty meters of the Corellian Sanctuary. Outside, three men—one of them very old—were scrubbing away at bright red paint that had splashed and run down the polished gold and black marble inlay of the little domed memorial. They looked up at him as he approached, frowning and suspicious. Ben wasn't sure what to say.

"What d'you want, kid?" said the youngest man.

"I wanted to look inside, sir." *Be polite; be humble.* Jacen had taught him that if you treated people kindly, they normally returned the favor. "Is that okay?"

"You a Jedi?"

The brown and beige robes were a giveaway. "Yes."

"Why do you want to see inside?"

"My uncle's Corellian." And it wasn't even a lie: he was genuinely as curious about Corellians as he was determined to complete the task that Jacen had given him. "May I go inside?"

The men looked at him, then at each other.

"I'll take him," said the old man.

Ben hesitated on the threshold. The doors of the arched entrance looked as if they'd been forced open. He followed the man into darkness and when his eyes adjusted, he was in a black-walled chamber that swallowed up the light. Then he looked up. The domed ceiling was studded with sparkling chunks of rough diamond set in constellations.

"They compressed the carbon left from cremations," said the old man. "Turned it into diamonds. That's the night sky as you'd see it from Corellia."

"Why?"

"Corellians who couldn't get home during the New Republic." The old man kicked through rubble on the floor of the chamber; some chunks bore black paint, signs of how the vandals had hacked at the plaster. "Next best thing to resting in home soil."

"Did you find all the stones they took out?" asked Ben.

"No."

"Who'd want to steal diamonds made from bodies?"

The old man frowned at him. "Some people don't care about that kind of thing."

The man was hurt and angry. Ben could understand that. He bent down and helped him pick up the rubble, checking each chunk for fragments of diamond, because that was, after all, a *person*. While they cleared the chamber, one of the younger men wandered in and stood watching. He was about eighteen, with short blond hair scrunched into spikes.

"We can't stand by and let them get away with this," he said.

"Who's them?" said Ben.

"Coruscanti."

"You know who did this?" Ben sensed an echo of half-hearted malice from the chamber, no real plans or hatred or intention to outrage. He finally understood what Jacen meant by *mindless violence*. Some people really did seem to do it without thinking very much. "Then you ought to tell CSF."

"Yeah, like they'd really take *that* seriously, I don't think. Not when they're looking for Corellians who planted a bomb."

Ben went to sweep up the remaining dust but the old man took the broom from him and did it himself. Ben sensed some resentment. He bowed his head, even though the man had turned his back on him, and walked outside into daylight that seemed painfully bright. The blond man went with him, and they sat down on the honey-colored marble steps that led up to the sanctuary.

"I'm Barit Saiy," said the blond man, and held out his hand.

Ben shook it gravely. "I'm Ben."

"So you've got Corellian relatives."

"Yeah."

"Whose side are you on?"

"I'm a Jedi. We don't take sides."

"You reckon?" Barit laughed, but not as if he thought it was remotely funny. "Everyone's going to be taking sides soon, what with this government trying to force its rules on everybody. I hate them. My granddad says it's like the Empire all over again."

"You *live* here, though."

"I was *born* here. So was my dad. My folks own an engineering workshop in Q-Sixty-five. Never even been to Corellia, yet."

"But you could live on Corellia if you hate it here so much."

"Would that stop them treating us the way they do?"

Ben was finding it hard to understand the *them* and the *us* of the conversation. He'd traveled the galaxy with his parents; he'd seen less of Coruscant than he had of a dozen other worlds.

But Barit wasn't just visibly angry: There was also a real sense of pent-up danger about him. Ben hadn't realized just what an emotional thing the Sanctuary was for Corellians living here.

Ben probed cautiously. "They said on the news that the bomb went off in the room of a Corellian man over here on business."

"They would say that, wouldn't they?" Barit had his elbows braced on his knees, right hand clutching his left wrist, looking around at pedestrians walking along the nearby promenade. "I bet they did it themselves."

"Who's they?"

"The government. CSF. Galactic security. They do that kind of spy stuff. If they plant a bomb and blame it on us, then it gives them an excuse to attack Corellia."

Ben thought of what he had done only a few weeks earlier: he'd sabotaged Centerpoint Station, Corellia's military pride and joy. And here he was sitting with a Corellian who thought the Galactic Alliance played dirty tricks and who treated him like a fellow Corellian. Ben felt a little thrill, the kind that came from having a secret identity, and then he felt . . . pretty bad about it all.

But he'd done what he had to.

Hadn't he?

"What do other Corellians here think?"

Barit shrugged. "There's a lot of us. And enough don't want to be dictated to by the Galactic Alliance."

Ben took that to mean that there would be a war after all, just as Jacen had warned—and just as Ben had felt when he sensed the anxiety in the Force. "So you'll be going back to Corellia to join the armed forces, then."

Barit lowered his voice. "Why do that, when we can fight better here?"

Ben thought about that for a moment. Adults often said things to him that they really shouldn't, seeming to think that he was too young to understand. Sometimes he was, though he always *remembered* what was said to him. But he wasn't too young to understand Barit.

It's just talk. We all say stupid things when we're angry.

Even so, he would remember it.

chapter five

My fee's five hundred thousand credits each for Han Solo and his son. If you want the Solo womenfolk and the Skywalkers, too—that'll be extra. I remember the Solo kids, but I don't think they'll recognize me again....

—Ailyn Habuur, aka Ailyn Vel,
bounty hunter, to an intermediary for Thrackan Sal-Solo

MUNICIPAL PORT,
LOWER CORONET, CORELLIA.

Han Solo had a smuggler's fine-tuned sense for avoiding trouble. But he was a little out of practice after years of respectability, and there was definitely a different skill needed to evade detection in a city in peacetime. He made his way to the *Millennium Falcon* under cover of darkness to check on the hyperdrive. It still needed work.

The distance from the rented apartment to the municipal landing strip was two kilometers. The *Falcon* nestled among a motley array of vessels, making what should have been an easily recognizable ship just one dented, scraped crate among scores of freighters, modified fighters, speeders, taxis, landing craft, and any number of heavily modified, shabby, and unidentifiable craft. Corellians were eclectic in their choice of transport, so one more vintage ship in a dubious state of repair wasn't going to draw much attention. In fact, the *Falcon* wasn't even the only ship of her class parked on the apron. There were, as far as Han could see, at least three others.

He ambled around the starboard side, pressed the security pad in his pocket, and lowered the ramp to board her. Once in the cockpit, he switched her to tick-over and the array of status lights and readouts flickered into life. This was *home*. It had been for as long as he could remember. This was where he had spent some of the most important moments of his life, where he had spent time with friends like Chewbacca, where he had found out who he really was. Permacrete and mortar meant nothing to him. The *Falcon* was more than home: she was family, too, and all the people he had ever loved had passed through her sooner or later.

He patted the console bulkhead lovingly. "Hi, baby," he said. "How you doing? Let's make you all better."

The hyperdrive was still off-balance. The coils and injectors needed a little more care spent on them to make sure that they released exactly the right amount of energy into the drive at the proper rate. Some of the repairs were simple mechanical stuff like finding the correct gauge of durasteel for the bolts on the housing and the shafts that created the fields. However advanced the propulsion system, it still came down to a point where huge forces created by energy had to be transferred to the good old-fashioned durasteel and alloy parts that held the drive and the hull together. Small vibrations became magnified; eventually, they smashed whole ships.

Han checked the automated system that sent sound waves through the hull to check for stress microfractures in the casing and airframe. There it was: stressing around the drive housing. He needed to replace brackets and bolts before he could risk taking the *Falcon* to full speed. He grabbed some tools and eased himself into the drive access space headfirst to see for himself. There was a certain comfort in getting his hands dirty and seeing problems as chunks of metal that could be fixed.

Okay, how do I fix Thrackan?

In theory, it was easy. Find out where he was at a given time and how to get to him, take a shot, and run.

But it wasn't that simple in reality. That was why men like Fett made their fortunes doing it.

And if I fix Thrackan, will there be another of his minions to take his place? Are we always going to be running?

No, it was just Thrackan. It was personal, like it always had been, and nobody else could hate you quite as thoroughly and efficiently as your own kin. Han tested the torque on the housing bolts with a hydrospanner and noted the illuminated display on the handle. There was a little play in the bolts: not enough for flesh and blood to detect, but discernible by sensitive equipment. If he needed to make a run for it in the *Falcon* right now, it would be a much slower one if he didn't want the airframe to shake itself apart.

"Aw, baby, I've neglected you . . ."

He set the spanner to extract the bolts one by one, let them fall into his hand, and padded them out with a makeshift pin of soft alloy before screwing them back in. That would cut down on the movement until he could find the right spares. "I promise I won't let you get into this state ever again."

"Touching," said a voice above him, and he jerked into a ball instinctively, knees tight to his chest, as the flare of blasterfire hit the deck a hand span away from where he'd been lying.

He rolled under the housing and reached for his hold-out blaster. Another bolt sizzled on the bulkhead to one side of him; he smelled singed paint and ozone. He was right under the housing now, too far under for whoever it was to get a clear shot at him unless they got down flat on the deck and fired at floor level.

Well, it wasn't Fett, that was for sure. He'd have been dead by now if it had been.

Han rolled over onto his belly with one elbow braced on the deck of the compartment to propel himself on the smooth surface and his blaster in his other hand. It was hard to see at this angle, but he spotted movement, and knew he was looking at boots.

"Come on out, Solo," said the voice. It was a man, probably young. He didn't identify himself: so he wasn't CorSec. *Chancer. Out for a bit of glory, a reward.* "Thought nobody would spot your ship, did you?"

Han held his breath, keeping an eye on the play of light that told him someone was creeping back and forth in front of the drive housing. He was trapped under a hunk of metal with only one way out. That was toward his attacker. *Fine.* He could do that, too. It only made him mad—mad that he hadn't set the intruder alert again, and even madder that someone was on his ship. It was the ultimate insult.

Lying flat under the housing, he had a 150-degree arc in front of him.

He flicked the blaster to the continuous fire setting with his thumb and braced his forearm on the deck. There was blood on the back of his hand: he must have scraped himself on something sharp. He hadn't felt a thing.

What if this guy had a gang backing him up? "Come and get me, kid."

Boots moved again. "You're stuck."

Han swung a stream of fire, left to right, just to make sure he hit something. There was a loud shriek of surprised pain. "And your dancing days are over."

Someone thudded onto the deck with a grunt of pain, and blasterfire hit something, because Han saw the flash and smelled the burn: but he hadn't killed anyone, and that meant he was still pinned down under the drive housing. He was working out just how fast he could get out from under the housing and realizing it wouldn't be a fast exit at all when he heard a startled "Uhh!" and a distinctive and very welcome sound.

Vzzzmmmm.

A lightsaber cut an arc through the air, once, twice, three times. Then there was silence. He waited, breathless.

"You can come on out now, old man." The voice was Leia's. Han detected a slight edge to it. "I've cleared up the mess for you."

"Thanks."

"Ever seen a Bothan well-spider?" Leia peered through the gap, on all fours. "They fight like you. They fire strands of caustic silk out of their burrows at predators. I couldn't help but be reminded. That and the gangly legs."

Han eased himself out of the drive housing space, realizing for the first time how many bruises and scrapes he'd have in the morning. It was one thing thinking you were as fit and fast as you ever were, but healing wasn't quite so quick at sixty as it was at twenty.

"You think you're funny, Princess, but you're not . . ."

"You're welcome. I thought I'd keep an eye on you."

"Because you sensed danger?"

"That, and I know how you shut the whole world out when you're thinking about this ship."

"Yeah, love's blind."

Han dragged himself out, catching his scalp on something and cursing. When he straightened up, Leia was standing over what Han could only describe as a dead guy. He was in civilian clothing and looked about thirty. He wouldn't be seeing thirty-one, that was for sure.

Leia held the lightsaber hilt in one hand, visibly jumpy. She tossed her head as if the novelty of having shoulder-length hair instead of a braid almost to her waist was taking some getting used to.

"Suits you," said Han.

"Feels weird . . . like my whole head's lighter."

"They say really long hair is aging for mature women, anyway."

"You looking for trouble, nerf herder?"

"Like we don't have enough?"

"I think we'd better disappear right now."

"What about the body?"

"Dump it out the air lock when we're clear."

"When did a nice girl like you learn to do things like that?"

"You taught me."

"Nice to know I have my uses." Han secured the drive housing cover plate, and they headed for the cockpit. It was like old times again, but old times he really didn't want to keep reliving.

"Where to?" said Leia.

"Coruscant," Han said. "For spare parts."

"And nobody on our tail there. Not trying to kill us, anyway."

"Luke can read me the riot act instead."

"At least the droids and the Noghri will be happy to have us back."

Han fired up the *Falcon*'s drive and hoped for the best. "I was planning on coming back once I've fixed the drive."

"That's smart," said Leia. She fell into the role of copilot automatically now. It was almost like having Chewie: almost, but that was a space not even Leia could fill. "Is this some macho thing? There's a time when a man's got to stop running and all that guff?"

"I'm going to be ready for Thrackan when the time comes."

Leia said nothing. The *Falcon* lifted clear, and Han laid in a course for Coruscant, ready to risk a jump to maximum velocity if Corellian Traffic Control had the same idea as the would-be assassin now cooling rapidly in the engineering space below. But the vessel slipped through the shipping lanes and out to the jump point with no more than a routine automated transponder exchange.

"I should have asked how that guy found us," said Han.

Leia didn't even raise an eyebrow. "I'll remember to leave you a moment for questions next time I stop someone trying to kill you."

Han took the *Falcon* as close to maximum speed as he dared. They spent the three hours it took to cover the twenty thousand light-years to Coruscant watching readouts and indicators, hoping the drive would hold together. By the time they reached Coruscant space, the *Falcon* had developed an uncharacteristic vibration that made her frame feel as if it were rolling on a sea every few seconds with an unnatural regularity.

Leia leaned forward in her seat and checked drive temperatures and profiles with visible anxiety. "You sure she's going to land in one piece?"

Han shrugged, knowing that wouldn't fool her one bit. "No. But trust me."

He picked up the Galactic City beacon at 750,000 kilometers and laid in a course to land at one of the public docking bays a long way from the center of the city—and unwelcome attention. What would they do if they knew who he was? Nothing. This was civilized space, where he might be asked some awkward questions about his Corellian sympathies, if anyone knew he had flown that mission with Wedge: but they didn't, and so he could drop in openly as Solo, Captain H., anytime he liked. If they *did* know he'd fought against the Galactic Alliance, they might just invite him in for a few questions, and a tangled game with lawyers would follow.

This was Coruscant, a planet run by law and conventions. People didn't disappear here—except in the criminal underworld.

But Han was cautious enough to stay with the anonymized transponder that identified the *Falcon* this time as a Tatooine freighter. There was a time when a visual check or a thermal signature would have betrayed her as a fighting ship, but she was old, and any number of eccentric traders flew modified fleet surplus warships these days. They had nice big cargo holds and handy defensive armament, which was just what was needed in some of the wilder parts of the galactic business community.

The console computer chatted silently with Galactic City ATC, swapping messages that blurred into streaks of illuminated text and symbols. The screen settled on a comforting message designed for human eyes: CLEAR TO DOCK AT BERTH BW 9842 TIME WINDOW 1245 TO 1545.

"Okay, prep for docking," said Han.

"You *never* say that."

"I never thought the drive might land without the rest of the ship before."

Leia watched the console with a slight frown, white and green lights from the instruments reflecting on her face. Han found he was studying her for signs of dismay, as if her confidence alone would make for a safe landing. The *Falcon* was vibrating noticeably now: nothing spectacular, but a regular, barely perceptible movement like a missing heartbeat every five seconds or so, with a slight murmur of moving parts that a pilot would hear only if he knew the ship as well as he knew his own body. And Han knew the *Falcon* that well.

So did Leia. She glanced at him and winked. "It'll be fine."

"Dropping to sublight."

"Sublight," said Leia, confirming the helm order.

The *Falcon* murmured again. Han found his knuckles straining white under the skin of his right hand as he clutched the yoke. The more tightly he held it, the more the vibration felt magnified into something to worry about.

"Engaging maneuvering drive." The drive kicked in with its own distinctive hums and resonance. *Come on, baby. Just a regular landing. You've done a million of them. Stay in one piece.* "Distance five hundred thousand kilometers."

"Adjusting angle of approach."

"Make twenty-four degrees."

"Correcting to twenty-four."

"Holding steady."

The navigation display showed a neat grid of lines and numbers with the icon that represented the *Falcon* aligned on the course that represented a safe approach to the Galactic City landing strip. A rhythmic shiver intruded into the familiar layers of sound and vibration that Han knew without even thinking about it as *normal.*

"Don't say it," Leia said sharply.

"Don't say what?"

"That you've got a bad feeling."

"Never crossed my mind," Han lied.

"Crossed *mine.*" Leia didn't even look up from the control console. "Because I've got one, too."

PLAZA OF THE CORE, CORUSCANT.

Lumiya was coming. She had answered Jacen's summons: she was heading for Coruscant, without argument or fear.

And he could feel her. He found he could track her—and her emotions—almost as if he could see her.

Ben sat beside him, unusually quiet, hands in his lap. He had taken to wearing a very small braid in his red hair, hardly long enough to plait and tied awkwardly with a scrap of brown thread, but Jacen could see it. The boy had his shoulders hunched up a little as if he was trying to hide it.

"Bad hair day?" Jacen commented. He found more to like and admire about Ben every day. The boy had growth spurts emotionally as well as physically, and the last few weeks seemed to have literally made a man of him. But Jacen wanted him to keep his sense of humor. He'd need it in the years to come.

"I . . . er . . . thought I ought to grow it." Ben's blush almost matched his hair. "Does it look stupid?"

"Not at all. But you're not technically an apprentice, so you don't have to wear it if you don't want to."

"I want to."

"Fine. Good."

"Who are we waiting for?"

I hate fooling him. But it has to be done. "A woman who's going to do some research for us. Military threat analysis." He took one more risky step—but Lumiya's old name was a common one, unlikely to draw any attention, and it ruled out slips of the tongue. "Her name's Shira. You might see her around from time to time."

"But we could get analysis from the Security and Intelligence Council."

"I like to have an independent view, as well. You can never have too much information." Jacen gave Ben a playful nudge. It helped him bury the shock that kept resurfacing after seeing his grandfather commit an atrocity. "Talking of which, you haven't given me your threat analysis."

Ben's eyes widened: he wanted to please. "Of what, Jacen?"

"I'm waiting to hear your impressions of the locations you visited."

"I didn't get much from the bomb site—not that the CSF would let me get too close—but the Corellian Sanctuary was . . . well, scary."

"Why?"

"I talked to some Corellians cleaning up the place. They really seem to hate Coruscant. I don't get it."

"Coruscant has had rifts with Corellia before."

"But they hate us and they live here."

"It's a cosmopolitan planet. Lots of worlds we might end up fighting have communities here."

"But Jacen, if they're talking about fighting us *here*—"

"Are they?"

"Well, a guy a little older than me. Probably just . . . *bravado.*"

Ben's sudden lurch into sober manhood, unsteady as it was, touched Jacen. "It's always interesting to note what sparks wars. It's often something relatively small, but for some reason it just tips the situation into chaos."

"That's the real enemy, isn't it?" said Ben. "Chaos."

Jacen almost shivered. It was another perceptive wise-beyond-age comment of the kind Ben was increasingly prone to. It might also have been the clarity of someone too young to have his thinking muddied and corrupted by convention.

It was also almost a *Sith* sentiment. Ben would make a good apprentice, and for all the right reasons. His sense of duty was starting to become tangible.

"I reckon so," Jacen said. "The galaxy works best when things are certain."

Jacen kept an eye on the movement of citizens crossing the plaza. He knew Lumiya wouldn't be so crass as to turn up in her exotic triangular headdress and trailing a light-whip. He could feel her coming, and it was almost a game to spot her by eyesight alone.

He hadn't warned her that he'd have Ben with him. He wanted to see how she reacted to Ben, and also how Ben reacted to her. Ben still couldn't recall what had happened out at Bimmiel, although he'd stopped asking now.

About a hundred meters away, Jacen caught sight of a middle-aged woman in a neat red business suit—plain tunic and pants—that was so dark it verged on black. She had a matching scarf wrapped around her head that covered her entire face; her eyes were obscured by a gauzy inset of some translucent silk. It was a practical fashion common on arid, dusty worlds and it seemed to be catching on in the capital, too. He knew it was Lumiya. He magnified his presence in the Force to get her attention, and she changed direction slightly as if she had spotted him like anyone else might.

The closer she came, the stronger the sense he had of a Sith making a conscious effort to conceal her presence in the Force, and almost succeeding.

"Is that her?" Ben asked.

Lumiya was close enough now for it to be obvious that she had seen Jacen and was walking straight toward him. She must also have seen Ben, but she didn't react at any level. She stopped right in front of Jacen, holding a black folio case in front of her with both hands almost like a shield. She had a soft, shapeless black bag over one shoulder: he suspected he knew what was in it.

"Master Solo," she said.

Nice touch. And even her voice was different. "I'm not a Master, but thank you, Shira." He turned deliberately to Ben. "This is my apprentice, Ben Skywalker. In an unofficial sense, of course."

"I'm sure I've seen you before," said Ben. He sounded genuinely baffled, but there was no hint in his emotions that he recognized her as Brisha, the woman he had taken a dislike to at Bimmiel. "Nice to meet you, ma'am."

"You might have seen me around the university," said Lumiya.

"I'm only thirteen," said Ben.

"Really? Oh, perhaps not, then." She proffered her folio to Jacen, suddenly a very convincing academic. "I've assessed the current military capacities of Corellia and worlds most likely to support it. Would you like me to go through the reports with you?"

Good actress. Lumiya's skill at creating illusions extended into the physical world, as well.

"I thought we might go to the Jedi Temple," said Jacen. *Temptation and threat in one package, for a Sith.* "There are quiet areas where we can talk. Ben, do you want to come, too?"

Jacen expected him to insist on coming; he was desperately anxious to learn, even if that meant sitting through meetings that even adults found boring. But Ben dropped his chin slightly as if about to admit something.

"Is it okay if I visit Fleet Ops? Admiral Niathal said I could."

Jacen hadn't expected that. "Of course."

Ben took his leave of them with a grave bow of the head and walked off across the plaza, every centimeter the young man.

"Luke's son is growing up fast," said Lumiya, lifting her veil clear of her eyes.

"Don't worry, he doesn't recognize you."

"Why have you brought me here?"

"I wanted to discuss what we began to explore back in your home."

"You've thought about it a great deal. I felt that."

"Oh, yes, indeed." Jacen got up and beckoned her to follow. He didn't like being a stationary target: there was little—if anything—that could present a serious threat to him now, but old habits died hard. "I've thought of little else."

"Have you decided to let me help you achieve your destiny?"

"Yes."

She searched his face, turning her head a little as she walked. He could only see her eyes—vivid, green, somehow permanently angry—but he felt her try quite deliberately to touch his mind.

"I'm at your disposal," she said quietly.

"You've never been in the Jedi Temple, have you?"

"No. It'll be interesting."

"You can suppress your dark energy, I hope."

"Is that what you're testing, Jacen?"

"I need to know how safe it is to have you near me," he said. "There's no better way to see if you'll be detected than to test if you can pass through the Jedi Temple unnoticed."

He thought she smiled. There was some movement of the fine, oddly unlined skin around her eyes, and it unsettled him. "I managed to infiltrate the Rebellion . . ."

"You weren't Sith then."

"I've hidden for decades." She replaced the veil. "I can hide indefinitely—anywhere."

This was arcane mysticism on a scale that only a handful of people in the galaxy had ever needed to consider. And yet Jacen found himself hailing an air taxi and getting into it with a Sith Master, as mundane and everyday an act as he could imagine. He savored the incongruity of it. They didn't speak at all on the way to the Temple.

For a moment, Jacen almost saw the funny side of it. Taxi pilots being what they were, he could almost imagine this one—a Weequay—telling his other passengers, "Yeah, I had one of them Siths in my taxi once."

But the pilot would never know.

What if she's using me? Who'll teach me the Sith way if I have to—

Jacen caught himself thinking that he might have to remove her if she proved to be bent on vengeance against the Jedi or one Jedi in particular. He knew exactly what he meant by *remove,* and he was once again surprised by the ease with which he took one small step further toward doing things he had been raised to regard as evil.

"Set us down here, please, pilot."

Lumiya walked beside him up the promenade leading to the Temple, and it felt as if she had cloaked herself completely. He could sense her unease, but any hint of darkness had been reduced to no more than the simmering passions found in any ordinary untrained human being. She passed through the huge doors of the imposing entrance and reacted just as any ordinary person with no Force sensitivity would: she stopped in her tracks and stared. If she hadn't been wearing a full veil across her face, Jacen thought she might well have been gaping, too.

"It's quite an exercise in material magnificence, isn't it?" he said.

"A statement of power," Lumiya responded, wonderfully ambiguous.

Let's see how much temptation you can stand.

He led her through the few areas where non-Jedi were permitted, and nobody stopped him: he was Jacen Solo, and no one would challenge his right to invite a mundane guest. That much took no Force techniques to achieve, because a confident air of purpose often opened more doors than an ID pass.

He took her into the Room of a Thousand Fountains. If anything would force her to show her true intentions—even a glimmer of a drive for revenge—it was proximity to a place of meditation, and he would spot it.

There was one more test beyond that, but he had to work toward it a little more carefully. And that was to put Lumiya within striking distance of Luke Skywalker.

There was nothing like seeing an old love who was also an old enemy to unlock someone's true emotions.

They walked in the vast greenhouse of exotic plants that had been collected from across the galaxy. Lumiya still exuded curiosity and a little surprise. There were only a few Jedi meditating there, but Jacen found a convenient bench between two assari trees whose branches swayed gently despite the absence of any wind. Water rushed over a huge granite boulder and tumbled into a stream that disappeared under a cover of bhansgrek bushes.

"I'd prefer you to stay on Coruscant," said Jacen.

"If that's what you want."

"I'll arrange a safe house for you." This wasn't the place to carry on a conversation in any detail. "And I'll want to discuss what my further instruction might consist of."

"Speed will be important," Lumiya said.

Oh, I know how fast events are moving. "Why?"

"I feel what you can feel—that we're on the brink of another war, and there are some wars from which people might never recover."

"I don't think there's ever been a time in our recorded history when there wasn't a war going on somewhere."

"All the more reason for changing the future, then."

Jacen took her around as much of the rest of the Temple as he could access with a visitor, but no Jedi reacted to her. She didn't betray a single emotion that indicated any agenda beyond what she claimed she had: to help him fulfill his destiny as the supreme Sith Lord.

He checked his chrono. A wild idea occurred to him, and he was getting used to listening to those as suggestions from the Force. The scheduled high council meeting would be ending soon.

All his study in a hundred different ways of harnessing the Force had come to a single point of fruition now. The only gaps in his knowledge of the Force were those of the Sith.

Sith techniques are just another weapon.

And they weren't inherently good or evil: they just existed, like a blaster, and you could just as easily use a blaster to murder as to defend. It all depended on who held it, and who stood within its range.

That much he knew.

"All right. How do I change the future for the better?"

"The next few weeks will determine what more you need to learn," said Lumiya.

"Did you arrange for that bombing to happen?"

Lumiya laughed, one of those little indignant snorts of disbelief.

"I don't need to create chaos, Jacen," she said quietly. "People are only too willing to do it for themselves. No, I had nothing to do with that."

He checked his chrono again. Yes, he had to do it *now*. It was time for her final test of sincerity.

"Let's take a walk," he said.

He led her through the corridors to the main lobby through which the passages to the high council chamber passed. Lumiya should have been able to detect Luke's presence, but it was essential that Luke not detect hers. Jacen concentrated on forming a Force illusion around her, not to make her appear as anyone else but to simply erase her presence as a Sith, in case her own subterfuge wasn't powerful enough to deceive Luke.

You're insane, he told himself. *What if you're wrong? What if Luke can sense her? Who's going to help you attain full Sith knowledge if Lumiya is killed or imprisoned?*

Jacen had thought of this test of Lumiya's intentions and so it was meant to be. He had to get used to that. He had to trust his reactions not as impulses to be doubted, but as *decisions.*

Steady. Trust yourself.

Jacen cloaked Lumiya in a Force illusion and projected his own unconcerned calm as Luke approached. It was an exhausting maneuver, nothing beyond him when dealing with ordinary people, but something that took all his strength when deceiving a Jedi Master of Luke's stature.

Luke strode toward them and glanced back over his shoulder a couple of times as if someone were following him. He acknowledged Jacen stiffly and paid Lumiya no more than polite attention, as if his mind was more on what was down the corridor.

Jacen strained to hold the Force illusion steady, like a ball of heat within his chest that he had to balance to keep it from touching his rib cage. That was *exactly* how it felt. And Lumiya . . . Lumiya, somehow nestled in miniature within that ball of heat, felt not vengeful or trying to disguise her intentions, but genuinely worried about being discovered before her work was complete.

Luke seemed baffled.

Suddenly Jacen realized that it wasn't anything in the office at the end of the corridor that was distracting Luke: he could sense something amiss and wasn't sure where it was coming from.

Luke was sensing Lumiya, but very faintly. Jacen knew it.

"Good morning, Uncle."

"Hello, Jacen." Luke's gaze rested briefly on Lumiya, but he concentrated on Jacen. "Morning, ma'am. Where's Ben?"

"Admiral Niathal is showing him around the Fleet Ops center." Jacen knew Luke was in a hurry to see Omas, the way he always was after a council meeting. "Have you time for a caf?"

Luke shook his head, as Jacen expected. "Sorry. Perhaps later." He was making an effort to disguise his uneasiness with Jacen in front of a stranger. He nodded politely at Lumiya, and then glanced briefly behind him again. "Ma'am."

They watched him go. Eventually Lumiya let out a breath. "You didn't have to do that."

Jacen kept the Force cover in place. "I think I did."

"My issues with Luke Skywalker are long over, Jacen."

"Really?"

"Yes. If I wanted to get to him, I wouldn't need you as a route. Please understand what's at stake here. This is beyond our own little personal grievances." She picked up her folio case. "I should go now."

He felt a surge of real anger in her. He believed her. Events were unfolding as they were because it was his *destiny*. He grew more accepting of it by the hour.

"I'll see you out," he said.

They walked back through the main entrance and paused halfway down the promenade to look back at the Temple. "So how does it feel to have walked in your enemy's camp?"

"I don't see Jedi as the enemy now," said Lumiya. "That's far too simplistic."

"What, then?"

"They're people with only half the picture who believe they have all the facts. It makes their decisions flawed."

"It's hard to want to see the rest of that picture."

"You already do."

He watched Lumiya walk away toward the taxi pad until he could no longer see her, only sense her. He was so engrossed in exploring the ripples she left in the Force and searching them for signs that he was startled by what touched his mind then, almost as if someone had tapped him on the shoulder.

He felt his *mother*. She was in trouble.

His future as a Sith Lord was very easy to lay aside for a moment while he reached out to find her.

CORELLIAN QUARTER, GALACTIC CITY, CORUSCANT.

I should have told Jacen where I was going.

Ben hadn't exactly lied to Jacen: he really *had* visited the Fleet Command Center, and Admiral Niathal really *had* showed him around the ops rooms. It just hadn't taken as long as he had expected. And now he was still desperately curious about the Corellians who lived on Coruscant and who were now quite possibly what Niathal called *the enemy within*.

Ben was having trouble working out what was truly Coruscanti on a world of a thousand species. But they were at war with other humans. What was *them*? What was *us*? How could Coruscant be both a separate world and the embodiment of the galaxy, *all* of it?

Maybe that was the problem.

Ben found himself in one of the Corellian neighborhoods near the heart of Galactic City, wandering along the catwalks among shops and homes and businesses. He was looking for an engineering workshop called Saiy's, owned by Barit's family. This looked like any other neighborhood: the names on the stores didn't look any different from those on the rest of Coruscant. The people looked like him. The more he saw of nonhuman species, the more Ben was intrigued by the ease with which beings could fight among themselves. It was as if the small differences mattered more than the really big ones—like you had to recognize something before you could hate it properly.

No wonder Jacen wanted to bring a bit of order to the galaxy.

Jedi weren't exactly invisible, but there was something about wearing a brown robe that gave you a *certain neutrality,* as Jacen called it. Ben ambled along the catwalks, taking in the detail; and although people glanced at him with vague curiosity, nobody bothered him.

Maybe they're seeing a kid and not a Jedi.

Ben was passing in front of a small grocery store when he heard the distinctive thrum of a large vessel behind him. He looked back to see a Coruscant Security Force assault ship, the kind the police used for patrols, making slow progress down the skylane with its side hatches open. Maybe the officers were looking for someone. But then he heard a booming voice from the vessel's public address system.

". . . do *not* use your water supply." The vessel was almost level with him now and the disembodied voice filled the narrow skylane, reverberating off the walls of buildings. "I repeat, contamination has been found in the water supply, and as a precaution all water has been cut off. Do *not* use your supply, because water standing in the pipes may be contaminated . . . please listen to your news station for updates . . ."

The ship passed, repeating its emergency message as it advanced, and Ben saw four blue-uniformed CSF officers standing inside the crew bay, one with a voice projector clutched in his hand.

"Contaminated with what?" said Ben. But he was talking to himself. People had come out of their homes and businesses to stand on the walkway and stare after the assault ship. One woman came out of a tapcaf with a holonews receiver and set it on one of the tables outside, and customers crowded around. Ben paused to watch.

The news channel was running a live report from someone at one of the water company's pumping stations. Problems with utilities were rare on Coruscant, but it still seemed to Ben like a lot of fuss for a routine problem. Then he heard the reporter use the word *sabotage*.

"What's he saying?" Ben asked, trying to peer between the customers for a better look.

"Someone put toxic chemicals in the water supply," said the tapcaf woman. "They've had to shut down ten pumping stations, and that means half of central Galactic City hasn't got any water." She slapped a cleaning cloth down on the table, clearly angry. "Which means I have to shut the 'caf until they sort it out."

"If it's sabotage, you know who'll get the blame," said a man clutching a small boy by the hand. "Us."

"Could be anybody."

"Disgruntled water employee," the tapcaf woman muttered.

"Maybe the water company screwed up and put the wrong chemical into the treatment plant," said another customer.

"And maybe it *is* us, because the government was asking for it."

The debate raged. Ben interrupted. "Who's *us*?" he asked. Identity was beginning to concern him. "Why would anyone living here want to poison their own water supply?"

The group turned away from the holoscreen for a moment as if they'd just noticed Ben, and the tapcaf woman gave him a sympathetic look. "People do stupid things when there's a war on," she said. "Don't they teach you that at the academy?"

"But there isn't a war," said Ben, and didn't admit he'd never been to any academy. He knew what a war was. War had to be declared: politicians had to get involved. "Not yet."

"Well, there is now . . ." The man picked up his son in his arms and began walking away. "Whether we want one or not."

Ben leaned over the edge of the safety rail on the walkway to see what was happening on the levels above and below him. People had done exactly what the tapcaf customers had: they gathered outside their shops and homes, talking and arguing. He could hear voices carrying. Traffic had slowed to a crawl. The police public address system boomed in the distance.

"Jacen?" Ben spoke quietly into his comlink, but Jacen wasn't receiving. The message service clicked in. "Jacen, I'm in the Corellian quarter and—" He searched for the words. But there was no point alarming Jacen. "I'm heading home."

Ben's sense of danger was becoming acute now. There was anger and violence building up exactly like the pressure before a thunderstorm; he could feel it pressing on his temples, making his sinuses ache, telling him to *get away, run, hide* at an instinctive level. He hoped he'd learn to read it better one day. Right now it was uncontrolled and animal. He ran back the way he had come, two hundred meters to the nearest taxi platform.

An air taxi was sitting on its repulsors, hovering silently over a dark pool of shadow. The pilot, a thin-faced human with a shaved head, glanced up from his holozine and opened the hatch.

"Senate District, please," said Ben.

"Where, exactly?"

"Rotunda Zone."

"Nah, I'm avoiding the center." The pilot looked at Ben as if he'd just arrived from Tatooine. "There's a riot going on over the water contamination. Should you be out on your own, lad?"

Ben was beginning to wonder the same thing himself. "How close can you take me to the zone, then?"

The pilot sucked his teeth thoughtfully. "The intersection of skylanes four-seven-two and twenty-three. Two blocks away. Will that do?"

"Okay."

Ben sat in the backseat of the taxi with one hand on the hilt of his lightsaber, fidgeting. He hadn't been worried when he'd infiltrated Centerpoint Station: that had been exciting in an unthinking, reflex kind of way, even though he stood a good chance of getting killed. It seemed impossible that anything could happen to him. But now he was among crowds that seemed ready to explode into violence, and although he was home in Galactic City, he was scared. There was something . . . *animal* about it all, something wild and unpredictable.

The taxi slowed and pulled in at a landing platform. Ben

could see police speeders ahead at the intersection of the two skylanes, diverting traffic the hard way. A CSF assault ship swept overhead as he stepped out onto the walkway, and his instinct was to follow its path.

So what are you going to do when you get there?

It was a good question, but instead of answering it rationally, Ben just headed for where his Force-senses told him he was needed. Jacen always encouraged him to trust his feelings; and this was as good a time as any. He raced down the walkway in the opposite direction from the rest of the pedestrians, who were doing the sensible thing and moving away from the riot area.

When he rounded the corner, he found himself at the back of a mob facing the Corellian embassy. The building was under siege; there was no other way to describe the barrage of missiles smashing against the permaglass front of the building and piling up in its marble forecourt. The embassy was in a plaza, not on a broad skylane with a thousand-meter drop beneath, making it an easy, close target for anyone hurling missiles. The CSF assault ship hovered overhead. Ben could see officers taking aim with rifles and then lowering them again.

Nobody on the ground seemed to have drawn weapons yet. But the crowd was screaming abuse.

"You scum! You poisoned the water!"

Ben dodged a lump of masonry that cleared the heads of the mob in front of him and landed at his feet, sending fragments flying.

"They should've pulverized your whole planet, not just stinking Centerpoint!"

The crowd roared and surged forward before falling back again, nearly knocking Ben flat. *He* was responsible for what was happening. He'd started this with the raid on Centerpoint. The falling sensation in the pit of his stomach stopped him in his tracks. He'd never seen people behave like this, but it was *all his fault*. He had to do something.

Another volley of permacrete shattered on the marble forecourt of the embassy, and CSF officers piled into the crowd with riot batons. But the more they tried to break it up, the more people seemed to press forward. The riot had a life of its own. Ben tasted a communal reflex rage, and it scared him more than anything he had ever experienced. For a split second he almost pitched in, too, his body very nearly overriding his brain.

In front of the embassy, a dozen Corellians—Ben assumed that was who they were—braved the hail of permacrete and snatched the lumps up to hurl them back over the heads of the CSF line. One of the men had a blood-smeared gash across his forehead, but he seemed oblivious to it. A CSF captain moved forward with a squad of officers, and Ben heard the Corellian tell him that they were supposed to be protected here, they were supposed to be *safe*—and then there was a volley of shots from above like projectile weapons firing and the air filled with acrid smoke.

It burned Ben's eyes and mouth. Dispersal gas: the CSF must have fired canisters from the assault ship hovering overhead. The crowd should have scattered, but instead people seemed to close in on one another and Ben was caught up in the panic. He fell. He was being trampled. Legs filled his field of vision and just as he curled instinctively to shield his head, a gloved blue arm reached out and grabbed him by the front of his tunic, pulling him free.

"Stupid kid—"

It was a CSF officer. The man had rescued him. Ben struggled to his knees, eyes streaming. "Come on, get out of here—"

Ben's attention snapped suddenly from his own predicament to a point behind the officer. He focused on a face he knew, a boy with short blond hair, Barit Saiy, and Ben was staring at a blaster aimed not at him but at the officer's back. He didn't think; he just pulled out his lightsaber with his free hand and saw the bright blue blade collide with a stream of white energy, deflecting it. It took a second, and when he blinked again to clear his streaming eyes he saw Barit disappearing into the mêlée.

The police officer stared at his lightsaber for a moment, one hand on his own blaster.

"It was a rock," Ben lied. "Someone threw something at you."

The officer pulled him to his feet. His face was streaked with gas-induced tears, too; he hadn't put on his respirator in time. "You're fast, kid. Let's get you back to the Temple, shall we?"

"I'll call my Master. He'll collect me." Jacen wasn't a Master, but the small detail of Jedi life wasn't important right then. Ben wanted to get away and follow Barit. "Thank you, Officer."

"Thank *you*, Jedi." The officer wiped his nose on the back of his hand and coughed painfully. "You saved me from a pounding, too."

Ben knew he had saved someone from something, but it was more than a man's life. However little he understood of politics, he was sure that a Corellian shooting a CSF officer would turn a bad situation into a disastrous one. Barit was in deep; Ben now felt a personal connection to the widening gulf between Corellian and Coruscanti, and sensed that Barit would play a part in something awful.

He wiped his face on the sleeve of his robe, nose streaming, and opened his comlink again. "Jacen? Can you hear me?" There was just the usual quiet hiss of a link that wasn't being answered, and the click of the message recorder. "Jacen, something terrible is happening."

chapter six

The bigger the galaxy, the sweeter the homecoming.
—Corellian proverb

JEDI TEMPLE PRECINCTS, CORUSCANT.

Ben was trying to contact him, but Jacen had his own problems at that moment. He sensed they were more critical: his mother was in trouble.

He felt her reach out to him. He felt both her fear and her determination, and the latter was winning.

Where is she? What's happening?

Jacen slipped into an alcove flanked by bushes in square ceramic pots and sat down to concentrate. Eyes closed, he could sense where she was, and she wasn't on Coruscant, but very near. It took him a few moments to realize she might be in a vessel.

Listen. Listen.

During his studies, Jacen had mastered a Theran technique that let him use the Force to hear remotely. He slowed his breathing and felt the buzz in his sinuses as if he were being woken too soon from an exhausted sleep. The buzzing filled his head, and then behind it, *within* it, he could pick out words and sounds.

He heard his mother's voice; and then he heard his father's.

". . . try another braking burn."

"Five seconds . . ."

Metal groaned. An engine boomed and sighed, a rhythmic rising and falling note, and it wasn't a reassuring sound. Jacen reached out with one word, the most that even he could send through the Force.

Together.

He visualized the *Millennium Falcon*. In his mind, he could see the plates of her underside and the transparisteel of the cockpit mounted on the starboard flank. He saw her as she should have been, whole and sound. He could feel Leia straining to use Force telekinesis, but he couldn't sense exactly where she was trying to apply it. He could only hear the tension in her voice and taste her growing anxiety.

And he could feel another presence, too: his sister, Jaina.

They hardly spoke these days, but twins could never cut themselves off from each other for long. She must have sensed their parents' crisis, too.

Whatever his mother was trying to do, Jacen could only guess. And guessing wasn't good enough when one was using the physical might of the Force.

Still in his Theran sound trance, he heard the *bip-bip-bip* of a sensor alarm, the kind that announced that a hull had been breached—or worse.

". . . drive's shaking loose and it's going to take the plates with it . . ."

That was what he needed to know. He was certain now that his mother was using the Force to stop the cracks in the drive housing from spreading and ripping the *Falcon* apart as the ship reentered the atmosphere. It was a massive task. She needed help.

Jacen filled his lungs with a long, slow breath and centered himself to try something he had never attempted before.

Mom, I hope you can handle this.

He pictured Leia sitting in the copilot's seat. Her emotions and her presence in the Force washed over him and he visualized himself in her place, behind her eyes, seeing what she saw. For a moment he was simply observing; but then a feeling like a sigh drained out of him and it was as if he were exhaling an infinite breath into his mother—no, *through* his mother. Now he was no longer sitting in the alcove between two topiary bushes, but staring at an array of lights and readouts and at hands that weren't his. Beyond the console, Coruscant loomed in the viewport.

If Jaina had joined the effort, she was hardly detectable. He had drowned out her presence in his own mind with the sheer strength of the telekinesis he was projecting.

Take this, Mom. Use me. Use the Force I'm channeling through you.

He heard her say "Uh!" as if something had startled her. Then he could feel pressure in his lungs as if he were running hard and fighting for breath. He had no idea how long it lasted. But he had the sense of clutching something tight to his chest, and an awareness somewhere outside his mind and yet at its core showed him the *Falcon* enveloped in the Force, the hull around her drive assembly compressed instead of expanding catastrophically.

He was sure he wasn't seeing what his mother was actually looking at, because he had none of the images of entering the atmosphere or landing. The scenes inside the *Falcon*'s cockpit were being supplied by his memory. He was simultaneously aware both of that rational fact and that his Force power was being funneled through his mother, helping her hold the drive assembly in place by telekinesis.

Then relief swept over him like a wave, making his scalp tingle and his heart pound. The *Falcon* was down safely. He *knew* it. Now he could open his eyes. When he did, he was almost surprised to find himself still in the grounds of the Temple in broad daylight.

Jacen opened his comlink. He felt Jaina briefly, but his mind was on his parents. "Mom? Mom, are you okay?"

Leia sounded breathless. "So much for sneaking in discreetly."

"Everything's all right, isn't it?" Jacen could hear his father muttering in the background. "I have to see you both. Stay where you are. I'm coming."

Jedi seldom ran flat-out in public, so Jacen avoided an undignified sprint with robes flapping and limited himself to a slow jog to the nearest taxi platform instead.

He was the new heir to the Sith legacy and he had seen his grandfather behave in a way that had almost shattered his world. But at that moment he was just a son who was more worried about his parents' welfare than the affairs of the galaxy.

Attachment had its place. Jacen let himself succumb to it and put aside his growing dispute with both his father and Jaina.

But sooner or later, he knew that a permanent rift in the family was a price he might have to pay.

SLAVE I, PREFLIGHT PANEL CHECK FOR ROONADAN.

Boba Fett had rarely carried passengers—not live or voluntary ones, anyway. The presence of this strange girl in his ship, which was more of a home than anything he owned made of stone and permacrete, bothered him. And yet he simply couldn't walk away from her.

Mirta Gev had a piece of his past. That mattered a lot when he was running out of future.

"You normally board ships with total strangers?" asked Fett.

Mirta slung her bag over one shoulder. "Are you going to kill me?"

"Nobody's paying me to."

"That's what I thought."

She boarded *Slave I* via the cargo hatch and went to follow him through to the cockpit, but he turned to block her path and gestured aft. "I don't like copilots. Stay put or I'll lock you in one of the cells."

Mirta didn't show the slightest dissent. She just paused and looked around, then sat down on a crate that was secured to the port bulkhead. She opened her bag and rummaged in it before pulling out a chunk of something that she unwrapped and began gnawing.

Fett stared at her.

"Dinner," she said. "I always carry rations. Just in case."

Fett fought back a reflex; his instinct was to tell her she was a smart kid. "Yeah, I don't do in-flight catering," he said, and swung through the hatch into the main section of the ship. The internal bulkhead shut behind him, because smart kid or not, he wasn't taking any chances with her.

He wasn't quite as agile as he'd been a year before. Just moving around in *Slave I*'s awkward spaces was uncomfortable now. It wasn't pure pain, but he felt that before long it would be.

Don't forget you're dying, Fett.

He settled into his seat and fired up the ship's drives. Checking the internal cam circuit that gave him a view of each of *Slave I*'s compartments, he caught a shot of Mirta leaning back against the bulkhead, eyes closed, arms folded across her chest, apparently dozing. Nothing seemed to faze her. He approved of that. There were always women in the galaxy—and men, come to that—who reckoned they were tough but seemed to think that was about a smart mouth and a fancy weapon. The truly tough ones, Fett thought, were the ones who could take anything in their stride and

finish the job. Mirta Gev showed every sign of being genuinely, quietly tough.

Fett didn't like anybody much, but he didn't *dislike* her,
although the thaw didn't extend to having her sit up front
with him.

He laid in a course to Roonadan. His stomach rumbled:
maybe he should have grabbed some of Beviin's coin-crabs
after all. He whiled away the next few hours watching the
stock prices from HNE and wondered what he might say to
Taun We when he finally caught up with her.

He had no doubt that he would.

Fett dozed, reclining in his seat. When he slept, it was
never deeply. The padded rim of his helmet was just soft
enough to stop short of cutting into his neck but too hard
for complete comfort when he let it take the weight of his
head. Sometimes he would drift in a few seconds of hazy
disorientation, half awake, sounds magnified, able to see
through a transparent barrier; he wasn't in the confines of
his helmet but somewhere else he didn't recognize. It was a
recurring impression. Taun We had once told him it was the
legacy of being gestated in a glass tank like the other clones,
and that they all had distant memories like that.

It was a kinship of sorts. He found his mind wandering,
thinking how they must have felt to know their days were
numbered, just like his were now. And that was another
kinship.

*I'm dying. Maybe dying feels like this. I ought to know by
now.*

The navigation sensors woke him with an insistent puls-
ing tone to warn him *Slave I* had dropped out of hyperspace, and he snapped upright and alert. His joints hurt; he
ignored the pain.

In the viewscreen the red-streaked crescent of Roonadan
grew larger until it was the entire sky. It was another heavily
populated planet whose habitable zones were crammed

with cities, but at least it wasn't as grim as Bonadan. Fett punched up the local data on his console and began his descent.

Roonadan still had a few green spaces and attractive buildings, and even a few wide rivers snaking through the northern hemisphere. It was the kind of place that was home to a mix of the highly educated scientists who developed products, the people whose task it was to make their lives more pleasant, and the majority who worked in the factories and laboratories that produced the goods that the elite invented.

It was exactly the kind of place Taun We might be, if she could take the sunlight. Kaminoans didn't like clear skies.

Fett disguised *Slave I*'s armaments with a sensor screen and prepared to land. If anything went wrong, he had the firepower of a small warship to get out of trouble—turbolasers, ion cannon, torpedoes, and concussion missiles. He'd added conventional armor-piercing detonite ordnance on the last refit just in case he was ever low on power and stuck in a tight corner. Leaving things to chance was for amateurs.

Banking over the capital city of Varlo, Fett thought *Slave I* should be his final resting place. He didn't want her left behind; he had a sudden vision of setting a course out of the galaxy in his final days and letting the ship carry him as far as she could on her fuel cells and then drifting forever where nobody would follow. It was reassuring.

Pack it in. You're not dead yet.

But if that's not an admission that you haven't a clue what your life's been about, then I don't know what is.

He picked up the automated air traffic control and set down at the first spaceport he could find. *Slave I* settled gently on her landing struts, the dampers yielding as she sank half a meter and then came to rest. The drive cooled, sending a characteristic decelerating ticking through the hull that eventually fell silent.

"Fett?" He glanced up at the screen that gave him a complete view of the cargo bay. Mirta had stood up and was stretching her arms like an athlete, pulling one arm across her body then the other. "Are you taking me with you?"

"No."

"So you're just going to leave me locked in here while you go off."

"I wouldn't let anything happen to this ship. You're safe as long as she is." He set the intruder defenses and stood up to check his personal weapons. Roonadan didn't have a no-weapons law like its sister planet Bonadan, but it was Corporate Sector and so some restraint was called for. "And don't mess with the controls back there. You won't like what happens if you do."

He waited for an argument, but she just sat down again and started dismantling her blaster. He paused to watch: she was calibrating and cleaning it. The kid certainly took her weapons seriously. Most people just expected their hardware to work properly without maintenance, which was a good way to end up dead. Fett was impressed that she wasn't among them.

He stepped out of the cockpit hatch and walked to the terminal building, checking data on the display that appeared in his visor as he walked. The planet was a research-and-development center. Somewhere there'd be a place where people whose job was to keep an eye on what companies did would gather to discuss business. Fett reasoned that it was a good place to start.

And like all commercial planets with plenty of job openings, Roonadan attracted a cosmopolitan population. A man in Mandalorian armor with a jet pack attracted almost as little attention as a Duros, but a lot less than the two blue-skinned Chiss who were wandering around the concourse in blue suits that matched their skin exactly. Fett took the opportunity to slip into one of the passport control lanes and select his most benign identicard for presentation to the female official securing the barrier.

The woman scanned the readout on the screen in front of her, then eyed his battle-scarred armor suspiciously. She didn't ask him to remove his helmet. "What brings you here . . . Master Vhett?"

There was a lot to be said for *Mando'a,* even if he didn't speak much of it. "Looking for security work."

"What kind?"

Now *that* was helpful. "Pharmaceuticals. Banks and personal protection got too rough."

She looked at him warily as if trying to squint past the visor. "I thought you Mandalorians were supposed to be hard cases."

"I'm not getting any younger."

"None of us are." She handed him back his bogus ID card. "They're always hiring here. Industrial espionage is our national sport." She jerked her thumb over her shoulder. "Head into town on the monorail and you'll find the job agencies on the main route. And if you don't get hired in five days, you're out of here, okay? We don't like vagrants."

So she had some knowledge of Mandalorians, but not of him. *Vhett* was just the pure *Mando'a* form of "Fett." It was surprising how close you could skate to the truth without anyone noticing. He touched his glove to his helmet in what he hoped was a deferential gesture and strode on.

Most of the time, one of his tactics was being Boba Fett and not disguising the fact. When you had that kind of reputation, it did a lot of the work for you: bounties found it was definitely smarter to surrender to him than to try to run, because there was nowhere to hide from Fett. But he felt a little discretion might get him closer to Taun We a lot faster. Time wasn't on his side.

Sometimes, too, it amused him to play a man down on his luck when he was actually one of the wealthiest individuals in the galaxy. But fortune wouldn't be worth a mott's backside if he didn't find a cure.

So when are you going to draw up a contingency plan? You never were much for long-term strategy. There'll come a point where you have to decide whether to go on looking for Ko Sai's data or to prepare for death. So what are you going to do with all those credits?

Boba Fett took the monorail into town with a dozen people who didn't have personal transport. They ranged from the obviously poor to the eccentric, and two Rodian tourists studying holomaps of Varlo. One of the passengers, a man a lot taller than Fett, was swathed in a black cloak with a hem that swept the dust and debris on the carriage floor, giving the cloth a permanent gray border.

Nobody even glanced at Fett. These weren't people who dealt with bounty hunters; he might have been a household name, but the households where his name was known tended to be those who could afford plenty and were motivated to pay it to solve their problems in a very permanent way. The people here didn't fit the bill.

Fett got off at the terminus and merged into an anonymous crowd of shoppers. The stores here were midmarket, the kind that clerical and technical staff would use. He walked into a clothing store and looked at the selection of men's fashions displayed as holograms above a dais.

"Is this the best you've got?" he said to the salesman.

"If sir wants to impress, sir needs to shop on the waterfront," said the salesman stiffly. "If sir has the credits, that is."

Fett assumed he meant one of the artificial rivers that he'd seen from the air. He looked over a voluminous dark tunic and cloak not unlike the one he'd seen the man wearing on the monorail. "I'll take this. And a holdall."

"Size?"

"Measure me."

"Might I see your credit chip, sir?"

Fett dumped two cash-credit discs—one hundreds—on the counter. "Will this do nicely?"

The salesman took a stylus from his jacket, flipped the discs over, and checked the holostamp under the stylus's beam of UV light. "Yes . . . sir." He flicked the stylus with his thumbnail and the instrument spat a thin beam of red light. "If sir would mind removing his armor, then I can measure."

"*Over* the armor."

"Sorry?"

"The armor stays. I'm not the trusting type."

The salesman hesitated for a moment but swept the laser across Fett from side to side and then top to toe, studied the precise measurements on the stylus's display, and shrugged.

"Large," he said.

"I can see you're a professional." Fett took the holdall and the clothing and headed for the nearest public refreshers.

It was cramped in the cubicle, but he slipped off his jet pack and rocket launcher, dismantled them into sections and put them in the holdall. The cloak and tunic draped over his armor just fine after that. Then he hesitated before removing his helmet.

It was the ultimate disguise. Apart from his doctor and a few Kaminoans, nobody knew what he really looked like any longer. He might even have changed too much for Taun We to spot him. He stared into the mirror above the basin and with a few seconds' detachment saw a man on the edge of genuine old age, hair mostly gray, face largely unlined, having been protected from sunlight for almost as long as he could remember.

Even the scars from the time he escaped the Sarlacc's acid gut weren't that conspicuous now. He could pass for any fit man in his early seventies.

Fierfek, *in a suit I might even look like a gentleman.*

And that was what he needed to be right now.

If he was going to find out where the scientists at AruMed lived, he had to look as unlike a bounty hunter as he could.

Boba Fett strode out of the refreshers and into public view without his helmet for the first time in his adult life.

chapter seven

Luke, you know very well that it's about a lot more than stopping Corellia having her own deterrent. It's tempting to reveal that little surprise in the Kiris Cluster to show people why we mean business. But for the time being we're just going to have to sit on it and hope we can persuade Corellia to disarm before our justification shows up on Coruscant.

—Cal Omas to Luke Skywalker and Admiral Niathal,
in a confidential discussion of the true scope
of the Corellian threat

GALACTIC CITY PUBLIC LANDING AREA 337/B.

They nearly crash-landed. So what? It wasn't the first time the *Millennium Falcon* had come close to disaster, and it wouldn't be the last. Han tried to look nonchalant.

But it had still given him a few moments of white-knuckled terror, the kind he didn't like Leia to see but that she could probably feel anyway. They both sat in silence on the lowered ramp of the *Falcon*, savoring the light breeze. Small taken-for-granted things felt precious when you'd survived by the skin of your teeth.

The *Falcon* stood in one of the hundreds of open-air bays that flanked the landing strip, just another aging vessel. Her hull made the occasional click as the metal cooled, and an ominous pool of coolant was growing under the drive housing. Han had put a pail under the leak to collect it, and now he could hear the fluid running over the rim of the container. The pipework around the drive had sheared at the welds.

"Well," said Leia at last, staring into the distance. As ever, she looked as if nothing serious had happened, just a little tired and close to irritation. "*That* was character form-ing."

"Don't suppose you could try Force-welding as well?"

"Try Jacen. He might be able to do just about anything these days."

"So what happened exactly?"

She shrugged. "No idea. It was like getting a Force booster pack from nowhere."

He's my kid and I don't know who he is anymore. But he comes up trumps when he's needed. So maybe I should shut my mouth. "That was handy."

"Jacen feels like he's very close," said Leia. "Let's do grateful, shall we?"

"Oh, I can manage grateful all right."

"Good."

Leia closed her eyes for a moment. "And Jaina's on her way."

My sensible girl. At least one of my kids still makes sense to me. "Who else knows we're here? Maybe we should have Luke and Mara over, too. Throw a barbecue right here. Invite the neighbors."

"Maybe fly a really anonymous ship until things cool down?"

"Well, *this* baby isn't flying anywhere for a while."

Han stood and walked back up the loading ramp. *Okay, get another vessel and head back to Corellia. Move to a new apartment. Breach Thrackan's security and shoot him. Then worry about another war.* The coolant level on the console indicator was showing zero. He went down to the drive bay, where he could smell scorched alloy and the throat-tingling whiff of the fluid. Stang, he was tired of all this. Was it ever going to end? A year with Leia, a normal year when nothing happened, nothing went wrong, none of the kids was in danger. Was that too much to ask?

When he came out through the main starboard hatch

again, Jacen was sitting on the ramp with his arm around Leia's shoulders, forehead resting against hers. Leia looked up, just a little warning glance, but Han didn't need to be told to show his son some appreciation. It was a reflex: he grabbed him as he stood up and hugged him so hard that he felt Jacen's ribs through his robes.

"It's okay, Dad," Jacen said softly. "Don't scare me like that again, though."

"I was going to say the same to you." This wasn't the time to mention taking sides. "You okay? You look worn out."

"Not as worn out as you."

"Things have been a little tense around here. Thrackan's put out a contract on us. You, too."

"It'll be fascinating to see him try." Jacen's frown seemed permanent now. "But you—"

"Hey, I might be ancient to you, but I can take Thrackan, thanks."

"My actions on Centerpoint provoked him. I feel responsible for your safety. What's the point of having a Jedi for a son if he can't look out for his dad?"

"You leave me to worry about Thrackan," said Han. *Yeah, you attacked Corellia, and you're my son, and I'm not sure how I deal with that.* "It won't be the first time. Just wait. He'll send Fett. I can handle Fett."

Leia gave a small snort of amusement. "You can brandish walking sticks at each other. He's not getting any younger, either. Why would Thrackan hire him?"

"Because he thinks Fett will psych me out."

"He thinks right, then . . ."

Han took it as making light of her fears, but Jacen didn't seem amused.

"Come back to my apartment, Dad." His tone was almost pleading. "Just in case someone's got your apartment here under observation."

"Wouldn't you know about that already?" said Han. Jacen's Force-senses seemed to beat scanners these days. He watched his son's face fall for a second.

"What makes you say that?"

"I don't know what kind of Force stuff you picked up while you were away all those years, but it sure comes in useful."

"Ah," said Jacen. He seemed reassured. Han wasn't sure what had rattled him. "Might as well take every precaution we can. Threepio's making a very convincing job of telling people he has no idea where you've gone, even the Noghri. He sounds positively annoyed about it—"

Jacen stopped and looked around. Something had distracted him—something Han couldn't see or hear, as usual. Then Han caught a flash of orange out the corner of his eye and turned to see a Galactic Alliance pilot walking between laid-up vessels on the apron of the landing strip. For an illogical moment his stomach churned, and then he focused on long brown hair pulled back in a tail and the fact that the pilot had an astromech droid keeping pace beside her.

Jaina. In a pilot's uniform.

"So when did she get *that* out of the wardrobe?" said Han. "She didn't tell us she was going back on active service—"

"No fighting," Leia said firmly.

Han was dismayed at how fast he moved from being glad to be alive to challenging his daughter's choices. He was still relieved to see her. She just reached out and squeezed his hand, oddly formal, and then did the same to Leia. She simply nodded at Jacen, which didn't bode well.

Han supposed that a Galactic Alliance pilot hugging people in public might have drawn some attention. He wished she would patch things up with Jacen, though.

"I'm not going to ask any obvious questions." Jaina patted R2's dome. "But I thought you could use some help with repairs."

"Thanks." Han ignored Leia's warning and the comment was out of his mouth before he could think too hard. "And why are you decked out in an orange flight suit?"

"Because I'm doing my job, Dad."

"Did Zekk get you back into this?"

Jaina could become her mother in an instant. She had that same look of sad patience. "Dad, I'm thirty-one, I make my own decisions, and you forget what I am sometimes."

"I never forget you're a Jedi. But that doesn't mean you should get dragged into the Alliance's wars against Corellia—"

"Dad," said Jaina softly. "I meant that I'm a fighter pilot. *That's* what you forget. I volunteered for active duty because this is my *job*."

R2-D2 trundled across to the *Falcon* and disappeared under her belly. Han heard a series of disapproving whistles and the occasional clank of metal as the droid examined her. Jaina stood her ground in front of her father, still sad-eyed, still looking as if she was searching his face for comprehension.

"You can't seriously believe that the Alliance is right, sweetheart," said Han.

"Dad, maybe I do and maybe I don't, but that's not the issue. I'm in uniform and that means I front up and earn it regardless of my personal views. That's what service is about."

Han took it as a rebuke. It wasn't, of course; but he knew deep down that he tended to emotion in wartime rather than cool professionalism. Yes, Jaina was a fighter pilot. He owed her the respect due to a professional warrior.

But it still broke his heart that his little girl—and she would always be that, even when she was gray-haired herself—

would be risking her life for a regime that seemed to want to re-create the bad old days of galactic totalitarianism. What had his own life been for if not to create a better world for his kids?

Don't do it, Jaina.

"I'd better get back to base," she said. Leia stood up and Jaina gave her a hurried kiss on the cheek. Han didn't give Jaina the chance to duck his, but Jacen hovered on the edge of the group, seeming to want to make peace with her and getting no reaction. "Wouldn't do for me to be advertising that the Solos are back. Watch your six, okay?"

"Take care of yourself, Jaina," said Jacen.

"And you." *Well, she managed that much,* thought Han. Jaina turned and took a couple of strides before glancing back at Jacen. "You don't feel right to me lately, Jacen. Are you in trouble?"

Jacen smiled as if he was getting her to thaw a little and was relieved. "Just busy, that's all."

Han watched Jaina go and tried not to meet Leia's eyes. *What was all that about?* R2 rolled back out from under the *Falcon,* and his readout began scrolling a long list of mechanical problems that had to be fixed and that would take a long, long time. Han stopped him in midbeep with an upheld hand.

"I know. Don't go on about it."

R2 whistled.

"I bet you can. You can fix anything. But don't rush, because it's time we got something less attention grabbing."

"At least come back with me while you sort out alternative transport," said Jacen.

"Good idea," said Leia. "And we can say hi to Ben, too. We've missed him."

That wasn't Leia playing the dutiful aunt. That was Leia checking up. Jacen said nothing, but Leia gave him a quick glance that Han spotted and didn't understand.

R2 beeped a cheery good-bye and trundled up the *Falcon*'s ramp. Han followed Leia, wiping coolant-stained hands on his pants, and couldn't get Jaina's comment out of his mind.

Are you in trouble?

Yeah, what *was* all that about?

JACEN SOLO'S APARTMENT, ROTUNDA ZONE, CORUSCANT.

Luke knew Ben would come back here sooner or later. He paced around the lobby of the apartment building, pausing occasionally to stare through the transparisteel doors. Something had happened to Ben, although all of Luke's Force-senses told him his son was alive and unharmed. But he wouldn't answer his link.

And Jacen had disappeared from the Force. Luke picked up echoes of him sporadically and then lost him again. He looked at Mara, wondering if she was able to detect their nephew any better than he could.

"Nothing," she said, and shook her head, apparently knowing exactly what was on his mind. It wasn't that difficult: he'd agonized about little else today. "Look, it's chaos out there. Ben's smart enough to avoid trouble. Let's take it easy."

Take it easy. What had he come to when Mara was the one urging *him* to calm down? He wondered how much of his own anxiety was caused by having nothing concrete to do yet in the coming war.

War. He'd thought it again. Somewhere along the line in the last few days it had changed from a threat to a certainty. Luke tried to separate it in his mind from the Force dreams of the man in the hooded cloak that still plagued him. He turned back to the turbolift and watched the cascade of lights on the floor indicator panel for a while until he heard Mara say, "Now, let's not be hasty, honey, okay—ah! Oh, no . . ."

Luke spun around to see Ben. The boy's eyes were swollen and streaming, and he wiped his nose as if he'd been sobbing his heart out. Mara stood frozen for a second and then went to wrap him in her arms. While he didn't push her away, he certainly didn't yield.

"What happened, sweetheart? Tell me what's wrong."

Ben coughed hard. "I got a whiff of riot gas."

"Oh, no." Mara put her fingertips under his chin and turned his face to one side to examine him. "You look like you've been burned. Can you breathe okay?"

"It's wearing off, Mom." He submitted to a hug. "I was in the wrong place at the wrong time."

"Let's get you to the medcenter for a checkup," said Luke quietly.

"I said I'm fine, Dad. *It wears off.*" Ben sounded annoyed. "Aren't you doing something about the water situation?"

Mara intervened. "The city authorities are looking after that."

"Is it the Corellians? Is it terrorism? They said so on HNE and everyone believes that."

"Why don't we go up to the apartment and get you cleaned up?" Mara steered Ben toward the turbolift. "Where's Jacen?"

Ben stopped at the lift doors. "I don't know. I was coming back from Fleet ComCen. Look, this is Jacen's apartment. I ought to ask him if it's okay to just go in."

"It's your home, too," said Luke carefully. So Jacen really did control Ben now. This was a boy who didn't even obey his mother when his life was at risk. It scared Luke, and then he found himself tearing his heart apart to be sure that he was genuinely afraid of Jacen's influence, tinged with darkness, or if he was just hurt that his nephew had more of a paternal relationship with his kid than he did. "Come on."

Ben usually sighed and showed dissent. But now he just nodded, resigned, as if he'd suddenly grown a lot older in a matter of days.

They rode the turbolift in an uncomfortable silence punctuated only by Ben's sniffs and coughs. His robe was dirty, as if he'd been rolling on the ground. When they got to the apartment, his first reaction was to head for the refresher. He stopped a few paces back from the doors and turned on his heel.

"Bottled water in the conservator," he said.

The water supply to most of the center of the city was still cut off. Luke turned on the taps in the kitchen to drain off any water still standing in the pipes and header tanks. There was no point taking any chances.

"I can feel that you're angry, Dad," said Ben hoarsely. He slopped a bottle of water into a bowl and soaked a washcloth to wipe his face. He flinched when the cloth touched his skin, but he didn't make a sound. "But it's not Jacen's fault. It's mine. I decided not to go with him when he had his meeting." He seemed about to expand on that but checked himself visibly. "I've learned my lesson."

"It's okay." Mara caught Luke's eye as Ben covered his face with the washcloth for a moment. Her expression said it all: *Is this the rebellious son we know?* "Let me get you something to drink. You sound awful."

They ended up in the living room, the three of them sitting as far apart from one another as the room would allow. Ben sipped a glass of juice and occasionally broke into a hacking, uncontrollable cough that left him wheezing with tears streaming down his face. His sobriety stunned Luke.

Maybe Mara was right. Perhaps Luke was too mired in his own anxieties about where he had lost Ben along the way that he was mistaking Jacen's motives. Apart from his terrible dreams and the darkness that trailed Jacen, he had nothing concrete to lay against his nephew, only evidence that Ben was settling down far better in his care than he ever had at home.

But they could sit in silence for a while. They didn't have to talk. Almost out of habit, Luke let himself drift to pick up impressions from the apartment and felt nothing beyond a sense of unease, as if Jacen was having problems.

A man having a difficult love affair. Maybe that's all it is.

But something told him that wasn't true. What he did begin to feel, though, was his sister, somewhere near—and Jacen.

The doors opened and Jacen walked in with Han and Leia. It should have been a family reunion of sorts, and a relieved one at that, but the expression on Han's face said otherwise. Luke decided to take the lead.

"It's okay, Jacen," he said. "We made Ben let us in. He got caught up in the rioting. Dispersal gas."

"I'm fine," Ben sighed. "It's wearing off."

"Well, we've all had a little drama in our day, then." Jacen ushered Leia and Han into the room. He radiated only concern and sympathy, nothing dark at all. "Mom and Dad nearly crash-landed, and Dad was nearly assassinated."

Mara got up to plump cushions around Leia. "Sounds like a regular day in this family . . ."

"We'll be heading back home as soon as we can find a replacement ship." Han barely made eye contact with Luke. "The *Falcon*'s not so hot right now. Artoo's carrying out repairs."

"Why didn't you let me know?"

Han shrugged. "We were kind of busy, trying not to plummet in flames. If Jacen hadn't projected the Force through Leia, you'd have needed a shovel to pick us up at the spaceport."

Luke tasted a chance to broker some peace, at least within

his own family. It didn't bode well for the galaxy if he couldn't persuade even his own family to stick together. "Corellia doesn't have to be home, Han. Come back. You're safer here anyway."

"Yeah, but there's the small matter of my being Corellian, which isn't fashionable right now, and your buddies attacking my homeworld because it won't roll over and be the Alliance's stooge while it plays at being the Empire again."

We should both know better. "Han, how long have we known each other?"

"Long enough for you to know that the way the Alliance is behaving should give you that proverbial bad feeling. The kind *I* get."

"Han . . . ," Leia said. It was a quiet warning. "Knock it off."

"No, let him have his say." Luke was suddenly conscious of Ben watching him, and this wasn't the way he wanted his son to see him—starting a verbal brawl with his best friend when all everyone needed right then was to be glad they were still alive. "I happen to think you're playing Thrackan Sal-Solo's game with this Corellian knee-jerk response to any suggestion of being team players."

"Whoa there, kid—whose team? *Yours?*"

"You can take this independence thing too far."

"Yeah, and you were quick enough to use my sense of rugged individuality when it suited you in the past, pal. But I can't pick it up and put it down that easy. It's who I am."

"Let's not argue over this," said Luke.

"We just did." Han shook his head. He stood staring at Luke for a few moments, looking more bewildered than angry. "They use you every time. Show me a government that hasn't used Jedi to legitimize its actions. You're like some galactic rubber stamp. Why are you backing Omas? You of all people. Does the name *Palpatine* ring a bell?"

"That was different. He was Sith."

"And Omas is a jerk, or at least a puppet for a whole mess of other jerks. Well, count me out. You've got my kids working for you, and that'll have to be enough."

"Oh, boy," said Mara. But Luke could sense her embarrassment and fear. "I love to see the grown-ups in action. Jacen? Let's make some caf for Leia while these two spray testosterone around the room. Come on, Ben. You, too."

"Yeah, I've had enough of this, as well," said Leia. She got up and stood between the two men, all weary annoyance. "Cut it out, Han. And you, Luke. We've got enough problems without having a civil war inside this family."

Luke felt an uneasy dragging sensation in his gut that he hadn't experienced for many, many years. It was self-doubt. Maybe Han had a point. Jedi had fallen into expedience before, and it had brought them down. The Force had ways of ringing that alarm bell. And Han was right: this was who he was—stubbornly independent, the one heading the opposite way when the crowds were streaming past him in the other direction, not because it paid him best—however polished his veneer of smart-mouthed, callous fortune hunter—but because he thought it was *right*.

And he would die rather than concede that independence. Han was Corellian. No, he was *Corellia*. Luke avoided generalizations, but Corellians were all like that, including those living here. It didn't fill him with confidence.

He sighed and held out his hand, genuinely wishing he hadn't said a word.

Han didn't take it. "I'm going to go see a man about a ship," he said, and stalked out.

Jacen walked up behind Luke and patted his shoulder. "I'm sorry, Uncle Luke. If I'd known you were here, I'd have called ahead to say they were coming. Dad's pretty strung out right now, and it's not just the politics. It's Jaina and Thrackan and now the *Falcon*."

It crossed Luke's mind that Jacen should have been able

to detect his and Mara's presence in the Force, but it was an unkind thought. Perhaps part of shutting down his own presence was becoming insensitive to others. Luke realized Jacen's Force skills seemed to be getting stronger and more subtle every day, and he felt uneasy.

"What did Han mean about projecting the Force?"

Jacen shrugged, once again the thoughtful man who felt compassion for every living thing. "Mom was trying to hold the *Falcon*'s hull together so—I suppose I added my Force-strength to it through her. Almost like we did against the Killiks to deflect their weapons."

"Almost," said Luke. No, they hadn't quite done that: channeling the Force was a new one to him. "You've developed some impressive skills lately."

Jacen was the only other Jedi Luke knew who could defeat Lomi Plo's illusion of invisibility. The trick was to have no doubts that could be turned against you as a diversion.

I have a lot of doubts. I think I have more doubts than certainties right now.

But as Jacen turned away from him, Luke caught a very faint touch of something familiar in his mind, almost like a trace of a familiar perfume. It was an echo; it felt ancient. Luke almost opened his mouth to inhale it.

Then he realized what it was. He knew *who* it was.

For a moment he thought it was emanating from Jacen, and then he realized it was purely coincidence. The revelation hit him like a body blow. He understood his Force dream perfectly now.

I know who the hooded man is. I know now, and it's not a man at all.

Luke sensed the barely perceptible trace in the Force of a woman who had once loved him, the Dark Jedi called Shira Brie who had degenerated into Lumiya, a Sith who was more cyborg than human. A woman who hated him, too, but whom he thought had vanished forever.

She was back.

She's here. I know she's here.

Lumiya . . . is here.

Luke tasted the presence of a dangerous, bitter enemy, and knew he had to find her before she harmed him and his family. It was just like her to take advantage of the unrest in the galaxy to cover her movements.

Jacen stared into Luke's face. "What's wrong, Uncle?"

Shall I warn Jacen that Lumiya has come back? Will he listen to me?

"It's nothing," said Luke. "Just unhappy memories."

chapter eight

Corellian militants have claimed responsibility for contaminating water supplies to parts of Galactic City with Fex-M3. The attack, which left four hunded fifty-six dead and more than five thousand with nerve damage, sparked yesterday's riots outside the Corellian embassy. CSF has doubled its police presence in Galactic City in a bid to prevent escalation of unrest. Galactic City authorities have declared a full terror alert and are asking the public to remain vigilant, but Admiral Cha Niathal has called for tough action to crack down on potential terrorists.

—HNE morning bulletin

OFFICES OF CHIEF OF STATE OMAS, SENATE BUILDING, CORUSCANT.

The HNE holocam hovered patiently as Chief Omas gave an earnest interview about the safety of Galactic City's water supply. Jacen stood back and watched from the sofa in the corner of the vast office.

Omas had a Naboo crystal jug on his desk and made a point—with subtle ease—of pouring a glass and sipping it occasionally while talking. There was nothing like a politician's personal display of confidence in the potability of Coruscant water. He even offered a glass to the reporter, whose expression told Jacen that he knew he was being subjected to a little spin. The man drank anyway. He and Omas looked as if they were playing a child's game of dare.

"Extra security measures are now in place at all water company stations," said Omas, cradling his glass. Jacen had learned—fast—that meshing your hands on the desk gave the most reassuring image, so the trick with the glass of water would be far from invisible to HNE viewers. "I'm confident there won't be a repeat of the sabotage earlier this week."

"Do you believe we're facing a genuine terrorist threat, or is this a random act?" said the reporter.

"It's a genuine threat, and it appears to be escalating." Omas didn't hesitate. "Even if we're not dealing with an identifiable formal terrorist organization."

"If you've identified that level of threat, then, do you feel you're doing enough to protect Coruscant citizens?"

This time Omas *did* pause for a breath. Jacen watched him calculate visibly, and he knew the politician was seizing an opportunity. "I can assure you that our security services are taking every possible action."

"But you've been criticized by some politicians for not going far enough."

"We've gone as far as the current law permits."

"Some of your colleagues are calling for the internment of resident Corellians."

"That's a *very* big step. We're not at war."

"By the time we are, won't it be too late?"

Omas managed a regretful smile. "Let's not be hasty."

Internment. That's my father you're talking about. Jacen caught himself bristling at the suggestion, and then felt guilty for considering his own family before those who were being caught in the crossfire of something that was a war in all but name. *Someone has to get a grip on this situation, and it's me.*

His eye was caught by movement in the outer lobby, visible through a transparisteel panel. The outline was broken by the etched designs, but he recognized Senator G'Sil, chair of the Security and Intelligence Council. As soon as the HNE reporter had finished the interview and left, G'Sil slipped into Omas's office.

"It's not my job on the line," he said, pulling up a chair. "But I think our friend from the media had a point. Sorry. Just a little benign eavesdropping."

Jacen knew why he had been summoned; he just wanted to see how they would broach the subject with him. Playing political games made him worry that personal ambition was driving him, but he was dealing with people whose stock-in-trade was maneuvering, so if he wanted their backing he had to maneuver, too. A Jedi was nothing if not pragmatic.

"I'm not comfortable with taking a hard-line approach," said Omas. "And it might not be my decision to make."

G'Sil gestured over his shoulder to the city beyond the room-width windows. "Take a look out there. We have a trillion people on this world. A few thousand—a tiny percentage—have been hurt directly by terrorism. The rest, though, think it's about to happen to them, and that's what we're dealing with here. Perception. Public confidence."

Omas raised one eyebrow. "Spin."

"*Reassurance.*"

Jacen had seen enough to add G'Sil to his list of allies along with Niathal.

"Fear breeds its own problems," said Jacen. "We have to limit that."

There was a moment's silence. Omas's shoulders dropped, and his presence in the Force was like a small piece of ice melting into nothing. His reluctance was tangible.

"Mara Skywalker isn't willing to take on a security role," he said. "You, however, seem equally able and a great deal more willing to do a thankless task."

"Define the task," said Jacen.

"Fill the gap between the army and the Coruscant Security Force."

"Why are you talking directly to me and bypassing the Jedi council?" Jacen asked. "I'm not even in the military."

"Because we're not asking you as a Jedi," said G'Sil. "We're asking you as Jacen Solo, and you'll be a given a commission and a rank. As colonel. I'd bet the council doesn't want to be tainted by messy stuff like this."

"They won't like it."

"Let's cut the PR-speak. As a democracy, we've never been very adept at running secret police. You know, the kind of shock troops that Vader had when . . ." G'Sil trailed off. "Sorry, Jacen. No offense."

"It's all right." Jacen meant it. He had come to terms with walking in his grandfather's footsteps, although he would not follow the entire path. "I'm not ashamed of Anakin Skywalker. And there are positive things I can learn from his example."

The office was suddenly and totally silent, as if both G'Sil and Omas were holding their breath until Jacen said it was okay to exhale.

"Do we take that as a yes?" G'Sil asked.

Stang, I walk in here a civilian and I'll leave as a colonel. Jaina won't like that at all. Jacen swallowed. "I'll need a security force to deal with it."

Omas looked to G'Sil and then back at Jacen. "CSF's Anti-Terrorist Unit is yours to command."

"No, I need my own team from the military and a few other sources, a team that's visibly separate from CSF. If civilian police are seen raiding homes and rounding up residents, it's going to make ordinary policing hard. Politically, it has to be separate—a Galactic Alliance special guard, if you like."

G'Sil nodded. "I agree. You have to keep the secret police separate from the nice, polite officers who police the street. Sends a message that ordinary law-abiding Coruscanti have nothing to fear, while demonstrating maximum force to the enemy."

Omas was sitting on the edge of his seat, elbows braced on the desk, one fist clasping the other as he stared down in defocus. "You said *rounding up.*"

"Internment," said G'Sil. "And that's not just spin. Corellians got at the water supply pretty easily. One relatively small bomb shut ten skylanes for half a day. It takes very few people to cause a lot of disruption on a crowded planet like this, and let me remind you that this is also a nervous planet not long recovered from another war. Makes folks paranoid."

Jacen could see the path ahead of him, the path laid down *specifically for him,* the inevitability of his destiny that Lumiya had shown him. Events were falling into place, and he was part of them with no option now but to accept his responsibility. "And we need to show any other world that might want to support Corellia that the Galactic Alliance isn't a pushover," he said.

Jacen noted the inclusion. *Who is this* we? *I'm not elected. I'm not a member of the Jedi council. I'm not even a Master.*

"Internment is going to take a Security and Intelligence Council vote." Omas seemed resigned but still salving his own conscience by doing things democratically. He gave Jacen an odd look, a faint bemused frown, as if remembering something, and looked a little past him. Then he appeared to focus again. "I'll need your lobby's backing."

"Assume you have it," said G'Sil.

Jacen was more concerned over whom he would need to carry out the task. His instinct was to seek loyal, dependable foot soldiers. "I'd like to recruit Captain Shevu and a team of his choosing," he said. He liked Shevu. The captain was uncompromisingly honest and had the feel in the Force of a man who wouldn't shy away from dirty work. "I'd also like a company of special forces troops. And I need access to Alliance Intelligence data." Jacen felt for a moment that he was standing outside his own body: *How did I slip into this so easily?*

"You'll want NRI officers, then."

"No." Intelligence hadn't dealt with the threat up to now,

so he had no idea whom he could trust. "This has to be seen as a fresh approach to the problem."

Omas radiated unease. "We've taken a step toward martial law."

G'Sil interrupted. "But this is technically a Coruscanti matter. It's not a Senate issue. You have the powers to put a temporary order in place for the planet."

"But Coruscant isn't just a planet. It's the Galactic Alliance, too. So I want full support for this, or things will fall apart when we start applying those special measures, as you like to call them. People tend to lose their nerve when they see force applied."

"A majority on the SIC would be legitimate authority to implement . . . special measures."

"And you can deliver that majority, can you?" said Omas.

"I'll call a special meeting now. Give me twenty-four hours."

G'Sil patted Jacen on the shoulder with evident relief and left. Omas, sitting behind his desk with the air of a man in a heavily defended trench, watched Jacen as if expecting him to break bad news.

"May I start assembling the personnel I need now?" Jacen asked. "Then we'll be ready to move when the authority is given."

"Very well. Let me speak to Admiral Pellaeon." Omas opened the comlink set into his desk. It was the same pleek-wood and lapis as the desk itself. "And I'll get Shevu seconded to you."

"You can explain all this to the Supreme Commander and CSF?"

"I'm very good at being plausible," said Omas. "But I doubt if CSF is going to object."

Omas looked as if he was going to add something, and

Jacen was almost certain of what it would be: Pellaeon would resign if this was forced on him.

That was what Jacen was thinking, too. When Niathal took over the defense role—and she would, nobody doubted that—her support would be a springboard for what was to come, what *had* to come.

But for the meanwhile, Jacen had to prove to Coruscant, and to a watching galaxy, that not only could order be imposed on chaos, it could also be imposed for the good of the majority.

He bowed slightly to Omas and left to make his way to the Strategic Command ops room, where he both felt and knew that Captain Shevu was still on duty despite the fact that his shift should have ended three hours ago.

Shevu was dedicated and forthright, and he'd have the best intelligence on where the Corellian troublemakers might be. Jacen could help him pinpoint them with the imprecise but highly reliable senses that the Force had given him.

They would make a formidable team, he, Ben, and Shevu.

VARLO, ROONADAN: WATERFRONT DISTRICT.

Just as the salesman had said, the waterfront neighborhood was chic and full of the well-heeled professional classes. The taxi took him along the artificial river, a canal with carefully constructed rapids and a manufactured current. There was even lush greenery along the banks, and parkland extended back to the rows of shops and trendy restaurants.

Fett, black cloak over his armor, felt utterly naked and concentrated on the fact that nobody would recognize him by his face. He decided he felt more at home in the kind of district where the bars were badly lit and a blaster was a necessity.

"I'm going to be working at AruMed," said Fett. "Where's the best place to buy a home?"

The taxi pilot glanced in his rearview mirror, and his eyes met Fett's. It was the first time in years that anyone had really looked into his eyes and not just tried to stare through the visor.

"Upper Parkway is where all the scientists buy a place. You a scientist?"

"I'm an anatomist." *Yes, I know precisely where to shoot any one of a thousand species for maximum stopping power.*

"You'll definitely want Upper Parkway, then."

"Nightlife?"

"Pricey bars. Skayan bistros and wine bars, mainly." The pilot wrinkled his nose disapprovingly. "I'm an ale man myself."

"How close to the AruMed labs?"

"Five minutes. Cozy little community."

"All human?"

"You got anything against nonhumans?"

"Just curious." Kaminoans hated sunlight. They were used to clouds, rain, and endless oceans. Fett doubted that an ornamental river would be water enough for Taun We. "I like to know my neighbors."

"Only ever seen humans up there."

Maybe you don't know how to look. "Drop me there. I want to check if I like the place."

Upper Parkway was every bit as smart as the taxi pilot had said. The apartment towers were interspersed with town houses—a real luxury on a crowded planet—and droids were still building properties on the edge of the park for which the neighborhood seemed to be named. From the end of the boulevard, Fett could see the gray monolithic building of the AruMed laboratories with its red illuminated sign, an easy walk for anyone living in Upper Park. And, as the pilot had said, the place had several attractive bistros.

He was perfectly at home rappelling from a roof to capture a prisoner or storming a building with blaster in hand. Walking into a bar and making cautious small talk was not his style.

But it had to be done. *Get it over with, Fett.*

Inside the bistro, everything was polished, orderly calm. He walked up to the bar and took a seat, browsing the menu. Without his helmet, he could actually eat something. The novelty of that idea seemed astonishing and reminded him how many things he had never done and now might never do if he didn't find that data.

"Can I get you something?"

Again Fett found himself looking into the face of a bartender, but this one was looking back as if he only saw a man, not a bounty hunter. Nobody else at the bar seemed to take any notice of him, either. He could usually bring nervous silence to a bar just by walking into it.

"An ale," he said. *It's so simple. It's what everyone else does.* "One of the Corellian ones."

A foaming glass appeared before him. "Visiting?"

Here's a man who makes a note of strangers. A cautious man. "Thinking of buying a place here."

"Good time to buy, too." The barman slid a glass bowl of some unidentifiable snack toward him. "Now that Aru-Med's expanding, the prices will go crazy."

Fett sipped the ale, almost totally distracted by the simple freedom of having a drink in public. He tried the snacks, too, which turned out to be salt-sweet and crunchy, like fried nuts. "Shares are doing well."

"It's those scientists they poached from SanTech. They say it's going to mean a big share of the gene therapy market."

SanTech. Fierfek. I guessed wrong. "Not Kaminoans, then?"

The bartender laughed. A man farther along the bar turned to look at him. "Ever seen one?"

Steady. "Yes. Knew one very well indeed."

The silence deepened. There was quiet, and then there was the silence of people taking serious notice, and the two did *not* sound the same.

"Customer here the other day said one had turned up at Arkanian Micro, but I think he was having a laugh," said the barman.

Arkanian Micro: well, if you deal in cloning, that's one more place to head. It was a knife-edge point in the conversation. Fett's stomach churned, and that rarely happened. *Wrong planet. But maybe the right track.*

"I knew a pathologist at Arkanian Micro," said a man sitting a little farther along the bar. "She said some interesting things about Kaminoans."

Ah, you're testing me. Do I work in the industry? Am I bluffing to get insider information? "What, that they'd never go outside in the sunlight? That they're obsessed with perfection?"

The man considered him carefully. "That they're gray with long necks and incredibly arrogant once you get past the polite exterior."

Well, that *confirms you've met one, or your friend has. Thanks.* Fett busied himself with his ale. Not many people knew that much about Kaminoans; over the centuries, only a handful of people had even known they existed, let alone seen them or had enough contact with them to describe their outlook on the non-Kaminoan world. But industry insiders here *knew,* all right. "Did Micro give them a nice dark hole to live in?"

"It was an issue," said the man, and looked satisfied.

So Kaminoans had probably defected to Arkanian Micro on Vohai. The intelligence was flimsy, but given that there was normally no intel at all on Kaminoans, it had a great deal more credibility.

Fett had already worked out his route to the Outer Rim

by the time he drained his ale, put his credits on the counter, and stood up to leave.

"I like this neighborhood," he said.

On the way back to *Slave I,* he did what he had done so many times: he used his datapad to carry out an automated purchase of an asset. He bought half a dozen homes in Upper Parkway and transferred them to one of his holding companies; they'd double in value inside the year. It was as near as he ever came to indulgence, but he would never live in any of them. They were an investment.

He never gambled. He *speculated.*

What are you investing for? Why did you ever invest? When did you stop and think what you were going to do with it all?

He hadn't. He was in it to succeed, to show how good he was. And the only person who would have cared how well he did, what a clever boy he'd been, was long dead.

Fett flexed his fingers discreetly as he sat in the back of the taxi, feeling the joints and tendons burn. The pain was still occasional rather than ever-present, but he knew it would get worse as his condition deteriorated. A few analgesics, when pain finally impaired his efficiency, would keep him going. No, he wasn't dead yet.

But if Ko Sai had been one of the Kaminoans—he noted that plural—who fled to Arkanian Micro, then her research on aging hadn't gone with her. The company would have exploited it to the full by now. Anti-aging was always the preoccupation of affluent civilizations. It earned big credits.

Maybe the talk in the bar was just rumor. No, enough hard detail had been revealed, and industry gossip tended to have a basis in reality.

But maybe Ko Sai had never managed to halt or reverse the aging process.

Then you're really dead, Fett. So shape up.

As soon as he was clear of the taxi he stripped off the robe and tunic, bundled it in the holdall, and put his helmet back on with genuine relief. It wasn't just a barrier against a world where he didn't truly belong: it was a piece of a kit, a weapon in its own right. He relaxed as the familiar welter of text and icons cascaded down the margin of the HUD and told him all was well with *Slave I*. He checked the various security cams remotely, staring through images of empty bays and secure hatchways at the permacrete strip in front of him. Even before *Slave I* came into view in one of the bays, he settled on an image of Mirta Gev. Still locked in the prisoner bay, she lay on the deck with her legs hooked over a bulkhead rail, fingers meshed behind her head, performing sit-ups.

He hadn't come across women like her before. He hadn't come across many men like her, either. Whatever was driving her, she was serious about it. Discipline was a fine quality. He came perilously close to *liking* her again.

Fool. She's ballast.

He opened *Slave I*'s forward hatch via his HUD link at thirty meters from the ship, climbed into the cockpit, and flicked open the internal comm system.

"Change of plan," he said. "We're going to Parmel sector, Outer Rim."

He waited for sounds of protest. Nothing. He checked the cam again to make sure Mirta was still there.

"Did you hear me?"

"Yes." She sounded a little out of breath and stood looking into the cam's lens. "You'll pay me sooner or later. I'm young. I've got time to wait."

She had no idea how pointed that observation truly was. Fett wondered if she knew he was ill, but there was no way she could know he was dying.

"Vohai," he said, and wondered why he volunteered the destination. She was making him drop his guard. *Nobody* managed that. He made a conscious effort to be himself again, untouched by anything beyond his own needs. "Sit up front where I can keep an eye on you."

He released the security locks on the aft compartments and fired up *Slave I*'s sublight drives. Mirta belted herself into the copilot's seat just as the ship lifted, the acceleration flattening her like a punch.

Fett paused. "I don't bother with the g-force dampers on takeoff."

Why did I say that? He'd developed a rhythm of barebones conversation over the years. His passengers were never volunteers. Nobody wanted him to catch up with them. This was how it went: they whined, and he slapped them down, with a blunt word or sometimes a blunt object.

Mirta didn't whine. He still felt the compulsion to slap down.

She stared ahead from the viewscreen. "I didn't pay for a ticket so I'm not complaining."

There was no answer to that. Fett took *Slave I* out on manual to check that he could still pilot without computer assistance. *So far, so good.* The illness was still just pain, not yet infirmity. Roonadan dwindled beneath them into a rusty red coin, and the viewport filled with star-specked void as *Slave I* cleared the planet. Then he took the risk of losing his main psychological aid to remaining aloof, and eased off his helmet. He expected Mirta to react; but she just glanced at him and then looked away again, apparently more interested in the starfield ahead.

"You're a clone, aren't you?" said Mirta at last.

She gets right to the point. "Got a problem with that?"

"No. I met a clone once."

"So did Ailyn. She killed him."

"Only because she thought he was you."

I don't want to chat. He didn't answer.

Mirta persisted. "But this clone said he'd fought at Geonosis."

"Couldn't have."

"Why?"

"Those clones were designed to age fast." Fett did a quick mental calculation, doubling the years. "He'd be a decrepit hundred-forty-year-old now."

"He was alive all right."

The clone army had been designed to mature in ten standard years, and then they carried on aging at twice or more the rate of ordinary men. Fett remembered feeling sorry for them as a kid, but his father had told him to be proud because they were perfect warriors. Sometimes he remembered that they were also his brothers. Whenever he met a stormtrooper going about Vader's business, he'd always wondered whether some remnant of his father's template— of himself—was behind that white visor. But he never asked.

"When did you meet him?" Fett asked carefully.

"Last year. I got in his way on a job."

"Bounty hunting?" *Where? Don't rush her.*

"Yes."

"A one-hundred-forty-year-old clone?"

Mirta studied his face for a moment, impassive. "He looked a lot like you, except for the scars."

"He'd be too old to even walk."

"Oh, he could walk all right. And handle a weapon. Big scary guy with a custom Verpine rifle and this long, thin, three-sided knife."

No clone from the Grand Army of the Republic could have survived, let alone have left the service. Their whole life was fighting: how could they have coped on their own? But clones were men, and they had been scattered across the galaxy in the war, so it was inevitable that some had fathered children. This had to be one of them. He was almost reassured to know that the clone bloodline hadn't been erased completely, but he wasn't sure why.

"You sure?"

"Yeah. He said his clan name was Skirata."

Skirata.

Fett jerked his head around and knew instantly that he'd displayed too much interest. But he knew that name. Back on Kamino in the years before the war with the Separatists started, his father had had a friend called Skirata: a short, tough, fanatical man who trained clone commandos and—according to his father—was the dirtiest fighter he'd ever known. He seemed to like that about him.

"What *else* did he say?"

"That he and some of his brothers left the army after Palpatine came to power. He wasn't very talkative. You're definitely related."

That made Fett pay *much* closer attention.

No clone from the Kamino labs could have survived this long—except unaltered ones, like him.

Or . . . one whose accelerated aging process *had been halted*. Only Ko Sai knew enough to be able to do that.

"I'm interested," he said.

"Why?"

He'd rarely needed to lie, but he lied now. "They'd be *my* brothers too, wouldn't they?" And then he wasn't sure how much of that was actually untrue. He had always been alone, just the way he liked it, and now he was suddenly curious about not being that way.

Mirta leaned back in the seat and looked up at the deckhead. The heart-of-fire was strung around her neck, which struck him as an odd thing for a bounty hunter to do with an object she'd retrieved. She was just a young girl, and girls liked baubles, but she didn't seem the type to go in for jewelry.

"He looked like you, more or less," she said at last. She tugged at the necklace like worry beads. "He had full *Mando* armor. Light gray. And these pale gray leather gloves with an unusual grain." She held both hands out above her lap, palms down, fingers spread, as if she was imagining those gloves on her own hands. "Really *immaculate* gloves."

Fett thought *gray* and an image of Taun We's long silver-gray neck and neat, yellow-eyed head dominated his field of view, as vivid as his helmet's display, right there in front of him and yet somehow *not* there.

If Mirta wasn't spinning him a line, then someone *had* managed to get hold of Ko Sai's data. And they'd made use of it.

But maybe she knew more than he gave her credit for. His father had taught him to watch out for traps. This was so close to what he wanted to hear that it triggered every suspicious nerve in his body, which was all of them.

If those clones survived, why haven't I heard about them before? If this kid's trying to set me up for something, she's got a lot to learn.

Even Ailyn had tried to kill him once. He glanced sideways at Mirta.

"Fierfek, you look *just* like him when you do that." She looked rattled. "It's the way you tilted your head."

Whoever the man with the gray gloves was, he seemed to have made an impression, or else she was an expert actress. She had a tight grip on the heart-of-fire as if to protect it.

Fett decided to make sure she was secured in the aft section when he needed to sleep. She still seemed to think that the goods she had to sell was Ailyn's location; maybe she didn't realize that she now had two things he wanted, and that was information on both his dead wife and—impossible, but he couldn't ignore it—his living brothers.

If she had known, she'd have asked him to pay for it.

But Mirta had the necklace. It was somehow all he could recall of Sintas Vel at that moment.

He suddenly missed her, and he knew he had no right to.

SENATE LOBBY 513, SENATE BUILDING, CORUSCANT: 0835 HOURS.

Admiral Pellaeon resigned as Supreme Commander of the Galactic Alliance Defense Force at 0800, a little too late for the main morning holonews bulletins, but early enough to interrupt drive-time programming for a few moments. He had objected strenuously—in private—to the powers granted to the Galactic Alliance Guard, but said nothing publicly. He was an old man. Nobody outside Omas's cabinet—and presumably the military—thought it unusual that he should let a younger officer take his place.

Jacen watched the news on the chamber's holoscreen, sound muted.

While he wasn't surprised that Pellaeon had finally gone, he still wasn't prepared for the speed at which events were moving. He wondered if Lumiya had influenced matters somehow. But she denied it. She sat beside him in the deserted lobby chamber, document case on her lap, face invisible under that dark red cowl and veil. The chamber was normally full of lobbyists and media seeking audience with Senators, but it was too early for the majority of the power brokers to be about their business. The Jedi council, though, was meeting Niathal in the Supreme Commander's suite: and it was interesting that she had not gone to see them, but that they had come to her.

Start as you mean to go on.

Jacen wondered what Uncle Luke would make of the Mon Calamari officer. She would replace Omas one day. He hoped Luke would see that coming and support her so that the war would be short and sharp, and so Jacen wouldn't have to take up the mantle Lumiya had thrust upon him.

There you go again. You know this is meant to be. You can't avoid it; Lumiya is part of the inevitable, just as you are. Submit to it.

"Tell me you didn't influence Admiral Pellaeon," said Jacen quietly.

"I didn't need to. He's furious about your appointment and he's old." Lumiya's voice was so low that Jacen almost had to amplify it with the Force in his mind. "By the time he decides he wants to return, it'll be too late for him to stop you."

The resignation of an elderly chief of defense was no shocking news story for HNE, merely a chance to recap on Pellaeon's distinguished career; but the succession of Admiral Niathal was significant. She was known as a hard-liner. Jacen switched the wall-mounted holoscreen to a Corellian news station where her appointment was provoking reaction. Thrackan Sal-Solo, Head of State, was holding forth on the certain threat to Corellia. With the audio muted, Jacen lip-read.

Sal-Solo announced that Centerpoint Station would be brought back online for the defense of Corellia within three months.

"You have an interesting selection of relatives," said Lumiya.

"All the more reason for me to do the decent thing and sort out the problems the various branches of my family appear to be visiting upon the galaxy."

"You're more like your grandfather than you think."

Lumiya knew Anakin Skywalker as her Lord Vader. He'd selected her as an intelligence agent. "I haven't failed to notice the parallels," said Jacen.

"And that makes you wary."

"I've seen the steps he took." *Literally, Grandfather: I stood behind you and watched you kill children.* "I have to do things a little differently."

"And you still want Ben Skywalker as your apprentice."

"Yes."

Lumiya emanated satisfaction, as if this was an extra

layer of vengeance on Luke, but he knew she was past that point. "That's a choice only you can make."

"If there's another candidate, I can't think of one."

"Are you still going ahead with the Galactic Alliance Guard?"

"Why wouldn't I?"

"You have an ally in the Supreme Commander now," she said. "You could go straight to the military solution."

"There's still a real job to be done in restoring security here. And Niathal needs time to stamp her leadership on the GADF. And Chief Omas."

"Commendable, pragmatic analysis."

Jacen wondered if he was taking a risk by having this discussion in the Senate Building. But if any of the Jedi council were as adept as he was at listening in the Force, he suspected they would be too tied up in their discussion with Niathal to hear. What would they be saying to her?

He could listen. He could snatch the sounds out of the air from behind closed doors at the far end of the floor and witness for himself, but it was irrelevant, and he didn't need to.

He knew they would be pressing caution on her.

He also knew Niathal would smile politely in that tight-lipped way of hers, twist her head sideways to stare them out, and say that she thanked them for their counsel.

Then she would ignore that counsel.

Jacen's mind leapt away from the business at hand for a brief moment and he found himself wondering why the Jedi Council hadn't given his grandfather the guidance he needed as a Padawan. If they knew he was the Chosen One, why had no Master from the Council taken on the role of training him?

Poor Obi-Wan. They dithered and left the task to you. Now they're dithering over another galactic war.

On the holoscreen, Corellian political commentators had worked themselves into a froth of outrage at Niathal's appointment. Jacen switched channels back to HNE just as the sound of footsteps began echoing down the long passage to his right. The meeting in the Supreme Commander's office had ended.

"Relax," said Jacen. He centered himself and projected a Force illusion around Lumiya to bolster her own cloaking of her identity again. He felt the sensation of a ball of heat building in his chest, and he nudged her with his elbow. "Go on. Brief me on the strength of the Corellian fleet and don't react to anyone passing by."

Jacen and Lumiya waited. The lobby and the corridor leading off it were empty. Eventually they heard boots thudding fast on the marble floor—Luke's, for certain—as if he hadn't much enjoyed the meeting and wanted to get out.

Okay, Lumiya, let's see how you react to Luke this time—and how he reacts to you.

Luke approached them, eyes downcast, distracted and frowning. He seemed about to walk past Jacen and then paused to acknowledge him as if it was an effort.

"Are you waiting for Niathal?" asked Luke.

"I'm paying my respects as head of the Galactic Alliance Guard." Jacen indicated Lumiya. "This is a colleague from the university's Defense Studies Department."

Luke nodded politely at Lumiya then turned back to Jacen. "Are you certain that's the right choice?"

"If I don't do it, who will?"

"Maybe nobody should," said Luke.

"If Chief Omas needs the job done, I'll do what I can."

Luke fixed Jacen with a frank blue gaze for a few moments, but he didn't look at Lumiya again, and—more to the point—Lumiya didn't look at him.

"Mind how you do it," Luke said, a slight frown still creasing his nose, and walked away. Jacen waited a full ten minutes, still holding the heat in his chest to maintain the illusion, before relaxing.

"I'm impressed by your ability to deceive Luke," said Lumiya. "And you appear to have no doubts or misgivings about it."

Jacen stood up. Lumiya had been given the best chance she had for decades to kill Luke Skywalker, and she hadn't shown the slightest inclination to take it.

"No doubts," said Jacen. "But no enthusiasm, either."

"That's as it should be," she said. "Tell me what your next task is."

There was no harm telling her. It would be all over HNE in a few days.

"Internment," said Jacen. "We're confining Corellians until this current wave of terror is contained. Come on. Let me introduce you to the officer who'll be in the Chief of State's office within the year."

Internment. Extreme, dangerous . . . and inevitable.

When you could let go of your own need to be the hero, the admired one, the respected, and face being reviled for doing a necessary job, then you had finally overcome the most poisonous attachment of all: the love of ego.

Jacen was prepared to be hated in pursuit of a greater good.

chapter nine

I heard stories about his grandfather when I was a boy, and Jacen Solo struck me as walking the same path. Vader liked a loyal military elite at his back, too. And sometimes ends do justify the means. The protest from the media and civil rights groups that greeted our announcement that a Galactic Alliance Guard had been formed to deal with the new threat to public safety was to be expected. It did not, however, make it any easier to hear myself decried as the new Palpatine.

—Chief of State Omas, Memoirs

CORELLIAN QUARTER, CORUSCANT.

Ben knew he was taking an insane risk by going back to the Corellian neighborhood, but he had to find Barit.

This time he made sure he was wearing regular clothes, not Jedi robes. He worried that he was a coward for hiding his status, but a sensible voice inside him said that there was no point in getting beaten up before he found out something useful. That was *pragmatism*, as Jacen called it.

Corellians didn't have a fight going with the Jedi. Just the Alliance. But the distinction between the two wasn't always clear.

He sauntered along the walkways, stopping to stare at things that made him curious, reminding himself that he was a thirteen-year-old boy and not a soldier this time. Nobody seemed to notice him.

All he wanted to do was to look Barit in the face and ask a simple question: what made him see Coruscanti as the enemy?

The fact that two governments were behaving like idiots didn't seem like justification enough for Ben. He didn't want to attack Corellians just because the government had a problem with Corellia: even the raid on Centerpoint Station hadn't been directed against *people*. He felt no hatred for Corellians at all.

But Barit, who wasn't that much older than him, had tried to shoot a CSF officer. He hadn't aimed at the mob stoning the Corellian embassy. He had tried to shoot a complete stranger who was trying to stop the riot.

Ben didn't understand, and he needed to.

The Corellian neighborhood was quieter today, as if people were waiting for something to happen. Some of the shops were closed. Ben stopped at a grocery store to pick up a bottle of fizzade and ask for directions to the Saiy workshops. He drank as he walked the kilometer or so to Barit's family business.

Ben found two men who looked about his father's age leaning over a large repulsor drive with hydrospanners in their hands. They glanced up sharply but relaxed when they saw him. *Just a kid.*

"Where's Barit?" he asked casually.

One of the men stood up. "Barit? *Barit!* Someone here to see you."

Barit emerged from a storeroom wiping his hands on a rag. He stared at Ben for a few moments as if he didn't recognize him and then didn't look pleased to see him. He walked out into the open air, and Ben followed him a little way from the workshops. There was an appetizing smell of frying and spices coming from an open doorway.

"Did you find your missing diamonds?" Ben asked. He meant the gems made out of Corellians' ashes in the Sanctuary. "Did anyone give them back?"

"No," said Barit. "The sort of people who smash memorials don't have consciences."

It wasn't a good start. Ben plunged in. "I saw you outside the embassy the other day."

"What were *you* doing there?"

"Getting a faceful of gas."

"Yeah. So was I."

Ben wondered what Barit had done with his blaster. He knew he could draw his lightsaber instantly from his pocket if he had to find out the hard way. "When I say I *saw* you, I mean I saw you with a weapon."

"Everyone carries a piece. Even you."

I have to know. "But why shoot at a cop?"

"You going to turn me in?" So he hadn't seen Ben deflect the blast. He had shot and run. "I didn't think I hit anyone. They never said—"

"I just want to know why you did it." *You aimed to kill, or you didn't care who you hit.* "The officer never did anything to you. He was just trying to stop a fight."

"Coruscant's against us. The Alliance is trying to kill us. We've got to defend ourselves."

"But that's not *people*. The CSF wasn't trying to do anything to *you*. How can you shoot at someone who wasn't aiming at you?"

"You wouldn't understand."

"I *want* to."

"You wouldn't."

"If you're that scared of us all, why are you still living here?"

"You'd like that, wouldn't you? Kick us out, send us back."

Ben didn't know how to respond. "You think you're at war with us?"

"We *are*. Maybe not properly, but we are."

"How can you think that when you *live* here? If you really believe that, how can you even *want* to live here?"

Ben stood staring at Barit in complete incomprehension. He had no idea what was going on in the Corellian's mind to make him feel that he was suddenly an alien on the planet where his family had been born. But he knew that it made him feel suspicious and wary of Barit in a way that had nothing to do with the fact that he was prepared to draw a blaster.

"Come on, Barit," one of the men yelled. "You going to be yakking there all day? Got jobs to do. Get on with it."

Barit looked at Ben as if he was memorizing his face. "Got to go. Thanks for not turning me in."

He walked back toward the workshop. Ben wandered away, the half-full bottle of fizzade still clutched in his hand, and wondered if he should have reported Barit to CSF.

It had never crossed his mind.

JABI TOWN, CORELLIAN QUARTER, CORUSCANT: 0400 HOURS.

This neighborhood hated the planet on which it found itself. And that was not a political or military assessment of the risk, but Jacen Solo's certainty of what he detected in the Force.

That alone was enough for a Jedi to act upon—if a Jedi was what he still was, he reminded himself.

Jacen could sense the resentment, anger, and danger that was simmering in this Corellian district of Galactic City, and that was why he had decided to begin his operations as the new commander of the Galactic Alliance Guard by raiding Jabi Town.

It was hard to seal off a neighborhood in a place like Coruscant. The intersections were three-dimensional and required six CSF traffic division repulsorlift ships for each skylane junction that Jacen needed to have blocked off. He stood on the platform of a military assault vessel, a matte-gray gunship not unlike its CSF counterpart, watching two of the CSF ships hover into position. It was still dark; the CSF vessels had no navigation lights showing. Jacen could only see them because the light pollution on Coruscant meant that Galactic City was never truly pitch black, and he could pick out the shape of the hull when it moved.

"Are you okay, Ben?"

Ben stepped forward. He hadn't said a word. He clutched his lightsaber hilt in one hand, and Jacen sensed he was agitated rather than excited. He had changed irrevocably from a boy who found missions an adventure to a young man who had a healthy degree of fear in him.

"I'm fine, Jacen."

"Comlink working?"

Ben fumbled with his right ear. "Do I really have to wear it?"

"You need to be able to hear what's going on between squads. You can't do that using the Force." Sometimes the non-Jedi solution to a problem was actually the easiest. "I'm not even sure I can handle that much voice traffic yet."

Jacen turned to the five squads of soldiers of 967 Commando in the troop bay, elite shock troopers whose specialty was siege busting and personnel retrieval, all of them handpicked because they were Coruscant-born and -bred, and human, with no possibility of secret sympathies with other worlds. Among them were volunteers from the CSF's Anti-Terrorist Unit, selected and vouched for by Shevu. They would be loyal. Jacen had come to value loyalty very highly lately.

He couldn't see their faces behind their riot visors and sealed black helmets. But they exuded no more than a sense of concentration and a little apprehension of the level that was normal for troops going into battle. They didn't know exactly what lay behind the doors of the Corellian quarter, but they knew they ran the risk of armed resistance and even explosives.

On the other side of the Corellian district, Shevu stood by with more squads, ready to storm buildings to search, subdue, and arrest. At the ends of the walkways, more soldiers of 967 Commando slipped into position and trained rifles on doors, ready to stop anyone escaping. The sniper troops had moved into positions on the rooftops around the block.

Jacen opened the comlink looped over his ear. "Squad commanders . . . no discharge of weapons unless you're fired upon first."

Shevu's voice cut in. "Can I suggest we update that to 'unless we perceive a real and immediate threat,' sir? Takes account of grenades and other weapons."

I'm thinking like a pilot, like a Jedi, not like an infantry officer. "Good idea, Captain. Revise that."

There was a faint murmur on the net as if troops had silenced their links for a moment and then opened them again. They'd exchanged comments. They might have said that their commander was an idiot for not establishing better rules of engagement from the start of the mission planning, but it felt more like approval that he could listen to advice. The Force might not have been useful for communicating routine detail, but it was perfect for discerning mood.

Jacen felt it was time to roll. Most would be asleep: 0400 was a good time to disorient humans and minimize resistance. Shevu had shown him medical data to confirm this but pointed out that it never, ever worked on Wookiees.

"Stand by," said Jacen.

Ben's lightsaber sprang into life, the blue light illuminating the troop bay. The 967's sergeant crackled audibly as his armor systems created feedback in the assault vessel's public address system. He adjusted something on the side of his helmet; silence descended.

Around two thousand people lived in this block of buildings, and Jacen had five hundred troops deployed: not a good ratio, but it was enough to get the job done. The assault ship hovered level with the walkway, and he leapt down from the bay, followed by the 967, who spread immediately to stack either side of doorways. Above them, Jacen could feel the adrenaline-fueled presence of roof teams and snipers.

There was a second of profound stillness like the pause of a pendulum before it swung back again.

"Go go go!" said Jacen.

The assault ships swung into the skylanes on either side of the block, and their arrays of two-hundred-million-lumen spotlamps turned the area into instant, blinding daylight. The 967 sergeant behind him relayed his voice via the assault ship.

"This is Coruscant national security. Stay where you are. I repeat, stay where you are." Jacen felt the vibration in his teeth and sinuses. The canyon of walls on either side concentrated the sound. "Officers will be entering buildings. Please cooperate. Be ready to show your identity passes."

One or two doors had already opened and some people stood on balconies in bathrobes, hands shielding their eyes against the ferocious white spotlamps. All along the walkways, there was a chaos of yelled commands and hammering on doors. There was no open area to assemble detainees to sort the Corellians from other passport holders who happened to be on the block, so commandos were going into the buildings and assessing the occupants where they stood, or taking them outside to stand against walls while their homes were swept for what had now simply become loosely termed as "threats."

People, devices, bad attitudes. They were all *threats.*

Jacen and Ben ran along the main walkway, lightsabers drawn, looking for where they might be needed. Around them, residents were already being led out of their homes, some silent and shocked, some swearing and struggling. Jacen glanced back at Ben: his face was set in fixed concentration, wide-eyed and made more shockingly white by the intense light. When he looked around, he could also see activity on the other side of the skylane where residents from the next block were starting to gather to watch the drama.

This will be on HNE in minutes. Everyone's got a holo-recorder these days.

Never mind. I have nothing to hide.

"Galactic Guard! Outside! *Now!*"

Ahead of them, a squad of four 967 troops confronted a set of locked doors. They leapt back from the doorway, flattening themselves at either side of the entrance. Jacen went to their aid.

"Ordnance, sir," said one of them. The voice was female. She held up the sensor readout—the Nose, as they called it—attached to the back of her left gauntlet. It winked red and orange. "The Nose sniffed something and the occupants aren't cooperating. Stand clear."

"Three inside." On the other side of the doorway, a commando with sergeant's insignia and the name WIRUT stenciled on his breastplate held a thermal imaging scanner against the wall. His comrade stood back a few paces and snapped a gas grenade onto the muzzle of his rifle. "If anything in there blows, sir, this isn't going to look pretty on HNE. You stand clear."

"Sergeant, I won't ask anyone to do what I won't do myself," said Jacen. "Show me the image."

The sergeant—Wirut—turned the imager to face Jacen. It had a pistol grip like a loudhailer, one end of the body a lens and the other side a display that showed red on black—three human shapes, moving around in an area that was probably set one room back from the frontage judging by the range shown on the display's grid.

"Ben, do you sense anything?" Jacen asked. "What does it feel like to you?"

Ben's sense of danger was becoming very acute. This was a good time to hone it to perfection. He half-closed his eyes in concentration. "Dangerous, but not right now. Soon."

"Explosives, but not assembled?"

"Is that what you feel?"

"Yes," said Jacen. He motioned Wirut back. "Hold the gas, trooper. You want them immobilized?"

"That's the general idea, sir, so they don't detonate anything."

"Fine." Jacen took a breath, visualized the interior of the ground floor and the door, and focused himself on the three people inside.

"Sir—"

Jacen didn't hear the rest. He sent a Force jolt through all three targets simultaneously, paralyzing them, and a second later the doors blew open not with the punishing shock wave of a conventional blast but the contained violence of the Force. The squad of commandos threw themselves flat. It was the smart thing to do in an explosion, clearly ingrained by hard training.

They froze, waiting for a shock wave that never came. Wirut got to his knees, and even if Jacen couldn't see his face, he knew the man was grinning.

"Nice trick, sir," he said, and stood up, rifle ready, to ease through the torn gap that had been the front doors. Jacen slipped in after him, followed by Ben and the rest of the squad. The three occupants of the house—a man in his thirties and two younger women—were crumpled on the floor of a back room, unconscious.

Wirut crouched down and checked them for a pulse. "Are they going to be okay?"

"It's harmless and temporary," said Jacen. "Just a shock to the spinal cord."

"You're going to put us out of business, sir," said the female trooper. "REBJ."

"I wish that were true, but I suspect you're going to be busier than ever." Jacen watched as one of the squad held

out his left gauntlet, following some trace. He was searching for the explosives. "REBJ?"

"Rapid Entry By Jedi, sir. Very handy. You'll be in demand."

The three detainees were brought out on makeshift stretch-
ers. Around them on the walkway, half-dressed civilians
and black-armored troopers milled about trying to load onto
more assault ships that were setting down or hovering level
with the pedestrian access.

"Just turned back an HNE speeder, sir," one of the troopers called to him. "Consider this operation prime time."

The night was lit well enough for news cams, too; Jacen
knew there was no such thing as a covert operation on this
scale in a heavily populated city. Ben leaned close to him.
There was a loud *whump* and the tinkling rain of shattering
permaglass as the 967 used frame charges on an apartment
block nearby to gain entry.

"Does that mean Dad will see what's happening?"

"I believe so," said Jacen.

"Oh."

"The only approval you need in your life is your own,
Ben. Are *you* ashamed of anything you've done?"

Ben paused, lips parted, eyes slightly defocused. He was
thinking about something very hard. "Only of things I
haven't done."

"Such as?"

"Not telling you about someone who tried to shoot a
CSF officer."

Jacen could tell from Ben's voice that there was a lot more
to it than that. He noted it mentally. "We can talk about
that later. Now go find a squad that needs assistance."

Ben raced off still clutching his lightsaber, the blue blade
leaving a ghost image as he moved. Across the chasm of the
skylane, Jacen could see the telltale flash of light from holo-
recorders as the neighbors opposite recorded the raid for
posterity, and—he had no doubt—for HNE.

He considered sending every holocam plummeting hundreds of meters to the ground with a multiple Force grab, but then decided he had to accept scrutiny. *If you're not prepared to do something in public, don't do it at all.*

And the raid was as much a statement of intent to others as it was to root out terrorists. It had to be seen to be done.

Jacen made a point of not shutting down his lightsaber. Even under the savage glare of the spotlamps, it was another green beacon, another symbol of Jedi involvement in something most Coruscanti hadn't seen in two generations. *This is what Jedi do, citizens. We act on your behalf. We don't just sit around and debate in our lovely new Temple that you paid for.*

Ben had an earnest and brief conversation with a squad sergeant and then stood back to wrench apart another set of doors using the Force. The light within streamed out dramatically, a hemorrhage of yellow light in a dark space between two pools of blue-white spotlight. Force-breaching caused a lot less damage than a detonite charge. Ben stood back to let the troops enter.

Jacen activated his secure comlink channel. "Shevu, how are we doing?"

"No fatalities so far, sir." Bangs and crashes of something heavy being handled interrupted the captain. "Still more than fifteen hundred individuals to process, but the resistant targets have been neutralized and the rest appear to be compliant."

Jacen translated mentally: *We kicked down a few doors and the rest have given up.* "Well done, Captain."

The sight of lightsabers being wielded in a roundup of Corellians would not play well to the Jedi council, Jacen suspected.

It was just the beginning. For a tempting moment he wondered how his grandfather had felt in the transition to becoming loathed, but to Force-walk into time to find out would have meant first finding *where* that had taken place, and he didn't know.

Jacen also didn't know if he could face more revelations like the last one yet. But pain always had to be embraced—sooner or later.

FLEET SURPLUS DISPOSAL LOT, GALACTIC CITY, CORUSCANT.

"Captain Solo, are you *sure* we can't accompany you back to Corellia?"

C-3PO seemed reluctant to surrender the case of clothes to Han, as if hanging on to the handle would ensure that Han took him, too.

"Yeah, nobody would ever notice a golden droid. You'd be invisible." Han didn't like the smell of the small shuttle he'd bought from the government disposal lot. It was alien: he hadn't realized how much of that small detail of the *Falcon* was embedded in his sense of comfort. He flicked through the controls on the console and despaired at the maximum velocity shown on the readout. "Stay here. Besides, you and Artoo can keep an eye on Jaina for us."

"Han . . ." Leia's voice drifted from the small cargo bay.

"Honey, *nobody* has protocol droids like him any longer. He'd be a—"

"Han, *you need to see this.*"

Han thought she'd found some mechanical fault he hadn't spotted when he handed over the credits. He made his way back aft to see her staring transfixed at the holoscreen in one of the coffin-sized cabins.

"Another bomb?" he asked. It was a cramped space; he could hardly see the screen without squeezing past her and pressing his back against the aft bulkhead.

"Try bombshell."

Han took a few moments to work out what he was look-

ing at. Riot police—no, *soldiers* in black armor were storming buildings, and the caption said JABI TOWN: DAWN RAID
ON CORELLIAN COMMUNITY. It was everything he expected
from the Alliance. They were playing the Empire all over
again, almost right down to the armor.

"Oh, you reckon this is going to shock me?"

Leia's mouth was slightly open and her frown made her
look as if she was close to tears. She held up her hand for
quiet and he saw it was shaking slightly.

"Jacen," she said hoarsely.

Han scanned the screen, expecting to see Jacen injured or
attacked, and then saw his son, his little boy who had always had a soft heart and who could feel pain for others, directing soldiers into buildings to drag out Corellians.

In that way of terrible and unimaginable things, it didn't
look real. His mind conjured up a scenario instantly: it was
a vile piece of fake propaganda. It was Thrackan's doing. It
was a *lie*.

But it wasn't. Leia put her hand to her mouth.

Jacen even had his lightsaber drawn. *And he had Ben
with him*. Ben was taking part in the raid.

Han couldn't speak.

"Honey, what's happening to him?" Leia's voice was a
whisper. "How can he do this?"

She turned up the volume. The voice-over faded in and all
Han could take in were the words, ". . . emergency powers
have been granted for the internment of Corellian citizens
resident in Galactic City . . ."

Han felt guilty that he saw not fellow Corellians being
herded into assault ships but himself being betrayed by his
own son. *You should be thinking of the bigger picture. You
used to be able to do that, you self-centered bum.* But as
much as he tried to be altruistic, the horror and outrage that
was replacing his shock was for himself and Leia.

Not even Jaina. Now I know what she meant when she asked him if he was in trouble.

All Han could think now was that they could be on the run from their own son—and that they'd be even less welcome back in Coronet if their identities were discovered.

"Threepio?" Han called. "*Threepio!* When the *Falcon's* ready, fly her over to us any way you can. Get back to the apartment *now* and call Jaina. Tell her we'll talk to her later. We have to go. Got it?"

"I have indeed *got it,* Captain Solo."

Leia said nothing. She eased past Han and settled in the cockpit. When things were bad, she usually became very calm and decisive. It was a barometer of how serious a crisis they were facing.

"Ready to lift," she said quietly, checking the status readouts as if she hadn't just watched her son turn into a monster on HNE in front of the whole galaxy. "Let's go."

chapter ten

To see a Jedi take up his lightsaber against civilians is shocking. But to see the son and nephew of the leader of the Jedi council doing it is heartbreaking.

—Master Cilghal, Jedi high council

PERIMETER FENCE, ARKANIAN
MICROTECHNOLOGIES: VOHAI,
PARMEL SECTOR: 1600 HOURS.

The bigger companies grew, the more complacent their security became. Fett could remember when Arkanian Micro was a tough nut to crack.

He knelt on one knee in the cover of bushes and used the scope of his EE-3 blaster to observe employees passing through the security gate.

"I could be useful," said the voice in his helmet comlink.

"Stay off this channel."

"Women can get access to places that men often can't."

Mirta was persistent. Fett bristled.

"You'll spend the journey back in the cells if you don't shut up."

She was still locked inside *Slave I*—hidden in the cover of a disused silo a kilometer away—confined to the crew section this time. She couldn't activate the ship's drives, but Fett had left a couple of comlink channels unguarded. If she was any good, she'd find them—and if she was double-crossing him, she'd use them and then he'd know who she was working with. So far all she had done was call him.

"Okay," she said, apparently unperturbed. "I'll stand by."

The only person Fett had ever trusted was his father. Neither of them was a natural team player. He could handle command when he had to, but he liked working alone, and the current task was a case in point. He could either talk his way into Arkanian Micro, or he could do what he did best, which was to observe, identify the weak point, infiltrate by force—and take what he needed.

Talking wasn't his strong point.

The staff moved in and out. A security guard on the gate and two sentinel droids scrutinized each individual going in *and* coming out, sweeping them with sensors.

Arkanian Micro had once buried its most sensitive laboratories in the polar ice of the planet, but now it seemed to prefer the softer suburbs and landscaped business parks. *Fat and lazy.* It was cheaper to build on the surface. Vohai hadn't suffered at the hands of the Yuuzhan Vong and it had grown complacent.

That was just what Fett needed.

He liked companies with tough security best, though, because they provided a handy pointer to the target. You didn't protect what you didn't value most. *Let's look for a few clues.*

Kaminoans wouldn't stroll out through the gates with a lunch box under one arm. Kaminoans liked cold, wet gloom. Vohai was pleasantly sunny much of the year. Fett called up the aerial view of the Micro complex on his HUD and worked out where he would place an office to ensure it had no natural light. The layout as seen in the frame that *Slave I*'s scanners had grabbed before landing showed a sprawl of building that was essentially a square core with a lot of thin arms radiating off it, and many courtyards. Humans—most species, in fact—liked bright natural light to work in.

But you wouldn't want one of those nice courtyard offices, would you, Taun We?

So, somewhere in the square heart of the complex, not on the periphery or in the strings of building that ran from it, was a lab or an office that a Kaminoan would feel at home in. *Me, too. Not the rain so much as the plain walls and the lack of clutter.* He thought of the simple toys and his austere childhood home and knew why possessions seemed a burden he didn't really want.

She's probably in there right now, building more clones. If she raises the alarm when she sees you, would you shoot her? Shoot someone old and weak?

He set his visor to full-range magnification by tapping the control plate on his left forearm—he preferred that to the blink-activated HUD system—and tried to get a better line of sight into the security booth at the gate. They were bound to have some repeater system. Every security station needed to be able to communicate with the rest. That meant there might be an indication of floors below ground.

From the air, only single-story buildings were visible. He needed to know if he faced a more complex layout once inside. It wasn't a good idea to get pinned down below ground level.

Fett needed a better observation point.

He looked around, calculating the angle of elevation he needed to get a clear view through the transparisteel window. If he sent a remote in closer, it would be spotted. He'd do this the old-fashioned way. Backing out of the bushes, he walked a hundred meters to the next lot and checked out the roofline. Fine: plenty of flat-topped warehousing to choose from. He slipped between two buildings, took out his rappelling line, and then decided a simple burn with the jet pack would save his shoulders a lot of wear and tear. He was up on the roof in under three seconds, lying flat and peering down the scope of the blaster to get a better look inside the security booth.

There was a status screen on the guard's desk all right. He eased along to the far edge of the roof on his belly and racked up the scope's magnification. The image shimmered, unsteady at that range, but he could see a grid of white lines on a blue background, with green lights winking at points along the grid—probably intruder sensors. There was nothing that indicated multiple layers.

One level. So far, so good.

The next step was to work out how the building was organized, and all that took was a little guesswork backed up by information that was usually public. Fett lowered himself from the roof on his rappel line, letting the pulley take the strain, flicked the cord clear, and settled down in the shelter of waste storage sheds to browse the local comlink directory system from his datapad.

It was fascinating to see how much information one could put together just by seeing how companies listed their departmental comlink numbers. Names and numbers scrolled across the screen of his pad.

Arkanian Microtechnologies . . .

DELIVERIES

PERSONNEL SERVICES

PUBLIC AFFAIRS AND INVESTOR RELATIONS

He scrolled farther. What was Taun We's specialty?

DEVELOPMENTAL SCIENCES AND EDUCATION

Taun We was an expert in human psychology. She knew enough about humans to make sure the ones the Kaminoans bred under the most unnatural conditions imaginable were conditioned enough to prevent them from becoming basket cases.

She wouldn't be splicing DNA. She'd have brought her little case of datachips with her as some kind of employment dowry, and Microtech would have been glad to have that data, but her day-to-day work—the work she loved doing—was making sure clones didn't go crazy. Profiling, testing, flash-teaching, accelerated socialization: giving clones the right attitude to be useful tools.

Hi, Taun We. I hope you're enjoying your new job.

Fett could have waited to see when she came out—almost certainly by vehicle, probably obscured from view—and followed her to wherever she called home. But it wasn't that much harder to walk in and find her. If he could get close enough to the building, he could use the penetrating terahertz radar sensor in his helmet's visor to look for a long body with pockets of low-density tissue, quite distinct from a human radar profile. It could see through walls. Infrared couldn't.

And it had been a long time since he had broken into a laboratory for data retrieval. A bounty hunter had to keep his skills sharp.

GALACTIC ALLIANCE GUARD HQ, QUADRANT A-89, GALACTIC CITY: 0830 HOURS.

Jacen came out of the GAG briefing room to find Mara standing with her hands on her hips as if he'd kept her waiting a little too long. She looked more under control than relaxed: her expression was carefully neutral, but he could feel the fear in her and see the dark circles under her eyes.

She stared. "When did you start wearing a uniform?"

Jacen glanced down at his black fatigues, hands held away from his sides. "I should have changed before we carried out the raids. Jedi robes and police actions don't mix."

"You're telling me. Luke's going crazy. Emergency meeting of the high council right now, in fact."

"I meant that all that loose fabric is . . . never mind." Luke's reaction was predictable. Jedi couldn't be seen getting their hands dirty, and certainly not his son. "You know why we wore robes originally? To fit in with the ordinary people. So I'm fitting in now, with *my* people."

Mara indicated her own battle jacket. "Sorry, Jacen. It's just a shock to see you in *that* uniform."

"I'm a colonel now."

"I'm not arguing. I just wanted to talk to you before Luke finds you. Is Ben okay?"

"He did very well. You want to see him? He's in the briefing room. We're just doing a wash-up with the squad leaders to work out what we'll do differently next time. And watching the news on the hour, of course."

Mara managed not to raise an eyebrow. "There's going to be a next time, then."

"You turned the job down. What did you think?"

"That it was going to be dirty."

"It is. But churning through war after war because we don't ever fully deal with unrest is a lot dirtier."

The briefing room doors slid open and a corporal from 967 Commando, Lekauf, stuck his head out. "Sir, you're on again!" he said with a grin. "Sorry, ma'am. HNE news."

"Don't let me interrupt you," said Mara. "Just passing."

Jacen took her arm. "Come in and meet my men." He wanted to reassure her about Ben. Unlike Luke, she didn't seem to want her son to be her little replica. She knew how to let go.

She recoiled visibly at the sight of Ben in black fatigues. He was sitting at the table with Shevu and the sergeants, cup of caf in one hand and datapad in the other, and even his body language had suddenly become adult. He was mirroring the adult males around him without even realizing. When he stood up to greet Mara, it struck Jacen that Ben would soon be as tall as he was.

"Ma'am," said Ben, all grave concentration. Not Mom: *ma'am*. "I didn't sense you coming."

"I just dropped by to say that I watched the holonews and—I wanted to see how you were feeling," said Mara. "Are you all right . . . son?"

Yes, he isn't your sweetheart when he's in uniform, thirteen years old or not. Jacen watched the unspoken interaction between them and detected the concern flowing both ways like a faint breeze, but whatever anxiety Mara had brought in with her had vanished and had been replaced almost completely by relief.

"Apart from getting up at oh-two-hundred, I'm fine."

"You're getting so *military.*" Mara managed a grin. "You sure you're okay?"

"Why shouldn't I be? It wasn't dangerous, like the assault on Centerpoint. Captain Shevu was watching my six."

Jacen found it touching that Ben had formed a bond with the 967. It boded well. Shevu was doing a fine job of stifling a smile, and his emotions—tired relief at the end of an operation, and a pleasant affection for Ben—were probably obvious only to Jacen's fine-tuned Force-senses.

"Here we go . . . ," said Lekauf, and turned up the audio on the briefing room's holoscreen. The image flashed up the tagline CRACKDOWN at the bottom of the screen and HNE anchors went into a recap of the morning's raid on Jabi Town. Four hours after the raids, the news emphasis had turned from the drama of hovering assault ships and commandos breaching doors to public reaction.

Admiral Niathal contributed a thirty-second defense of the GAG's actions—967 Commando was, after all, now part of her special operations forces—but it didn't appear that defense was necessary.

Jacen, braced for opprobrium, was taken aback by the reactions of Coruscanti asked for their opinion on the streets and walkways of Galactic City.

"It's about time," said one man in a business suit. "I think Colonel Solo did what we should have done a long time ago. We're too scared of upsetting other governments. Well, Corellia, not anymore."

Mara murmured, faintly sarcastic. "Ooh, you've got fans."

"Didn't plan that . . ."

"I know."

"I hope Luke sees it that way, too," said Jacen, knowing that he wouldn't. "And Admiral Niathal."

"I'll try convincing him."

Jacen beckoned her out of the way of the soldiers, who were staring fixedly at the news coverage with the air of men who knew that public perception was as much a part of the war as any weapon they carried.

"Tell me straight, Mara—are you still happy for me to be training Ben?"

She brushed a loose strand of hair from her eyes in a way that suggested she was buying a few seconds of thinking time. *Even Mara's wary of my reading her emotions.*

"I think it's hard to accept that my little boy's turned into a soldier overnight, but that's something I should have seen coming when we wanted him to be trained as a Jedi."

Jacen still felt a flutter of hesitation around her. "I know you're still troubled by all this."

"Okay, let me ask *you* a question."

"Go ahead."

Mara's eyes were fixed on his now. "Is there someone in your life who's causing you some pain?"

"I don't understand." He really didn't.

"A woman. Jacen, I'm not prying. I just need to know if you're having a difficult time."

He thought of Tenel Ka and Allana. He hardly dared do that these days, in case Lumiya sensed his secret and they were put in danger—more danger than they were already in.

"Yes." It was so true that it hurt. "There's someone I would like to be with that I can't."

Mara exuded pure relief. The frown lines between her eyebrows vanished and she almost smiled. "That's all I needed to know, Jacen. I'm sorry you're having problems. I won't mention it again, but if I can do anything, you let me know, okay?"

Jacen nodded. He couldn't imagine anything that Mara *could* do, but it was comforting to know she was willing.

"Thanks, Mara," he said. "You're probably about my only friend these days."

She shrugged and waved discreetly to Ben before disappearing through the doors. Jacen could guess what was happening in the council chamber without using his Force-senses to listen. He'd let the side down. Jedi didn't raid people's homes with black-clad shock troopers.

A Jedi's job is to solve a problem without taking lives. I think I did that today. Sitting back and not getting involved while people get killed in an endless cycle of wars doesn't count as not having blood on your hands.

Jacen was jerked out of his thoughts by a cup of caf being thrust in front of him. "I don't think things are quite that bad, sir."

It was Corporal Lekauf: young, sandy-haired, and solidly optimistic. Jacen accepted the caf and they both stood watching the HNE coverage of the raids again, the outraged reaction from the Corellian ambassador and Senators, and the imminent threat of severing diplomatic relations.

"I'm never sure if all this is aimed at Coruscant or the Alliance," said Lekauf.

"Separating the two is a real political conjuring trick."

"I'd rather see more unity than separation, sir."

"Me, too." Jacen found he enjoyed the company of 967. They all had the corporal's general optimism. "How long have you been in the army?"

"Since I graduated, sir. Four years."

"What made you sign up?"

Lekauf smiled, almost embarrassed. "My grandfather served under your grandfather in the Imperial Army, sir. He always talked about how Lord Vader put himself in the front line. Meant a lot to him, that did."

Jacen patted Lekauf's shoulder. It was humbling to see how loyalty could last generations. Whatever sins Anakin Skywalker had committed as Vader, there were still those who recognized his qualities as an inspirational commander. Jacen decided it might be safe to walk back in time and watch him again.

He wasn't repeating his mistakes. He was simply building on Anakin Skywalker's missed opportunities.

"Let's make our grandfathers proud, then."

DUR GEJJEN'S HOUSE, CORONET, CORELLIA.

That Gejjen kid didn't seem quite so pleased to see Han this time.

"You going to invite us in?" Han filled his doorway, blaster held at his side, and Gejjen stared at it, wide-eyed. "We're feeling kind of unwelcome out here."

Gejjen stood back, eyes still on the blaster as Han and Leia slipped into his hallway. Han flicked on the safety.

"Where have you been?" asked Gejjen.

"We ran into a well-wisher and had to make a run for it," said Leia. "And before you ask, yes, we know what's happening on Coruscant."

"Sal-Solo is having a field day with it." Two small children emerged behind Gejjen, and he shooed them back into the room. "The Solos' son imprisoning innocent Corellians. Inspiring headlines."

Han snorted. "I'm glad I don't shock easy. Does this mean he's changed the contract on me to read *extra dead*?"

"*Us,*" Leia muttered.

Gejjen ushered them into his front room, and Han noted that the blinds were drawn.

"Where are you staying?"

Han didn't sit down despite the mute offer of a chair. "That's our little secret."

"Okay." Gejjen didn't appear offended; paranoia seemed a normal part of political life. "My sources say there's more than one taker for the contract."

"Fett doesn't play well with others."

"Told you it wasn't Fett," said Leia.

"Fett or no Fett, Captain Solo, the threat is real. And while we're appalled at what your son appears to be doing, Thrackan Sal-Solo is pursuing his line for his own ends, not Corellia's, so as far as we're concerned, we still have common cause."

"Who's we?"

"The Democratic Alliance. We understand how hard it is for you."

"You think?"

"You're here, aren't you? We know you put Corellia first."

"I'm going to deal with Thrackan myself, thanks."

"We can't be seen to do *that*, of course, but we can probably give you useful support."

You load the blaster and I fire it. Yeah, I get the idea. "I just need times, locations, and access."

Han was aware of Leia staring at his back, a kind of sixth sense that owed nothing to the Force and everything to more than thirty years of marriage. He turned slowly, expecting to see a weary frown of disapproval, and saw only wide-eyed resignation. Sometimes she looked just the way she had when he first met her.

"Just keep feeding me information about Thrackan's location," said Han. "Your party representatives have access to that, right?"

"When he's taking part in government business, yes. Itineraries, meetings, that kind of detail."

"Good."

"So what's your plan?"

Han gave him a slow, wary smile. "If I told you that, you wouldn't be able to deny involvement, would you?"

Gejjen went to a desk in the corner of the room and took a datachip from a drawer. "Floor plans," he said. "Government buildings. They're not illegal, just only available for inspection in libraries and civic offices. They might be useful."

"Consider me a librarian."

"Dur," said Leia. "If Thrackan Sal-Solo *were* to fall from power, would your party be in a position to form an emergency government?"

Gejjen was now focused totally on Leia: *that* was what really interested him, the seizure of power. Han chose not to be offended.

"With my colleagues, the Corellian Liberal Front, and those in the Centerpoint Party who'd like a change of leadership, yes."

So that's how a coup happens. In some guy's living room while his kids are playing in another room. "Hey, you telling everyone my cousin's days are numbered?"

"If you think you're the first person this year to come up with the idea of neutralizing him, you'd be very much mistaken," said Gejjen. "Corellia doesn't want to be his personal toolbox any longer."

"We'll keep contact to a minimum," Leia interrupted. "And we'll keep changing our comlink code. I hope the next time we meet is when the crisis has passed."

Leia herded Han out into the street and they walked a tortuous path to the center of Coronet, doubling back on themselves to check that they weren't being followed. There was a lot of air traffic heading into the spaceport and a general buzz of tension in the city itself. It felt like a world bracing itself for the worst.

They came into the main boulevard where the apartment rental office was located. They'd lease something small and anonymous in the center of town, Han decided. Something nobody would expect the Solos to want to live in.

It's just like old times again. Living on the edge.

"Do you think Gejjen's cronies are setting me up to do their dirty work?" he asked.

"What, that the assassination contract is a ruse?" Leia shook her head. "You heard Jacen, you saw the holonews, and there's the small business of the guy we shoved out the air lock."

"Oh, yeah, him."

"I'm not encouraging you to do this."

"But you haven't told me not to."

"I'm not making your decisions for you, Han. I'm your wife, not your mother," Leia said.

"But you're a Jedi, too . . ."

"It sounds like a case of self-defense to me."

"Not a coup?"

"*That's* a separate issue."

"Diplomacy's a fascinating spectator sport," Han said.

"It's about managing the inevitable with minimum loss of life."

"Yeah, ours."

Han cared about Corellia in that abstract way people did when their home—even their unhappy home—was being attacked by outsiders. He'd never thought of himself as a patriot; he simply felt Corellian to the core. But there was one thing that still drove him above all others, and that was Leia and the kids.

"Thrackan doesn't stand a chance of taking three Jedi," said Leia, as if she did a little telepathy on the side. "It's you I'm worried for."

"Jedi *have* been known to get killed."

"It's not very gracious of me, but I kind of wish Jacen had shot him after all."

"You and me both."

The rental agency office was crowded when Han and Leia reached it. There was a line of people, some with young children, some elderly, waiting with bags and cases of varying sizes.

"You just arrived from Coruscant, too?" said the harassed-looking woman at the main desk.

"Well—" Han didn't get the impression that she recognized him as Public Enemy Number One. "Yeah, we just got in."

"You're ahead of the rush, then." She handed him a datapad. "Register your details. We've only got one-bedroom apartments left. Will that be okay?"

Han glanced at Leia.

"We just want a roof over our heads," she told the woman.

"We're all shocked at what's happening on Coruscant, ma'am. But you're safe now. Who'd have thought it? Han Solo's son, too."

"Yeah, we're shocked, too," said Han, and meant it.

They signed a lease as Jav and Lora Kabadi and found themselves disguised quite by accident as just one couple in the first wave of Corellians fleeing Coruscant to avoid internment. The irony wasn't lost on them.

"Nice timing, son," Han muttered.

SENATE CHAMBER, CORUSCANT: EMERGENCY DEBATE ON INTERNMENT POLICY.

Jacen sat next to Niathal on the Mon Calamari delegates' platform and listened to Corellia's Senator Charr haranguing Chief Omas about the abuse of human rights on Coruscant and the lack of consultation with the Senate.

"We have no option but to withdraw our ambassador," said Charr.

"Is that Coruscant or the Alliance we're talking about?" Omas asked.

Charr hesitated. "Isn't that one and the same, Chief of State?"

"I think the honorable representative for Corellia understands that the action I took was to ensure the safety of Coruscant citizens, which is a responsibility given to me by the Coruscanti local authority, and so does *not* require sanction by the Senate. So which entity do you wish to withdraw representation from?"

There was a general murmur of support but significant scoffing from some of the Outer Rim delegates. Omas stood his ground. At the moment, Corellia's allies were a minority, but that would change unless they were given a good reason *not* to line up behind her.

"How do you feel about that blockade, Admiral?" Jacen asked quietly. Senatorial platforms detached from the walls of the massive chamber and hovered into the void between them for delegates to deliver impassioned but noncommittal speeches against terrorism and the need for unity.

"Are you asking if I could mount one now?"

"I'm assuming you can. Do you still favor one?"

"Yes, because that's the most robust stance I can persuade the Senate to allow. And blockades are very *flexible* responses," Niathal said.

"If it were carried out on behalf of the Alliance, that is."

"We live in a world of blurred lines."

The debate was remarkably subdued, all things considered. Jacen began to wonder if the backlash he had expected was actually his fear of the Jedi council's opinion. If anything, he appeared to be . . . popular.

That didn't make him comfortable. He wanted to remain

aloof from anything that might sway him, and even a Jedi could enjoy being liked a little too much.

Jacen and Niathal joined Omas in the Chief of State's cabinet room, where Senator G'Sil was already waiting. Omas didn't look happy and sat down at the head of the lapis-inlaid table with slow deliberation.

"Well, let's be grateful today's events went as well as they did."

G'Sil looked up. "Where are we housing the internees?"

"Just over half of them had Corellian passports in the end, so we've put them in an old barracks block for the time being," said Niathal. "The rest were allowed to return to their homes. The question is how far we plan to go with this, because we have a lot of Corellian citizens resident here, and if we have to intern them all by force it's going to be a labor-intensive job."

"Immigration reports growing numbers looking to leave."

"I'm getting very uneasy about this, Admiral," said Omas. "The images on HNE might have played well to the jingoistic element on Coruscant, but it reminded a lot of us of Imperial excesses."

"You *authorized* the action." Niathal fixed Omas with that head-tilted stare. "What did you *expect* it to remind you of?"

Jacen cut in. Niathal had dispensed with any pretense of disinterest in Omas's job the moment she had been appointed Supreme Commander. She was going for broke.

"We're simply doing the same as the terrorists, except we caused no serious casualties," said Jacen. "A small action creating a disproportionately large impact. This is as much a propaganda war as anything."

"You planned to scare Corellians out?"

Niathal lowered her voice. "No, we planned to make it clear we would deal with threats to the population of Coruscant."

"And that's why you go in and do your own sleight of hand, is it?" Omas was addressing his remarks to Niathal even though it had been Jacen's operation. "One massive overreaction makes it look as if you have the whole situation under control?"

"If that's how you want to see it, Chief Omas, yes." Jacen answered. *It's me you're dealing with, not Niathal.* "No deaths. A reassured public. A clear statement to any who want to kill and maim civilians that they won't be tolerated. Removing truly dangerous individuals from our streets. And also sending a message that if Corellia can be stopped from pursuing a destructive path at the expense of the common good, then *any* world can. Or would you rather let the enemies within erode our society? These are people who are happy to accept the benefits of being a Coruscant resident, an Alliance citizen, but don't want the effort of being loyal to it. If that's my sleight of hand, then I'll sleep soundly tonight."

Omas looked about to speak but simply glanced down at his hands as if making a conscious effort not to respond. He was too wily a politician to take on both Jacen and Niathal in front of G'Sil. If he lost, G'Sil would smell blood.

"If you'll excuse me, I have to talk to the Corellian embassy." Omas stood up and walked to the doors. "I'd appreciate a schedule of your next operations in advance."

G'Sil watched him go. "It's always a shame when HNE isn't here to record a really great speech."

No, Senator, that's not the game I'm playing. You have no idea, do you? No idea at all. "You might be surprised to know I meant every word," said Jacen. "I know what a war looks like and I want this one to be the *last* one."

G'Sil seemed to take his comment as youthful sincerity. "Now, there's a wish with a lot of meanings," he said. "Let me go and calm Omas down. He's finding it hard to adjust to Jedi who aren't nice, tidy parts of the high council. Funny how we can attack Corellian territory without turning a hair, but we lose our nerve when we kick down a few doors on our home turf."

I never wanted to take on the Jedi council. But nobody here can see anything except in terms of personal ambition.

"Are we both after the same job?" Niathal asked Jacen. It was always hard to tell if a Mon Calamari was joking. Jacen sensed that there was a tinge of amusement in her mind, but not much.

"I don't want to be a politician," he said. "You'd make a fine Chief of State, but I wouldn't."

Niathal's mood changed like the sun coming out and Jacen felt relaxed goodwill and . . . *respect.* He'd meant what he said; she'd taken it as a deal struck between them.

"What job do you want, then? Jedi council?"

Oh, not that. She was already seeing him as a rival to Luke. From a political point of view, it had its own inevitability, but she couldn't have known that the Jedi didn't feature in his plans at all.

"I'm not even a Master." He had a moment of cold clarity in which he saw exactly what he wanted, and it stood outside him, a vision to observe and not be part of. "What I want is for the trillions of ordinary people in the galaxy to be able to get on with their lives knowing that it's being run by a stable form of government. The vast majority of folk just get smashed by the fallout from the power struggles of a handful. I want to see that stop. I want to see power meaning *duty,* service, not a prize."

Niathal adjusted her tunic, straightening the braid fastening. "Well said. For someone whose whole family is an elite, you have a refreshingly *military* take on the exercise of power."

Jacen had cut free from his attachment to a heroic reputation, but it was comforting to be reassured that he wasn't deluding himself. He savored a small moment of relief, and dreamed of a secure galaxy for Tenel Ka and Allana.

chapter eleven

Chief of State Cal Omas today authorized new emergency measures to crack down on continuing unrest in Galactic City. Corellian passport holders now have forty-eight hours to report to their local CSF precinct and opt for repatriation or face internment. The move has been condemned by Senate representatives from Altyr Five, Obreedan, and Katraasii. Meanwhile, anti-terrorist squads raided homes in the Adur quarter overnight and seized explosives and blasters. Ten men and three women have been charged with conspiracy to cause explosions.

—HNE lunchtime news bulletin

ARKANIAN MICROTECHNOLOGIES HEADQUARTERS, VOHAI.

If there was a weak point in any perimeter, Boba Fett would find it. And he had.

He watched a small bird—a hummer, bright scarlet—perch on the top of the four-meter-high perimeter fence that ran for six kilometers around Arkanian Micro's headquarters and noted that there was no reaction from the guards in the gatehouse.

There was no point having a security system so sensitive that birds could set it off. And if a bird could get over that fence, then so could Fett.

Security cams didn't cover much beyond a hundred meters around each guarded gate. It all depended on the sensors that detected entry at any unsupervised point along or over the fence, and that was a weak point for a man with a custom disrupter.

The sensors projected a slim movement-sensitive ellipse along the entire cross section of the fence, generated from ground level and extending two meters on either side of it and—if the sweep from orbit by *Slave I*'s scanners was correct—two hundred meters above it to thwart aerial incursions.

Or intruders with jet packs, of course. Fett didn't take that personally.

But the sensors didn't react to small objects. Fett stood back from the two-meter line and took two long wires with gription clips. He cast one like an angler, looping it out from shoulder height just as he had when fishing for devees from the landing pad of his Tipoca City home as a kid. The clip snapped on to the mesh of the fence, insubstantial as a hummer. Then Fett cast the other wire two meters along the fence, attaching a second gription clip.

He now had two long lines that enabled him to attach his disrupter without breaching the sensor field. Standing inside the bight of the wires, he plugged them into the casing of the disrupter and pressed the key. He was now as good as inside. As far as the detection system could tell, there was an unbreached perimeter; the wires were effectively a loop in the fence, and the bypassed section of fence itself didn't exist.

Fett adjusted the controls of his jet pack and soared over the fence, landing carefully within the bypassed zone. He memorized the section, visible only by looking for the gription clips. The palm-sized disrupter itself nestled unobtrusively in the grass beyond.

Fett sprinted to the cover of the wall and jetted to the flat roof. Normally he would have fired his grappling hook and climbed, but speed mattered now. It was worth the extra jet pack fuel. He lay on his belly and crept across the roof, his visor almost touching the gravelly surface as the penetrating radar scanned for people within.

It was a huge area to cover. He pressed a medical sound sensor, more sensitive than the military ones, to the roof to pick up what signal he could. From the sound of the conversation immediately below him—a woman recording someone's educational details—he had landed over the personnel department. And he was still crawling across offices that had external windows. Taun We would be somewhere far from daylight, right at the center.

It took him more than two hours to edge his way across what seemed to him a featureless charcoal-gray cinder plain, listening for clues to what lay beneath and watching the radar outlines of bodies moving. He hoped that the disrupter would still be there when it came time to leave, but if it wasn't, it would be far easier to make a run for it on the way out than on the way in.

This is really hurting my hips. And my chest.

Fett lifted his body slightly and took his weight on his knees and elbows. He heard the clink of glass dishes and the *wusshh* and *umppp* of chiller cabinets opening and closing. He saw people sitting, probably at a long bench and others clustered around a table. The outlines of the inorganic objects were almost impossible to make out, but he was used to assembling a mental image from the scant cues provided by the movement and shape of bodies.

He'd seen a few labs in his time. He knew how Taun We liked hers laid out. When she'd had a leg cloned for him a few years before, her Tipoca laboratory had still been just like it was when he was a kid and she had first shown him around.

He heard the occasional word that sounded like a conversation about a scanning microscope. *Could mean anything. But I'm over the labs, that's for sure. Next vent I find, next point of entry, I'm going down there.*

He checked the chrono readout in his helmet, shifting his focus and feeling the beginning of a headache. *Three hours. Too slow.* The longer he took, the more vulnerable he was to discovery.

You don't quit now, Fett.

And then he heard it: just a couple of words. It wasn't even anything from which he could derive meaning. But he knew that tone, that pitch, so very well that it was like hearing his own name whispered in a crowded, noisy room; everything else fell silent as his brain filtered out all irrelevance.

It was Taun We's fluting, gentle voice. He forgot the raw ache in his sternum and felt the adrenaline course through his body, erasing every pain.

Gotcha . . .

He frame-grabbed the coordinates in his HUD, got to his knees, and scouted around for an air vent. There was a biohazard containment opening fifty meters across the roof, the kind of hatch that a hazmat team would use to enter the building if it was ever contaminated and sealed. And he knew it would yield to the lock overrides on his wristband. He hadn't met a lock, seal, or panel that didn't.

And it was designed to take someone wearing a full hazmat suit. For once, his jet pack wasn't an encumbrance as he took a security blade from his shin pocket to bypass the breach alarm and opened the hatch.

He slid down the vent and found himself standing in a chamber with two doors leading off it. Both were locked. When he switched to his HUD's normal vision, the glow around him was that dull amber emergency lighting, and a safety notice on the wall read: LAST INSPECTED 6/8/1/36.

He adjusted his helmet's sound sensors and listened. The corridor outside was clear. A quick flick back to the terahertz radar scan confirmed it. He made his way down the corridor, checking as he went, following the occasional sound of Taun We's voice until he found himself outside an office with two shapes visible inside on his helmet scanner: one dense human body and a Kaminoan one with its characteristic abdominal spaces.

Fett ducked into the nearest alcove—a fire control station—and waited for the human to leave. Eventually the doors opened and a woman left. The lock panel at the side of the doors flashed again, but Fett slid a blade from his override system into the slot and the doors parted with a whisper.

He took the precaution of locking them behind him. Leaning over the desk, a tall creature with a long graceful neck and small, round gray head was engrossed in work at a data screen.

Taun We didn't turn around. "Please leave the file in the tray."

"Nice place you got here."

Kaminoans never showed emotion, but the speed with which Taun We whipped around and the way her head jerked back on seeing him told him she was surprised.

"Boba?"

"Oddly, there's only one."

"How . . . did you find me?"

"It's my job, remember?" Fett walked slowly across the room and propped his backside on the edge of her desk. He lifted his helmet. "Let's say I followed the money."

"Koa Ne sent you to—"

"No. He wants the data back, but that's not why I'm here."

Taun We stared into his face, blinking slowly. She knew him about as well as anyone alive, and that wasn't a long list. She looked . . . old, very old.

"Are you all right, Boba? Is your leg functioning properly?"

"No. In fact, my whole body is giving me a few problems."

"Can I be of help?"

"I'm suffering from tissue degeneration. Liver problems. Autoimmune diseases. Tumors. My doctor says I have a year or so to live if I'm lucky." He reached in his belt for a datachip. "Take a look at the tests."

Taun We took the chip with long, thin fingers and slid it into her dataport. "Ah," she said. "I see."

She got up and went to a cabinet, and Fett's natural mistrust of the galaxy kicked in. If she could run out on her own government, she could betray him. He clicked his blaster just as a warning.

Taun We turned slowly and glanced at the blaster. "Do you think I would wish to draw attention to the fact that you tracked me down and gained access to my secure office?"

"You stole data and defected. Never had you down for that kind, either."

Did I ever care about Taun We? I think I did.

Fett thought that it was funny how you never truly recalled how you felt as a child, except for the defining moments: and he was defined by his love of his father, and he knew it, and he was *proud* of it. When the idea occurred to him that it was *all* he was, he shook it off.

I miss Dad, every single day, every single minute. I want to live up to him.

Fett motioned Taun We to sit down with the barrel of his blaster. She settled in the chair, hands clasped, and didn't react at all: no fear, no surprise, no affection. She was ice, control, indifference.

You brought me up—more or less.

"Boba," she said. She still had that soothing, musical voice. He wasn't sure how long Kaminoans lived, but she had to be coming to the end of her life. "I regret that I don't have the skills to help you."

You're the nearest I ever had to a mother. And that scares me sometimes.

"I guessed as much," said Fett. "I just want your data. And some information."

She's completely cold. I was just another experiment she was pleased with.

"My data belongs to Arkanian Micro."

"The data belongs to the Kaminoan government, but seeing as they aren't paying me, I'll take it to cover my expenses."

"I can't hand it over."

"So I'll take it." Fett slipped the data breaker from a pouch on his belt and flipped it over in his left hand. He selected the docking interface that fit Arkanian Micro's computer system; the device had a dozen different plugs that rotated into position on a wheel. "Or copy it, anyway. I don't plan to sell it—yet."

Taun We blinked slowly. She had the eyes of the Kaminoan ruling class: gray, not yellow, not low-caste blue. "It will ruin Arkanian Micro."

"Tough."

"And it will ruin me. Do you feel no compassion for me, Boba?"

"No. I don't believe I do. Not now."

Taun We appeared to be considering the revelation, head tilting slowly from side to side on the long column of her slender neck like a tree swaying in a breeze. He wondered if that reaction was just her expertise in human psychology taking a knock: she didn't know his mind as well as she thought. She still reminded him of a nahra artist, a Kaminoan mime-dancer. He'd always been baffled by nahra as a kid, because Kaminoans didn't feel a thing and yet they loved a kind of ballet that mimed emotions they didn't appear to have.

That summed up their lives—and his, he realized.

Time for analysis later. Get to work.

Still holding his blaster on the scientist, Fett took three paces to the computer console and slid the data breaker into the port. The device sparkled with blue and green status lights to show that it was searching and downloading, and he let it gather a lot more data than he needed. He wasn't a thief, but other Arkanian Micro data might come in handy—and even save his life. He was just taking custody of a copy of it.

"I don't make deals," he said. The status bar indicated that five thousand exabytes of data had been swallowed whole. Complete genomes took a lot of memory. "But here's a promise. Tell me all you know about Ko Sai, and I *won't* hand this data over to the highest bidder. That'll make sure you're still of use to Arkanian Micro."

"She's dead."

"I still want to know everything."

Taun We paused for a moment, blinking slowly at the blaster. "Are you going to take me back to Kamino by force?"

"No. I don't need the credits."

"But would you kill me, Boba?"

He paused. *For this, I would.* "Yes."

She still seemed puzzled, not hurt, or afraid, or betrayed. "Very well. Ko Sai thought the cloning program would be destroyed, so she defected to the Separatists during the Battle of Kamino to save her life's work."

"And her own skin."

"We are not materialisic, Boba. It was not about payment. It was about pride. About excellence."

Fett slipped the data breaker back in his belt. "Get on with it. Where did she go?"

"I have no idea where her journey took her next."

"What happened to her?"

"She was . . . traced."

"By who?"

Another pause. Whatever it was, it was giving Taun We problems. "Clone intelligence units. And one of your father's commando instructors."

Fett swallowed hard. He hadn't expected *that*. "And?"

She indicated the braided Wookiee pelts strung from his

right shoulder plate. "She fell prey to the Mandalorian penchant for souvenirs."

"Interesting," said Fett. *No, it's astonishing, it's terrifying, it's hope, it's everything.* "So the clones got their revenge."

"We assumed so. Packages arrived. Parts of a Kaminoan body whose genetic profile was Ko Sai's."

Fett found that unnecessarily brutal. Kill a prisoner if you were paid to, kill them if you *needed* to; even retrieve parts if you *had* to. But mailing Ko Sai home a piece at a time sounded like a vengeful, elaborate message. "And her data?"

"We can only assume they took that, too. It has never been recovered."

"What was special about it?"

"Ko Sai's triumph was controlling the aging process. She knew how to manipulate it better than any other biologist. We were interested only in accelerating it to mature clones faster, but I can see how many would find slowing the process and its therapeutic potential an attractive commodity. She claimed she was able to achieve it in the laboratory."

Mirta had met an original Kamino clone, she claimed. *A clone who couldn't,* shouldn't *be alive today.* Fett found a slew of puzzle pieces dumped in his lap, all fitting together. Impossible clones, dismembered Kaminoan scientist, missing cloning data. "You got any names?"

Taun We stiffened. "Do you remember that aggressive little human called Skirata? The one who . . . threatened my colleagues with a knife so frequently?"

Yes, he remembered Kal Skirata, all right. Sometimes his father swore he was the best of the bunch; sometimes he just swore at him and lashed out. Jango Fett rarely lost his temper, but Skirata had a talent for making that happen. He was ferociously and uncompromisingly Mandalorian.

As a lonely kid on Kamino, Fett had narrowly escaped being forced to learn *Mando'a* from Skirata's wildly unpredictable special forces trainees, six cloned ARC troopers who answered only to him. They were intelligence units; the Nulls, as everyone called them, the first batch of clones, and they had turned out crazy, hypersmart, and dangerous. They had disappeared when the war ended.

Yes, this was a neat pattern. Skirata lived for his clones. He'd want them to live out full lives like ordinary men. He would have wanted Ko Sai's data and expertise very badly. Butchering her to get the genetic technology he needed to stop the accelerated aging would have been nothing to him, just a means to an end.

And if one of Skirata's clone troops was still alive and fully active today when he should have been the equivalent of a 140-year-old, it meant that they'd found a way to stop the accelerated aging process—Ko Sai's way.

That's *what I need.* That *will save my life.*

Fett was suddenly enveloped in a sensation of vivid awareness, like a pleasantly cool shower on a hot day; the colors around him seemed instantly vibrant, the sounds crystal clear, the smells sharp. Adrenaline coursed through him. He'd found what he was looking for—or the route to it, at least.

He'd never failed to track a bounty. *Never.* Even if a few had escaped in the end, he had always found them.

I'll find you, too.

"Useful," said Fett. Holding the blaster level was making his forearm ache. He'd never felt that before. "You keep quiet about this and I'll keep this data to myself. Got it?"

"Agreed," said Taun We. "And if—when you find Ko Sai's data, we would give you an excellent fee for its return."

He suddenly thought of Sintas, her eyes brimming with tears of joy as she held baby Ailyn. No, Taun We couldn't possibly care about him like a real mother.

Taun We's first thought was for her science.

"Maybe I don't want to sell it," said Fett.

"What do you plan to do with your legacy?"

"What?"

"You're dying. And even if you succeed in finding Ko Sai's data and it can help you, then you still face the question of what legacy you will leave behind."

"Why does that worry you?"

"I believe it was a concern to your father. He told Count Dooku that he did not want a son—he wanted an *apprentice* to be Jaster's legacy."

That stung. Maybe Taun We didn't mean it the way it sounded. He remained deadpan and wished he had kept his helmet on. "Jaster Mereel was more than Dad's mentor. He was a father."

That seemed to mean nothing to Taun We. "And what is that legacy?"

"To be Mandalore. To make sure Mandalorians survive, whatever happens. And I'll live up to my father's pledge just as he did before me."

Taun We remained glacial. "We will exceed any offer."

Dad was always looking back at Jaster Mereel, feeling he had to live up to him. Maybe I was a second chance to do that.

"I'll let you know."

Jaster's legacy. Beviin's got a point. More Mandalore, less business.

Maybe she said it to wound him. No, Kaminoans didn't care about anything, even if they were almost your mother.

He put on his helmet and turned to leave. Would she raise the alarm? She wouldn't want anyone to know that her data had been compromised. All she cared about was her work, as she always had, and that would buy her silence. If Arkanian Micro ran any security checks, they would find nothing missing and no botched attempts at slicing their system. It was between him and Taun We.

"I would like to know if you find Ko Sai's research, and if it cures you," she said.

Fett resisted the urge to ask if that was personal or professional concern. "If I'm still around in a couple of years, you will."

He left the way he had come in, crawling back up the hazmat access hatch with the aid of his grappling hook and covering the distance to the edge of the roof in a rapid crawl. The disrupter clips were still in place. Checking around him, he jetted over the fence, released the clips—and as far as the fence sensors were concerned he had never been there.

Slave I's ramp lowered via his remote helmet link and he stepped up it, wondering why he clung so fiercely to his father's ship. It was a wonderful vessel, but it meant more to him than just the best his fortune could buy.

I'm in my seventies now, and I've only just started to be more than someone's son. Doesn't mean I love you any less, Dad, but I can't look back forever.

Boba Fett wasn't certain what would fill that void and show him his purpose in life, but he knew now that it lay ahead of him, and not behind him frozen in memories.

He stood in front of *Slave I*, an icon of his childhood, and wondered where the line between trademark and trap was drawn.

"So you didn't trash the cockpit," he said, opening the conversation for once.

Mirta was wiping the console. It looked remarkably shiny: Fett kept a clean, well-maintained ship, but this time it looked polished. "Did you get what you came for?" she asked.

He kicked *Slave I* into life and lifted her clear, looping under the monorail that snaked two kilometers above Vohai's surface. "I did."

"What now?"

Fett took refuge behind his visor. He was torn now. He

needed to find that impossibly old clone, and he wanted to see Ailyn, and he wanted to know how Sintas had died.

Mirta knew—or claimed to know—all three answers. Sintas's fate now wasn't urgent; and he could find Ailyn for himself, because he could find Han Solo, and where Solo was, Ailyn would follow.

So he needed to track that clone of Skirata's. Even if he didn't have Ko Sai's data, he might be good for a tissue sample that a Kaminoan could examine and reverse-engineer.

Still too many uncertainties. Still too many variables.

Fett decided it was time to reveal his interest, but *carefully.* "Where did you run into that clone?"

"Coruscant. Seemed to be a regular trip for him." Mirta stared straight ahead as usual. "So where are we heading?"

To find Han Solo, because that'll lead me to Ailyn.

He staged a conversational diversion. "You've got the necklace. You tell *me* where we're heading."

Mirta took the leather cord from her neck and stared at the shimmering stone in her palm. "Let's try Coruscant."

Aha. Fett had never taught Ailyn anything about bounty hunting, but she had obviously learned that you could often hide better on a planet that was one vast city of a trillion people than you ever could in a cave up a mountainside on the Outer Rim.

Fett laid in a course for the galactic core; zero, zero, zero. *Slave I* was about to make the jump to hyperspace when the comlink console flashed impatiently in front of him.

The point of origin said CORELLIA, even if the sender had tried to disguise the source with multiple relays. Fett didn't get a lot of calls from Corellia, and when he did they usually weren't the kind that he wanted to take in front of Mirta Gev.

"Time to eat," he said. "Get back aft and see what you can find in the stores for us."

Mirta obeyed in silence, without a hint of dissent on her

face. It was the response of someone used to following orders, not a woman who spent her time in the kitchen. "Okay."

"Not insulted by that, are you?"

Mirta looked at him as if he were mad. "My father was
Mandalorian. So I can fight *and* cook."

Fett realized how little he knew about the small details of
his own culture. Next time he saw Beviin, he'd ask the man
to explain all that. He waited for Mirta to close the internal
hatch behind her and then switched the call to a secure circuit.

"Fett here. Make it fast."

There was a slight pause. "And this is Thrackan Sal-Solo,
Corellian Head of State. I've got a proposal for you."

SQUADRON TRAINING SECTION
AIRSPACE, CENTAX 2.

The XJ7 below Luke jinked to port and fell away beneath
him with astonishing speed. Even for him, Jaina Solo was a
serious challenge in aerial combat.

Or maybe I'm slowing down.

Luke throttled his own XJ7 into a dive, plummeting into
the moon's canyons in pursuit of Jaina. He'd thought she'd
had enough flight time recently not to need to sharpen her
skills, but when Jaina said she was returning to active service, she *meant* it. She went on exercises with the squadron
just like the new intake, colonel or not.

It was a live-fire exercise, too. Some of the pilots had
never been shot at for real. It tended to change their perspective of warfare.

Beneath them on the valley floor, a droid anti-aircraft
battery let loose with ion cannons. The red bolts of energy
soaring up at him seemed to merge into a single field with
the red halos of the XJ7's engines as Jaina zipped between
the bolts, rolling instantly through 180 degrees to narrow

the fighter's profile and sending a stream of fire into the ion cannons.

She leveled out at the bottom of the canyon behind the battery, and Luke dropped down behind her, shaving the canyon floor so closely that the downdraft from the XJ7 threw up a cloud of tiny pebbles that hammered under the fuselage.

Luke sent a volley of fire after her, aiming a few degrees wide of her starboard wings. The canyon wall spat plumes of pulverized rock in her path, and she skimmed over it.

She broke comm silence, which wasn't like her. "Don't play, Uncle. It won't help me."

He realized he could have taken a serious shot and he still might not have hit her. But he couldn't fire in earnest on his niece, even if he knew she could almost certainly evade it. It was the *almost* he didn't like.

"I'm breaking," he said, and climbed sharply to level out at a cruising altitude. "See you back at the mess."

Centax 2 was a sterile moon with the usual sprawl of military facilities arranged like a warehouse floor covered in boxes. The base would win no prizes for architecture. If war broke out for real—and Luke always found the *for real* proviso painfully ironic—then it would switch overnight from a training squadron to an operational air station. The switch seemed close to being thrown. Luke lifted the canopy of the XJ7 and climbed out of the cockpit to slide down the ladder wheeled into position by ground crew.

I used to do that a lot faster, too.

He waited at the entrance to the mess until Jaina's fighter swept into the hangar on repulsor power and settled in the bay next to his. When she slid out and took off her helmet, her face was taut and anxious.

"You're up to speed," Luke said comfortingly, walking toward the doors to get her to follow him. "Are we allowed to wear flight suits in the mess?"

Jaina managed a smile and indicated her own orange suit. "Don't worry, I'm the colonel. I'll provide top cover."

It was the first chance Luke had grabbed since the Corellian internment row to talk to Jaina alone. She radiated misery. Anxiety about "skills fade" and being "fit for role"—phrases that had peppered her conversation rather too liberally in recent days to convince Luke—was good tech talk for the sake of the squadron, nothing more. She was Jacen's twin. Whatever was happening, it was happening to her more acutely than the rest of the family.

"After you," said Luke.

The mess was a warren of compartments with one large section where food was served and eaten, and a lounge area almost the same size that was scattered with comfortable seating and sparse entertainment, the main focus of which was a huge holoscreen on one wall. It was wide enough to be seen comfortably from the refectory area while pilots and ground personnel waited for meals to be dispensed.

Most of the pilots in the lounge area had their backs to the refectory and were watching the screen. The lunchtime HNE news had started, and that now meant complete silence descended: everyone was waiting and watching for the little twitches from the politicians that would mean that the squadron's *warned* status would switch immediately to *mobilized.*

Jaina reached over the counter to scoop some vegetables onto her plate just as the top headline boomed to fill the entire complex. It didn't, of course, but Luke felt that it did. He froze.

"And today's top story—the roundup of Corellian nationals continues as thousands leave Galactic City in a voluntary repatriation program."

The screen was filled with a shot of 967 Commando shock troopers advancing down the walkways at either side of a Coruscant residential skylane, one squad preceded by the now familiar figure of Jacen Solo in a stark black cover-all of the kind favored by special forces. That would have been bad enough, but the only other person in any kind of uniform with his face visible was *Ben*.

It was very, very quiet in the mess now.

My son. How did I ever let Jacen do this to him?

The shock troopers all wore fully enclosed helmets. It was sensible equipment for a soldier to wear, but that didn't make it look any less menacing. Luke could hear not the commentary pounding in his ears but Han's voice saying that the Alliance was rapidly turning into the Empire.

"Colonel Jacen Solo, speaking earlier, said—"

Luke managed to look at Jaina, whose face was stricken. There was no other word for it.

And it was clear that most of those watching the screen had no idea who was standing behind them in the refectory.

"Old family tradition, terrorizing the population," said one captain, feet propped on a low table. "Just like his grand-father all over again. When's he going to go for a nice black cloak and helmet? And lots of troopers in lovely white ar-mor?"

Some of the officers in the mess laughed, but most looked as if they wished they were somewhere else. Luke had grown adept at reading the ebb and flow of trouble waiting to ex-plode, and it surprised him again just how finely balanced it was between tempers fading and sudden explosion.

This time it was Jaina who exploded. Her fists were balled. Luke, caught off-guard by his own shame at Ben's appear-ance, failed to block Jaina's Force push as the captain hit the wall of the mess, upending his chair. Jaina lunged forward. Luke managed to shove in front of her. Two other pilot offi-cers stepped in, sending chairs tumbling to stop their com-rade from doing anything else stupid.

"He didn't mean it," said one. He didn't seem to see Luke. "Sorry, Colonel."

Jaina was flushed, eyes wide. Colonels didn't take swings at other officers, using the Force or not. It was bad discipline. Luke wanted to get her outside, but she needed to let it be known she was back in control. Nobody enjoyed serving under an officer who couldn't control her temper.

The captain was hauled to his feet. He looked more winded than injured. "Go on," said one of the officers, "Apologize to the colonel. You were out of line."

The captain's expression said that he thought he'd got it about right, but his mouth did as it was told. "My apologies, Colonel Solo."

"We're all getting a little tense," said Jaina. "I should have found a less assertive way to ask you to retract what you said about my family."

And now the captain appeared to realize he was also facing Luke Skywalker. "Sorry, sir . . ."

It hurt because everyone's saying it, thought Luke. *You're just the messenger.*

"Forget it," he said. "Jaina, let's take a walk."

There was no natural vegetation on Centax. They found a spot in the shade of a hangar and sat down on a couple of crates.

"We can fence around this or we can blurt it out," said Luke. "I prefer blurting, personally."

"Saves time."

"I don't know what's happening to Jacen."

"Neither do I, Uncle."

"Try a guess, then."

"I don't know *him* anymore."

"That's a scary thing for any twin to say."

"There's something *dark* about him now. He shuts me out. He even manipulated me against the Chiss."

"I know." *Yes, he's good at that.* "It's . . . worrying."

"I can't trust him now."

Luke didn't want to hear it said aloud, but he knew he

had to listen. Mara sensed it, too, but was satisfied that it was the opposing passions of a messy love affair that were creating the darkness. Luke thought of the images he had seen in recent days and knew that the darkness was separate from any problems Jacen had in his love life. It was graphic enough to be captured on holocam.

I want my son to stay away from him.

Luke thought of Lumiya and his dreams of the hooded figure, which was surely her. But those signs of impending disaster were new; Jacen had opened the rift with Jaina by tricking her into attacking the Chiss several years earlier.

Jedi were used to seeing what ordinary people couldn't. Being deceived—something regular folk learned to live with from an early age—was especially threatening for them.

But you're not fooling me, Jacen. You're turning to the dark side.

"Uncle Luke, this is none of my business," said Jaina, "but if I were you, I'd get Ben a new teacher."

Luke knew she was right, and he also knew that Mara would fight that every step of the way.

And so would Ben.

BRAVO COMPANY 967 COMMANDO, VEHICLE CHECKPOINT: GALACTIC CITY, LOWER LEVELS, 2330 HOURS.

"We left the best till last," said Corporal Lekauf.

Ben was confident in his lightsaber skills, but the lower levels of Galactic City made him envy the soldiers' armor. It was the first time he'd been to the city's grim heart, and it wasn't like the Senate sectors at all.

In fact, it wasn't even like the slightly seedy Corellian neighborhoods, where there had been a pleasant sense of normal family life going on—at least before the raids had begun. At night, the lower levels were genuinely intimidating. Ben kept one hand on the hilt of his lightsaber.

One soldier from Bravo Company set a vehicle barrier across the end of the road, a chain of small spherical droids whose armament and stinger cords could stop a vessel attempting to pass anywhere up to thirty meters away. There was another one at the far end of the street; the only level below this one was made up of utility tunnels.

I really hope we don't end up going down there.

Standing well behind the barriers were small knots of people—human and other species—who looked as if they might cut Ben's throat just out of curiosity.

"This is horrible," he said.

"Beats doing this in broad daylight with HNE breathing down our necks," said Lekauf. Maybe he had a point: the media never cared what happened to residents of the lower levels. "We can just go in and clear this place out."

"This isn't a Corellian neighborhood."

"Not all the threats are Corellian." Lekauf turned at the sound of jogging boots, and Ben followed his gaze to see Captain Shevu approaching. The only way Ben could tell the 967 apart when they were fully armored was by the name tags on their chest plates and their variations in build and height. Shevu had a single discreet gold star on his helmet; Lekauf had two thin gold stripes; and Witur, one of the sergeants, had three. Apart from that, they were an anonymous mass of black plastoid plates over black fatigues.

The CSF—some of whose ranks had volunteered for transfer to the 967—had already nicknamed them "Stormies." Everyone seemed to see parallels with Ben's grandfather's day. Ben wasn't ashamed of his lineage and he wasn't ashamed of the work he had to carry out: he just didn't understand how it all got this bad so quickly.

But, so far, nobody had been shot or badly injured. Every Corellian who had been detained was alive and well—or had been deported. It must have been hard, Ben thought, to be sent home if the only home you had ever known was Coruscant: but in that case, why weren't they loyal to the planet where they'd been born?

Just as he'd thought he was growing up, Ben felt like a kid again, a kid who had missed something important that all the adults knew but weren't telling him.

"Okay, listen up," said Shevu. He gathered two squads around him, pulling in Ben and Lekauf, too. "Best intelligence is that Customs and Immigration got a tip-off about three Corellian agents and a bounty hunter they made contact with, and CSF tracked them down here." The location was an apartment block with some boarded-up windows that sat between a sleazy bar and a brightly lit building whose business Ben wasn't sure about, except that the staff all seemed to be women. "That's who we've come for— names are Cotin, Abadaner, Bolf, and Habuur."

Shevu handed Ben a datapad with pictures on it; the squads were receiving the images via the HUDs in their helmets.

"They know we're here," Ben said.

"Not much they can do about it, then, except come out when we ask nicely," said Lekauf.

Shevu tapped the charge indicator on his blaster rifle. "Double-check them against your feature-recog software, because they're going to be seriously armed and you might need to put them out of business permanently. Colonel Solo's covering the rear exits with two squads if things don't go to plan."

It wasn't a raid so much as a siege. Ben had learned an awful lot about storming buildings in a very short time. He didn't feel that he was much use, but Lekauf reassured him that he could do things no ordinary soldier could when they needed him to.

"Okay, let's start this like good guys," Shevu said. He

turned toward the front of the apartment block, and there was an audible click from his voice projection unit. He was about to use the loudhailer setting.

Ben braced for painfully loud noise.

"This is the security forces." Shevu's voice vibrated off the buildings, slow and carefully enunciated. People still in the street behind the barricades scattered and ran for cover. "Cotin—Abadaner—Bolf—Habuur! Surrender your weapons. Come out of the building and keep your arms above your heads. You can come out now, or we will enter and detain you."

Maybe I could try mind influence, thought Ben.

A bolt of blasterfire spat from a window, and the squad returned fire as if by reflex.

Okay, maybe that isn't going to work.

"We tried," said Shevu. "Blasters only. No projectiles. Don't want anything penetrating walls, because we've got civilians in there." He opened the loudhailer again. "Residents! Stay in your homes with your doors closed. Armed security forces are entering your building. I repeat—stay in your homes."

He shook his head, muttering about CSF failing to evacuate the apartment block in advance, and signaled the squads to enter. Ben could see at least two squads on the roof clambering into a maintenance access hatch. There were no stairways in some of these blocks, which meant each turbolift lobby was a potential killing field; it took guts to step out of a lift into the unknown. But that, Lekauf told Ben, was what armor was for.

"Wirut," Shevu ordered. "Put a flash-bang through that window on my mark, will you?"

"Sir," said the sergeant, and slipped a charge into the feed of his grenade launcher.

"Squads, when you access the fourth floor we'll light them up from here. Count us down."

Ben couldn't hear the response. He *really* wanted a helmet with full comlink. But what he lacked in technology he almost made up for with his own Force-senses. Now that he focused on the shattered and gaping window where the blasterfire had emerged, he could feel the fear and hostility inside. There was a lot of general fear in the building, almost certainly the cumulative terror of other residents who were stuck inside the block.

"Once we've neutralized the main targets, we'll do a sweep of all the apartments just to be certain," said Shevu. "Can't guarantee that CSF identified everyone. Ben, are you up for playing sniffer droid for us?"

"*Yes sir!*" It wasn't a game anymore, but he desperately wanted to play his part.

"Who do we lift, then, sir?" Lekauf asked. "Anyone with a criminal record? That's pretty well the whole neighborhood."

"No, only the ones we think *we* might be interested in," said Shevu. "Or we'll be here all night."

The raid was surprisingly quiet. Ben could see the occasional flare of light through windows as blasters discharged, and heard the accompanying faint *bdattt-bdattt-bdattt* of rounds. It was as if the whole neighborhood was holding its breath, waiting for the fighting to be over. Without the comlinks to the rest of Bravo Company he couldn't tell how far they had penetrated the building, and Jacen was not only silent but shut down in the Force. Ben couldn't feel him at all. He wondered if his Master—and Jacen *was* his Master, whatever the Jedi council said—now hid his presence instinctively as a defense mechanism.

Then Wirut reacted as if someone unseen had tapped him on the shoulder. He aimed his grenade launcher and there was a whoosh of gas as the flash-bang shot into the building. Ben caught the fallout of the deafening sound and blinding light even from twenty meters away, and his ears took a few seconds to hear the shouts and the hammering sound of blaster bolts as soldiers stormed the apartment.

Silence fell. Shevu cocked his head as if listening, and the faint wail of a child somewhere inside made Ben's hair stand on end.

"Okay," said Shevu. "Two targets down, two unaccounted for. Ben, with me. Let's work our way down from the top."

Every apartment that opened its doors voluntarily to them was full of suspicious, hostile faces that were clearly no strangers to visits from the authorities. But Ben sensed no purpose or immediate danger. He kept close to Shevu, and when they emerged on the next floor, Jacen was already crouched outside one apartment talking earnestly to a couple of 967 men. He beckoned Ben to him.

"What do you sense in there, Ben?"

Ben closed his eyes and imagined the rooms beyond the double doors. He'd seen the interiors of enough apartments in the block now to picture the layout within. When he concentrated he felt the prickling in his throat that indicated an immediate threat, and his mind was drawn to one room where a man and a woman—he knew that, and wasn't quite certain how—had some grim purpose.

"I don't like the feel of that either," said Jacen. He seemed particularly troubled by it. Ben thought he would have been used to violent intentions by now. "I think that's our two missing targets."

"The old-fashioned way, sir?" One of the 967 held up a roll of detonator ribbon.

"Let's try a little REBJ," said Jacen, drawing his lightsaber. The squad with him stacked on either side of the door. "That's what you call it, isn't it? Rapid entry by Jedi? Okay, here goes rapid . . ."

Jacen held up his left hand and lowered it along the line where the two doors joined, not touching them. He was a clear meter away. The doors shot apart, slamming back into the housing on either side, and Jacen's lightsaber seemed to have a life of its own as he deflected red blaster bolts that flared from inside the apartment. Ben should have known better than to stand behind him and Shevu went to pull him aside, but he fended off a stray blaster bolt and piled in behind Jacen on blind instinct.

Two people inside—yes, a man and a woman, he'd been right—aimed at Jacen, but the blasters flew from their hands as if snatched by an unseen hand.

The woman, about as old as Ben's mother, dark hair scraped back from her face and a tattoo across one eye, scrambled to reach for something—probably another blaster—but Jacen slammed her flat against the wall with the Force and pinned her there. The man lay slumped against a chair, groaning. The squad poured in, and the two prisoners were cuffed and dragged out.

Shevu eased off his helmet and stood wiping his forehead on the back of his glove. "You're going to have to give us a list of your *functions,* sir," he said with a faint smile. "Can't quite keep up with your box of tricks."

"Neither can I sometimes," said Jacen. He turned to Ben. "You okay?"

"Fine," said Ben. It was over for the time being. They could go back to barracks. He could feel the shaking in his legs that always followed an adrenaline rush, and the relief made him feel almost tearful. He bit his lip discreetly.

"You were going to tell me something a few days ago." Jacen always seemed to know how Ben was feeling. He knew exactly when to ask a question and when Ben would find it hard not to answer. "Remember?"

"About what?"

"Something about reporting someone."

Ah. *Barit.* Ben suffered indecision again. Barit hadn't actually shot anyone, but he'd tried pretty hard. Was it right to turn him in? He might have already been interned or deported. But he might not. And whatever sympathy Ben might have felt for him, he might try again.

You're in this now. You know what the stakes are. You're not here to be liked.

And Jacen needs you. He needs you to be loyal.

"The family is called Saiy," said Ben. "They run an engineering company."

chapter twelve

MIRTA GEV TO AILYN HABUUR
AM RETURNING TO CORUSCANT
HAVE NOT RECEIVED YOUR REPLIES TO PREVIOUS MESSAGES
PLEASE CONFIRM RENDEZVOUS POINT
HAVE HEART-OF-FIRE
—Mirta Gev's comlink text to suspect Ailyn Habuur,
intercepted by Galactic Alliance Guard signals squad,
passed to Colonel Solo for evaluation

JACEN SOLO'S APARTMENT, ROTUNDA ZONE.

The one thing you could count on with Corellians was that if you knocked them down, they got up again and again and *again*.

Jacen had been too preoccupied with the anti-terror operations to devote time to sensing what Thrackan Sal-Solo might be doing from a strategic point of view: Fleet Intelligence seemed to have that under control. But he knew that Centerpoint would remain an issue as long as it hadn't been totally destroyed, and this morning his uncle didn't disappoint him.

Jacen had joined the billions of Coruscanti whose morning now began by switching on the HNE news even before the first cup of caf to check how close to war they were getting.

HNE was running an interview from Corellian holonews with Sal-Solo, in which he announced work was about to start on restoring Centerpoint Station to operational status.

Jacen wasn't sure if Sal-Solo had the capacity to do that or how long he might take to achieve it, but it was perfect timing. If this didn't persuade the Alliance to authorize the blockade of Corellia, nothing would. Striking at Corellia's industrial orbitals would have achieved far more, far faster, but he knew a blockade could achieve the same ends in time.

Time means lives. Time means more chaos. We always think that time will resolve things, but it never has.

He forgot about caf and breakfast, left Ben to sleep off the previous night's operation, and went straight to the Senate. Niathal, always an early riser, had beaten him to it. He found her in Omas's offices and he knew the admiral and he had one thing in mind.

Omas was watching the holoscreen he now had running permanently in his private office.

"Diplomacy by holonews," he said irritably.

Niathal nodded at Jacen to sit beside her, a little psychological display of unity in front of their reluctant Chief. "Did you think Sal-Solo would pick up the comlink and ask if it was okay to start work on Centerpoint again?"

Jacen glanced discreetly at her. Her expressions were becoming as easy to read as her emotions. She was *satisfied*.

"I don't think we have any choice," he said. "We can't ignore this."

"I hate that phrase." Omas turned down the audio volume. "Because it's usually true these days."

"It's going to take two fleets to isolate Corellia," said Niathal. "I'm asking you for authority to pull the Third and Fifth Fleets back from exercises on the Outer Rim."

Omas wore an expression of weary resignation, but the edge in his voice said different. "I need authority from the Senate first."

"Getting two fleets into position to begin a blockade takes time. You start on the Senate procedures, and we'll get the logistics in hand. Then we'll be ready to deploy as soon as the authority is given."

"We?" Omas asked pointedly, looking at Jacen.

"The Defense Force," Niathal said stiffly.

Well, you catch on eventually, Chief, thought Jacen. *Yes, we've taken sides, and she's not on yours.*

"Don't jump the gun," said Omas. "I have to table this as an emergency motion. We have to carry the rest of the Alliance with us."

But it was a foregone conclusion as far as Niathal was concerned. Jacen followed the admiral out into the corridor and into her offices at the far end of the floor. They didn't speak until the doors were closed behind them and she had pressed a key set in her desk.

"Just to be certain," she said. "This is the secure link that doesn't go via Fleet ComCen."

"You're recalling those two fleets, aren't you?"

"I don't have to ask the Senate's authority to move assets already committed to exercises."

"So you just bring them back home for exercises . . . here."

"Almost." She hit a few more keys. "No point letting the enemy prepare for a blockade, or it just prolongs the thing. I've drawn up plans for the blockade."

"Total exclusion zone?"

"No, *two* exclusion zones. One to stop Corellia resupplying Centerpoint from the surface. If we rely purely on isolating Corellia from the outside, then the embargo will take years to bite. If they can't get matériel up to Centerpoint, then that does the job a lot faster."

Jacen thought about the mass of industrial orbiters strung around the planet.

"That means creating two picket lines as sterile zones."

"That's why I need both fleets. I'm going to share the plan with the fleet commanders. Then they stand off a couple of hours' jump from Corellia and they're ready to deploy the moment the Senate gives the word."

"You're sure you can trust them?"

"They're both Mon Calamari. Yes, I trust them."

"Omas is getting cold feet."

"They can get as cold as he likes, but Sal-Solo is not just refusing to disarm, he's rearming. I think that'll get the Alliance's attention."

Jacen heard Lumiya's voice within him, reminding him of the inevitability of it all, and that if he embraced his role—his duty—he could bring order to the galaxy.

He thought of his five years of studying every arcane school of Force philosophy and wondered what more Lumiya could show him to bring him to the status of a Sith Master. He couldn't imagine it. So he simply seized the tenuous ideas and thoughts that welled up in his mind, not knowing their source or validity but eager to accept that his intuition might be the key.

He was running on instinct, not intellect.

Feel, don't think.

Even the Jedi taught him that.

See, you don't think of yourself as a Jedi any longer.

Jacen had no idea whose voice that was—his, Lumiya's, another's entirely—but he surrendered to it.

"I would like to play a role in the blockade," he said.

Niathal projected a holochart of the Corellian system onto the wall and stood back to study it. "You're a fighter pilot, aren't you? Like your sister."

"I'd like a command."

"A ship?"

"A squadron. I'm confusing you, aren't I?"

"I thought you already had quite a substantial command as head of the Galactic Alliance Guard."

"I'd like to show that I'm prepared to fight in the front line," Jacen said.

"I think everyone knows that from your combat record."

"That wasn't against my father's homeworld."

"Ah, the ultimate loyalty test," said Niathal.

"If you like."

"Very well. You can have temporary group command. That'll include the squadron your sister commands. Unusual to have one colonel under another, but it's not unknown. If that doesn't demonstrate that the Solo family puts nation before family, I don't know what will."

It's more than that. I have to have the respect and support of more than one admiral. I need the rank and file to see me as their own, too, just in case you can't deliver their loyalty—or you change your mind about me.

"Thank you, Admiral."

Admiral Niathal gave him a tight-lipped smile and moved icons of battleships around her chart with the motion of one finger.

"Time I brought the exercises to an end, then." The icons had become a three-dimensional net around Corellia, separating the planet from its industrial facilities, which lay entirely in orbiting stations far above the pleasantly rural planet. The Corellians' wish to keep unspoiled countryside free from industrial sprawl now made them very vulnerable. "I'm calling Endex five days early. The commanders know what I have in mind now."

Niathal went to her desk comm, and the message that would effectively start the war was, ironically, one that usually brought maneuvers to a halt.

Jacen watched the small screen as the encryption program took the plain-language text and wrapped it in a secure algorithm.

ENDEX ENDEX ENDEX.

"End of exercise," said Niathal. "And the start of the real war."

SLAVE I, EN ROUTE TO CORELLIA.

"What's up with you?" Fett asked.

Mirta kept chewing her lip. It was a very discreet habit, but Fett was alert to small detail. Hunters had to be.

"Where are we heading?"

"Corellia."

"You said Coruscant."

"No, *you* said Coruscant." Fett switched the navigation display to a three-D holochart so that she could see it shimmering above the console in front of the viewscreen. "I've got business in Corellia first."

She fell silent, and seeing as she hadn't said a great deal on the journey anyway, he wasn't shocked. But something had agitated her.

Maybe it was the messages she kept sending to Coruscant. Ailyn wasn't answering. Fett wondered when Mirta would work out that monitoring transmissions to and from *Slave I*—even those made via private comlinks—was part of the ship's security system. Maybe it was time to shake Mirta down a little.

"I've lost contact with my customer," Mirta said at last.

Points for honesty, then. "She might not want to pay up. Is it just the necklace, or did you have information for her?"

"Information, too."

"You weren't stupid enough to give her that data over the comlink, were you?"

"No."

"Then she'll pay up."

"I'm—I'm more worried about her safety. She was on a job."

I know. "Yeah, dead customers don't pay."

"Exactly." But Mira's voice sounded small and afraid for once. Maybe she wasn't quite the experienced bounty hunter she made herself out to be.

Fett decided that Ailyn was too sharp an operator to risk transmissions when she was hunting someone like Han Solo. She was his daughter, after all: some of his genes must have made her what she was. And few bounty hunters made enough credits to be able to afford Fett's line in secure communications kit.

She'd be there, somewhere.

He opened his own comlink. It didn't matter if Mirta heard this. "Beviin," he said. "Beviin, I have a job I'd like to discuss with you."

It took awhile for Beviin to answer. *"Mand'alor?"*

"Beviin, Thrackan Sal-Solo wants us to fight for him. Defending Centerpoint Station."

"Yes, it's all over the news. He was on HNE this morning about rebuilding it yet again. War's about to kick off. Solo's son is head of the Alliance's secret police and the Corellians are really *a'denla* about it—"

"Assemble as many commandos as you can. Meet me on Drall in two days at Halin's Bar."

"It closed down five years ago. Try the Zerria. Same street."

I'm out of touch. Too much time on Taris. "Okay, make it the Zerria."

"I can probably get half a dozen together by then. Almost everyone else has headed back to Mandalore."

Six? Six! Too busy to do their duty? "Why?"

"It's harvest time. Quite a few of us have farms."

"Aren't the women supposed to look after that?" Beviin had an adopted daughter. Fett couldn't recall her name, but he was sure she was old enough to run a farm. "What happened to the rapid response force?"

Beviin's voice chilled perceptibly. "If there was a *real* war on, we'd be pretty rapid . . ."

Fett was almost distracted by the idea of his Mandalorian troops doing something as banal as farming. He'd never thought much about what they did when they weren't deployed. But they had wives and children, and *lives*.

"Whoever you can get in two days, then."

Fett closed the link. Mirta stared at him, clearly appalled.

"So you disapprove of fighting for Corellia?"

She shrugged. "I was thinking that you don't know much about what's happening on your own world, considering you're supposed to be the Mandalore."

"I don't even live there."

"The Yuuzhan Vong hit the Mandalore sector as badly as anywhere, Fett." It was the first time she'd addressed him by name. "Everyone's still rebuilding. You know what your name means? 'Farmer.' *Vhett*. It's *Mando'a* for 'farmer.' "

"I know that." *Dad came from Concord Dawn. He said his family were frontier farmers. How did he get a Mandalorian name, then?* "I'm more of a blaster and jet pack man myself."

"How can you rule a nation when you don't know the first thing about it?"

"It's not a nation, and I don't run it. I'm a figurehead when they don't need me to fight, and a commander in chief when they do."

"A mercenary for your own people."

"The irony isn't lost on me."

"You're out of touch. More Mandalorians are heading back home."

Home. "There aren't that many. And what's home?"

"You've no idea how many *Mando'ade* there are, have you? Plenty. Not just your troops and bounty hunters. People who've kept their culture alive all across the galaxy. Just like your father was adopted by Jaster Mereel, the culture gets passed on."

"You know a lot about me."

"More than you know about yourself, obviously." Mirta was actually angry. Fett could see the color in her cheeks.

Her voice had tightened and raised a pitch. "My dad said a *Mand'alor* should be like a father to his people."

"I don't need a lecture in responsibilities from a kid."

"Well, your daughter wanted to kill you because you walked out on her and her mother, so I'll take it that responsibility isn't your strong suit."

Fett was used to fear, deference, or awe. He hadn't seen much defiance in his adult life—not for long, anyway. Mirta didn't seem to care if he dumped her out of the air lock.

My own kid. I had what Dad wanted so badly, and I threw it away.

"I was sixteen," he said. "Sintas was eighteen. The only females I knew as a kid were a Kaminoan and a changeling bounty hunter. Doesn't equip you to be a family man. I tried."

"Yeah."

Fett never let himself get angry. To be angry, you had to care; and the only person he had ever cared about was his father.

But this girl had touched a nerve. "Maybe I'd have grown up a nice guy if a Jedi hadn't cut my dad's head off in front of me."

"It's hard to lose a parent."

"Where are yours?"

"Dad's dead."

"Mother?"

"Haven't seen her in a while."

"You'll grow up as bitter as me, girl."

"Already have," said Mirta. "Already have."

There was nothing more to say. He'd already said too much; and he had to warn Beviin not to mention that they all knew that Ailyn was hunting Han Solo. He laid in a course for Drall and wondered what he would say to Ailyn when he finally caught up with her.

For the first time in his life, he suspected it would be *Sorry*.

HIGH COUNCIL CHAMBER, JEDI TEMPLE, CORUSCANT.

Luke knew events had reached the point where he could do nothing to pull the Alliance back from confrontation with Corellia; there was only damage limitation. A blockade was the least destructive option.

He had already decided not to press Cal Omas to step back from the brink. He wasn't even sure that Omas could do that if he wanted to. The Jedi council sat in a grim circle, as it must have done many times in the face of war over the millennia, and seemed to look to him for an answer.

Corran Horn—Corellian, stubborn, unperturbed—was there. At least Jacen had the decency not to round up a senior Jedi Master in his purges.

"I think we've exhausted diplomacy," Luke said.

"A blockade is simply going to rally other worlds to Corellia's cause," said Horn. "And don't think I'm saying that as wish fulfillment because I'm Corellian. I'm just reading the mood like everyone else."

"Attacking Corellia directly isn't going to achieve anything different. And letting Corellia have its way is going to encourage every other government to follow suit."

"Then the only question is to ask what the role of the Jedi council is going to be in this."

"Same as it's always been," said Kyle Katarn. "Looking for a peaceful solution, but ready to fight for the Alliance if called upon."

Cilghal interrupted. "With respect, Master Skywalker, there is a question we all appear to be unwilling to mention."

"Which is?"

"The actions of Jacen Solo."

Luke avoided Mara's eye. She was sitting to one side, staring intently at her datapad on the table in front of her, and she didn't use her standing as secretary of the council to ask Cilghal to table the question formally. Mara had never been one for slavish adherence to procedure.

"If you want to raise that, let's be specific." Luke fought down a reflex to turn to Mara and say, *See? They noticed it, too!* He knew perfectly well what he saw. The only reason he wasn't doing something about it was his own family interests, his own need for peace with Ben and Mara. *And that's not good enough.* "I think we've all noted the prominence of Jacen in events involving the Corellian community."

"Since you're frank enough to say so, then may I ask if you have misgivings about a Jedi being seen to act against civilians like this?" Cilghal squirmed visibly, but Luke admired her courage for confronting him when nobody else seemed willing to point out that his nephew was behaving badly by Jedi standards—by *any* standards. "With your own son accompanying him?"

I'm the Grand Master. I have a duty. Sorry, Mara.

"I'm deeply troubled by it."

There was a collective intake of breath.

"Is that it?" said Kyp Durron.

"I have no control over Jacen. He exists outside the Jedi order, and he isn't Ben's Master, and Ben is not his apprentice."

Luke could feel—and see—eleven pairs of eyes turning to Mara. Luke knew it was unfair to expose a family argument to high council scrutiny, but this was no longer just a couple disagreeing over their child's education. *Jacen is turning dark. I have to have the courage of my convictions.*

Mara looked up and her expression was set like permacrete in neutral calm. "I'm not sure if I should take part in this discussion. I have to declare an interest."

"Let's put this another way," said Katarn. "It's an embarrassment for the Jedi order to see the son and nephew of the Grand Master kicking down doors with the boys in black."

"But you accept that the Galactic Alliance Guard is acting legally?"

"*Unpalatably* but legally, yes." Katarn and Cilghal had now formed up into a definite but respectful attack, as if they were relieved that they weren't imagining it all. "It's the involvement of Jedi in it that we're most uncomfortable with."

Ah. *We.* Luke was ripped apart at that moment: he had either to humiliate his wife or deceive the high council because of his own personal fears. It didn't matter that his word was law here. He *knew* he was on thin ice.

"I am, too," he said at last. "I'll be asking Ben to withdraw from operations with the Guard."

"He's thirteen," said Durron. "You should be *telling* him."

Mara said nothing, but Luke could feel her boiling inside. He knew what would happen when the meeting was over. But she had the grace not to argue with him in front of the high council.

"Jacen's clearly popular with the public," Durron added carefully. "And more than one of us in this chamber has gone to some extremes and come back okay, so maybe we should be making an effort to help him identify more with the order."

"Meaning?" said Luke.

"It's time he became a Master. We all know what he can do."

Luke had a sudden image of his father. His sense of déjà vu was both comforting, because his father had been redeemed, and terrifying—terrifying because Vader had once been a Jedi prodigy, too, a decent young man, but the dark side had claimed him nonetheless. And it might well claim Jacen. Luke could taste it.

It's not frustration at not being a Master. He's gone dark. And he's not the only darkness I can feel.

Luke wondered why Lumiya had come back and knew it wasn't to see how much her old homeworld had changed since she'd been away.

But it wasn't the time to mention Lumiya. He turned his mind back to Jacen's status in the order.

"Let me think about that," said Luke.

The meeting broke up shortly afterward. Mara said nothing to Luke until they were well out of earshot, sitting in their speeder on the way back to the apartment.

"I want Ben away from Jacen," Luke said at last.

"Honey, we've discussed that . . ."

"I'm sorry it came up in the meeting, but I can't turn a blind eye to it any longer. It stops *now.* No thirteen-year-old should be out on raids with Jacen's secret police."

"Or with Jacen at all, right?"

"Mara, *everyone* sees it."

"He's having a bad affair."

"Bad affair? He's *interning Corellians*! You heard Cilghal. I'm not delusional. Have you spoken to Leia? Han?" *Don't mention Jaina.* "I haven't heard a word from my sister and my best friend in days. If you genuinely believe there's nothing odd or worrying about Jacen right now, then open up that comlink and call Leia and ask her what *she* thinks."

"Okay, and if she says yes, her son's turning into Palpatine, what do we do? Drag Ben away from him kicking and screaming?"

"If need be, yes."

"When did you last talk to Ben?"

Too long ago. "When he came back after being *gassed.*"

"Well, I speak to him most days and he's a changed kid.

He's happy, he's respectful, he's calm. He's *grown up*, Luke. Jacen did that."

"Well, bully for Jacen. I still don't want our boy being trained by him."

"So *you* can tell Ben he's back to square one, then."

"I will."

"And then you can work out who's going to take him on."

"Maybe *I'll* have to do it for a while."

"Oh, *that'll* work . . ."

And this was why they had come to this point: because there was *nobody* else who could handle Ben like Jacen could. Luke was no further forward. But he *could* ask Jacen not to take him on raids.

As for Jacen being seen as the Jedi who kicked down doors . . . he couldn't touch him. People were reassured by his hard line. And even if the Jedi order threw him out—by whatever mechanism they might have to draw up for that—Jacen would *still* be a massively powerful Force-user, and nothing could take that from him.

It was probably better to have him inside the tent than outside throwing rocks. For the time being, anyway.

Mara wasn't stupid. So why wouldn't she concede that Jacen was *dangerous*?

"There's something else you need to know, honey," said Luke. "And it's not good."

"It can't be worse than this."

"It could be." It was time. Luke couldn't hold it back any longer. He was grateful for the autonavigating skylanes of Coruscant, because he doubted if he could have flown straight unaided right then. "Lumiya's back. I don't know where, or how, but she's back."

chapter thirteen

Unless Corellia reconsiders its intention to make Centerpoint Station operational again, in contravention of the Senate instruction to all member states to disarm, I have no option but to authorize sanctions against Corellia in the form of traffic interdiction. A naval blockade of Corellia will begin at 0500 tomorrow unless undertakings are given that Corellia will not rearm. This means that no vessel will be permitted to enter or leave Corellia or any of its industrial orbiters.

—Chief of State Omas,
to the Senate and the Corellian ambassador

ALLIANCE FLEET FLAGSHIP **OCEAN**,
CORELLIAN SYSTEM, 0459 HOURS
CORUSCANT TIME.

Admiral Cha Niathal checked her personal chrono and then looked up at the bridge bulkhead to check the ship's readout.

"Any signals?"

Jacen hadn't seen Flag Lieutenant Vio's eyes leave the comm console for an hour. If Corellia had backed down, he'd have known.

"None, ma'am," said Vio.

"I'll take that silence as a *get lost,* then," she said. "Flag, make this to all ships. Interdiction measures are now in force. Corellia is under blockade."

The ships had taken up stations in two distinct zones, one encircling Corellia at two hundred thousand kilometers, the other between the surface of the planet and the orbiting factory complexes and shipyards where Corellia's industrial heart lay. Corellia was cut off now from outside traffic and—

more significantly—from its own factories and power stations.

Jacen watched the deployment of the ships, from destroyers to fast patrol craft, on the tactical holodisplay that mirrored the larger chart in Ops. Nearly three hundred small craft now patrolled the inner cordon, ready to stop traffic movement from Corellia's surface to the industrial orbiters. Beyond the orbital ring, destroyers and cruisers waited for the inevitable.

"Anyone laying bets as to who comes to Corellia's aid first?" Jacen asked Vio. He knew that crews couldn't resist that kind of thing.

Vio didn't blink. "Jabiim and Rothana are obviously favorites . . ."

"Rothana?" Jabiim was always swimming against the tide. Its national sport was intransigence. "Why Rothana?"

"More to observe than support. Shipyard rivalry thing."

Niathal eyed the holochart and waited. There were a million flights a day through inner Corellian space; the first confrontation would come very soon.

"I was going to ask why the Supreme Commander is out here and not back at Fleet Ops running the show from there," Jacen said quietly.

"Same reason the head of the Galactic Alliance Guard is on the front line." Niathal watched the unnaturally frozen chart that should have been showing the transponder icons of thousands of commercial vessels going about their business. "To be seen."

Ocean hummed and throbbed with the mechanical voices of a thousand systems, feeling almost like a living creature to Jacen. It was fascinating to be close to something that had no living substance and so wasn't transparent to his Force-senses. He could only influence *Ocean* using the physical Force. He couldn't *feel* her.

He sought Ben in the Force, magnifying his own presence

to reassure him. The boy was back on Coruscant, safe in the care of Captain Shevu. He'd wanted to accompany Jacen, but, as Jacen pointed out, he needed his liaison to stay with the Guard. Ben was enjoying his newfound status as part of a team that respected his skills, and took little persuading.

He had shaken off his father's shadow for the first time. Ben now truly believed he was a person in his own right, and not just the Skywalker kid. Jacen admired his resilience: he knew what it was to be the child of political celebrities, but being a Solo carried nothing like the stifling expectation of being Luke Skywalker's son.

"*Ansta* has contact at five hundred thousand klicks, ma'am," the comm officer announced.

Niathal didn't move a muscle. "So Admiral Cheb gets first bite."

Jacen could feel Jaina's anxiety, many decks below in the hangar. He knew she couldn't feel his, because he had withdrawn from the Force, cloaking himself against detection. For a moment he considered reaching many light-years away, into the Hapes Cluster to brush gently against Tenel Ka's presence, but he didn't dare. He tried not to think of her at all. Even thought might put her at risk of discovery if he was careless. Lumiya's Force skills were still not to be taken for granted, and Tenel Ka and Allana were in a far more dangerous position than he would ever be.

It was time to make his impressions on the thousands of officers and ratings in the interdiction task force. "Permission to put Rogue Squadron on alert five, ma'am?"

"Carry on, Colonel Solo."

Reputations spread like wildfire in ships. Jacen knew what he wanted his to be: the officer who would never shirk his responsibility, and who would never ask anyone to do what he wouldn't do himself.

It made you friends. Jacen knew he would need every one of them in the months to come.

HIGH-SECURITY CELL BLOCK,
GALACTIC ALLIANCE GUARD HEADQUARTERS,
CORUSCANT.

Ben checked his comlink and saw that he now had five calls waiting from his father. When he was with Jacen, he felt shielded from the weight of Luke's presence, but now he felt very alone and *hunted*.

He was pretty sure his father could sense where he was. He hated that. He felt he had no privacy. But so far the interference was purely calls, even though Luke must have known that Jacen had joined the blockade.

Ben concentrated on the matter at hand, which was learning from Captain Shevu. Shevu was head-to-head with another captain, Girdun, having one of those whispered angry fights that adults had.

"We have *rules*," said Shevu. "And until the Senate tells me those rules have changed, I live by them."

"Yes, and let's hear you taking that fine moral stance when someone gets assassinated and we might have stopped it."

"Prisoners get five hours' break from questioning in twenty-four. You want to do it different? Not on my watch."

The man and woman they had detained in the apartment block were in separate holding cells. The man was a small-time Corellian agent—possibly called Buroy, possibly not—who had been identified from the NRI's database. The woman was probably Kiffar, judging by her facial tattoo, and her name was Ailyn Habuur. Shevu had taken a comlink from her and it had stored three messages since she'd been captured, all from someone called Mirta Gev.

Shevu got his way. Girdun stalked off.

"You don't have to stay," said Shevu, tapping the security code into the cell's lock.

Ben was afraid that if he went back to the apartment, his father would find him and confront him, and that he wouldn't have the will to stand up to him. Either that—or they'd fight, and Ben hated having fights. "I might be able to help."

The doors slid open. Shevu gave him a dubious look. "This is just a regular interrogation, the way we did it in CSF. If you can mind-influence, great. If not, don't worry."

"You know we do that?"

"I don't think it's classified information somehow."

Ailyn Habuur was sitting at a table, hands on the surface in front of her. She was handcuffed, and her face still bore the marks of the scuffle when she was arrested. The tattoo that surrounded her left eye was unnerving, and she was the hardest-looking woman Ben had ever seen: wiry and un-smiling, with thin, sinewy forearms that made her look as if she spent her time strangling people.

"Okay, ma'am," said Shevu, sitting down opposite her. "You keep some unsavory company."

"It's not illegal to be a bounty hunter."

"Depends what you're hunting."

"Not illegal to be in the same apartment block as Corel-lians, either, but I see you're working on that."

"Look, ma'am, this is how we do things." Shevu was quiet and polite. "You give me a good reason why you're holed up with a Corellian agent and carrying some serious hardware, and why you chose to shoot it out with the Nine Six Seven, and I let you leave. Otherwise I tend to think you're a threat to security. And in that case, you stay here until you rot, if you're lucky."

Habuur slid back in her seat, all ice, and then glanced at Ben.

"What's the kid here for?"

"Training."

"You start your thugs young on Coruscant."

Shevu laid Habuur's comlink and datapad on the table in front of her. Ben watched, feeling how stressed she was. There was something unfocused about her, as if her hostility and anxiety were directed at something that wasn't in the room.

"You like spacecraft for some reason?"

Habuur shrugged. "Beats walking."

"You got a lot of images of them on your datapad." Shevu switched on the 'pad and showed them to her. "Who did you have under surveillance?"

Habuur just stared back at him. Ben craned his neck to get a look at the images on the 'pad, but it was all just a blur from this angle.

Shevu went on, still with that tone of bored patience. "Just cut the poodoo and tell me why you're here. If it's just some lowlife you've been sent to vape, I'm too busy to worry about that."

"Don't I get a lawyer?"

"Under the emergency powers I've been granted, no. You get zip."

"You'll be banging my head on the table pretty soon, then."

"Want me to call your friend?"

"I don't have any."

"The one who keeps contacting you."

"Who?"

"Mirta Gev," said Shevu.

Habuur's face was completely unmoved, but Ben felt the little flare of strong emotion—fear, dismay, yearning—well up and surround her like an energy field. Shevu reacted to it, too. Ben wondered how non-Force-users could sense things that well hidden.

"She was recovering some jewelry for me." And that sounded like the truth. The whole timbre of her voice and the feel of the Force around her changed. "My mother's necklace."

"Looks like she got it."

Habuur said nothing and remained apparently relaxed in

the durasteel seat even though the muscles in her jaw had started to twitch. Shevu got up and beckoned Ben to follow him outside.

The captain closed the doors. "Go and get Girdun for me. I want to check out this Mirta Gev again. If she's on her way here, I'd like to welcome her to the capital personally, especially if she's armed like madam in there."

"Are you happy leaving her with Girdun?"

Shevu frowned slightly. "That's a very grown-up question."

"He feels pretty nasty."

"That's a Force judgment, is it?"

"Yes."

"It's spot-on. He's a former New Republic Intelligence officer. He's used to different rules than the ones we had to follow as police." Jacen had cobbled together a very mixed bag of men and women for 967 Commando; Ben found some of them frightening, and he could see the differences in *cultures,* as Shevu called it, among those from the Intelligence Service, the police, and the military. "But he wouldn't dare cross me on this."

"Okay." Shevu was very much in command, even if the two men had the same rank. "Right away."

Shevu went back into the interrogation room, and Ben went in search of Captain Girdun, trying to walk briskly and not break into a run. He found the man in the barracks' gymnasium. The 967, being newly formed, didn't have a proper headquarters yet and had taken over a Fleet Reserve training center.

Girdun, who never looked at ease in his black uniform, stood talking to a couple of sergeants. Somehow it took Ben a few seconds to see the ranks of people behind him, sitting cross-legged on the floor with their hands on top of their heads, fingers meshed. Some of them looked like the kind of people Ben would avoid at all costs, and some looked pretty ordinary. Most were male.

"Latest haul," said the sergeant. "Nice tip-off, kid."

Ben still scanned the gymnasium—silent except for the heavy sense of people breathing nervously—in the way of someone who felt he ought to recognize one of the prisoners.

He did.

His gaze jerked to a halt on a blond boy a few years older than he was. Barit Saiy sat in the ranks of Corellians arrested during the night, staring at Ben with an expression of utter loathing.

"Yeah, great tip," said Gurdin, distracted. "What did you want me for?"

Ben knew at that moment that he would never be a child again. He wished more than anything that he could.

chapter fourteen

Ke barjurir gar'ade, jagyc'ade kot'la a dalyc'ade kotla'shya.
Train your sons to be strong but your daughters to be stronger.
— Mandalorian saying

ZERRIA'S BAR, DRALL, CORELLIAN SYSTEM.

"*Mand'alor!*" said a voice Fett didn't recognize. "*Gal'gala?*"

The soldier took off his Mandalorian helmet and gave Fett a stiffly formal nod. A baby's handprint in charcoal paint adorned the helmet of his gray-blue armor, a curious foil for the Verpine rifle slung over his left shoulder.

"This is Ram," said Beviin. "Ram Zerimar. He's our star sniper. For those *delicate* jobs."

Zerimar nodded politely. Fett wanted to ask about the handprint but didn't.

Mirta gave Fett one of her subtly admonishing looks. He was attuned to them now. "And he says he wants to buy you a drink," she said.

"Later." Fett returned Zerimar's nod. *Not even my own men see me without the helmet.* "Let's talk first."

There was nothing like half a dozen fully armored Mandalorian warriors to guarantee you a table to yourself in a crowded bar. Beviin introduced them: Zerimar, Briike, Orade, Vevut—and Talgal, the only woman, and one who looked as if she ate Yuuzhan Vong for appetizers. Apart from Beviin, none had fought with him against the Vong and he didn't know them. He studied their faces while they looked suspiciously at Mirta.

"Bounty hunter," said Fett. "Mirta Gev. Mandalorian father."

They thawed instantly. Fett watched their shoulders relax. They all muttered *"su'cuy gar"* like a chorus. It was a pretty logical greeting for warriors, apparently: "So you're still alive." Warriors didn't expect much from life and they frequently didn't get it.

"So how do you feel about defending Centerpoint Station?" Fett asked.

There was a disinterested silence. He watched them chew it over for five seconds, and he suspected they'd have spat it out like rotting meat if he hadn't been *Mand'alor.*

Orade—buzz-cut blond hair, broken nose, a brush of gold beard on the point of his chin—folded his arms on the table and made a fresh scrape in the polished surface. "What do *you* think?"

"I think Sal-Solo is a self-serving sadistic liar, but then most of my customers are. He's also going to lose, and losers can't pay." *Actually, I can't be bothered. I've got bigger things on my plate.* "But I'll hear him out. How do *you* feel about it?"

"Unenthusiastic," said Vevut. Another stranger: he had long, black, woolly braids bound with gold rings, and the dark skin of his left cheek was scored by an impressive scar. He drained his ale and clicked his fingers at a nearby droid. "Maybe we wait and see before we commit ourselves."

"If you really thought it was worth it, you'd get the whole one hundred behind you, *Mand'alor,*" said Beviin. "But I'm with Vevut. Wait and see. Things have changed since the Vong invasion."

Vevut turned in his seat, armor creaking, to look meaningfully at the service droid. It lurched toward him. "Yeah, we're not so desperate for work. Farms keep us busy enough."

"Sir!" said a droid's voice. "Sorry to keep you "

"About time. I'd like another ale."

The droid pirouetted, reflections of the bar's garish lighting bouncing off its polished dome, and tilted as if bowing.

"I am Forre Musa, an artist droid, dedicated to your entertainment," said the droid.

"I'd rather have another ale," said Vevut, voice low. Mirta's eyes kept darting toward the doors. Fett's peripheral vision never lost sight of her hands. "But what kind of entertainment?"

"Oh, it's of the highest intellectual quality, sir," Forre Musa said. "I can read you important works of political allegory, comments on current affairs with a unique perspective, great literature—all my own work, of course—and sagas. What's it to be?"

"We'd rather hear some jokes," said Mirta.

"I don't do jokes. I am a *serious* artist."

Mirta raised her blaster. "Shame," she said, and fried his speech circuit with one clean, point-blank shot. "We could do with a laugh."

The bar hung on one silent second as the fizz of shorting circuitry cut through the buzz of conversation. Then everyone went on drinking. Vevut and the others roared with laughter. Mirta appeared to have passed their test of destructive humor.

Even the Dabi bartender seemed pleased. He rearranged the glasses and polished one thoughtfully while his other pair of arms rummaged in a drawer and pulled out an insurance claim flimsi.

"I'm glad you did that," he said, scribbling happily on the form while also working up a good shine on the glass. "He was killing trade here. The droid company wouldn't give me a refund."

"Glad to help the local economy," said Mirta.

"Free ale all around."

"I like her," Vevut said.

"Then teach her to play Cheg," said Fett. He indicated the Cheg table in the center of the bar. "I want to talk to Beviin."

Cheg was a remarkably noisy, violent pursuit for a table-top game. Fett watched for a few moments as Mirta caught on to the rules rather too fast, whacking the small puck across the tabletop with her knuckles as she shoulder-charged Orade for possession of it.

"It's okay, I told them to stay off the subject of Ailyn's bounty in front of her," said Beviin. "So how did you pick up a stray? Never known you to do *that*."

"She offered to lead me to Ailyn because she's done a job for her."

"You can find Ailyn easily enough on your own. Solo's been seen on Corellia. All you have to do is wait."

"The kid's got my wife's necklace. I want to find out how." Fett wondered whether now was the time to come clean with Beviin about his illness, but he decided yet again that it could wait. "And some other personal stuff I'm interested in."

"You like that kid."

"I ought to space her. She spent the flight here beating me up for being a rotten Mandalore."

"So she's not blind."

"You got a problem with the way I do things?"

"Yeah, and so have a few others now. Don't get me wrong. Nobody's after the job—nobody that *I* know, anyway. But the Vong war was a wake-up call. We need more than a symbol."

"Mandalores aren't administrators. Mandalorians can run their own communities—anywhere. They just need . . . general leadership when it's called for."

"Well, maybe it's called for now. Everyone's still rebuilding across the galaxy and it's time we did, too."

Fett sat with his hands flat on the table. He could hear the guffaws of laughter and occasional exclamations in a language he should have understood but didn't.

"Mandalore's still in one piece. So is the rest of the sector."

"Just. And you don't spend much time there."

"A lot of Mandos don't," Fett said.

"They're not the *Mand'alor.*"

"Why does this matter now?"

"People get an idea and start to think differently. It spreads. We lost a lot of people in the war. Makes everyone think hard, that does."

"Ask me straight. Don't hint."

"Come home and help our people."

"How?"

"Shysa pulled us together once. Now it's time for you to do the same."

"I'm a soldier. The war's over." *And I'm dying. I'm the one who might need to find a new Mandalore, not you.* "You need someone who can run an economy."

"Then what's the use of being *Mand'alor*? No heir, no clan, no sense of duty. You're not Mandalorian. You just wear the armor."

It was a dangerous retort, but Beviin didn't seem to care. Fett didn't even take it as a challenge—just a Mandalorian's forthright view that he felt fully entitled to express. There had always been a Mandalore, chief of clans, the leader anointed by the last Mandalore or the one who snatched the title from him, always on his deathbed, which was invariably in combat. The ancient mask that was the Mandalore's mark of rank was always at risk.

Maybe it's obvious I'm dying. Maybe they're looking for who'll lead them next.

"You're saying I should be a conventional head of state. We don't *have* a state like that."

"These days we might need one."

"Get a bureaucracy and sit in meetings and get slow and flabby like every other world?"

"There's more to it than that and you know it." It was oddly difficult to take offense at Beviin. "We need to make sure we're warriors with a citadel to defend, so we can pick our battles and not rely on the whims of *aruetiise*. Foreigners. It's the spirit of the times, like I said."

It didn't sound crazy put that way, but Fett felt it had nothing to do with him. Mandalorians were defined by family above all else, and that was one thing he'd sought and never found after his father was killed. *I tried: Sintas, my Journeyman Protector days . . .*

Thinking about his estranged family was painful. But remembering why he'd been exiled from Concord Dawn was something he couldn't allow himself to do. He locked down his emotions. *Death really messes you up.* He was alone. He was fine that way.

Beviin seemed to be waiting for a reply.

"And who's driving this *spirit of the times*?" Fett asked.

"Nobody, really," said Beviin. "But there's this guy called Kad'ika that we're all hearing about. Thinks it's time we looked after ourselves—*really* looked after ourselves. Not just gather in the clans and unite when we're threatened, but build Mandalore itself into something new."

I never heard that. And I never miss intelligence. "So he wants to be Mandalore?"

"No, they say he wants *you* to be Mandalore."

"Then he can come and tell me himself. Whoever he is."

The name *Kad'ika* told Fett something. The *Mando'a* suffix *-ika* made it a child's name, a diminutive of the name *Kad*. Fett suspected that a Mandalorian who still had a childhood nickname and seemed confident to wear it almost as a badge would be anything *but* little. In the past he'd hunted several big, dangerous targets with trivial names that belied their muscle and firepower. They'd seemed to bask in the irony.

He'd killed them anyway, but they'd been a challenge.

A professional took no chances and never underestimated the task at hand. Fett added Kad'ika to the list of potential quarry that was big and dangerous until proven otherwise.

"It means 'little saber,' " Beviin said helpfully.

"Cute," said Fett. *One more complication, one more mystery. Stick to your priorities, Fett.* "I'm heading for Corellia now."

"You'll have to beat the blockade, then."

"I will. You still flying Gladiators?"

"We are."

"Form up and follow *Slave One,* then. Let's see if the Alliance remembers that we fought against the Vong for them."

Fett decided to stay busy. He needed to find his cure, he needed to see Ailyn, and he needed not to dwell on the unhappy past.

Corellia's ills would do the job for now.

CORELLIAN BLOCKADE, INNER EXCLUSION ZONE.

Rogue Squadron maintained formation behind Jacen's XJ7 as the fighters patrolled the exclusion zone around Corellia. It took five standard hours to circle the planet at maximum speed.

The squadron was flying a cube pattern around a cluster of orbital units that made up a shipyard, probably a less glamorous target than Centerpoint but a significant one nonetheless.

And somewhere aft of his port wing, mistrustful and angry, was Jaina. Maybe it was his instant elevation to colonel. She'd worked for her rank. He could feel her, a bright fire of resentment and anger. Zekk was on his starboard side. For a few moments the squadron touched minds in a battle-meld, but it didn't feel as united as it once had.

I've lost you, Jaina. In the end, I might lose everyone's love, maybe even Tenel Ka, but it has to be done.

Jacen shook himself out of regret and the squadron broke into six paired patrols, fanning out into the orbits of the industrial space stations and shipyards—and Centerpoint Station.

How close could his squadron get before the Corellians opened fire? Would they fire at all?

If the orbital stations didn't have fighter craft embarked— and that was always a possibility—then all they had was their close-in defense systems, the ones they never expected to have to use. Jacen switched to the main ops comlink to hear the voice traffic between other squadrons' pilots and Forward Air Control.

"Unarmed maintenance transport inbound for Centerpoint. Moving to intercept."

"Copy that."

"Visual on the transport. Confirmed unarmed."

"Intercepting now. Range five kilometers."

"He's holding course. Let's see who blinks first."

"He's slowing."

"And now you've got company. Corellian fighter range ten kilometers moving to transport's position . . . fast . . ."

"Got him on scanner . . . now visual, too."

It was the first test of wills.

"Back off, pal—"

"Whoa, that was close."

"He's locked on to me."

"Cleared to engage."

"He's breaking off—transport is altering course."

Zekk cut into Jacen's comlink circuit. It seemed Jacen wasn't the only one listening to the chatter. "Shouldn't we be there?"

"Centerpoint isn't the only game in town. Patience, Zekk."

Centerpoint might have been the political focus, but Jacen knew the leverage would be in the factories and power stations orbiting Corellia. There was a total of a million workers in those orbiters, people with families down on the surface who cared about them.

"Contact, bearing twenty-five by forty from datum." Zekk's XJ7 blipped on Jacen's onboard scanner as it peeled off to investigate. He watched as Zekk pinged the vessel with his sensors; the shared display outlined a big, ungainly ship that appeared to be one large tank. "Okay, profile looks like a replenishment ship—water bowser and food. Panic over."

"Turn it back, then."

"What?"

"Orders are to turn back *all* vessels."

Zekk's comlink made a slight pop as if he'd switched it off for a moment. "But it's just water and catering. It's not industrial or military."

Zekk didn't get it sometimes. Jacen wondered why he saw angles that other Jedi didn't. "Those orbiters can only recycle and condense so much water a day. The shortfall has to be topped up."

"You think that's worth doing . . ."

"Rule of three."

"What?"

"Three minutes without air, three days without water, three weeks without food. That's how long a humanoid can last, and they're mostly Corellians on those orbiters. The first thing every commander should learn about a siege. There are ten thousand workers in that orbital yard alone, and they're *not* going home just yet, and they're *not* going to be resupplied. That makes people sweat."

Zekk's comlink popped again. Maybe he was silencing

the audio to swear for a moment. "Who's this shapeshifter and what has he done with Jacen?" he said sourly.

"Just turn back the bowser, Zekk. I'm not running a popularity contest."

"Very good, *sir.*" Zekk's tone said otherwise, but Jacen watched him roll his XJ7 into a dive and head straight for the water tanker.

Jaina's voice was almost a whisper in Jacen's comlink. "Is this policy?"

"Turn back all vessels means turn back all vessels. Do you have a problem with that?"

"Just a humanitarian one."

"It'll bring Corellia to the negotiation table a lot faster without shots being fired."

"Well, you're in command," said Jaina, all acid. "*Colonel* Solo."

Jacen wondered if any other squadron was quite as casual in its attitude to orders as Rogue. He doubted it.

It was a long sortie. For the next three hours the squadron harried supply vessels and transports, turning some of them back simply by flying uncomfortably close. Others were more persistent; it took a concussion round detonated close to their bows to make them alter their course and head back down to the surface. For once, the XJ7s' business was about being visible, conspicuous, and intimidating.

"We only have to keep this up for a few months," Zekk said wearily. "Piece of cake."

"Try this for size," said Jaina. "Check your scanner. Three assault fighters on our six. I think Cousin Thrackan is fed up with us already."

Jacen looped his XJ7 into a climb, tracing a complete arc almost without thinking about the maneuver, and found himself looking up through his canopy at the approaching Corellian fighters as they crossed beneath him. Even with g forces normalized and no sense of orientation, Jacen still had a clear sense that he was above them, upside down, just like flying combat missions in a planet's atmosphere. He could see and feel Jaina—and see Zekk—flying wide of him, far below, canopies facing him; they had looped in the same plane to come up on the Corellians from the rear, rather than climbing above them. *Did we discuss this move? Or did I just think it?* No, it was silent habit reinforced by that twin bond. Jacen feared it was the last thing he would ever truly share with his sister, but it was one more pain he had to face. She couldn't follow him on the path he was taking any more than his parents could.

He savored the final remnant of true understanding between them and accelerated into the loop to drop down behind the three fighters, right himself, and skim at top speed just meters clear of their canopies. The three fighters broke formation and scattered. Without any verbal commands, the three Jedi pilots latched on to their individual targets, Jaina and Zekk close enough on the tails of theirs to show little eddies of ionized gas on the nose shields of their X-wings. Jacen's target seemed to be under the impression that he was chasing *Jacen.*

Corellians were excellent pilots, but they weren't Jedi. The marginal difference in reaction speed and orientation made for much bigger gulfs in performance at high speeds. Jacen seized that advantage. He let the fighter sit close on his tail for a couple of kilometers and then plummeted away from it, perfectly aware of his own position in space relative both to it and to Jaina and Zekk, who were also locked in their respective games of tag.

It was just sparring. This was a game of brinkmanship; a game of maneuver and countermaneuver to test each other's nerve. A game to show that if it came to a shooting match, the Alliance would win.

Jacen thought this right up to the time he saw the display

on his screen blip red with the warning that the Corellian had a missile lock on him. He sensed anything but a bluff.

You're really going to shoot, aren't you?

The Corellian fired.

Jacen didn't feel in danger; he had deflectors, the XJ7's robust airframe, and his own skills. He also had chaff to deploy. Instinctively, he fired the small decoy in his wake and it fragmented into pieces that looked, to a missile, very much like a target.

But if you want a fight, you've found one.

The missile exploded on his tail, and the rain of fragments peppered his hull. The Corellian fighter was still hard behind him and now he meant business. Jacen also knew that his opponent would aim the next missile manually, overriding its smart guidance to thwart more chaff.

That's what I'd do, anyway.

Jacen could have sent the Corellian spiraling harmlessly away by using the Force to tip his wings. He could have stopped his drives dead and left him drifting. But this pilot was one more asset that was ready to take their lives. He and his starfighter had to be removed permanently.

You started it, my friend.

Jacen flipped the XJ7 ninety degrees and shot up vertically as the Corellian disappeared beneath him and overshot. Jacen was back on his tail, staring into white engine halos and closing the gap until he was close enough to fire the laser cannon. The starfighter exploded in a ball of white light.

Jaina? Zekk?

He felt them weaving between the two remaining Corellian fighters and then saw the enemy vessels break and shoot off toward the planet. He didn't think they were retreating. He suspected that they were regrouping to assess the rapid escalation of the conflict.

A few hours into the blockade, the shooting had already started.

"Congratulations." Jaina's voice over the comlink was flat and unemotional, although she didn't feel that way in the Force at all. Jacen sensed her as *resigned*. "You've made the history books. You fired the opening shot of the real war."

SLAVE I, ENTERING CORELLIAN EXCLUSION ZONE, OUTER CORDON.

"Warship *Ocean* calling unidentified vessel," said the Alliance. Fett listened in silence, *Slave I*'s scanner profile presenting the almost undetectable thermal and magnetic signatures of a speeder bike. He was, for all intents and purposes, invisible—unless someone was lucky enough to get a visual on him. "Identify yourself."

"This is Mandalorian vessel *Beroya*." Beviin's voice oozed cheery comradeship. "Need a hand?"

"Why would we need that, *Beroya*? We've got two fleets deployed here."

"You weren't that choosy when you needed us to fight the Yuuzhan Vong."

Fett prepared for a maneuver that would either get him through the blockade in one piece or solve all his worries about terminal illness—because if he miscalculated, he'd be vaporized along with *Slave I*.

And so would Mirta Gev, of course.

"Do it," Mirta whispered.

"Wait . . . ," said Fett, fingers resting on the recessed pad that would punch *Slave I* into hyperspace. "Just making sure the trajectory is clear."

There was a moment's pause from *Ocean*. He heard the comm officer swallow. "Since when has Mandalore been part of the Alliance? You planning to bill us for this?"

"Just being comradely," said Beviin. "But strictly speaking, we couldn't be part of any alliance even if we wanted to, because . . ."

Nice diversion, thought Fett. If Beviin started on his theory of Mandalorian statehood, *Ocean*'s comm officer could be pinned down for days. It was now or never.

"*Now!*"

He hit the hyperspace jump control once and hit it again almost a heartbeat later.

In a second *Slave I* accelerated from a few thousand kilometers per hour to half the speed of light, and then decelerated again. Fett's stomach felt as if it had detached from his body.

It was the equivalent of slamming the ship into a rock face, but it punched *Slave I* past the blockade fast enough to show up on a scanner as nothing more than a brief burst of energy. The huge forces made *Slave I* shudder and groan, and Fett found the surface of Corellia looming in his viewscreen. He'd cut it too fine. He couldn't correct the angle of approach before the ship hit atmosphere. He struggled to correct the flight path, slamming on the burners and giving *Slave I*'s hull one more set of impossible stresses.

"You always this lucky?" Mirta asked. Her voice was tight and strained. Fett didn't look at her. If she had any sense, she'd be scared rigid. He certainly was. Only idiots didn't feel fear.

"Let's see," he said. Fear, yes; but fear never paralyzed him. It just made him sharper.

Slave I hit the atmosphere, and the hull temperature sensor jumped into the red. The emergency computer kicked in, correcting as best it could, but now it was simply a case of waiting to see if *Slave I*'s hull—and airframe—could handle the worst possible reentry.

Mirta, to her credit, was completely silent. Fett wouldn't have blamed her if she had allowed herself a scream or two.

"Have you done this before?" she asked, voice shaking.

"Once."

"That's encouraging."

Corellia filled *Slave I*'s viewscreen. It was sobering to note how much of a planet a ship covered when decelerating. They were over Coronet; Fett recognized the city. The big park that was split in two by the speeder highway hadn't changed. The hull sensor had settled back into the yellow zone, and apart from some ominous creaking *Slave I* had slowed enough for a normal vertical landing on her downjets.

"Coronet ATC to unidentified Firespray, I have you on visual . . . you're a little big for a speeder bike, aren't you?"

"*Slave One* here," said Fett. *Oops.* He disabled the decoy system and the ship resumed her normal profiles. "Your scanner must be having problems."

"Just can't get the maintenance staff these days. You're cleared to land in the priority bays. Follow the red lights."

"It's nice to feel welcome."

"President Sal-Solo is sending a speeder for you."

Slave I settled on her dampers, and Mirta let out a breath loud enough for Fett to hear. But he never allowed himself that degree of relief. One danger had passed, and now he simply moved on to the next one: holding Sal-Solo at arm's length, getting off Corellia again, finding that clone, and getting him to surrender his secrets.

And facing Ailyn, which suddenly felt more dangerous than anything he'd ever done in his life.

Why does a man who's dying anyway worry about crashing?

"Come on," he said. "Help me secure the ship. I don't trust Sal-Solo any farther than I can spit."

"You're letting me come with you?"

"I'm not letting you sit in *Slave One* for a few days." Fett set the intruder countermeasures, this time including the self-destruct. He didn't trust *anybody*, but there was still a scale of distrust, and Sal-Solo was up there with the Hutts. "Just do as I tell you."

"Is that because I'm useful, or because you want to keep an eye on me?"

"Because I don't want to have to hunt you down and shoot you before you tell me what happened to my wife," he said. He wasn't sure if he said it to shock, or because he meant it. He didn't have to care either way. "I did love her. I just didn't know how to be part of a family."

Do I mean that? Yes, I think I really do.

Fett didn't let Mirta see all the codes that turned *Slave I* into a booby trap for anyone insane enough to try breaking into her, but the girl learned the basic routines fast. By the time they climbed out of the forward hatch, there was an airspeeder waiting on the permacrete strip and three men in business suits standing in front of it with hopeful expressions.

A Corellian stepped forward—dark-haired, young, but with an air of being well into middle age—and held out his hand for a few awkward seconds before realizing Fett wasn't about to shake it.

"Welcome to Coronet, sir," he said. "We represent the three main political parties of the Corellian Assembly. We hope you'll be able to help us."

So Sal-Solo had sent his minions. Okay, that was understandable. Fett checked his weapons status in his HUD, just in case things didn't go quite as planned, shoved Mirta in the back of the speeder, and then sat up front with the driver. That appeared to surprise his welcoming committee.

"I'm Dur Gejjen, by the way," said the young-old Corellian, commendably unfazed. "It's *very* good to meet you."

Gejjen would be trouble. Fett could feel it.

chapter fifteen

We're under siege. The Galactic Alliance has violated our airspace, marooned civilian workers on orbiters without food and water, and opened fire on our defense forces. The Alliance has committed more acts of war against us. We'll stand alone if we have to, but I invite other planets to ask themselves this: which of you will be the Alliance's next target? Support us while you still can."

—Thrackan Sal-Solo in a speech to the Corellian Assembly, broadcast live on HNE's Corellian affiliate network

SENATE BUILDING: DAY THREE OF THE CORELLIAN BLOCKADE.

An ocean of people—perhaps half a million—churned and surged around in the plaza in front of the Senate Building. Jacen could see a very long line of hundreds of blue-uniformed CSF officers with riot shields and visors pulled down, forming a defensive barrier across the face of the building. It was a protest: not exactly a mass riot, given the population of Galactic City, but it wasn't a welcoming committee for the heroes of the blockade, either. Judging by the position of the police lines, there appeared to be two hostile factions yelling abuse at each other—Coruscanti versus the pro-Corellian lobby. Coruscant and the Galactic Alliance were indivisible.

Jacen could hear a chant taken up by thousands of voices.

"The—Empire's—back! The—Empire's—back! The—Empire's—back!"

It was hard to tell, but Jacen assumed it was a taunt from the dissidents, and not Coruscanti enjoying the prospect of firm government. But his exploits had gone down very well in the Alliance's heartland. He kept an eye on HNE and the news holozines.

"Pity I couldn't stay in the front line," said Niathal. "That's the worst thing about command. Anchors you to a desk."

"I'll remain hands-on for as long as I can," Jacen said. "I'd like to show my face on the blockade line. Good for morale."

"You have an office in mind, then . . ."

"Don't worry. Not yours."

"And I note that you haven't gone back to wearing Jedi robes."

Jacen dusted a speck of lint from his black GAG uniform. "I don't see any point in provoking Uncle Luke or the Jedi council. I know they don't enjoy being identified with my actions."

"Ironic, seeing as the Public Affairs Office says polls indicate the popularity of the Jedi council has increased a little."

"Jedi are supposed to be beyond populism, Admiral."

As Niathal's staff airspeeder slowed to skirt the crowd, Jacen glanced out of the window and noted the new mix of species and allegiances forming the army of protesters. "Well, we rounded up the Corellians, and now their places are being filled by others." He identified various nationalities by clothing, hairstyles, snatches of language. "Look, isn't that a couple of Rodians?"

"As long as you don't see any Mandalorians . . ."

The closer to the lobby that the speeder edged, the uglier the mood of the crowd appeared to become. A group of CSF officers drove back the crowd with none-too-gentle shoves emphasized with batons to let the speeder through. Jacen and Niathal got out, and he took the precaution of throwing up a Force-shield around them.

Jacen almost didn't feel *danger* now, not in the sense he always had. He merely took account of circumstances and reacted accordingly. As they stepped out of the speeder, a hail of stones, old food containers, bottles, and other debris flew at them. All of it bounced back from the Force-barrier, some of it hitting the upturned riot shields.

Jacen turned and stepped forward into the crowd: he didn't enjoy displaying his Force powers in such a vulgar way, but there were times when they could make a point. He held his hands a little way from his sides, closed his eyes, and pressed outward with his mind as if lifting his arms.

Nothing violent. Mustn't cause a crush, or a stampede. Innocent people will be hurt.

The crowd closest to him fell back a few paces, some of them looking around frantically to see what was pushing them back. More missiles rained from farther back in the press of bodies, accompanied by shouting and shoving, but they simply bounced off the Force-shield, and Jacen stood calmly staring back into the mass of people. A breathless silence spread from the line nearest to him like a fast tide engulfing a shore. Even some of the CSF officers seemed frozen to the spot.

Everyone knew about Jedi, but very few ever saw them in action—or felt them.

"Go home," said Jacen. "Just break it up and go home before I have to *do* something about it."

They didn't run, of course, but he had made his point; the respite gave the CSF line a chance to push the rival groups apart again, and Jacen followed Niathal into the Senate Building and up to the Chief of State's office.

Luke Skywalker was already there, Mara sitting beside him, and he didn't look pleased to see Jacen.

"We are still *not* at war," Omas insisted, staring out the window at the crowds. "Does the council still support the blockade?"

"As the only alternative to full-scale war or backing down on disarmament, yes." Luke wasn't looking at Omas.

His gaze was on Jacen. "How much impact is the blockade having?"

Niathal looked up from her datapad. Jacen wasn't sure how she regarded Luke; his uncle didn't feature in their conversations. "We've intercepted or turned back around seventy percent of vessels trying to enter or leave the two exclusion rings, but in terms of volume of cargo and personnel, that's nearer ninety percent. We're stopping the big vessels but losing some of the small ones. All in all—it's biting already."

"Should we revise our policy on stopping traffic movements around the shipyards?"

"Nonviolent way of leaning on the civilian population," said Jacen. "When dad doesn't come home when he's due back from the yards, it focuses families, and families lean on governments."

Luke stood up and watched from the window with Omas. "And what about these people, Jacen? You've cracked down on the Corellians. What about all the non-Corellians I see down there?"

Mara gave Jacen a careful, *don't-take-the-bait* look. He could feel the tension between her and Luke, and he knew it was more about Ben than about politics or personal rights. "If any other national group or species threatens the security of Coruscant or the Alliance, then I'll deal with that, too."

"Within the law."

"Yes, within the law. I realize you don't approve of my methods, but someone has to carry out the damage limitation."

"We've had a dozen terrorist incidents in a few weeks," Luke said. "I'm sorry that lives have been lost, but we need to get that in perspective when it comes to how we treat billions."

That got Omas's attention. He turned from the window.

"I invite you to tell the Coruscant public that, Master Sky-walker. The fact that they won't see it that way is why terrorism is always so effective. And the Senate doesn't see it that way, either. The Security and Intelligence Council now has full emergency powers to take operational decisions on the handling of public safety."

Luke stood his ground. Jacen had thought he was indecisive and afraid of banging heads together, but when he did take a stand, he was adamant. It was just a pity that he took a position on the wrong issues.

"I'm still uncomfortable with the armed forces being used against civilians."

"Define a civilian with a blaster who doesn't like the government, then," said Jacen.

"The legitimate government has taken the decision." Luke's tone was even and controlled. "I'm just dissenting, and as the members of the Jedi council aren't the elected representatives of the people, then an opinion is all that it is."

Niathal was watching the exchange with faint interest. "This is an exquisite ethical argument, but right now I'm more concerned with stopping Corellia repairing an orbital weapon that was capable of taking out the Yuuzhan Vong and that will, if brought back online, ruin the Alliance's entire day."

Omas almost twitched. The power play was luminous in its visibility. "What would you prefer to do, Admiral? We failed to destroy it last time."

"We can reduce a planet to molten slag from orbit. Let's not rule out the possibility of needing to do that to Centerpoint—even if it would be best preserved to defend the Alliance."

"It's populated," said Luke.

"So are warships."

Omas interrupted, looking at his chrono. "I don't think

this takes us any farther forward. I have a delegation from the Corporate Sector Authority coming to see me soon." He jerked his thumb over his shoulder at the protest still going on below, which had turned ugly now as far as Jacen could see. CSF officers had waded in with batons, and the telltale cloud of white gas from a recently fired dispersal canister drifted on the air, clearing a space as protesters scattered. "Don't be surprised if we see the planetary allegiances going on down there reflected on the blockade line."

Jacen took the unspoken instruction to leave, and Niathal followed him. As Niathal peeled off to go to her state office, Luke caught Jacen's arm—just a brief touch, nothing more. But Jacen sensed him flinch as if he'd had an electric shock.

"Have you got five minutes, Jacen?" Luke indicated a side room.

Jacen smiled. "Ah, we all fall into corporate euphemisms fast, don't we?"

"Sorry?"

"It's code for 'Come in here and let me read you the riot act,' isn't it?"

"It's code for 'We want to talk to you about Ben, in private.' "

Jacen inclined his head politely and suppressed his detectable feelings further so that he presented quiet bewilderment to Luke and Mara. The doors of the side room closed behind them.

"Where *is* Ben?" Luke asked.

"Captain Shevu is keeping an eye on him at the barracks."

Mara spoke for the first time. She'd been uncharacteristically silent in Omas's office. It was a sure sign something was wrong, because Mara always had a view, even if it didn't match Luke's—*especially* if it didn't match Luke's.

"Jacen, Luke's worried about Ben going on these raids with you."

"He's perfectly safe. Safer than when you sent him to attack Centerpoint with me."

"Actually, it's not his physical well-being that concerns me the most," said Luke. "I'm worried that instead of being taught to use his Force skills for good, he's using them to bust down doors and round up civilians."

"It all depends on your definition of *good,* doesn't it?"

"I want Ben to go to the academy and get himself straightened out for a while."

"Normally I'd say that's your decision to make as his father, but he's a Jedi, and he has a job to do at which he's actually very good—identifying threats."

"He's thirteen years old, for goodness' sake."

"And you thought that was old enough to send him on a commando raid. I hate to question your logic, Uncle, but this isn't making sense to me." *Go on, say it. Tell me that you think I'm turning to the dark side. That's what you think, isn't it? Let's have it out in the open. Accuse me.* "He isn't using violence. Why is it okay for Jaina, Zekk, and me to fly combat missions that end in the deaths of other pilots, but it's not all right for Ben to find terrorists and help arrest them?"

Luke pinched the bridge of his nose. Mara's face was ashen; she looked drawn and strained.

Jacen decided to make his move. He could carry on without Ben as his apprentice, but sooner or later he would need one, and Ben was progressing by leaps and bounds. He *liked* the boy; he wanted to see him make the most of his potential. "I don't want to put you on the spot, Mara, but do you agree with this?"

"I think we need to talk this through with Ben," she said carefully. "He's settled down well, and I think we need to discuss this when we're not so tired and irritable."

"Actually, no," said Luke. "I think there's something that needs to be said right now. Jacen, you need to know that Lumiya is on Coruscant. You know who Lumiya is, don't you?"

It took all of Jacen's control to maintain his façade of ignorance and use the past tense, relegating her to history. "Yes. She was a Dark Jedi."

"She's back. She's here. I had terrible Force dreams about a hooded figure threatening us all, and then I felt her somewhere near."

Look patient, as if you're humoring him. "What's this got to do with Ben?"

"I don't know yet. But I feel it has *everything* to do with Ben. Don't put it past Lumiya to engineer events to serve her purposes."

"Okay." Jacen feigned a half smile as if embarrassed. "I'll be on my guard."

Luke appeared slightly deflated, as if he had heard his own words repeated back to him and had second thoughts about them. "When Ben's finished whatever he's doing today, ask him to come and see me. He's not answering his comlink."

There was no point having a confrontation. Ben wouldn't listen to Luke, and Jacen could sense that Mara wouldn't, either. "Whatever Ben wants, I'll go along with it," he said.

Jacen left and walked out to the turbolift lobby. He was torn between returning to the blockade and concentrating on his security role, but the latter was clearly more urgent. Outside, the protest had been broken up and CSF assault ships were loading handcuffed men and women who had been arrested. The situation was going to get worse before it got better. It was time to get back to the GAG headquarters and have Shevu brief him on progress with the detainees and especially the bounty hunter they had picked up.

There was one other urgent task, though. He opened his comlink and keyed in the code on his secure link.

"Lumiya," he said. "I need to talk to you."

GALACTIC ALLIANCE GUARD HQ, QUADRANT A-89, GALACTIC CITY.

More rioting had broken out in one of the commercial zones, and a couple of the GAG intelligence officers were poring over images being relayed back to them via helmet cams worn by CSF riot squads. Ben watched them for a while, trying to learn how they recognized faces and tracked the movements of what they called "persons of interest" around the city. When a Jedi relied on his Force-senses, he never learned how to do the thinking that regular people had to do to solve problems. Jacen always reminded him about that, telling him not to let his brain rust just because he had Force powers.

"Are we doing riot control now?" asked Ben.

One officer turned to him, but his eyes were still on the screen. "That's CSF's problem. What we're looking for are faces we might know from the last job." The intel officers were ex–CSF Anti-Terrorist Unit. He pointed to a figure masked by the press of bodies. "I think we've got an old buddy here who we could never quite nail on explosives charges."

They seemed pleased. Ben looked forward to accompanying them when they *turned his place over*, as they put it. It was interesting to learn how many terrorists had pretty basic criminal backgrounds; Ben's impression of them as fanatical people with a political cause wasn't the whole picture. It seemed that a whole range of people ended up getting involved, and for all kinds of reasons. He was learning more every hour.

"Ben?" Shevu leaned around the open doors. "Colonel Solo's back. Report to him in the cell block."

"Yes, sir." Ben found himself marching down to the cell block, which happened to be the fastest and most dignified way to move without breaking into a run. He found Jacen with Captain Girdun, having one of those hissed close-quarters conversations that showed they were angry with each other. The words *results* and *unacceptable* drifted toward him. Jacen stopped and motioned Ben forward with a crooked finger; Girdun was clearly dismissed for the time being.

"I saw the news," said Ben. "Nice shooting."

"Shooting's never *nice*." Then Jacen switched from annoyed to benign in an instant. "But sometimes necessary. Look, your parents want to see you. Will you do the diplomatic thing and visit them?"

"Dad's mad at me, isn't he?"

"What makes you say that?"

"He always is. I never do things right for him."

"He's worried about you, and he needs some reassurance that I'm not teaching you bad ways." Jacen put his hand on Ben's shoulder. "He'd rather I wasn't teaching you at all, but your mother is okay with it. In the end, I can't make him or you do anything, but for what it's worth, try not to have a fight with him."

Ben heard the meaning clearly enough: he'd be sent to the academy. He couldn't face that now. He might have a lot to learn, but he felt he'd passed the point where he could go back to lightsaber drill and meditation. He'd done *real* work, made a real difference, and he knew he would have no patience with theory again.

Perhaps Jacen could teach him more diplomacy. It seemed to be almost as handy as Force-listening and disguising your presence, two other things that Ben badly wanted to learn.

"Okay," he said, filled with dread. "I'll visit tonight."

"Now let's see what Ailyn Habuur has to say for herself."

The bounty hunter had been in custody for nearly a week, and this was the first time Ben had seen her since Shevu had questioned her. She hadn't been a glamorous woman to start with, but she looked terrible now; Girdun didn't appear to have taken good care of her in Shevu's absence. There were bruises on her face. She was leaning forward, arms braced on the table, breathing with some effort.

"I really need to know who you were sent to kill," said Jacen, reasonable and earnest. He sat down at the other side of the table and indicated to Ben to take a seat near the doors. "Was it Chief Omas?"

"I'm just a debt collector." Habuur wasn't quite as defiant as she had been a few days earlier, but she wasn't cracking, either. "Don't let the blasters fool you."

"You were carrying enough hardware to take out a platoon. You were with a known Corellian agent, so I know which government is paying you."

"Like I said, debt collection . . . it's a competitive business."

"If you've come to Coruscant, you're looking for a high-value Alliance target."

"You've got all you're getting out of me. Can I call a lawyer now?"

Suddenly Habuur's head slammed down on the table without warning. Ben flinched at the loud crack. Jacen hadn't lifted a finger. Habuur pulled herself upright again, blood trickling down her chin. She looked more surprised than hurt, although she appeared to have broken a tooth.

"Nice trick, Jedi boy."

"I've got plenty of those."

"I'll bet."

"Let's try again. Was Omas your target? And who else is working with you?"

Ben still didn't believe what he'd seen. He believed it the

next moment when Jacen used the Force to crack her head on the table again.

"Jacen . . . ," said Ben. This wasn't right. And it wasn't Jacen. "Jacen, should you—"

"Later." Jacen glanced back at Ben, startled, as if he'd suddenly remembered he was in the room. "Go and wait outside."

Ben realized he should have waited a long way from the interrogation room where he couldn't hear anything, but he felt he had to stay close, as if distancing himself too much would have somehow allowed Jacen to do worse things than he was already doing. *So he hurts people. I was pleased that he shot down an enemy fighter, but that guy's dead. So why do I feel bad when I see him hurt someone?* Ben took out his lightsaber and stared at the hilt, trying not to listen to the interrogation. *This is a weapon.* He'd been trained to use it to defend himself, but he also knew that it was a blade packed with enough pure energy to slice off someone's head or cut clean through armor.

He'd never killed anyone.

What was a lightsaber for, then, if you couldn't face the fact that it killed people? He tried to think of Jacen as using a weapon—his Force powers—to defend the Galactic Alliance against people like Ailyn Habuur, but all he could feel was that Jacen, a man he respected more than his own father, was hurting a woman who couldn't defend herself.

He heard things he knew no kid should have heard. But still he couldn't walk away. He sat there for an hour, then two, staring at his hands, hearing the raised voices, then the thuds and occasional cries of pain, and then only Jacen's voice repeating the same question over and over again: *Who sent you, and who were you sent to kill?*

Ben couldn't bear it. *Jacen, you have to stop.*

Girdun and Shevu appeared at the double doors at the

end of the corridor and took one look at Ben before walking briskly to the interrogation room.

"Jacen's in there," Ben said weakly.

"Oh, boy." Shevu nudged Girdun. "Come on, we can't let this go on."

"He's the commander."

" 'Dun, you moron, he's going to kill her. That's not how we do things."

"It was how *we* did things."

"Really? Not on *my* kriffing watch." Shevu appeared to have lost his cool. Ben watched, not wanting to stop them because he knew deep down that he should have stopped Jacen somehow. Shevu overrode the lock and Ben tried hard not to look inside the cell. "*Medic!* Get a medic, someone."

Jacen snapped at Shevu to get out, but Girdun bundled in behind him and the two officers laid Habuur flat on the floor and tried to revive her mouth-to-mouth. Ben watched as they took turns pumping her chest, hand on fist, checking her breathing and pressing fingers on her throat to try to find a pulse. Jacen stood back.

"Where's the kriffing medic?" Shevu demanded.

Girdun felt her neck, then her wrist. "No pulse."

"Ben, *call the medic.*"

Girdun shook his head. "Too late. She's gone."

Ben stared in horror. Habuur looked terrible. He'd never seen a dead person before, not like that, not with his own cousin standing over her as if it was just a little inconvenient for her to die before she'd answered his questions.

"What were you *thinking,* sir? We can't handle prisoners like this. You've got to report it. If you don't—"

"I've entered people's minds before and they've always been fine afterward," said Jacen. He seemed surprised that his Force technique had caused so much damage to Habuur, but not sorry. Ben noted that. Ben was forgotten in the brief panic, invisible once again to adults having a fight. "We *have* to know who she was working with."

Shevu stood his ground. He didn't seem in awe of Jacen at all. "You should have left this to me, sir."

"Time is critical in assassination attempts. They could be out there *now*."

"I know that, and I also know that you don't let prisoners die during questioning. I have to report this."

"You report it, then, Captain, but right now I have to find out who she was after, and my only lead is some woman called Mirta Gev."

"There's the Corellian agent, sir," Girdun said, straightening up. "He doesn't know who Habuur was after, only that Corellian Intelligence told him to give her a safe house and provide weapons."

"Some agent, if he yielded that much."

"I'm very persuasive, sir," said Girdun.

Shevu rounded on him. "We don't want another dead prisoner."

Jacen looked through Shevu as if he weren't there. "Get working on him, Girdun, just in case."

I have to do something. Ben couldn't bear to think of someone else dying like that woman had. He had an idea: work through the information again, just like the ex-CSF men had told him. It was stupid, because Jacen was smart enough to have spotted anything useful, and the World Brain's network of Ferals—enslaved spies—knew plenty. If his Force powers couldn't shake the information out of Habuur, then Ben stood little chance of doing any better. But he decided to use the tricks that ordinary people had to when sorting through information.

"Can I see the datapad, please?" Ben fought to stay calm. He had moved from disbelief to shock. He didn't know why Jacen had done what he did, but he had to have a reason. It had to be that Ben just didn't understand it yet. He had to stay calm. But he wanted to run back home to his mother and—yes, his father.

You can't keep doing that. It's not a game. You've grown up now. You can't do the things you do and then run home when it gets scary.

Jacen handed him the datapad, suddenly all reason and concern. "You sure you're all right, Ben?"

"I—I just never saw a dead body like that before."

"It's okay. You want to go home? I mean home to your mom. It's okay if you want to."

"I'm okay."

Ben took the datapad and retreated to the nearest empty room. It was the cleaning droid's station. He settled down on an upturned bucket and tried to look through the data in a sensible and rational way, but it was hard when you'd seen your hero do something terrible.

There. He'd dared think it. Jacen wasn't perfect.

He flicked through the images in the datapad, hundreds of them, and they were all pictures of vessels just as Shevu had said. He had to scroll through them a number of times before the idea that was nagging away at the back of his mind suddenly became clear and he spotted what was in a lot of the pictures: not every one, but most of them. Sometimes it was just a detail, and sometimes it was almost half the ship, but it was the same class of ship.

It was a YT-1300, an old Corellian transport model that was still a common sight around the Core Worlds. They ran forever. Uncle Han's *Falcon* seemed ready to run for eternity. Ben had a flash of insight.

Ben trotted down the corridor and approached Jacen cautiously, hoping that he was right—and hoping that the information might save the Corellian agent from Girdun.

"She was after Uncle Han, Jacen." Ben handed back the datapad. "That's the ship they were doing surveillance on.

It's in more than half of the images. They thought he was still here. She was looking for the *Falcon*."

Jacen shut his eyes for a moment and swallowed. "I assumed she was in the right place. I assumed, Ben. That's a lesson for all of us—never *assume* anything." He concentrated, eyes closed, holding the datapad in his hands as if he was visioning something in the Force. "She didn't feel focused on Dad, either."

I thought you could do anything in the Force, Jacen. Why did you miss that? What blinded you to it?

Jacen opened his eyes again, looking as surprised by the oversight as Ben was.

"You're right, Ben. I feel it. Well done. So this Mirta Gev might be connected. The woman who's been trying to contact her." He fumbled for his comlink, uncharacteristically shaken. "I can tell Dad we've got one of the assassins Thrackan sent after him. Now all he has to do is watch out for this Mirta Gev."

Jacen hugged Ben with genuine relief. Ben could feel it wash over him. Shevu came out of the cell and gave Jacen a completely blank look that Ben could tell didn't fit at all with what he was feeling, but Jacen was too tied up with calling Uncle Han to take any notice.

Ben knew what Shevu felt, and he felt a little of it, too.

Sometimes you have to do things you don't like and kill people because you absolutely have to.

Jacen was right. But it was still horrible, and he didn't think he would ever find it easy. He left Jacen to his call and decided it was time he faced his father.

CORELLIAN ASSEMBLY BUILDING, CORONET: OFFICE OF THE CORELLIAN PRESIDENT.

It was an awfully big office, and offices that big usually meant small-minded men occupied them. Fett remained dismayed by the ease with which the likes of Thrackan Sal-Solo bounced back from disgrace and even treason charges to hold high office again and again. The galaxy was a moral cesspit. It got what it deserved.

"You beat the blockade, then," said Sal-Solo, leaning back in his splendid apocia chair and holding court in front of the opposition party representatives. He smiled charmingly at Mirta, who didn't smile back. She didn't charm easy, that girl. "How would you like to work for Corellia?"

"Specify your requirements regarding Centerpoint."

"The Alliance sabotaged it but I'm embarking on repairs and it should be fully operational in a few months." Sal-Solo used the pronoun *I* a great deal. Fett listened in vain for the word *we*. "Once it's online, the Alliance won't be able to make us disarm. *Ever.*"

"Then why do you need Mandalorian assistance?"

"Repair crews haven't been able to land on the station."

"Try recruiting on Nar Shaddaa. You need smugglers to run blockades, not soldiers."

"But when we do land crews, we'll need someone to defend the station. It's the Alliance's prime target."

Fett didn't care for Sal-Solo. He didn't care much for anybody, but this man was what Mandalorians called a *hut'uun,* a coward, the lowest form of life. Mirta had taught Fett a few choice *Mando'a* words against his will, but it seemed to be a fine language to curse in. "How much?"

Sal-Solo's eyes flickered as if he had to look to his colleagues for some mandate but was deeply unhappy about being seen to do so. "One million credits."

"Per man."

"Yes."

"Per month."

"That's a ludicrous figure."

"It's dangerous work."

"I was thinking of a flat fee. It's only going to take a few months."

"We don't do open-ended contracts. Months turn into years on construction projects." Fett really didn't want the work at all, and he knew the commandos didn't. "And no start date yet. Call me again when you put a crew on the station and we'll talk. But it's a million per man per month. If we do it, we'll be bearing the brunt of Alliance attacks and they'll probably cream your fleet first, which means we'll be defending your interests on our own."

"How many men?"

"That thing's bigger than the Death Star. A hundred at least."

Fett watched Sal-Solo's face fall ever so slightly. Two of the other three politicians looked grim. The third, Gejjen, seemed perfectly happy. Maybe he knew something about Corellia's budget that they didn't.

"I hope you didn't mind my dragging you all this way for such a brief meeting," said Sal-Solo, still directing the occasional insincere smile at Mirta. "I'll be in touch."

"Always worth visiting Corellia," said Fett. *Yes, always worth getting inside a government building and recording the layout and weak points. Always worth finding out what your opposition buddies want. Always worth tracking down Han Solo and waiting for my daughter to show up.* "I might stay a few days."

The politicians laughed politely.

But not for too long. I need to track down Ko Sai's research and that clone with the gloves.

"Got time to show me around?" Fett asked. He figured he might as well record what he could. "Nice place you've got here."

"Shall I do the honors, Mr. President?" Gejjen offered.

That didn't surprise Fett one bit. He beckoned to Mirta, who walked behind them with sullen disinterest as Gejjen showed Fett the fine state rooms—everything paneled in gilded apocia—and the offices. All the while, Fett's helmet and gauntlet sensors built up a handy plan of the whole Corellian government complex, even the parts that Gejjen didn't show him. That penetrating terahertz radar had been a *very* good investment.

The grounds were beautiful, too. Fett assessed the height of the walls and the nature of the security patrols while admiring a row of trees with pale blue blossoms whose crowns were trimmed into cubes.

"I realize you're a busy man, Fett," said Gejjen. "But may I make a proposal?"

Fett kept an eye on Mirta, who also seemed to be checking out the layout of the complex judging by her eye movements. Her Mandalorian father should have taught her the value of a helmet. "Wondered when you'd get around to it."

"Our President doesn't enjoy our full confidence. Would you remove him for us?"

I thought you'd never ask. "How permanent?"

"Totally."

"Who's paying?"

"All the opposition parties. Together, we can outvote the Centerpoint Party, and without Sal-Solo they can be quite sensible."

Fett considered the contract. Timing was the issue. He wanted to pursue Ko Sai's data as soon as he could. *And after you see your daughter. Last time you saw her, she was too young to talk.* "When?"

Gejjen handed him a tiny datachip. "When can you complete the task?"

"When I've checked you out." Fett tapped the datapad link on his forearm. Yes, the chip was valid. "One million."

"You people deal in round numbers."

"I could make it three million. Yes or no?"

"Yes." Gejjen tapped his own datapad. "There. Half a million up front. Balance on completion. Can we offer you a room? A speeder back to your ship?"

"It's a nice day," said Fett. "I'll walk."

Mirta matched his pace along the broad boulevard leading from the government building. She had been commendably silent. She was agitated, though: she sneaked a glance at her comlink.

Ailyn still hasn't responded to her. "Say it," said Fett.

"What?"

"That I should stay out of Corellian politics."

"For a million? If you don't do it, I will. Sal-Solo gives me the creeps." She slipped the comlink back into her pocket. "When are you going to do it?"

"More pressing business first."

"What's more pressing than a million credits?"

Okay, girl. It's time.

They were on Corellia, and so was Han Solo. Solo was the bait for Ailyn. And one thing Fett could always do was find Han Solo. He could almost think like the man now.

And he was getting tired of a kid thinking she could fool him.

"I'm here to find Han Solo." He could see her expression even though he wasn't looking directly at her; the helmet display could take an image from a wide angle. She blinked rapidly, but the rest of her face was utterly composed. "Because Ailyn's looking for him, and when I find him, I find her."

Fett didn't break his stride. His joints ached and he wanted to sit down and rest, but he kept walking.

"So I don't get paid," she said.

"I'll pay you because I said I would. But don't play me for a fool."

She shrugged unconvincingly. "So shoot me."

"You've still got your uses."

"How'd you know Solo is here?"

"I know Solo. And my sources are better than anyone's. He's here."

"Ah," said Mirta. "Ah."

She'd get paid. Felt couldn't understand what was worrying her. He always kept his word.

chapter sixteen

Mom, Dad, please don't ignore this message. We've caught Thrackan's assassin because she made the mistake of looking for you on Coruscant. Her name is Ailyn Habuur and she isn't going to trouble you any longer. But she might have a female accomplice called Mirta Gev. That's all we know right now, but stay sharp. Mom, Dad, I love you. Please try to understand what I have to do.

        —Jacen Solo, encrypted comlink message to his parents

JACEN SOLO'S APARTMENT, ROTUNDA ZONE.

"I came as soon as you called."

Lumiya was waiting for Jacen, looking for all the world like an insurance saleswoman with a taste for couture clothes rather than a Sith adept.

"It's been a difficult day," he said, and grabbed his hold-all to pack a few things. That much of him was still Jedi: he owned almost nothing except the kit he needed as a pilot and a colonel. "I need to discuss some things with you."

"I could sense your anxiety."

"Luke is aware you're here. He doesn't know where you are exactly, but he feels some echo of your presence."

"You mustn't be alarmed for me. But we have to accelerate your progress toward full Sith knowledge in case Luke finds me and prevents me guiding you."

"Are there techniques to teach me?"

"Not techniques so much as *awareness.*" Lumiya spread her arms and the room was suddenly both calm and charged with dark energy. It felt to Jacen like sitting in the company of dangerous men in a beautifully appointed office, a veneer of grace over savagery. "Technique is for apprentices. You know all you need to know. It's within you. You only have to become aware of it and embrace it."

"You make it sound like pain."

"It *will* be."

"You know what it is, then. Tell me. Or warn me."

"No, I don't. I can only guide you toward awareness and encourage you to step across the line. It's a different rite of passage for everyone who attempts it, because it's about breaking their own personal limits."

The room was soothing, an illusion that was almost a meditation chamber. The light around them was deep blue and distorted as if filtered through water. Jacen thought it was ironic that her power and energy could only find an expression in illusion, useful though that was. She could change nothing permanently.

He could, though.

"I killed someone today."

"You're a soldier. Soldiers have to be prepared to kill."

"I killed in a way I didn't think I ever could. I'm appalled at what I can do. I don't enjoy this."

"If you enjoyed it, Jacen, you would not be the one destined to become the Sith Lord."

The logic was both seductive and horribly true. He was now on a path of pain; he had to do what he dreaded most. That was why it was becoming easier each day, although it hurt so much. It was *right*. It was exactly what Vergere had taught him when he was in the hands of the Yuuzhan Vong. He had to suffer to become the "glorious creature," the shadowmoth who had to struggle and panic to emerge strong from its cocoon, to be changed—into what he needed to be. *A Sith Lord.*

There had never been an easy path destined for him to fulfill this prophecy. Vergere had known that. She had *known*, even then.

"You knew my grandfather. Did he have to pass this way?"

"Yes."

"Then why didn't he succeed?"

"He wanted power. Not political power, but the power to shape reality for those he loved. It diverted him and it flawed a great man. He also lacked your breadth of education in the Force. That's my belief."

Jacen thought of his astonishing lapse in failing to spot the simple truth that Ailyn Habuur had been sent to assassinate his parents, not Cal Omas. It was the kind of thing he should have been able to divine from the Force through a number of techniques, and yet he hadn't. He hadn't seen it coming.

I've been blinded by personal preoccupations, by family ties. That must be the reason.

"Sith lore teaches that we shouldn't avoid love and anger," said Jacen. "How can that be true if it was Anakin Skywalker's flaw?"

"You don't *have* to avoid it. You have to be able to pass through it and draw strength from it. Look at the Jedi now, all with their families and children, all fettered by them. Luke's little wife ignores what she feels about you and looks for any excuse not to believe it because she puts her son's happiness first. Luke doesn't confront you because he fears alienating his wife and son. If they faced those fears and drew on them, they might well thwart our plans. But they won't."

Jacen knew she was right. "And Ben?"

"Ben will make a fine apprentice for you once he stops being defined by his father's name and resenting it. He's already on the path." Lumiya lowered her voice as if afraid to make the next suggestion. "You must become a Jedi Master."

"Isn't that what I *don't* need?"

"Ben needs you to be his Master so he knows he's made the break from his father's control. The Jedi council needs to show it values what you do for the Galactic Alliance if it doesn't want to be seen as undermining government, because there are always those who will use that against them." She paused. "Besides, why *shouldn't* you be a Master? If what you've learned over the last few years doesn't qualify you, what does?"

"Lumiya, if I lobby for this, it's going to look like a weakness they can exploit."

"You don't have to, not yet. Let me shape opinion."

"Influence the Jedi council? Oh, come on now . . ."

"You have allies there apart from Mara Skywalker. Let me plant the idea in a few places—outside the council, of course. Ideas take on a life of their own."

"Like Admiral Niathal's."

"She already had ambitions. She merely needed not to be ashamed of being bold."

"Is there anyone else you've influenced to act?"

"I haven't had to influence much. This is a galaxy in search of order."

Jacen needed to ground himself again. Attractive as Lumiya's reassurance was, he trusted his own feelings most. He would go back to the Jedi Temple tonight and see for himself—hear for himself, *feel* for himself—what was true and not true.

And he would risk time-walking to his grandfather's day again. He had to face it.

"You'll be ready to understand what your final passage must be very soon," said Lumiya. "I know it."

"So do I," said Jacen, and clapped his hands together once in a burst of Force energy. The beautiful blue underwater illusion vanished like shattering ice on a pond, and he was back in his sparse apartment again with a bag to pack and a war to win.

SKYWALKERS' APARTMENT, GALACTIC CITY.

The apartment doors opened before Ben could press the entry key. Luke felt him coming, a turmoil of emotions in the Force.

Is that what I do to him? Is he that scared of me? I think I preferred it when he just ignored everything I said.

"No need to look so scared," said Mara. She took Ben's shoulder and steered him into the living room. "We're just worried about you, that's all."

She sat him down and gave Luke a warning glance as he walked into the room to attempt to pull his son back from the brink. Ben was still wearing his black fatigues, which were actually no more than the standard special forces uniform but somehow looked a great deal more sinister. He certainly didn't look like a Jedi.

You tried to force him to be what he didn't want to be. This is what happens.

"Are you okay, Ben?"

"Yes, Dad."

"I'm not angry with you." Luke pulled up a chair. "But we see the kind of things Jacen is doing lately and we wonder if you should be part of it."

Ben just stared back at him. Luke had seen that expression on children's faces before, but they had been refugees, children from war zones who'd had to grow up faster than was reasonable or decent and who never went back to being carefree kids again.

"I'm learning a lot," said Ben.

"I'm not sure if it's the kind of thing you ought to be learning."

"Why, sir?"

Ben had always called him Dad. Suddenly he had become *sir.* Luke caught Mara's reaction, a little mental flinch beneath the reassuring smile that seemed set in place.

"It's violent, Ben."

Ben swallowed. "Jedi do violent things. We fly star-fighters with laser cannons. We use lightsabers. How many people did you kill when you fought the Empire?"

Luke was stopped in his tracks. He found himself forming the words, "But they were all . . ."

All what? All evil? All people who didn't matter? Most of them had just been swept up on the wrong side—soldiers, pilots, people in uniform, even civilians, just cannon fodder—and it had been easy to see the good guys and the bad guys back then. Now he couldn't put his hand on his heart and say that he truly believed he had killed only evil men.

"I killed a lot of people," Luke said.

"And so did I," said Mara pointedly. "And I was on the other side."

Ben looked as if he was measuring his words. He'd acquired a little gesture—a habit of looking down at the floor, chin on his chest, and pursing his lips—that was pure Jacen. "But I haven't killed anyone. I know I've saved a couple of lives in the last few weeks. Just because it looks bad, it doesn't mean it *is* bad."

Luke had no answer. His gut instinct and his recurring dream of the hooded figure had not changed one bit, but his intellect was saying something else. It was whispering *hypocrite*. Mara caught his eye.

"Ben, how would you feel if I asked you to go to the academy for a while?" Luke asked.

"Now?"

Luke had expected an instant eruption of indignation, not merely a one-word question. "I'd thought that, yes."

Ben looked down again, an echo of Jacen. "Are you going to make me?"

"I'd rather not."

"Then I'd like to carry on with the Guard a bit longer.

There are things I need to understand before I study again. Things I can't work out at any academy."

Luke's Force-sense told him that Ben meant *exactly* what he was saying. He wasn't playing for time or manipulating the situation.

"Okay, son," said Luke. "We'll talk about it later."

They had a meal together, their first as a family in what seemed like a long time, and for a while Luke could almost pretend that nothing was wrong. Ben got ready to leave.

"Could we spend some more time together when all this stuff has calmed down?" Ben asked.

It was the assumption of an innocent child that the situation would resolve itself in a time scale he could imagine: days, weeks, months. Luke wished it were true.

"That would be great," he said.

When Ben had gone, Luke waited for Mara's reaction. It took a while.

"Now look me in the eye and tell me that Jacen is corrupting Ben," she said.

"I never used that word."

"You didn't tell him you wanted him to stay away from Jacen, either."

"Okay, Ben has grown up very, very fast."

"And he's making sense. Nobody's ever asked that question before."

"What?"

"How we can justify what we've both done in the past. It's easy for me to look back and know what I did, but what about you? Ben's got a point."

"You're remarkably tolerant these days," said Luke.

"I'm a lot older now, and I'm more concerned about my own family than the galaxy's problems," said Mara. "It knocks the edges off a girl."

For a moment Luke wanted to believe that he'd overreacted to Ben and Jacen, and that Mara was right. His mind said that what he saw on the surface was true. But his gut said otherwise. It said that what he saw in his dreams was more real than his waking hours.

"I'm glad we could sort that without having a fight and Ben storming out," said Mara.

Everyone believed what they wanted to believe. If it hadn't been for that echo of Lumiya—and he couldn't have been mistaken about that—then Luke would have believed it, too.

KEBEN PARK, CORONET, CORELLIA.

He's going to have your wife and kids killed. That's all you need to know.

Han Solo wasn't one of life's natural-born killers and he knew it. For all the times he had fantasized about killing his cousin Thrackan, from his teenage years right up to a few hours ago, he now wondered if he could actually aim a blaster at him in cold blood and pull the trigger.

The man deserved it. But that didn't mean Han could do it.

He was going to try, though. Jacen might have intercepted Ailyn Habuur, but there was another potential assassin out there, this woman Gev. And if there wasn't, then Thrackan would just keep coming anyway, year after year. He'd blighted Han's life for as long as he could remember.

The plans that Gejjen had given Han were the public kind that any Corellian taxpayer could examine in the public library. The itinerary of the President could change, too, so that meant Han would have to do some serious recce work before he felt confident about taking a shot. For a scumbag, Thrackan didn't seem to surround himself with the massive security typical of most paranoid tin-pot despots. But maybe he thought people loved him as much as he loved himself, and seeing as he had been voted back into power yet again after a career of sleaze and treachery that would have embarrassed a Hutt, he was probably right.

Han found a good vantage point in the park overlooking the government offices and Presidential residence. The G.O., as Corellians now called it, was one large complex, a tasteful little village of colonnaded low-rise buildings in the classical style set in well-kept formal gardens. The park around it sloped gently up an artificial hill that provided a safe gradient for board-skiing when it snowed. Han found a seat at the top of the hill and took out some breadsticks to chew on, every bit the regular man having his lunch in the park. He even fed the gliders that gathered to watch for crumbs.

I'll need to get him in a confined space. I'm not a sniper.

Han wondered if he should have put aside old feuds and hired Fett after all. At least he'd have known the job would be done right.

Okay, he has his regular weekly press conference today, which means he has to be in his office either side of that slot. A nice grenade launcher. No, he'll have staff with him. It's not their fault their boss is a scumbag.

Whatever it was going to take to eliminate Thrackan, it was going to have to be close, personal, and point-blank. And then there was the matter of getting out again.

Han broke off a piece of breadstick and rubbed it into crumbs between his fingers before scattering it on the grass in front of him for the gliders. They descended in a flurry of wings. *Okay, maybe take him while he's in transit: but that means a sniper shot, too. Or a drive-by. Or a . . . no, this is all going to suck in innocent bystanders. I have to get him alone in his office.*

If Fett did this for a living, then Han understood why he wasn't the sociable type.

The gliders flew up in a sudden spiral like one animal and left him staring at a snowfall of crumbs. He finished the bread and walked down the hill, working out when the next public guided tour of the building would give him a chance to get inside and look around.

If I take Thrackan out and get clear of the building, will Gejjen turn me in?

No, this bounty-hunting business wasn't like fighting as a soldier at all. Han strolled through an avenue of trees that led past a construction site for a new sports stadium; work had ceased. There must have been plenty of places that were running short of materials now that the traffic between the orbital factories and the surface had been largely stopped. When Thrackan was done and dusted, he thought, that could be his new job. He was great at running blockades. He could teach these kids a thing or two.

Han was just wondering if Leia had managed to get hold of Jaina by comlink when he heard a sharp hiss like a jet and felt as if someone had run up behind him.

He spun around and was face-to-face with a Mandalorian visor that he knew far, far too well.

"Long time no see," said Boba Fett, and Han went for his blaster without thinking.

Fett brought Han down with a forearm smash under the chin and sent him sprawling. Han tasted blood in his mouth and his head rang so hard he was convinced the sound was real and external. Getting hit by an armor plate was a lot harder to bounce back from than a bare fist.

He shook his head to clear it and propped himself up on one arm. He was now staring into the sawn-off muzzle of an EE-3 blaster.

"Every time I see you, that thing's had a few more gizmos added," said Han.

"You make it sound like I pursue you."

"You do."

"Your glory days are long over, Solo." Fett encouraged him to get up with a jab from his boot, blaster still aimed, and picked up Han's where it had fallen. "Nobody's put a decent price on your head for years. I'm after someone who matters."

"Funny, I thought you'd taken Thrackan's contract."

"Shut up and give your ego a rest."

"What are you here for, then?"

"Sightseeing. You want an audience?" Fett shoved him into the chaos of bricks and durasteel that lay where it had been left and toward a site office, one of those temporary cabins that could get up and walk to a new position on their own repulsors. Fett bypassed the lock with something on his gauntlet and waved Han inside with his blaster.

"So what can I do for you?" Han asked, settling on a chair covered in permacrete dust. "Need another carbonite caf table for your Hutt buddies?"

"If I'd wanted you dead, I could have looked the other way when you had that spot of trouble with the Vong." He still hadn't holstered his blaster. "I need you as bait."

"Terrific."

"No risk to you."

"It's the word *bait* I tend to notice."

"My daughter accepted Sal-Solo's contract on your family. I shouldn't get in a fellow bounty hunter's way, but I need to find her and you're the best way to do it."

"Can't you call her like a regular father?"

"She's sworn to kill me."

"She's a chip off the old block for sure."

"So I'm going to sit on you until she shows up. You can do it the easy way or the hard way."

"I remember your *easy* way."

"You can do it *dead* if that's easier."

"You must want to see her real bad."

Fett perched in the edge of a desk between Han and the

door, one boot on the seat of a chair. He glanced toward the door as if waiting for someone to show up. Han calculated whether he'd be able to charge whoever came in and make a run for it before Fett fired, and he realized he couldn't. Then he heard rapid footsteps—too light for a man—and wondered if Leia was going to rescue him again. Her timing was usually great.

But it wasn't Leia.

A very young girl with short brown hair, cold dark eyes, and an earnest, humorless face ducked into the cabin and closed the doors. She was wearing armor; not a full set like Fett, but armor all the same, and that meant another bounty hunter.

"She's still not answering," said the girl. She stared at a comlink in her hand as if willing it to melt. "If she doesn't know Solo's here, she won't come."

"You don't usually work in a team." Han was getting worried now. Fett doing things that were out of character scared him more than the alternative. "You need hired help these days?"

"This isn't a team," said Fett. "This is an arrangement."

"Okay, if I help you out, what's in it for me?"

"What do you want?"

It was worth a try. Fett was the master at this kind of thing. "Help me assassinate Thrackan Sal-Solo."

Han could have sworn Fett actually sighed. "Too late. One of his political rivals already booked me to do the job."

"Well, that's just great. Who? No, let me guess. Nice young man with dark hair? Dur Gejjen?"

"Might be."

"He gave me a few tips on how to whack Thrackan, too. Looks like he isn't sure I can do the job."

The girl stared at Han as if she'd have to clean him off her boots sooner or later. "*Can* you?"

"It's not as easy as it looks, is it?"

"It is," said Fett. "Now, about my daughter."

Han thought of Jacen's comlink message, which he had read several times but not answered. Bounty hunting was a small world. He took a chance. "Is your daughter called Mirta Gev by any chance?"

The girl's hand went to her blaster as she fixed Han with an unblinking stare. "*I'm* Mirta Gev, Granddad."

So this was it. It *was* Fett's double cross after all. He was working for Thrackan. Han decided to go for it. "Just my kriffing luck—"

He exploded out of the chair, head down, and charged the girl. She was a lot heavier than she looked and that armor plate on her chest really hurt, but nowhere near as much as the stock of Fett's blaster against the back of his head. He fell on all fours and the girl brought her knee up in his face just as he pitched forward. That hurt a lot, too.

"Solo, you forgot a few things since we last met." Fett hauled him to his feet and shoved him back in the chair. "Don't take on two bounty hunters at once. Now, how come you know Mirta's name?"

"Why should I tell you?"

"Because I'm going to kill your sleazebag cousin. Show some gratitude."

Fett meant it. Han couldn't work out what was going on, except he wasn't dead yet, and Fett wasn't the man to indulge in long gloating speeches before he claimed his bounty.

"My son says they picked up a hitwoman in Galactic City called Ailyn Habuur and that—"

"*Osik!*" the girl hissed. Her face was instantly white and shocked.

"—and if you're Mirta Gev, then you two might both be after me and my family."

"I'm not hunting you, old man." Mirta was upset: that

was clear. "I was looking for Habuur." She took a breath. "I recovered some items for her."

"She must owe you plenty, judging by the look on your face," said Han. He looked at Fett, but a man with a helmet betrayed nothing. He was just very still.

"Ailyn's my daughter," he said quietly, in a voice that sounded as if it belonged to a totally different man. "Real name's Ailyn Vel. So your son's got her, has he? I think I know the kind of job he does."

"She was cannoned up and ready to kill me, pal."

"I need to see her."

"Well, let me go and sort Thrackan and I'll put in a good word for you with my boy. Maybe he can arrange visiting rights."

"And maybe I'll tell your boy that he can pick his dad up in a body bag if he lays a finger on my daughter. Maybe I'll finish the job for her, because you're no use to me as bait now."

Mirta was staring at Fett as if she wasn't sure what was happening. He'd certainly said something she wasn't expecting.

"Looks like we're *all* stuck," said Han.

"No Sal-Solo, no contract on you."

"Well, that's a win-win situation if ever I heard one."

"Get your Jedi son to release my daughter."

"If you let me have a crack at Thrackan," Han said.

"I'm not splitting the bounty."

"Just let me split his skull."

"Deal."

"Okay. Deal."

Fett held out his hand to Mirta for her communicator. "Call your wife and tell her you've run into an old friend and that you're going to be late getting home."

"She'll sense there's something wrong. She's got this Jedi danger sense."

Mirta Gev raised her blaster and held it to Han's head. "Can she bring people back from the dead, too?"

"Okay, point taken. I'll make it convincing."

"Move it," said Fett. "Don't want to miss the President's news conference. It's going to be his last."

chapter seventeen

Jedi are seldom public figures and rarely risk controversy. But Jacen Solo's extraordinary record in recent weeks—leading the war on terrorism, even flying combat missions in the Corellian blockade— marks him out as a man less concerned with the esoteric spiritual preoccupations of the Jedi order than with doing his bit for the Galactic Alliance. He's the perfect counter to those critics who demand to know what taxpayers get for their credits from the Jedi order. But, ironically, he still has almost no status within the order itself. He doesn't even hold the rank of Master.
—HNE's *Week in Focus*, political commentary

THE JEDI TEMPLE, CORUSCANT: 2215 HOURS.

Even the Jedi council had its business hours. Jacen always found that amusingly unspiritual. He could enter the Temple at any time, but he needed to be in the council chamber itself, and that required a little deception.

It also needed a massive Force effort from him, because he had to make himself invisible at the same time as shutting down his Force presence and flow-walking back in time. He doubted he could hold all three elements together for long. He had to enter the chamber, listen and look into the past, and leave no trace of his visit.

Jacen, back in his traditional robes again, wandered around the Temple archives room browsing the datafiles until there were only a few Jedi left reading at the terminals. They would hardly notice that he had disappeared among the shelves and not walked past them again. Concentrating on his body as if it were a shell, he used the Fallanassi skills he had learned to project an illusion of being nothing, of having transparency, and drew his Force presence so far inside himself that he vanished to all Jedi senses. A woman lost in thought while she stared unblinking at a screen took no notice of him when he sat down next to her. Now he could walk into the council chamber itself, unseen—he hoped.

The Temple, whose rebuilding had struck Jacen as a needlessly expensive statement of power, was now working in his favor. He had marshaled the courage to look into his grandfather's past again, and this was the place he needed to be to do that, on the site of the very chamber where Anakin Skywalker's fate had been decided. He slipped through the doors and stood within the circle.

The inlaid marble floor was said to be identical to the one on which Anakin would have walked. Jacen stared at it, wondering if he might see the floor through Anakin's eyes. He had felt his emotions. And he had seen through his own mother's eyes; it might be possible to do both at once.

Listen.

He felt the soles of his boots become part of the marble as if he were growing into the polished slabs like a tree. His head buzzed. Snatches of conversation washed over him until—like picking out the sound of his own name in the crowded, noisy room—he heard *Anakin.*

He felt as if he were braking on a long slide down a hillside. He felt the jolt in his mind, and the sounds in his head became clear. He didn't recognize the voices, but he could easily work out who some of them were.

"*So is he the Chosen One?*"

"*Qui-Gon believes so.*"

"*But what do we believe?*"

"*Skywalker is exceptional, but he's past the age of being trained.*"

"*But is he the Chosen One?*"

"*If he is, then training him becomes irrelevant. He will either find his path or not.*"

"*A logical argument you make, but direction is needed.*"

"Then who will train him? Who can train him? Perhaps nobody can take on the challenge."

"But if we do not train him, regret it we may."

"And none of us can take on a Padawan, and we have more pressing problems to deal with."

The last speaker was Mace Windu. Jacen recognized him from recordings, and his heart sank at how easily they had abdicated responsibility for Anakin considering that he was the Chosen One. Jacen sought parallels, more clues to where Anakin had gone astray on his path to show him the pitfalls to avoid.

This time he needed to see what had happened. He shut out the time-echoes of the voices again and slipped into a corner where he could hide if his Force-invisibility failed as he flow-walked into the past. The effort of sustaining all the techniques at once was making him sweat.

His head pounded and the image of the chamber blurred for a moment, but then it cleared and Jacen felt as if he had woken with a start. The Council sat in their ceremonial seats or appeared as holograms, and one of those present in the flesh was Anakin Skywalker, now a young man, and a very angry one. He was standing in the center of the chamber in a black cloak, arguing with Mace Windu and Yoda.

"Allow this appointment lightly, the Council does not. Disturbing is this move by Chancellor Palpatine."

"You are on this Council, but we do not grant you the rank of Master."

"What? How can you do this? This is outrageous! It's unfair! I'm more powerful than any of you. How can you be on the Council and not be a Master?"

"Take a seat, young Skywalker . . ."

Jacen watched for a few moments and both pitied and understood Anakin, and knew that he wasn't following his path, not at all. *Poor Grandfather: gifted, exceptional, dismissed, barely tolerated, largely untrained, abandoned.* No wonder he resorted to crazed, desperate violence. Had he received the training that Jacen had, if he had been able to perfect his powers and experience all uses of the Force—even those the Jedi academy shied away from teaching—then the galaxy might have been a very different place.

I'm the second chance.

The Jedi Council dropped the ball. And they paid for it.

Jacen had accepted his Sith destiny, but now he understood not only that it *had* to happen, but *why*. Everything in his life had led to this point because Anakin Skywalker's destiny had been subverted and warped by well-meaning but blind Masters, sending him off on a tangent to do a flawed Palpatine's bidding instead of realizing his own full power.

I'm more powerful than any of you.

It was a boy's expression of anger, but it was true. And, as history repeated itself because it had no other choice, Jacen was more powerful than any of them except Luke. And he was growing closer to Luke's strength by the day.

When he achieved Sith Mastery, he would surpass him. He hadn't yet thought how Luke and he would coexist after that point had been reached. For a brief and tempting moment Jacen considered Force-walking into the future, as he had done before, but his instinct said to leave it alone for the time being.

Power. Power was a vulgar, personal word, shot through with ambition and petty vanity. Becoming a Master was a necessary political step in achieving the ultimate order. Beyond that, it had no meaning, but Jacen would still seek it—purely as a tool.

He could maintain the time flow and invisibility no longer. He snapped out of the past and held his presence in check long enough to leave the chamber and pause farther down the corridor to catch his breath. A maintenance worker appeared from a storeroom and stared at him, surprised.

"Good night, friend," said Jacen, and mind-rubbed the memory from the man as he left.

SLAVE I, CORONET CITY SPACEPORT, CORELLIA.

"How do you breathe in this thing?" Han grumbled.

"Try shaving in it," said Fett.

Han Solo adjusted the Mandalorian helmet with both hands. The spare armor that Fett kept stowed in *Slave I* as a backup was just what he needed to get them right up close to Sal-Solo. The body plates weren't fitted, so they attached to Han's clothing without too much trouble, but the helmet was a custom job and he was struggling with it.

"I can't see," said Han.

Fett activated the HUD.

"Whoa . . . what *is* all this?" Han put his hand on the bulkhead as if he were falling over. "I can't balance—"

"Data display and three-hundred-sixty-degree vision." Fett shut down most of the feeds and the blink-operated controls so that Han saw only what he'd see with his own eyes. It would take him days to get used to the 360-degree field of view without crashing into things. And there was no point confusing him with the rest of the display that rolled and flashed constantly inside the visor. If he blinked at the wrong time he'd either blow himself up or wipe billions off the stock exchange. He only needed to be able to *see*. "Never worn a helmet?"

"Yeah, but I don't recall stormtrooper helmets being quite this fancy inside."

"That's cheapskate defense procurement for you. Try walking."

Han paced up and down the narrow galley in *Slave I*'s cargo section, turning his head left and right. Mirta watched him with cold indifference. But Fett had come to know her well enough to realize that the news of Ailyn's capture had knocked her sideways. Maybe there was a really big bounty hanging on that necklace.

"Okay, I can do this," said Han. "I can see well enough to blow his brains out. So explain this to me."

"We just walk in and ask to see your cousin. Then we get him on his own. Then we kill him."

"Then *I* kill him."

"I agreed to kill him and I will." Fett didn't have time for this. "You can take a shot, too, if it makes you feel better."

"And he's just going to let you stroll in?"

"Yes. He asked for some Mandalorian assistance. I said we'd think about it. I've thought."

"What assistance?"

"Defending Centerpoint."

"But you took a contract to assassinate him," Han said.

"Gejjen made me an offer and I accepted. I didn't accept Sal-Solo's. I'm a man of my word. A contract is a contract."

"So we pose as your Mandalorian henchmen."

"He'll want to see us."

"How do we find our way around? It's a maze in those offices."

"Already done the recce and recorded the data." Fett projected the holoplans of the Presidential offices onto the cargo bay bulkhead. The penetrating radar had built up a detailed three-dimensional walk-through image. "Getting in is easy. Next two stages are getting him on his own, because I don't like collateral damage, and getting out again."

"Can't Gejjen help you do that?"

"How's he going to explain a dead President?"

Mirta looked up. "He'll blame it on the Alliance, because that's very handy for him."

"She's good," said Han.

"Either way, we get out fast. I suggest we exit via this route to his bunker, which leads to *this* tunnel that comes out in the park." Fett traced the illuminated transparent chart with the finger of his glove and considered how bad a firefight might get if they were trapped in that tunnel. Mirta only had a small bag with her: that meant not much kit—not *enough* kit. "You want a helmet, girl?"

"No."

"You'd better be fast, then."

Han stared at the chart, seeming more comfortable within the confines of the helmet. "Thrackan's got a bunker?"

"Civil emergency center. He's got direct access from his office."

"You don't trust him either."

"He has no honor. But that's irrelevant."

"I don't think I'll ever understand you, Fett. You kill without blinking and yet you're taking an awfully big risk to find a daughter who's tried to vape you."

"He's all heart really," said Mirta.

"I must be, because you're still alive," said Fett.

Han eased off the helmet and took a deep breath. "And I never had you down for a double act, either."

"We're not," said Fett. But Mirta had her uses, and she never gave up. He liked that.

"He needs me for ballast," Mirta said sourly.

Fett checked the charge on his blaster. The adrenaline rush of carrying out a job on the spur of the moment like this had made him forget his illness for a while, and it left him with a pleasant sense of omnipotence. The pain in his stomach and joints—a persistent tenderness that sometimes peaked into a sensation almost like toothache—was always there now but it could still be pushed into the background without his reaching for painkillers. He wondered how long he'd be able to do that.

Nobody ever survived the Sarlacc, but I did. If you want something badly enough, push yourself hard enough, you can do anything.

Even survive against all odds.

Even restore an empire.

Even heal a rift with your only child.

Yes, he could do anything. He was Boba Fett. He was what his father had made of him, and that was a survivor.

"*Oya,*" said Mirta.

"What's that mean?" Fett asked.

Mirta checked her blaster. "Let's go hunting."

GALACTIC ALLIANCE SHIP **OCEAN**, ALLIANCE THIRD FLEET, CORELLIAN EXCLUSION ZONE: DAY SIX OF THE BLOCKADE.

"Well, *that's* going to make life interesting for Omas," said the hologram of Admiral Niathal.

A line of vessels—some freighters, some individual warships, some starfighters, and some whose profiles didn't match anything Jacen had ever seen—had formed up in line astern a Corellian cruiser, *Bloodstripe,* at 50 kilometers from the Alliance picket blockading Centerpoint Station. The ops room crew of *Ocean* watched the unmoving ranks of lights on the scanner; the commander of the Third Fleet, Admiral Makin—another Mon Cal with an unflinching approach to warfare—stood beside the hologram of Niathal with his arms folded.

"I make that one Bonadan *Cutlass*-class . . . a couple of Fondorian fighters . . . and that's an Atzerri freighter," said the weapons officer. "They've been on station for the past hour."

Makin turned to face the image of Niathal. "May I have conformation of orders, ma'am?"

"Maintain the exclusion zone and deny access to *all* vessels," said Niathal. "And if an Alliance vessel is fired upon or otherwise threatened, then you may engage."

"Colonel Solo," said Makin. "Put Rogue Squadron on alert five."

"Awaiting your orders, sir."

"Let's see who blinks first this time."

Jacen made his way to the hangar deck where a row of XJ7s stood with canopies open and ground technicians running preflight checks. Jaina and Zekk were leaning against a bulkhead talking in hushed voices, and Jacen chose not to use his Force-senses to listen.

Jaina greeted him with a hostile stare and a definite sense of pushing him away in the Force. "Good of you to drop in, Colonel Solo," she said. His instant commission had really irked her. "Who's minding the shop back at Secret Police HQ?"

Zekk greeted him with a nod. "Now, Jaina. We have a guest star. Be nice."

Jacen chose not to take offense. "Mission brief, people." *It doesn't matter. Pass beyond it.* "Some other fleets have fronted up on behalf of Corellia, some of them civilian vessels. They're lined up, daring us to take a crack at them."

"We've been watching the scanner repeater." Zekk nodded in the direction of the bulkhead, where a large holoscreen mirrored the tactical information from the ops room. "This is going to get tricky. One wrong move—"

"—and we suck in a lot more enemies." Jaina completed Zekk's sentence, a holdover from their time as Joiners. "Do we have orders to engage?"

Jacen could feel her mistrust and sorrow. It was a real weakness in a squadron if pilots had lost faith in their commander, but it wasn't his military judgment she would question. It was his morality.

"Only if fired upon or placed under serious threat."

"I'm glad we're clear," said Jaina. She picked up her helmet from the bench, lowered it into place, and fastened the chin strap. "Are we just going to buzz them, or try to drive them back?"

"Right now none of them are in the exclusion zone. If that changes, we turn them back."

"I love a standoff," said Zekk. "Are they letting supplies through to the shipyard orbiters yet?"

"No. Total exclusion zone means total exclusion zone."

"Even in Corellian space."

"Not our problem, Zekk. The legality of that is for the Senate to argue later. Okay, time to turn and burn."

Three XJ7s didn't constitute a major confrontation, but Jacen was clear how far he would allow things to proceed. This was another game that could easily escalate. The three starfighters came up well under the line of assorted vessels and looped around to take up positions between them and the Alliance picket ships ringing Centerpoint on the outer side. Moving to intercept across that huge curve of alloy and durasteel meant a fast dash, but that was what XJ7s were made for.

Jacen watched his cockpit console display for movement. He reached out carefully in the Force to test Jaina's state of mind: She was, as ever, focused on the job at hand, but a persistent ripple of hostility—there was no other word for it—tinted the slow eddies.

He felt a strong shove back against him in his mind.

Get out of my head. He could grasp the meaning as clearly as if she could share words with him. *Back off.*

Jacen wondered if Zekk could sense this, too. He didn't attempt to test Zekk's feelings, but he shared an emotion with both of them instead: he sent *calm.*

They waited, silent, watching their screens.

One of the Fondorian fighters eased out of the line and past *Bloodstripe.* It advanced slowly toward Zekk, who was holding position on Jacen's starboard wing.

"Steady," said Zekk.

The Fondorian slowed almost to a halt and then suddenly peeled off to one side. Zekk matched its maneuver instantly and harried it for ten kilometers at close range until it swung around and headed back to the line behind *Bloodstripe*. Now all the vessels pulled forward to form a line level with the Corellian cruiser.

"They're going to go for it, Zekk," said Jaina.

"Yeah, I feel it . . ."

"Here we go."

Jacen said nothing. *Bloodstripe* didn't move, but the ships to either side of her did. They spread farther apart, and for a moment he wondered if they were simply going to try to draw Alliance ships away.

But the picket ships at their back had orders to remain on station. Their laser cannons could very nearly cover the whole run of Centerpoint's access bays, and Jacen was sure *Bloodstripe*'s commander knew that. This was a gesture. This was provocation.

"Hold steady," said Jacen.

Then the Atzerri freighter picked up speed and came straight at them. Jacen had it on visual now. It was an old ship and lightly armed to deter piracy. But it was picking up speed.

"He's coming right at you, Jaina," said Jacen. "If he hasn't changed his mind at two kilometers, give him a reminder who's in charge here."

"I'll buzz him."

"You be careful," said Zekk.

The freighter showed no signs of slowing. It was coming at the picket head-on, and its course appeared to be about to take it between the XJ7s and within three klicks of one of the Alliance destroyers. The only question was when it was prudent to block its path.

"That's close enough," said Jaina, and edged forward to

skim over the freighter's casing, nearly shaving its antennae. The freighter didn't waver.

"He needs another reminder," said Jacen, and set off after Jaina to block the freighter's path.

"Bonadan cruiser breaking on the far side." Zekk's voice was a whisper. "Leave that to me."

Resolute, one of the picket destroyers, cut in on the shared comlink. "Laser cannon targeted, Rogue Three, just in case he gets any ideas."

The cruiser was a legitimate target; it was an armed warship. The Atzerri freighter, though, needed more careful handling. Firing on a civilian vessel was a political risk, not a military one. Jacen set a head-on course for the freighter's long panel of viewports set across the width of its nose. Jaina had looped back and was making a second pass to block the ship.

"Blink . . . ," said Jacen.

The freighter held its course.

"Go on . . . blink."

They were on a collision course. It wasn't high speed, but in space even a low-velocity collision could be disastrous.

"Don't play this game with me, friend," Jacen said.

He could now see the figures moving on the freighter's brightly lit bridge. He was close enough to see the color of their overalls. *Not yet.* Red, blue, a few green; humans, all of them. *Not yet.*

Thirty seconds more on this course would smash him into their viewport.

Steady . . .

If he didn't pull up in twenty seconds, he'd be dead. He was no longer aware of Jaina, or Zekk, just the rust-streaked ship with its band of white light that now filled his field of view. He became a pilot again: not a Sith Lord-in-waiting, or a Jedi with all the knowledge of generations, but a pilot at one with his fighter.

Ten seconds . . .

Jacen surrendered himself to instinct. He jerked the controls and the XJ7 climbed high and fast just as the freighter made a last-second dip below the plane of collision. Jacen knew he had missed the hull by meters. When he reached the top of his climb he looked down and saw that the freighter's aft ports had opened: small laser cannons were trained on him. Not all ships had all their armament mounted forward; freighters expected sometimes to be chased in pirate-infested space lanes.

"Got you," said Jaina. "Jacen, I'm targeting their cannons—"

There was a staccato exchange of white and blue streams of fire beneath Jacen as he arced down into a dive and came up behind Jaina. The freighter fired again, and then Jaina was clear of the stream and coming about for a second time. Jacen watched one cannon mounting shatter and break into a shower of shimmering particles, and then the other.

The freighter slowed and began to turn. Jacen sent a one-word message to Jaina in the Force: *Fire.*

He felt her resist him.

He switched his comlink to Jaina's channel alone. "Finish it, Jaina."

"I've disabled both aft cannons. He's heading back."

"He opened fire. Do it."

"Jacen, the ship's damaged and he's retreating. I can't continue the attack."

"You know the rules of engagement."

"I won't do it. It's a civilian vessel and right now he isn't presenting a threat—"

"That's an order."

"It's outside the ROE."

"It's legitimate. I repeat, take him out."

"Colonel Solo, I'm refusing that order."

Jaina cut her comlink and swung back to the picket line. Jacen seethed. She was crazy. Civilian or not, the freighter had opened fire. Retreating or not, it still had functioning cannons. It was a clear threat.

Jacen lined up the icons on his console and sent a spread of five torpedoes into the freighter.

"Jacen, what the—"

That was all Jacen heard from Zekk. A ball of gold light plumed from the starboard side of the freighter's hull, then another and another, and suddenly half its flank was in fragments and hitting ships alongside. The line flanking *Bloodstripe* broke and scattered. On his screen, Jacen saw the pinpoint images of small lifeboat ships disgorging from the cruiser to go to the freighter's aid: half of the ship had blown away.

"Rogue squadron, bang out *now*." *Resolute*'s commander cut in. "We're opening fire. Get out of there."

Jacen dropped immediately under *Resolute*'s arc of fire and headed back to *Ocean,* picking up Zekk and Jaina as he went. He could feel Jaina's fury as she trailed him in silence.

Zekk opened the comlink. "Anyone want to tell me what happened back there? Jaina, why did you break off?"

Jacen answered for her.

"Colonel Solo refused a direct order," he said carefully. It broke his heart, but he had no choice. *My sister. I've really lost her now. Why won't she see what has to be done?* "She's now suspended from duty."

PRESIDENTIAL OFFICES, CORONET, CORELLIA: 1830 HOURS.

"Do take a seat," said Thrackan Sal-Solo. "I wasn't expecting to see you back so soon."

The doors to the office were open, and a couple of Sal-

Solo's staff sat at desks in the adjoining room. Fett perched on the edge of one of the fine brocade chairs and motioned to Han to sit down. Mirta simply stood to one side, arms folded. Sal-Solo didn't seem to expect to be introduced to Fett's new associate.

He'd meet him soon enough.

"Did you have second thoughts?" asked Sal-Solo.

"Just seeking clarification," Fett said. He noted the position of the door that led to the emergency bunker. "Can we discuss this in private?"

"How private?"

"Is this room soundproofed?"

"Yes."

"Then shut the doors and give your staff the rest of the evening off."

For a man like Sal-Solo it wasn't an unusual request. Fett was counting on it; he hadn't been paid to silence any bystanders. The doors closed, and they were as alone with Sal-Solo as they were ever likely to be.

There was a panel of comlinks on the desk. Fett was pretty sure one of them would be a priority button to summon help. He was also sure that Sal-Solo carried more than one blaster.

Don't make a hash of this, Solo. Clean shot. I should never have let you tag along, but you're my ticket to my daughter now.

"Tell me again what you have in mind for Centerpoint."

His HUD showed nobody in adjoining offices. Beyond two rooms, the penetrating radar became less efficient. *Why will I give anything to see Ailyn now after fifty years? Amazing, the power that mortality has over your mind.* He rested his hand on his blaster rifle. He always carried it rather than sling it across his shoulder; Sal-Solo seemed unperturbed by it.

Mirta didn't take her eyes off him. Han was silent but visibly tense. Fett could see it in his shoulders.

"Once Corellian forces breach the blockade, we can resupply the station with technical equipment and reactivate it. We'd hope to position your men inside to stop further sabotage. It's a huge station to make intruder-proof."

Okay, watch me carefully . . .

"Like I said, one million credits per man per month."

Fett counted the seconds. Han twitched.

"Cheaper than an army, I suppose," Thrackan said at last.

"A hundred Mandalorians *is* an army," said Fett.

And then Han leapt from the edge of his seat and slammed across Sal-Solo's desk, knocking him flat into the wall and upending his chair. Sal-Solo pulled a hold-out blaster from his jacket while they struggled, and Han head-butted him. The blaster went flying.

You moron. You blew it. Han pulled off his helmet with one hand and had his cousin by the throat.

"You scum—"

Fett launched himself across the desk and pinned Sal-Solo down. "Just *do* it, Solo," he snapped. "Kill him. Or I will. It's not sport."

Mirta covered the doors with her blaster. At least the girl knew what she was doing.

"I've waited years for this, Fett."

"Make it fast, then." Fett assumed Han wanted to make his cousin suffer before he killed him, which was sloppy, but then family feuds were always too emotionally charged. "Remember what you agreed."

Han had a stranglehold on Sal-Solo's throat. The man's eyes bulged. "Never again, you scumbag." He dug his fingers into the skin. "You *never* mess with me or my family again."

Sal-Solo found a defiant, strangled voice. "You think the bounty hunter I decoyed you all with on Coruscant is the only one hunting you?"

"What do you mean?" Fett grabbed Han's wrist to stop him choking Sal-Solo before he answered. "What decoy?"

"I tipped them off about her. Too busy following her to worry about the others. They're coming, Han, and you don't know how many. You'll never be able to sleep soundly again."

Ailyn. You set up Ailyn. You used my little girl.

"Back off, Solo—he's mine," said Fett, and held the blaster to Sal-Solo's head.

"No, he's *mine*," said Mirta, and rolled across the desk to fire three bolts into Sal-Solo's forehead.

It was a split second of total silence and then two seconds of chaos. Han was cursing that he'd been cheated; Fett put two rounds into Sal-Solo to be sure he'd finished him. *And that's for Ailyn, too.*

"You should learn to shoot first, Solo," said Fett. "Now get down that passage fast. Run for it."

"But *I wanted to take him*—for all he's done to me."

"Go on, then—put a few more through him. Have your vengeance. Then shut up and get moving."

The room might have been soundproofed, but the sound of blasterfire could penetrate a long way. Fett wasn't sure Han could do it. But Sal-Solo was dead already and Han no longer had to face shooting him in cold blood. At last he fired. Fett grabbed him and shoved him through the door to the passage as Mirta retrieved the spare helmet.

She was a smart kid—even if she had taken a shot she shouldn't have.

They ran down a single flight of steps and into a long passage lit by yellow emergency lamps. Fett's helmet sensors picked up movement two rooms above; running feet. Someone was coming. He took the full set of security blades out of his pocket and set their interference pattern to block all comlinks except his own. This wasn't the time to let anyone call for backup.

Then he shoved Han ahead of him and forced him to run. The fool was still staring back at his cousin's body.

"Now my side of the bargain, Solo," Fett panted as they ran. "My daughter. I have to see my daughter."

chapter eighteen

*The Galactic Alliance is in turmoil this morning as more planets
withdraw representatives from the Senate in protest at fighting in
the Corellian blockade. Atzerri's ambassador to the Alliance de-
scribed the destruction of one of its freighters as "an act of war."
Chief of State Cal Omas told HNE earlier that the exclusion zone
would remain in place until Corellia disarmed and that the Atzerri
vessel had opened fire after repeated warnings.*

*There has been no response from Corellia's President Thrackan
Sal-Solo.*

—HNE morning bulletin

LUMIYA'S APARTMENT,
SAFE HOUSE, GALACTIC CITY.

Jacen rubbed his eyes, trying to erase the dream he'd had on
the flight back from Corellia and that was still vivid in his
mind.

He hoped it was a dream and not a vision. As the turbolift climbed to the three hundredth floor of the apartment
tower, he tried to shake the image from his mind and failed.
In the dream, he was staring at his hands, lightsaber clutched
in one, sobbing.

*That's what you dream of when you send your own sister
for court-martial. Deal with it.*

No, he wasn't proud of what he'd done to Jaina, but it
had to be done. He let the misery wash over him and didn't
flinch from it as he opened the doors of Lumiya's safe house
apartment with a brief focus of Force energy. Inside was a
surprisingly comfortable suite of rooms scattered with objects that he thought he recognized from her asteroid habitat. She'd been back home to pick up a few things. Somehow
he hadn't thought of her as needing material trappings.

"You're very upset," she said, emerging from another room. Jacen was startled by her appearance. "Your grandfather found me drifting in my starfighter after Luke Skywalker had fired on it and left me for dead. Vader saved me. So my life is inextricably linked with your family. Did you know that?"

"You see that as destiny."

"*Inevitability.* Which is why you should stop feeling guilty about your sister."

"I'm having bad dreams about it. I wasn't expecting that."

"Do you want them to stop?"

"No. They are what they are. I have to embrace them."

"Be sure you know the fine line between dreams and visions. They may tell you what you need to know—what I can't tell you."

"Which is?"

"How you progress from where you are now to what you have to become. I can guide you in techniques, but their application must come from you."

Jacen sat down, careful not to touch any artifacts in case one had a use he didn't yet know. "This is what I don't understand. I spent over five years perfecting my use of the Force, learning techniques from all species—not just the Jedi way. What more can there be? Where does a Jedi adept end and a Sith begin? You see, I never really believed that it was purely a line between good and evil. Some days I can't even define those terms."

"It's *acceptance*," said Lumiya. "The willingness to surrender to what the Force asks of you. To stop denying it by rationalizing denial as self-discipline and avoidance of powerful emotions."

"That sounds as if I should simply do the first thing that comes into my mind."

"You already know you should."

"Why am I different from my grandfather, then? The more I do, the more I feel I'm doing exactly as he did. Was it really only his preoccupation with his wife that stopped him achieving order?"

"He started his training too late and was still inexperienced when he was exploited by a man who wanted power. You're a mature man with a lifetime's training and nobody is using you. You won't make the same mistakes."

"It can't be that easy."

"It won't be. It'll be painful."

"More painful than turning on your own sister?"

"Oh, yes . . ."

"That's my destiny?"

"That's the price you pay for bringing order to the galaxy. This is your *sacrifice*. Now do you see why weak men like Palpatine saw only *power*, and why they were defeated?" Lumiya's hypnotic voice was almost disembodied. Jacen watched her mouth, and had no sense of being spoken to by another living being. It was an oracle, a dispassionate revelation. "There is *nothing* in it for you as Jacen Solo."

He'd lied. There *were* worse things already than suspending Jaina. There was the look on Ben Skywalker's face when he saw Ailyn Habuur's body. He'd gone too far invading the woman's mind; she hadn't been up to the physical strain. He wouldn't make that mistake again. But Ben's trust in him had taken a body blow. The boy still didn't understand that doing things his father's way led to an endless cycle of war and chaos. Luke wouldn't face the need to take extreme measures. Luke wanted to feel *good* about himself.

That was attachment.

"How do you feel when you see Luke Skywalker now?" he asked.

"I feel nothing," said Lumiya. "I only remember."

"What should I do next?"

"I can't tell you. Deal with what troubles you most."

"My apprentice, Ben. He's wavering."

"Don't seek his approval."

"I don't."

"Don't set an example and hope that he'll follow it. Put him in a position where he has to discover the truth for himself."

She was, as she had been at Bimmiel, painfully right. Ben had to learn what his father never had—that there were necessary evils.

And there was no better place to learn that than in the Galactic Alliance Guard.

EMERGENCY MANAGEMENT COMPLEX UNDER KEBEN PARK, CORONET, CORELLIA.

For a couple of old guys, Han thought, he and Fett were keeping up with the girl pretty well. Then he realized that the underground passage sloped downhill.

The corridor that ran from Sal-Solo's Presidential suite to the emergency management bunker stretched for a kilometer under Keben Park. All they had to do was keep running. What happened after that Han had no idea, but it wasn't the first time he'd run headlong and trusted to his instincts and luck.

Besides, he was with Boba Fett. That man could escape anything.

"Where does this come out?" Han panted.

"Leads into the bunker complex. Then two exits out of there to the surface."

"Two?"

"Two exits are always better than one."

A long way behind—but not far enough—pounding boots echoed. They were now in a dimly lit tunnel with a hard, tiled floor and large stenciled signs every few meters with helpful messages like GOT YOUR RESPIRATOR? and SECURE ALL DOORS—YOUR LIFE MAY DEPEND ON IT.

"We're not going to run into company ahead, are we?"

"Not unless we're really unlucky." Fett pounded along behind Mirta. "They only staff these places in civil emergencies."

"Like a war?"

"Yeah, that'd qualify . . ."

Mirta had her hand blaster held at shoulder level as she sprinted, a testimony to the benefits of unfashionably flat boots and sensible clothing. "They'll have a *real* emergency on their hands if they get in the way."

Doors ahead of them opened automatically and bright lights flared into life on the ceiling. If this was all set to trigger when staff entered, then they had to be alone down here, or the lights would already be on.

Alone except for the guards chasing them, of course. *Had* to be guards. Han was tuned to the sound of guards' boots. Fett came to a halt as they entered a lobby with six doors leading from it. Three were marked TRAFFIC CONTROL, WATER & POWER, and CENTRAL E.M. CELL. The other three weren't marked at all.

"Which one?" said Han.

Mirta stepped behind them, blaster sweeping an arc, while Fett froze. Han realized he was focusing on some display in his helmet's HUD.

"Two exits via the main E.M. room here, but if we get stuck there are hatches to accessible vents from the other rooms." He indicated his jet pack. "I don't do vents."

"E.M. room here we come—"

The running footsteps behind were much, much louder

now. A bolt of blasterfire spattered plaster ten meters from them. Fett broke off and extended his left arm, sending a long jet of flame down the passage behind them that made a loud *ha-whompp* sound and blew billows of gray smoke back at them. Curses and shouts rang down the passage. The flamethrower had slowed their pursuers but not stopped them.

"Move it," said Fett.

The E.M. door didn't open automatically. Mirta hit the heel of her hand on the square red key at the side a couple of times and the doors parted. They were already halfway into the room before Han realized that it was full of desks in rows with comlinks on each of them. The walls were covered completely in holomaps and display boards; the place was ready to handle whatever disaster hit Coronet when the warning sirens sounded.

A bewildered man in a white shirt looked up from a datapad and stared at them.

"You're early," he said. "We weren't due to staff the—oh, boy—"

A blue streak of blasterfire spat from the doorway and Han, Fett, and Mirta fired at the same time, driving back two security guards. The man ducked, arms covering his head, while they traded blaster bolts and Fett shot out the doors' lock panel, sending the two halves slamming shut.

"Health and safety inspection," said Han as the terrified man flattened himself against the wall. "Keep up the good work."

They burst through one of two doors marked EMERGENCY EXIT and were back in a yellow-lit corridor again, running for their lives. It sloped uphill. Han really noticed that now. His thigh muscles screamed for a rest. Behind them, there was the sound of blaster bolts smashing through doors and the pounding of those boots again. The guards didn't give up easily.

"Your jet pack isn't going to be much use to you down here, pal," said Han.

Fett didn't break his pace. He got to the end of the passage and spun around, nearly knocking Han against the wall. Then he bent forward at ninety degrees to the ground, hunched his shoulders, and tapped at the panel on his left forearm.

"You reckon?" he said, breathless. "Mind the backwash, Solo."

A *shwoosh* of hot air and a blinding flash of yellow light nearly flattened Han as the small missile on Fett's jet pack skimmed the back of his helmet and shot down the corridor, trailing vapor. The explosion deafened him for a few seconds. Fett grabbed his shoulder and shoved him ahead.

"You know how much these MM-nines cost?" Fett grumbled.

Han's ears were ringing. "There's got to be safety regulations on that thing." But he could hear the thuds and cracks of falling rubble. They ran.

Ahead, a patch of light that was brighter than the yellow gloom of the tunnel kept Han running at an automatic, animal level. *Escape. Just escape. Worry about everything else later.* He'd expected Mirta to be halfway across the park by now, but she was standing by the exit doors, pumping blasterfire into them until they parted.

Cool evening air washed into the musty passage. The tunnel emerged in the slope of another artificial hill on the far side of the park.

"All clear," she said. "Go on, *run*."

Mirta didn't strike him as the type to care whether he lived or died. But, like Fett, she had her reasons for wanting him in one piece. Fett could have left them both stranded and escaped with his jet pack, but he didn't let Han out of his sight.

"Call your wife," said Fett. "Get her to pick us up. We can't run all over Coronet at this time of night. Too conspicuous."

They crouched in the cover of thick bushes near the highway, and for a second Han had one of those out-of-body views of himself in his mind that sometimes left him reeling. Three Mandalorian assassins, fully armored, hiding from the Corellian Security Force in a nice, normal park as a government coup began a kilometer away. He opened the comlink.

What am I doing here?

"Hi, honey," said Han. "Can you give us a lift?"

Leia's voice was, as usual, all resigned calm. "Who's *us?*"

"Some Mandalorian buddies I ran into."

"That's nice. I'm watching a lot of police activity from the apartment."

"Ah, that'd be Cousin Thrackan . . ."

"How is he?"

"Dead," said Han, his stomach torn between nausea and a lifetime's worth of relief. "Very, very dead."

GAG HEADQUARTERS, GALACTIC CITY, CORUSCANT.

"What happened to Barit Saiy?" Ben asked.

Shevu consulted the custody file and shook his head. "Not here. No record of transfer to CSF custody, either."

"But every prisoner should be logged in and out, right?"

"Right." Shevu stared at his datapad, lips compressed in a thin line. "I don't like prisoners who disappear." He managed a smile at Ben. "Maybe he was repatriated and nobody logged him out. We sent back a *lot* of Corellians in a hurry before the blockade."

"Yeah . . ."

"It's hard when you get personally involved," said Shevu quietly. "Best to stand clear and do everything by the book."

"Jacen doesn't."

"Colonel Solo is my commanding officer."

It wasn't an answer that made any sense on the surface, but Ben was learning fast: Shevu was saying that he wouldn't give an opinion on Jacen's behavior, whatever he thought of it. He was angry about Ailyn Habuur. Ben was distressed too. Jacen was all he wanted to be, and then suddenly he killed a prisoner—carelessly, not in anger, but she was still dead—and Ben wasn't sure he knew him as well as he'd thought he did.

Is this what I want to be?

"I understand," said Ben, and went off to the now empty gymnasium to practice his lightsaber skills with a remote as a target.

The small sphere danced and spun in the air as he swung and sliced, leaving a faint trail of light behind the blue blade with each stroke. When he became swept up in the movement and stopped concentrating, he always found himself on the edge of one perfect movement after another. It didn't feel like a series of actions; it felt like one, his first and last stroke, frozen and repeated over and over again. There came a point as he pursued the darting silver sphere when his mind was completely blank. Not just clear; *blank*.

And in those moments he saw things.

It was as if his conscious mind had stopped its relentless chatter and left a door wide open. Then his mind wasn't pure white light any longer but a detailed image with layers of data that he could understand intuitively but not *read*.

It stopped him dead in his tracks. The remote, responding to him, froze in midair.

Jacen was summoning him.

The remote presence of other Jedi was something he had

grown up with, the way other kids heard their parents calling them. But this was different. He was being summoned, not called. It was an order. He felt it.

He retrieved the remote and ran to find Jacen. He could locate him easily these days, as if Jacen had an overwhelming presence in the Force like a signpost when he wanted it. Sometimes, though, he disappeared completely. Ben *really* wanted to learn to do that, too.

Jacen was sitting in one of the administration offices, staring at a holomap on the wall with his hands cupped over his mouth and nose as if he was thinking about something that upset him.

"Jacen?"

"Ah, Ben. I wasn't expecting you to come so quickly. I hope I didn't interrupt anything."

Like I had any choice. But Jacen always treated him like an adult. "Just lightsaber drill."

"I'm looking at the areas we have to sweep now. We've got a running battle going on between Atzerri and Coruscanti in the lower levels, according to CSF, and the bomb disposal teams are investigating ten more suspicious packages. We deal with one problem, and another three spring up in its place."

"What did you want me for?"

Jacen indicated a chair and motioned Ben to sit down. "It's time I gave you more responsibility. We only grow when we're given the chance to."

Ben tried to imagine what extra responsibility he could be given. He had already gone on anti-terror operations and sabotaged weapons that could destroy whole worlds. It was hard to top that when you were thirteen.

"You can detect weapons and explosives. You're really good at it." Jacen jerked his thumb in the direction of the holomap on the wall. "Go on. See if you can sense anything by looking at the map."

Ben jumped up out of the chair and scanned the map. Like most holomaps of Galactic City, it was multilayered and he could peel away levels of each grid or dive deep into them by touching the light grid with his finger. He passed his hand above the surface to concentrate on the Force and found nothing.

Perhaps it wasn't on that section of the map. He tapped his finger against the far left of the display, and the map shifted west to take him farther from the Senate Building and toward the business districts. He found himself drawn to a quadrant a few kilometers southwest of the Senate, but he sensed nothing specific.

"In there somewhere."

"Good." Jacen stood right behind him and put his hand on his shoulder. Normally that was reassuring, but right then Ben had a sudden memory of Ailyn Habuur. "Go on."

"Something's about to happen." Ben felt he was being tested. "Do *you* feel it?"

"Yes, I do. And the World Brain's Ferals report activity there."

"What is it, then?"

"I want you to work this one out for yourself as part of your training. I'll be there to help you out if you need it, but I think it's time you learned to make decisions. I trust you."

For a few moments Ben was wildly excited at the trust Jacen was placing in him. Then he lapsed back into being torn between fear of failing and remembering Ailyn Habuur.

"Do you trust *me*, Ben?" Jacen asked suddenly.

"Of—of course I do."

"Tell me the truth."

Jacen could sense *everything*. Sometimes he seemed almost telepathic. Ben knew there was no point lying to him, and he didn't want to. He wanted answers.

"Okay, I don't understand how you could hurt that woman so badly," he said. "You're not a bad person. You don't like violence. It scares me, because I don't think I could ever do that and that means we're different, and I wanted to be just like you and now I'm not sure."

Jacen didn't look upset or offended. It was hard to tell how he had taken the admission.

"I can understand that," he said quietly. "And we all have to find out for ourselves how far we can go and what we're prepared to do. You won't know until you have to do it."

Ben wasn't sure that he understood, but he knew he had to go through with this. It couldn't be that different from what he'd been doing for the last couple of weeks. He knew what he could do—and what he wasn't prepared to do. He was certain of that.

New black GAG assault vessels—CSF ships in new livery— were waiting for them at the landing pad. Captain Shevu leaned out of the troop bay of the lead ship, hanging on one of the overhead straps with one arm.

"Quadrant H-Ninety's not secure yet," he told Jacen. "They've barricaded the skylane intersections with speeders."

Jacen jumped up into the bay and hauled Ben aboard. "Are they still in position?"

"CSF wants a bit of backup before they move. There seem to be a lot of Coruscanti involved."

Jacen frowned. "You sure?"

"Sure. Not every taxpayer here seems to agree with the Alliance line."

Ben pondered that as they rose into the air and banked left to head for H-90. It was an ordinary neighborhood as far as he knew: shops, bars, apartments, and a market, with a cosmopolitan population. He'd assumed that it was the non-Coruscanti section that was the source of the growing discord and danger that he'd detected by concentrating on the holomap. It had never occurred to him that the people he thought he was protecting would object to being protected.

Every day brought new revelations about the confusing adult world. Just when he thought he'd worked it out, he found he hadn't. Jacen and Shevu shouted a conversation above the noise of the drives that filled the open bay. Coruscant lay like a map beneath them, filtered slightly by haze.

"It started when CSF arrested someone for painting antigovernment slogans on the local Galactic City Authority offices, sir. There's a full riot squad deployed now."

"Any more incidents?"

Shevu paused and put his hand to his ear, concentrating on his comlink earpiece. "Twenty public order arrests. No serious casualties. Pretty quiet."

"Worse to come, though, Ben?" Jacen asked.

Ben nodded. The wind whipped the legs of his uniform. "Yes." Shevu simply looked at him with that intense stare that said he preferred hard facts to Force impressions. Confronted with that expression, Ben had his doubts, too.

"I think that's a safe bet any day of the week," said Shevu.

The assault ship swooped low over a skylane that was clogged with speeders of all sizes at each intersection. CSF vessels had formed up behind them at a careful distance; the focus of the activity was an apartment block, where a noisy protest was taking place. Someone had sprayed PEACE NOW and STOP KILLING CORELLIA on the awnings that covered sections of the walkways so that the message was visible from the air.

The crowd along the walkways looked like a complete cross section of species, and when the GAG ship dived lower to observe, it was met with jeers and obscene gestures. For a peace protest, it was getting pretty aggressive; Ben kept an eye out for blasters. The crowd seemed on that edge between simmering down and exploding that he was getting used to seeing. The ship lifted higher and hovered above the CSF line until a speeder bike rose to meet it. The sergeant astride it flipped up his visor as he drew level with the bay.

"Tip-off that they might be hoarding weapons somewhere. We're deciding whether to go in and search the area and risk a full-scale armed riot, or wait until they get bored and go home."

Jacen, Ben, and Shevu surveyed the scene from a safe height. "Want us to go in?" Jacen asked. "We don't have to worry about community relations like you do."

"Yeah, I heard that," the sergeant said warily. A chant rose up beneath them: *The—Empire's—back! The—Empire's—back!* "Not planning to deploy in white armor, are you? That'd *really* start them off."

"Very funny," said Shevu. He lowered his helmet into place, suddenly becoming anonymous behind the shiny black visor. "Okay, you want us to root out a few?"

Once Ben was physically close to the area, he could feel much more specific disturbances in the Force, little whirlpools of threatening darkness. He felt something else now. "It's *big* weapons."

"We were kind of hoping for *small* ones, but . . ."

Ben could feel a growing anxiety that was almost like itching deep in his ears, so deep that it nearly touched the back of his throat. He was close. He craned his neck and looked out as far as he could from the open bay, hanging on to the safety line.

"I know where they are," he said. He looked to Jacen to confirm his feeling. Jacen just looked at him, waiting. "What do you think?"

"What do *you* think?" asked Jacen. "Your call."

"It feels . . . really dangerous."

"So decide. Do we go in or not?"

Ben wavered. "If I'm wrong, we might start a full riot and people might get killed."

Shevu powered up his blaster. The faint whine cut through the rumbling voices and the throb of repulsors. "Ready when you are, sir."

"You have to make the decision, Ben," Jacen said. "You have to decide what you think is right based on the intelligence you have *now,* and then stand by your actions."

Ben hesitated. He wasn't sure now if Jacen would stop him if he thought he was mistaken. He had to make his move.

"That block *there,*" said Ben, pointing down at a stack of apartments over a scruffy restaurant. "Take us in."

Although Ben was sure—*almost* sure—that he could deal with blasterfire or missiles hurled at him, he was scared. The crowd below loomed larger, some turning and running away as the assault ships closed in, some rushing toward the vessels. At ten meters, Ben jumped, using the Force to stop him smashing into the walkway. People scattered. He heard Jacen thud down behind him and he didn't look back as he ran for the door of the restaurant. Black-suited GAG troopers passed him and secured the doorway, and Ben drew his lightsaber simply because he was operating on blind instinct now.

There was nobody in the restaurant. The tables were empty and he ran between them, heading for a door at the back. Behind him he heard shouting, screams, and blasterfire: he had to be right about this now. He stopped at the doors at the back, not sure whether to force them open, and saw that it was Shevu behind him, not Jacen, covering his back, blaster aimed.

I can't stop now.

Ben opened the doors with a Force push and stepped through, lightsaber held in both hands, and found himself in the kitchens, a jumble of durasteel racks, ovens, and sinks flanked by cupboards and storerooms. He concentrated, trying to feel for where people or arms might be hidden, and went instinctively toward a hinged door with a hand wheel on one side. He didn't sense a person, but he sensed something indefinably dangerous.

"You *have* to remember to wear an earpiece," Shevu whispered through his voice projector, and pointed to the hand wheel, indicating *get over on that side* by stabbing his finger. Then he made a circling motion.

Turn the hand wheel.

Ben held his lightsaber in his right hand and slowly wound the wheel with his left. The door hissed as a seal broke and a mist of chilled air tumbled out into the warm kitchen. Shevu held up two fingers, then one, and jerked his fist down.

Two, one—go.

Ben wrenched the door open and Shevu aimed inside. It was pitch black and the blaster's targeting spotlight punched into the darkness of a cold store, highlighting mist. Ben fumbled for the lights. Frost-rimed boxes lined shelves; unidentifiable joints of meat hung from hooks. Nobody was hiding in there.

Ben covered Shevu as he rummaged around in the cold store. The captain emerged with a long metal cylinder in one hand. His helmet was already iced over.

"Know what this is?" he asked.

Ben stared at the object. It was a tube. "Grenade launcher?"

"Close. Shoulder launcher, for small missiles. Part of one, anyway. There's about a dozen in there."

"That shouldn't be on the menu."

"Kriffing right it shouldn't be."

"Okay, let's go up one floor," Ben said.

"That's your Force-sense talking, is it?"

"Yeah."

"Okay, works for me."

The turbolift was tiny and they huddled inside. Ben hated lifts. It was the moment when the doors opened that was worst: his Force-sense would tell him if there was a welcoming committee outside, but he still had a sick feeling in his stomach as the doors parted and he saw into the lobby beyond for the first time. This time he was sure there were people around. He pointed to the left. Shevu darted down the passage and trained his blaster on the first door, gesturing Ben to stand to one side as he blew the lock panel. Then Ben sent a surge of energy ahead of him in a shock wave to flatten anyone inside.

Like a stun grenade, it provided a few precious seconds to overpower an enemy, but it didn't leave them temporarily deaf and blinded. The two men inside—and Ben had spotted them only when he was well inside the room—scrambled up from the floor and he lunged forward with his lightsaber. His reflexes took over. A blaster bolt shot past him. He thought it was from Shevu's weapon and as he saw one of the men raise his arm he brought the saber down in an arc. It felt like the skirmish was taking forever, but he knew somehow that it was seconds. Another bolt of white light flared and he deflected it without thinking. Then there was silence.

The air in the room smelled of burned fabric and rasped at his throat. He could feel his pulse pounding in his temples.

"Well, they're about as dead as you can get . . ." Shevu still held his blaster on the two men as he stared down at them. "Why'd you block my shot like that?"

"Did I?"

"You did."

"But you shot one."

"No, one of them fired at me."

Ben looked at his hands as if they weren't his. He was holding the lightsaber two-handed as usual and his grip was shaking. He'd killed both of the men. They both looked about Jacen's age and he didn't like what he saw.

"You okay?"

"Were they both armed?"

"Bit late to worry about that." Shevu squatted down, laid his blaster beside him, and began searching the bodies. Ben heard pounding boots, and two GAG troops entered behind them. "Well, one definitely was. Can't find a weapon on the other."

Force forgive me. I killed them. I killed a man who wasn't armed. I didn't even think.

Ben leaned against the wall and slid down it a little, bracing his legs. Around him, more GAG troops were running down passages, checking rooms. He heard cupboards being wrenched apart and shouts of, "In here! Clear!"

His head sank into his hands. He wanted to look, but he couldn't. Someone took his arm.

"Ben, get up." It was Jacen.

"I'm sorry—"

"Ben, get a grip. You've got work to do." Jacen pulled him upright gently but firmly. "Go on. Look. You should have searched the bodies instead of leaving it to Shevu."

"He wasn't armed."

"Stop it. His buddy *was,* and the place is stuffed with rocket launchers and hardware."

Jacen steered Ben toward the two men on the floor and held him by both shoulders from behind to make him face them. Ben switched off. He felt a numbness spread through his mind and all he saw was shapes. He didn't see people. He knew he would later, but right now something had cut in to cushion him from what he was seeing.

"You made the call, Ben." Jacen's voice was low. From the corner of his eye, Ben could see Shevu watching, or at least he was facing in their direction, head turned as if he was focused on them. "Mostly we get it right, but sometimes we don't. You got most of it right today. Maybe you got all of it right, but it might take us days to find out if that man was a threat or not. Either way—you can't afford to let it get to you."

He turned Ben toward the door, and one of the GAG troops took his arm and led him out into the passage. The noise outside was leaking into his awareness; he felt the Force torn and twisted by a riot in progress. He'd started it. It was all his doing.

He caught a snatch of conversation.

"He's a kid." Shevu's voice. "He's a boy."

"He's a Jedi and he has to *learn*," Jacen said. "He was already handling weapons at the same age you were learning to add."

Ben took a breath and surrendered himself to blind reflex again. By the time he got out onto the walkway, CSF officers were using snare rifles on parts of the crowd that wouldn't disperse and the air was hazy with smoke. The thrum of assault ship drives made his back teeth vibrate. A CSF officer grabbed him and bundled him into one of the police personnel carriers and he sat with his back against the bulkhead, silent and stunned, until a familiar face appeared in the hatchway with his visor pushed back.

"Hey, Ben," said Corporal Lekauf. "You okay?"

"Kind of."

"It's never easy, kid."

"What isn't?"

"Killing someone. You need someone to talk to, I'm here—anytime."

Ben knew he should get out of the carrier and get back to fighting, but a small, scared voice inside said that he was only a kid and it wasn't fair and that he wanted his mom. He shook himself out of it. Mandalorian boys his own age would already be warriors. They'd spit on Ben for being such a baby. He pulled himself to his feet and scrambled out of the personnel carrier, stumbling back down the walkway as if wading through deep snow.

At some point—and it was probably only moments later—Jacen caught his arm and passed him to Shevu. They were pulling out. The black assault ship drew level with the walkway and Shevu heaved Ben aboard. On the flight back to base, Ben sat sandwiched between Shevu and Jacen, thinking that if they moved he'd just collapse.

"It doesn't get any easier," Jacen whispered. "The day it gets easy is the day you have to stop this business."

Ben found his voice somehow and it didn't sound like his own. It echoed in his head. "Will you teach me to shut down my presence in the Force, Jacen?"

"Why?"

His instinct was that it would protect him one day. He also had another reason. "So if I want Dad not to find me, I can."

"You can't hide from your father every time you do something he doesn't approve of."

"I know, but I just want . . . to be on my own sometimes. *Really* on my own."

Jacen studied his face as if looking for something. "You did okay today, Ben. You don't have to hide."

The last few weeks had been a constant series of cliff edges that Ben felt he had stepped from and somehow he hadn't fallen. But they had changed him each time, and he had a sense of never being able to step back onto the cliff edge again. And today—today really *had* changed him. He knew it. He wanted his old self back, but he knew that the Ben he had once been was gone forever.

He wanted to cry. But he was a soldier now, and he had to live with what he did.

Dad must have gone through this, too. And Mom.

He wondered if he would ever be able to talk to them about it. He doubted it.

chapter nineteen

What is he playing at? Either he's running the Guard or he isn't. I know he gets results, but he has to make up his mind about whether he's a fighter pilot or a special forces colonel. I don't know if he just likes playing with X-wings, or if he's trying to score points with the admirals. Maybe both.

—Captain Girdun, in a message to his wife, on the subject of Colonel Jacen Solo

THIRD FLEET BASE, CORUSCANT.

It was a dream: a real dream, Luke hoped, the kind caused by eating too close to bedtime or enduring too much stress, and not a Force-vision.

But it had woken him early. His son Ben appeared, head in hands, crying, sobbing: "It's too high a price. *It's too high a price.*"

That didn't sound like the kind of thing Ben might say, but then Ben was changing into a man almost before his eyes now. Luke sat in the deserted wardroom of the Third Fleet's shore base and waited for Jaina. He let his gaze rest on the row of ship's badges that were hung neatly along the pleckwood paneling behind the bar.

No, military discipline was none of his business. But Jacen Solo was.

Jaina arrived still wearing her orange flight suit and sat down in the chair beside him with slow care.

"Thanks for coming, Uncle Luke."

"I wanted to hear your side of it. I don't believe Jaina Solo would ever turn tail and run during an engagement."

"I'm suspended from duty."

There was no point telling her that the gossip had already ripped through the fleet: she'd refused to obey an order to attack. It was the kind of thing that got a high-profile Jedi pilot a lot of attention.

"What happened?"

"I didn't think it was . . . appropriate to continue attacking a civilian vessel when it was retreating."

Luke knew the answer but he asked anyway. "Who ordered you to do that?"

"Jacen."

"Had the ship fired on Alliance vessels?"

"No, but it breached the exclusion zone and it had targeted Jacen. I took out its aft laser cannons, but it was still capable of firing. Then it withdrew from the exclusion zone and Jacen ordered me to open fire on it." Up to that point, Jaina had been detached and professional, couching everything in military terms. Then her frown deepened. "It was just *wrong,* Uncle Luke. He wanted destruction. He wanted to teach them a lesson. I *felt* it."

Luke chewed over the complexities of rules of engagement. Technically, the freighter was a proven threat. It could still attack Alliance ships even if it had moved outside the exclusion zone. *Technically,* Jacen was right.

Had it not been Jacen, Luke would have chalked it up to the split-second decisions people had to make in battle and accepted it sadly. But it *had been* Jacen's order—one more incident that showed Luke how far toward the dark side his nephew had moved. The Jacen he had known was gone. And Lumiya was around. She was back, and that boded ill.

She was here. He'd have to find her.

"Mom and Dad are going to be so ashamed of me," said Jaina. "Please don't tell them. I'll do it myself when I'm ready."

"They know the kind of person you are." Luke reached

out and took her hands. "But why haven't you defended yourself?"

"Because if I told everyone what happened, they'd think I was whining. You know: everyone else has to do as they're told, but Jaina Solo thinks she's above orders."

"I know you're right, Jaina."

"You wouldn't have fired, would you?"

"I meant that I know Jacen is turning to the dark side, and that it's beyond anything that you or I did when we ventured there."

"I don't want to be right."

"Neither do I."

"You're arguing with Mara about it, aren't you?" Jaina said.

"Sometimes."

"She can't see what he's like these days?"

"She sees, but she has another explanation. And we live in difficult times."

"We always do. That's no excuse."

"So what are you going to do now you're that grounded?" Luke asked.

"Until I face a court-martial—no idea. Can I be of use to you? I'd go find Mom and Dad, but I don't think that would help them right now."

"I'll think of something. How's Zekk taking this?"

"Trying to be understanding. I don't want to be understood. I just want this insanity to stop."

"Me, too," said Luke. "Come on. Come and have lunch with me and Mara. We don't see enough of you these days."

"Do you stay in touch with Mom and Dad?"

"If you mean do we talk . . . not much. But I'm always in contact with Leia. I'm afraid it's your dad I've lost touch with." Luke could remember the time when the three of them had been inseparable; it had been impossible to imagine then that there would ever be rifts or that they'd be fighting on opposite sides. "I miss him."

"I'd bet he misses you, too."

Luke thought of straightforward battles against evil and how he had never given the gray areas a second thought. He missed that, too.

On the way back to the apartment, the traffic lanes seemed slower than normal. The stream of airspeeders was backing up. Luke switched to the holonews traffic channel to find out where the delay was and heard a new fact of daily life in Galactic City: a number of skylanes had been closed and the traffic rerouted while CSF officers cleared up after a riot.

"We'd better get used to this," Jaina said. "The Alliance just upset a whole new bunch of people, as well as Corellia."

Somewhere, Luke felt Ben in sudden, brief pain: not in trouble, not in danger, but in emotional pain. It was faint, almost like an incomplete memory, and then it was gone again as if it had been snatched back under cover. He wondered why he hadn't picked up anything before. Alarmed, he opened the comlink and called Mara.

"Honey, is Ben with you?"

"No." Her voice tightened. He heard the pitch rise. "What's wrong?"

"Can you feel him? Is he okay?"

"I can't feel anything. No sign of him."

Jacen. Luke knew his nephew could disappear from the Force when he wanted to. Maybe he could mask the presence of others. Ben would be alongside him, he knew that much. And he couldn't feel Jacen at all.

"Okay, honey. Just checking. I'm on my way home with Jaina."

He shut the link and looked for another route home. There was no point chasing Ben and having another fight right now. The last time they'd spoken, Ben had seemed close to working things out for himself. Forcing a Jedi to do anything was always of questionable use, even if that Jedi was your little boy.

"You have to get Ben away from Jacen," said Jaina, unprompted.

"I know," Luke said. "I'm trying to get him to make that choice for himself. If I force it, I'll make Jacen a martyr in his eyes."

"Am I wrong to think this about my own brother?"

"What do your senses tell you?"

"That he's going to somehow break my heart one day."

"Yes," said Luke. "We need to make sure that never happens."

But it already has, he thought. *It already has.*

THE SOLOS' APARTMENT, CORONET, CORELLIA.

"You got to hand it to Gejjen," said Han. "He must have had all this planned."

Fett had already worked out a fast exit from the Solos' shabbily anonymous apartment. From the window he could see the red flashing lights of Corellian Security Force speeders racing across the city: when he checked his bank account—one of them, anyway—he was already one million credits better off. Gejjen certainly paid promptly.

Mirta gave Han a wary look. "Forget Gejjen. Call your son."

Leia Solo—and despite the decade that had passed since he had last seen her, Fett had still recognized her immediately—had a comlink pressed to one ear. "I'm trying." She stared at the comlink in exasperation and then snapped it shut. "He's not answering. Let's try the Jedi way. That usually gets his attention."

She clasped her hands in front of her and closed her eyes for a moment. Fett didn't care for Jedi: they were an aristocracy, winners in a genetic lottery, and there was something about the lack of merit required that rankled with Mandalorians. But for all the lightsaber trophies he kept on display from Jedi bounties, Fett knew they had their uses.

All I care about now is seeing Ailyn. Corella can burn for all I care.

"You doing some of that Jedi mind stuff?" Mirta demanded.

Leia opened her eyes and didn't look amused. "I'm reaching out to my son in the Force to make him realize I need to talk to him. He'll know it's me."

On the wall, a holoscreen showed a harassed-looking news anchor relaying the news that the President had been assassinated. The Deputy President, Vol Barad, suitably respectful, paid tribute to Sal-Solo and said that an emergency meeting had been called with leaders of all the political parties to "work out a way forward."

"First time he's been allowed out in public since Thrackan came to power," said Han. "He must think this is his lucky day."

"Come on, Jacen," Leia muttered.

Han, fixed on the holoscreen, snorted in contempt. "Oh, here's our little buddy now . . ."

Fett turned to see Dur Gejjen being interviewed. He was consummately calm and grim-faced, and spoke of his shock at the news. He was rather convincing: a dangerous young man, Fett decided, and one who'd have a fine political career. He'd eat Han Solo alive. Maybe Leia would be able to handle him.

"He's talking about a coalition government . . . ," Han muttered.

"Dividing the spoils," said Fett.

"Thrackan must have ticked off more people than I thought. I didn't realize even his own party hated him that much."

"Maybe they'll build a statue to you, Solo."

"Hey, it's your happy little partner who whacked him, pal."

Mirta had started pacing up and down the apartment, now watching both the doors and the windows. Leia opened her comlink. "Try again . . ."

"Thrackan said there were still other assassins out there," Han said quietly.

Fett shrugged. "Not now they know he's dead."

"You sure?"

"If they're not going to get paid, why would they want to kill you?"

Han frowned slightly. "I suppose that's bounty hunter logic."

Fett wondered if he should point out to Han that he had more to fear from Gejjen and his cronies than from an honest hired killer, but Han should have been able to work that out for himself. Anyone who could hire a hit on a rival politician would have no compunction about doing the same to Han Solo.

Fett was glad he worked in a trade where the rules were nice and clear.

Then Leia said, "*Jacen!* Jacen, this is urgent—" and the room fell silent. Fett killed the audio on the holoscreen. Mirta stared at him, unfathomable. Listening to one side of the conversation was agonizing. *What does she look like now? Is she married? Does she have a family? How will I get her to listen to me?*

And what am I going to say to her?

"Jacen," said Leia. "Thrackan's dead . . . don't ask . . . no, ask your father about that . . ."

"Ailyn," Mirta interrupted. "Ask him about Ailyn."

Leia nodded emphatically. "Jacen, this is important. You said you arrested a bounty hunter called Ailyn Habuur. Your father did a deal about Thrackan . . . no, *listen,* Jacen,

I need you to listen . . . now Thrackan's dead, the woman isn't a threat, and her father wants to see her very badly . . . Jacen?"

Fett felt sweat beading on his top lip despite his helmet's environment controls.

"Jacen, repeat that . . ."

Leia's gaze fixed in mid-distance and then flickered as if she'd heard a reply she wasn't expecting.

"Jacen, her father is *Boba Fett*."

Whatever Jacen had said, Leia was having problems understanding it. She closed the comlink and ran one hand over her hair, not quite looking at him or Mirta.

"I'm sorry," she said. "I don't know how to tell you this, but Ailyn Habuur died . . . under interrogation."

No. No. I was going to talk to her. I was going to put things right—

Fett told himself that he didn't care about anything or anybody, and that Ailyn was a stranger, but it was a lie. The fact that he had last seen her as a baby and that she had tried to kill him didn't change a thing right then: she was his *daughter*. He was dying and he wanted to see her.

He reeled. He had no answer. He looked at Mirta Gev, and she stared back at him, and her face was stricken. There was no other word for it.

Then she leveled her blaster at him. Instinct made him reach for his, and the next thing he saw was a streak of white fire coming at him almost in slow motion, and Leia Solo reaching out both hands as if she could seize the very energy with them.

Mirta's blaster flew high in the air and clattered across the tiled floor.

chapter twenty

Investigations are continuing into the assassination of President Sal-Solo, but we have reason to believe that this outrage was the work of Alliance agents. This will not weaken our resolve to maintain Corellia's independent military deterrent. Following an agreement among all parties, Corellia will now be governed by a coalition of the Democratic Alliance and the Corellian Liberal Front, which represent the largest bloc of representatives, with an advisory role for the Centerpoint Party.

—Statement from the new coalition administration of Corellia

Leia stood between Mirta Gev and Boba Fett. Mirta fell back against the wall hard as if she'd been thrown against it. Leia stood over her, but the girl just stared past her at Fett, defiant but pinned down by the Force.

The air stank with the ozonic smell of a discharged blaster. Fett had his EE-3 trained on Mirta, but Han noticed that it was slowly lowering to his side.

"I want to know what all that was about," Leia said, as if Mirta were just a naughty kid who hadn't done her homework rather than a bounty hunter who'd tried to take a shot at Boba Fett.

Mirta's eyes brimmed. Han hadn't thought of her as the crying kind. Maybe it was a *very* big bounty she'd just lost.

"I was delivering *him* to her." She indicated Fett with a contemptuous jerk of her chin. "She wanted to kill him for certain this time."

Fett didn't say a word. He slung his blaster rifle over his shoulder with a slow, deliberate movement and stood the way he often did, hands a little away from his sides, weight on one foot, as if he was going to whip out one of his astonishing array of weapons.

"But why shoot him? Now that she can't pay you, what's he—"

"He ran out on his wife and baby, that's why. Yes, the great Boba Fett didn't have the guts to stand by his family. He left her, and she had to bring up Ailyn on her own, and she died because he wasn't there being a proper husband and father. If . . . she couldn't kill him, then I *will*."

Leia crouched over her. Tears were streaming down the kid's face now and Fett was absolutely still. "Why? What has he ever done to you?"

Mirta gulped in air, choking back sobs. Han resisted the urge to play dad and comfort her.

"Because she was *my mother,* and I promised her that he'd *die,* that's why. So he's my grandfather—in name, anyway." She rounded on him, scrambling to her feet. "You didn't know that, did you? You didn't know because you didn't *care.* You never even tried to find out what happened to Ailyn until now, and it's too kriffing late for us all. Fifty years—*fifty years!*"

Han would remember this for years to come and still not believe it. Fett's shoulders heaved visibly as if he was taking a deep breath. He still said nothing. It was a lousy way to be reunited with family; Han almost felt sorry for him.

Mirta stood staring into the mask of his helmet as if she could see the man behind it. Then she punched both fists into his chest plate as hard as she could, face contorted with grief and rage, and knocked him back a couple of paces. He just took it. She punched as hard as she could, and Fett let her until Han saw that her knuckles were bleeding and he decided she'd had enough. He grabbed her shoulders and pulled her back.

Fett still hadn't said a word.

"Hey, c'mon . . . c'mon . . ." Han held Mirta until she stopped struggling, "It's okay, kid. It's okay. Take it easy." Her mother was dead. Okay, she was a contract killer, but that wasn't the girl's fault. He caught Leia's eye and could see that she was horrified. Whatever Jacen had said that he hadn't heard had upset her. Maybe the detail was too graphic to share. "Fett, don't you have anything to say to this kid? She's your family."

"He's not!" Mirta snarled.

Fett simply turned to Han. His voice was as flat and unemotional as ever. "I want Ailyn back. I want her body."

"Leave that to me," said Leia. "We'll sort it out."

Han couldn't take it in. He'd had some bizarre days in his life, but this was getting near the top of the scale. "Sweetheart, you're placating *Boba Fett* . . ."

"His daughter just died."

"He didn't even *know* her."

"Han—"

"She was sent to kill us. You forgot that small detail?"

"Han, you remember when Anakin died?"

The reminder of his son's death stopped him in his tracks for a moment. The pain was as fresh as ever. "But we *loved* Anakin! We raised him! Fett didn't even—"

Leia held up her hand for silence. "Don't, Han. Nobody knows what Fett feels or doesn't feel. And neither of us would be standing here now if he hadn't saved us from the Yuuzhan Vong. Okay?"

Leia's compassion always humbled Han, but he felt she was wasting it on Fett. She had a point, but she was being way too kind to a man who'd nearly killed him more than once.

But Fett had kept his word. Thrackan was dead, even if the girl had probably fired the fatal shot. And there were no more contracts out on the Solo family—as far as Fett knew, anyway.

Han patted Mirta's back. She was shaking now. He felt sorry for her, not Fett. "You two better sort yourselves out. Fast."

"He's all you've got, Mirta," Leia said quietly. "Trust me, however bad things are, your family is all you have in the end."

Don't get too cocky about your diplomatic skills, honey, thought Han. Mirta might have been tear-streaked, but she also looked murderous. She'd killed one man tonight and she didn't look like she'd have any trouble making it two.

Han thought it was high time he and Leia worried about their own skins. Could they live on Corellia openly now? He picked up his comlink to call Dur Gejjen, but stopped as Fett suddenly took off his armor plates, chest and back, and dumped them on the chair. He held his arms at his sides.

"Pick up your blaster, Mirta Gev," he said. Leia moved as if to stop her. "No, let her do it."

And the kid did. She bent down and took the blaster in both hands and held it level, right hand grasping the grip, left cupped beneath to steady the shot, and aimed at Fett. She was deadly calm now.

Fett reached up slowly and lifted off his helmet.

He was gray and scarred and *hard.* It was the first time Han had ever seen his enemy's face. It was far less than he had imagined and all the more shocking for that. It was a face that was as unfeeling as a slab of rock. They said your life was etched in your face over time, and Fett's life must have been utterly cold, brutal, and alone.

"Go on," said Fett. He was staring straight at his granddaughter. "Do it."

Stang, she's going to . . .

Mirta wasn't crying now.

"I said *do it.*"

She held her aim for a count of five and then lowered the blaster. Han wondered if Leia had given her mind a little gentle influence but decided not to ask, not just yet. Then she sat down on the battered sofa, blaster on one knee, fingers still tight on the grip. If Han had expected a tearful reconciliation, he had the wrong family. Fett's ice-water blood definitely ran in her veins.

Leia watched warily as if she was expecting Mirta to change her mind. Fett replaced his armor and stood by the window again, watching the police activity in the city beyond, blaster at his side.

Leia broke the silence. "Now everyone's calmed down, I'll talk to Jacen again; we'll arrange to recover the body, and then you can leave." She walked out into the kitchen and Han followed, wondering if he'd hear blasterfire the second his back was turned.

"When did *you* become Fett's best buddy?" he whispered. "Remember that little vacation I spent encased in carbonite thanks to him? Okay, so he saved the day when the Vong—"

"Han, I don't know how to tell you this, but I think it's going to be Fett who bears the grudge." She stared at the comlink as if she dreaded talking to their son again. "I'm not sure you're even going to believe me."

"I'm not a mind reader. What do you know that I don't?"

"Jacen killed Fett's daughter. Personally."

"Yeah?" Han lowered his voice still further. "That's the idea. She was going to kill *us*."

"He killed her while he was interrogating her."

Han had to think about that for a couple of seconds. Jacen was more of a stranger with every passing day. He was becoming the Alliance's bullyboy, the head of their secret police, although there was nothing very secret about them.

But he didn't kill prisoners. He *couldn't*. Only monsters did that kind of thing. Jacen couldn't be a monster. He was his boy, his sweet kid.

"No."

"I think he tortured her, Han."

"No."

"So you see why we have a problem."

"I refuse to believe that . . ."

"Do you think *I* want to believe it? How does anyone accept that their kid turns into something terrible?"

"It *had* to be an accident."

"I want to believe that, too. Right now I'm just waiting for Fett to ask who actually did it, because he'll want to know sooner or later. You would. We both would."

"He hadn't seen the woman since she was a baby. You think he cares?"

"I'm going to assume he does. People have feuds within families, but when an outsider gets involved, they tend to gang up. What do you think Fett's going to do? Shake your hand and say, *Okay, Han, so I handed you over to Jabba the Hutt and your son tortured my daughter to death, so we're even . . .* you think he'll say that?"

Han's brief relief at knowing Thrackan would no longer be around to harass him and his family was rapidly being replaced by the fear that Boba Fett would put him at the top of his vengeance list. Fett had a reputation for never giving up. He never had.

Han leaned back against the wall, not sure what scared him most: having Boba Fett as a real personal enemy, or knowing his son had turned into a killer. He settled for the latter.

"Jacen?" Leia's voice was all calm reason. Han wondered how she did it, but she was a lot tougher and cooler than he'd ever know how to be. "Jacen, I need you to do something for me. It's important."

CHIEF OF STATE'S OFFICE, SENATE BUILDING, CORUSCANT.

"Well," said Cal Omas. "Where does *this* leave us?"

Senator G'Sil rubbed his forehead with one hand, and Jacen watched him carefully. Luke, in turn, watched Jacen.

He could feel his uncle's focus on him, his suspicion, his dread, his calculation.

There's nothing you can do about it, Uncle Luke. You had your chance. Now we'll do things the Sith way.

"This wasn't our doing," G'Sil insisted. "The Intelligence Service definitely had no hand in assassinating Sal-Solo. That man had so many political enemies that Corellian Security will be interviewing suspects until Mustafar turns into a ski resort."

"We still have agents in Coronet, though?"

"Of course we do. But it's still not our handiwork—we wouldn't be so stupid as to hand Corellia a free pass to recruit other planets to its cause."

"We're not being believed," Luke said slowly.

Omas looked exhausted. "People believe what they want to believe. So who do we have to deal with now? Who's really running the show in this multiheaded beast of a coalition cabinet?"

"Dur Gejjen," Jacen said. *So Dad really did it. I don't believe it. He killed Thrackan.* "And he came to my parents before Sal-Solo was killed with a suggestion that a regime change might be in the cards."

Omas looked to Luke as if expecting some input. "What does Intelligence have to say about him, then? I can just about remember his father in the Human League days."

"Don't expect him to disarm any faster than Sal-Solo," said G'Sil. "Forget the assassination, except as an accelerant to finding Corellia more allies. The overall situation hasn't changed."

"Where's Niathal got to, by the way?"

Jacen looked up. "She's on her way. She's being briefed by the commanders."

The blockade was biting. Corellia could feed itself, but for everything manufactured it relied on its orbiting industrial stations, which were now mostly cut off by Alliance pickets. It was also losing starfighters and ships: without the repair and refueling facilities in the orbiting shipyards, which had also been successfully isolated, its fleets were seriously compromised.

Jacen considered how he would get Ailyn Habuur's body to Corellia. He could beat a blockade alone. *No, it was Ailyn Vel. So you killed Fett's daughter. He has a Mandalorian army that could take on the Yuuzhan Vong. Avoid him for as long as you can.* If Fett were placated, his parents could at least live on Corellia without looking over their shoulders the whole time. He considered explaining to Fett that he hadn't planned to kill Ailyn, but Fett probably didn't know exactly who had killed her, and it was better for everyone to leave it that way. There was no point adding more enemies to the list.

He's Mandalorian, remember. Long memories, short fuses.

"Are you with us, Jacen?" Luke asked.

Jacen jerked back to the here and now, caught unawares for once. "Apologies. Just considering logistics."

"The Jedi council feels that we should open formal talks with the new Corellian government and offer them a way out."

"They'll turn it down."

"Nothing's lost by offering," said Luke. "Do we need Senate agreement to do that?"

"Technically," Omas replied. "But seeing as over a hundred planets have withdrawn their representatives in protest now, I think we can assume that those left wouldn't object if we did."

Luke seemed to be optimistic about the prospects of a breakthrough even if his expression was grim. "Why would Gejjen and his cronies want to remove Thrackan if they didn't want a change of policy?"

"No better time to remove a rival than under the cover of

war," said Jacen. "It probably has nothing to do with disarmament, and everything to do with old, festering resentments."

"Sometimes I'm glad I'm a simple farmboy," said Luke.

"And the Alliance isn't formally at war with anyone, Uncle."

"Oh, that makes all the difference, then. Because a growing number of planets seem to think they're at war with the Alliance."

Omas interrupted Luke. "Gentlemen, if the new Corellian administration refuses to disarm, then we have no choice but to formalize a state of war. That changes the legality of the situation and gives us different laws to deal with matters."

"More powers." Luke's voice was almost a whisper.

"More *emergency* powers," said Omas.

G'Sil glanced at Luke with a benign smile that did nothing to conceal from Jacen that the Senator was thinking . . . *weakling.*

"I'm not a great student of history," said Luke. "But I think we've been here before somehow. Before I was born, of course."

"Do you have an alternative?" Omas asked. "I really would welcome the Jedi council's views if there's a concrete course I can pursue. But right now I have three broad options: to allow Alliance planets to maintain their own independent defense forces, to continue as we're going, or to mount a much more aggressive campaign to force disarmament. If you have another option, now is the time to put it forward."

Luke shook his head. "You *know* I haven't. But I can't sit here and not express my unease, either."

Jacen turned his head and caught G'Sil's eye for a fraction of a second, and knew that they were thinking exactly the same thing. *Well, your conscience is clear, Uncle. It's some-one else's responsibility now, isn't it?*

Omas stood up and began collecting flimsi sheets from his desk. It was the diplomatic way he indicated to any meeting that the talking was over and now he was going to do something. Jacen wondered if Omas ever slammed his fist on that beautiful inlaid desk. He doubted it.

"I'm going to make a formal approach now to the new Corellian administration and offer them talks on disarmament," Omas said. "Maybe we'll all get a surprise. Maybe the blockade made them see sense."

Jacen genuinely hoped it had. He wanted to see order restored, and he didn't enjoy being despised by his uncle. He turned to Luke to at least take his leave of him courteously, but Luke walked past him with a formal nod of the head and left.

Yes, it hurt. But a lot of things would hurt. Jacen accepted it as part of the price he was paying. He opened his comlink and called C-3PO.

"Threepio?" The droid, at least, always greeted him as if he was pleased to hear from him. "Has Artoo finished repairing the *Falcon*? Tell him to hurry up, then. I'm flying her back to Dad."

chapter twenty-one

The Galactic Alliance has offered settlement terms to the new government of Corellia. We hope that those terms will be accepted and that we can put an end to the blockade. We do not want war. This is our last chance for unity.
      —Chief of State Cal Omas, speaking at a news conference

CORONET CITY. SPACEPORT.

Fett occupied himself with carrying out panel checks on *Slave I* and tried not to think about the fact that he had lost a daughter and acquired a granddaughter in a matter of a day.

This was why it made sense to live alone. Families, wives, and kids were painful. They got in the way.

Mirta was, as far as he knew or cared, still at the Solos' apartment. How had she fooled him for so long? He couldn't believe he hadn't worked out who she was. But if you hadn't seen your daughter for more than fifty years, there was no reason to recognize her daughter.

You have a family. Like it or not, you have a family.

She might have had more than one child. What would he do about that, then? What if he had more grandchildren out there, all raised to hate him as thoroughly and efficiently as Mirta had been? No, he should have spotted it right away. When he looked into her dark eyes, he could see his father now. He could see his *own* eyes.

He could see his own hatred, too. He resented the galaxy, and Jedi in particular, for having to grow up without a father. It wasn't surprising to see that hate and resentment reproduced faithfully in a granddaughter.

Now he waited for Goran Beviin to shake down his network of contacts and tell him what Leia and Han Solo either didn't know or didn't want to tell him.

"*Mand'alor,*" said the comlink.

Fett pounced on it. "Beviin? What have you got for me?"

"I'm very sorry about Ailyn, *Bob'ika.*"

I don't want your sympathy. "I need intel."

"Ailyn was being held by Jacen Solo."

"I know that. But who was interrogating her?"

"Like I said—Jacen Solo."

I'll kill him. Fett felt his stomach settle into that cold place of detachment that preceded a strike. His thoughts fell immediately to the best weapons and strategies to add another Jedi lightsaber to his collection, the first that he would truly savor and not regard as just another job. *No, remember what Dad taught you—stay professional. Stay cool. Understand the enemy.*

"This had better be accurate."

"*Mand'alor,*" said Beviin, "this comes from the Coruscant Security Force. Some still think well of Mandalorians, thanks to your father's friends."

"I'm touched."

"You should be. The CSF bar is full of gossip about Jacen Solo, because some of his Galactic Alliance Guard are ex-CSF men. Some of them really don't like his way of doing business."

Fett had taken little notice of Coruscant's descent into martial law yet again. He'd seen it all before. But now it was personal.

"I want to know *everything.*"

"Jacen Solo is a regular little *chakaar.*"

"I take it that's bad."

"He uses Jedi techniques that don't quite fit their peace-and-justice image. Apparently one of his officers was complaining that he uses the Force to beat answers out of prisoners without laying a finger on them."

Something went *ping* in Fett's memory. "Go on."

"They say he killed Ailyn with the power of his mind." Beviin swallowed audibly. "Just say the word, and we'll find him."

Jedi. Arrogant, power-hungry barves who don't care who they trample over. Nothing changes. "Not necessary."

"You're going to go after him yourself, then?"

"Ailyn was a bounty hunter. She knew the risks."

"*Bob'ika,* you can't mean that . . ."

I ought to, but I don't. It hurts. It doesn't hurt as bad as losing Dad, but it hurts somehow. "Forget Jacen Solo. Leave him to me."

"He's a real piece of work. Word is that he ordered his twin sister to fire on a civilian vessel, and when she refused, he suspended her from duty. What a lovely, happy little family the Solos must be."

Ah. I think I know where this is going. "What else? Anything, no matter how trivial it seems to you."

"He doesn't even wear Jedi robes now. He struts around in a black uniform. Luke Skywalker's boy is his minion. That really upsets the CSF boys. The kid's thirteen."

"He's a grown man, then."

"*Aruetiise* see a thirteen-year-old as a child."

"He rather enjoys his power even for a Jedi, this Jacen Solo."

"You know what they say about him? The older ones who remember the Empire say that it's like having his grandfather back. They say he fancies himself as the new Vader."

Ah. Fett's jumble of memories from nearly forty years earlier fell into place. *Ah.*

"Anything else?"

"No, *Mand'alor*. Is there anything else you want me to do?"

"Keep an eye out for a Mandalorian with gray armor and gray leather gloves who claims to be a clone who fought at Geonosis."

There was an audible pause. "I'll ask around."

"And don't be tempted to go after the Solos' son. Leave him."

"If you say so."

"I say so."

Fett sat staring at the control panel in *Slave I*'s cockpit for a long time after Beviin had closed the link. So the Solos had a feud running within their own family—and their son was the man behind the new hard-line politics of the Alliance. He thought he was the new Vader.

And he killed prisoners without touching them.

They didn't teach *that* at the Jedi academy on Ossus, Fett was pretty sure of that. He'd taken his father's advice on learning how his enemies thought very seriously. He knew a lot about Jedi.

I know plenty about Sith, too.

Vader had been the master of causing pain and death without so much as a touch of his finger. Fett had rather liked Lord Vader. He paid well and he paid on time. He never asked his people to do what he wouldn't do himself. In some ways, Fett missed him.

I've seen the galaxy ruled by Sith, and I've seen the galaxy ruled by Jedi. I still made a profit. In fact, I didn't really notice the difference, and the galaxy was still a mess at the end of it. It's not my problem. And it's not the Mandalorians' problem.

So Jacen Solo wanted to be just like his grandfather. Maybe he wanted to be a Sith Lord, too.

Maybe I'll let him.

There was no better way of exacting revenge on the sanctimonious Jedi than to let them rip themselves apart all on their own.

He wouldn't have to punish the Solos at all.

It would take time, but that was fine. It was one more reason to make sure he beat his illness. He wanted to be around to see it.

CORELLIAN EXCLUSION ZONE: **MILLENNIUM FALCON** INBOUND.

Jacen would have been happier flying alone, but with Thrackan Sal-Solo dead there was no longer a reason for keeping C-3PO and the Noghri away from his parents. Corellia knew the Solos were back.

"*Millennium Falcon,* this is Alliance warship *Revival.* You're approaching a total exclusion zone. Alter your course ninety degrees. I repeat, your course is taking you into a military exclusion zone and we *will* open fire if you proceed."

"Oh dear . . . ," said C-3PO. "Master Jacen, do be careful."

"Relax. I can handle this."

Jacen switched to an open channel. "*Revival,* this is Colonel Jacen Solo of the Galactic Alliance Guard."

"Your transponder is showing as the *Millennium Falcon,* a Corellian-registered vessel."

"Apologies, *Revival.*" He sent an encrypted identification code to the warship's comm officer. "I have a rendezvous to make within Corellian space. They won't fire on the *Falcon* now that Sal-Solo is gone."

"We weren't advised of this, Colonel."

"It's a classified operation. Put me through to your commanding officer and I'll have him verify it."

"Won't be necessary, sir. Just identify yourself clearly on your return."

"I'll be back in a different ship. Don't be too quick to open fire, will you?"

Revival didn't jump to his command, but that was a good thing. They were taking security seriously. He steered through the line and into the exclusion zone that had trapped an orbiting ring of industrial stations and fleet bases in limbo, cut off both from contact with Corellia itself and from outside supply lines.

It couldn't have been much fun now on board the shipyard stations. Civilian workers did weeklong shifts and were then shuttled home, but they weren't going anywhere now, and they weren't being resupplied. Sooner or later their food would run out. Jacen had heard that they were already on limited water rations: as he'd calculated, recycling water met only some of their normal consumption needs.

When Jacen crossed the planetside limit of the exclusion zone he switched to the civilian transponder, looking to any ground-based traffic control like one more small ship that had beaten the blockade. Lots did. They just didn't make much of a difference to the overall supply situation, that was all. Once clear, he took up station at the rendezvous point and went aft to the cargo bay for a final check on Ailyn Vel's body bag, lying in the conservator on a repulsor gurney.

C-3PO trotted along behind him, all anxiety. "Allow me, Master Jacen."

Jacen held up his hand to the droid in polite refusal of help. "It's okay, Threepio. I'll do it."

What's happening to me?

Jacen pondered how he had moved from the kind of Jedi that Luke was proud of to one who could kill prisoners and even other Jedi. Somewhere in that five years of seeking Force knowledge, something had changed him. He wondered at what point he would be able to bring Lumiya into the open.

His parents' shuttle came alongside the *Falcon* and docked with her cargo hatch. Leia was first into the bay, and although her first move was to hug him it felt formal, distant, as if she was holding back. His father trailed behind, looking broken. There was no other word for it. He made no attempt to embrace him.

"Hi." Han glanced past him at C-3PO. He didn't normally take that much notice of the droid. "Hi, Threepio. Are the Noghri with you?"

Jacen ignored the snub. "Hi, Mom. Hi, Dad." What did you say at times like this? He plunged in. "Yes, they're in the cabin. Have you heard from Jaina?"

"No."

Leia cut in. "You want to tell us something?"

Jaina hadn't told them about the court-martial, then. "No. She's fine. Not flying combat missions." If she wanted to keep the matter to herself, that was fine by him. "I'm sure Zekk's keeping an eye on her."

"Is there anything else you want to tell us, Jacen?" Leia was talking to him as if he were a kid who'd done something terrible. "Anything at all?"

"What, exactly?"

Han sighed with that roll of the head that always told Jacen he was in trouble. "Son, we're collecting a corpse from you. That should give you a clue."

"She was hired to kill you. She never got the chance." Jacen opened the conservator hatch, and cold air rolled out. He indicated the large black bag lying flat on the durasteel gurney. "What more is there to say?"

Han now stood between him and his mother. "I need to know what happened. For my own sanity."

Leia scratched one brow, clearly embarrassed. "I think we both need to know, Jacen."

"Okay, Dad, I was interrogating her and she died. Do you really want to know the details?"

"It kind of makes a difference, Jacen."

"I used a mind-invasion technique to make her talk. She must have had some physical weakness. She died of an aneurysm."

"Can we take a look?" Leia asked. "We have to hand her over to Fett. We don't want any surprises."

She'd look anyway. Jacen had to face this sooner or later. He decided sooner was better. He hauled out the gurney, then opened the bag down its gription seam.

"There," he said.

Leia and Han looked. His mother simply swallowed hard, but his father turned away with his hands on his hips, head bowed. Jacen waited while Leia composed herself, then fastened the seam again.

"Did you put those bruises on her face?"

This is the price you pay. He could almost hear Lumiya reminding him, but it would take a long time for him to forget the look of utter betrayal on his mother's face at that moment. This felt like his lowest ebb.

"I believe so."

"*You believe so.*"

"Yes."

Leia nodded a few times, silent, staring off to one side. "Okay. Not much more I can say, then." She took the repulsor gurney's handle and moved the body back into the conservator. "We'd better be going."

Jacen waited for his father to say something, but Han wouldn't even turn around. Jacen went to the hatch to board the vessel they'd flown to the RV point and expected Han to relent and say something, but he didn't.

I can't just end it like this. I'll make him speak to me. I have to. Why can't he understand?

"Did you really kill Thrackan, Dad?"

Han turned and looked him in the eye, but there was no spark of recognition. "Hey, maybe it runs in the family. If I can kill in cold blood, so can my boy. I'm glad we understand each other."

Jacen went to take his father's arm. "Dad, don't do this—"

Han shook it off. "Get away from me."

"Dad—"

"I don't know who you are, but you aren't my son anymore. My Jacen would never do the kind of stuff you do. Get out. I don't want to know any more."

Jacen's last sight of his parents was his father turning his back and his mother standing by the hatch as the doors closed, staring at him as if she was about to burst into tears.

Dad's right. What am I?

He shook off the misery and shame as one of those weaknesses of the old Jacen Solo and reminded himself that his life wasn't his own now. His destiny was Sith. He turned the battered vessel toward the blockade and allowed himself the brief luxury of reaching out in the Force to Tenel Ka and Allana while he was still far, far from Lumiya.

GAG HEADQUARTERS, CORUSCANT.

Captain Shevu was swearing under his breath as he stared at a data screen in the administration office. A clerical droid stood to one side of the desk, forlorn and silent, occasionally reaching out an arm and withdrawing it quickly each time Shevu looked up and glared at it.

Ben hovered in the doorway, wondering if Shevu was going to round on him, too. The officer wasn't happy.

"Do you know when Colonel Solo's due back, sir?" *Don't say Jacen, not in front of his men.* "He's late."

"Colonel Solo comes and goes as he pleases," said Shevu. "Can I help with anything?"

"Are you any good at finding dead bodies?"

"Well—"

"Sorry, Ben." Shevu dismissed the droid with a sharp look. "We appear to have lost a dead prisoner, and seeing as they don't stroll out of here unaided, I'm trying to find them. You can't file an incident report without a body."

Ben's stomach sank. "Ailyn Habuur, right?"

"Right. Nobody signed out the body. But it's gone."

And so is Jacen. But he was going to see Uncle Han. Ben tried to think of an answer that would take away the nagging dread he felt about Jacen and Ailyn Habuur. "Does it matter?"

Shevu had a way of dropping his chin and staring unblinking at you that made it clear he thought you were an idiot. "Yes, Ben, prisoners who die in custody always matter and you don't just dump them like garbage. What do you know about her?"

Ben shrugged. "She was angry and scared."

"I hear from my CSF colleagues that someone was asking questions about her."

"Is she someone important?"

"I don't know. Do you?"

Ben shook his head. He got the feeling that Shevu was being cautious about what he said to him and—obvious, this—that he didn't like Jacen very much.

"Why don't you go and visit your parents?" Shevu made it sound like an order. "If Colonel Solo comes back in the meantime, I'll tell him I sent you home."

It was good to have the decision made for him. Ben wondered if the events of recent days would show on his face so clearly that his father could read them. He hoped so. He wasn't sure that he could bottle them up much longer.

Mom would understand better. She'd told him a few stories about being the Emperor's Hand. She'd done some bad things, she said. But it hadn't made her a bad person, so perhaps Jacen was like that: perhaps he just did a few things that were terrible but he could learn from them and never do them again.

Ben called first and got an automated answer. The Jedi council was in session, so he went to the Temple and waited in the archives for an hour. The meeting went on, and he knew better than to even try to interrupt. So he occupied himself looking for data on Ailyn Habuur.

The Jedi archives were vast, an odd mix of ancient texts and hard data. They said that between the archives and the meditation areas, Jedi could discover anything about the outer and inner worlds that they wanted to if they put their minds to it.

He didn't find an Ailyn Habuur in any public records— not even in the Kiffar records—but he found a lot of Ailyns and Habuurs. He found thousands. The size of the task daunted him, and he wondered if it mattered whether he found out or not.

Then he found himself looking for the names *Nelani* and *Brisha*.

He'd made a deal with himself not to ask any more questions about that missing chunk of time out at Bimmiel that had somehow ended with the Jedi Knight Nelani Dinn and a weird woman called Brisha both getting killed. He accepted that a lot of things had happened that he didn't fully understand, but they still puzzled him, and Jacen wasn't telling him.

How had they died?

How did Brisha and Nelani die?

He had to know. The feeling inside him said that what had happened to Ailyn Habuur meant he *had* to ask, because it changed everything. They were connected somehow.

Nelani was easy to find, because he knew she was a Jedi and that narrowed his search. But there were thousands of Brishas, too—some names, some places—and he didn't have the time to go through them all. He wasn't even sure what he was looking for, or if he would even recognize it if he saw it. He made up his mind to ask Jacen when the time seemed right.

Ben took the turbolift to the council chamber floor and waited in the lobby until the meeting broke up. His parents, deep in conversation, walked down the corridor as if they hadn't spotted him, and he wondered if he had accidentally mastered the art of disguising his presence. Funny; he'd resented being invisible to grown-ups until only a few weeks ago, always ignored like a kid. Now he wanted that invisibility in the Force.

But not right then. At that moment he really wanted his mother and father to know *exactly* where he was, and to help him find out where he was going.

He wanted to tell them how bad he felt about Ailyn Habuur and Jacen.

But that was wrong. If he had a problem with Jacen, he ought to do things like a grown-up and have it out with him like a man before whining to his mom and dad.

Besides, there were other things he wanted to talk about.

"Hi, honey," said Mara. She looked him up and down and he wished he had changed out of his uniform. "What's wrong? Have you been waiting long?"

Ben hugged her and then turned to his father to give him an awkward embrace. He wasn't sure how he had to behave with him now. Most of the time he'd wanted not to be just Luke and Mara Skywalker's kid, but at that moment he was almost relieved that he was.

"Can we go have lunch, Dad?"

"Sure. Something really *is* wrong, isn't it?"

Ben should have told them right away, but he'd thought about it a little more and he was ready now. He *needed* to talk.

"I killed someone," he said. "And I feel really bad about it."

chapter twenty-two

I regret to announce that the Corellian government has declined our offer of talks unless the Galactic Alliance undertakes to recognize the right of Corellia to maintain its own independent defense force and deterrents. As the Alliance is unable to accept a refusal to disarm, we are now in a state of war with Corellia and her allies.

—Chief of State Cal Omas,
in a brief statement to the Senate

MILLENNIUM FALCON
EN ROUTE TO CORONET.

Even sitting at the *Falcon*'s controls again couldn't make Han feel any better. He wanted events of the last few days to wind back like a holorecording so he could erase them and do things right this time.

Corellia loomed larger in the viewscreen. At least they could land openly now and the worst thing that would happen would be a few jeers about being a traitor—if anyone remembered that far back. A few weeks was a very long time in a war. And he didn't care any longer if the Solos were a political embarrassment to Luke. Luke had made his choice.

And my son is turning into a monster.

Leia reached across and put her hand on top of his as he gripped the forward thruster controls.

"It's eighty kilos per square centimeter."

"What is?" asked Han, distracted.

"The yield stress of durasteel. You look like you're testing it."

Han let go of the controls. The autopilot was active anyway. He had been gripping the yoke for comfort because he felt it was about all he *did* have a grip on at that moment in his life. "Is it us? Did we raise him like that? How did we do it? How come Jaina isn't like that?"

"I don't know what's happening either."

"I thought I understood all this dark- and light-side stuff. So it's all part of the one Force. So what did I meet back there that used to be our Jacen?"

"Honey, you have to calm down."

"Jacen tortures prisoners to death. How can I calm down? Is he going crazy? Does he *feel* different to you?"

Leia was always the sensible one with the cool nerves and the ability to make everything sound as if it were under control. He was the one who did the physical stuff. That was the way their marriage worked, and it had withstood some pretty terrible tests. Now she looked as if she couldn't make things right again.

"Okay," she said. "Jacen feels . . . changed to me. Maybe this is what's getting to Jaina. She's very unhappy. I can sense it."

"At least she's not flying missions. She saw sense."

"But she hasn't contacted us, which usually means there's something she thinks we'd be better off not knowing."

"You think you could maybe trade Force telekinesis for telepathy if you get the chance? That would *really* come in handy."

Han rubbed his hands over his face and then checked the control console. They'd land in an hour. But Thrackan was gone forever. That was something. And the *Falcon* was airworthy again, which was another plus.

"When Fett sees the state of the body, he's going to work it out for himself," said Leia.

"Maybe he won't look."

"He doesn't strike me as the squeamish sort, honey."

"He never saw her for fifty years. It's not like he cares about her. What sort of father doesn't see his kid for years?"

"Well, we didn't see Jacen for five," Leia pointed out.

"That was different. Are you scared of Fett?"

"I like to give him a wide berth."

"I'd like to say I can take him anytime, but I have my doubts."

Leia closed her eyes for a moment as if marshaling her thoughts. "We'll deal with it if and when it happens. It might not be our biggest problem."

"What, that our son ticks off the galaxy's most lethal bounty hunter? What's higher than that on the list?"

Leia got up from the copilot's seat and made her way aft to the hatch linking the cockpit to the cargo bays. Han knew she was going to take another look at Ailyn Vel's body; maybe she was going to make her look a little more presentable for her father, or somehow gather information from her last moments in those Jedi ways. He didn't ask.

"I'll tell you what's a bigger problem than having a feud with Boba Fett," she said. "Having a son who kills when he doesn't have to."

Han wondered if it was the first time Jacen had done that, and felt ashamed for even thinking it.

Then he wondered when Jacen would do it again.

CORONET CITY SPACEPORT, CORELLIA.

Mirta was waiting for Fett when he opened *Slave I*'s forward hatch. She didn't have a blaster in her hand, so he gave her the benefit of the doubt.

He was feeling both his age and his illness right then. Dull pain gnawed at him. He ignored it. "The Solos are bringing back Ailyn's body," he told her.

"I know. I want it."

Here we go. "You don't have a ship and you don't have any credits. What are you going to do with her?"

"What are *you* planning to do with her?"

"Bury her."

"Little late to take care of your daughter now."

"Don't you think I know that?" Fett noted that she was wearing the heart-of-fire around her neck. "So she gave you the necklace as a lure for me."

Mirta clasped her hand around the stone. "No, I really did recover it."

"So what happened to Sintas?"

"Why do you care?"

"Because I loved her. And not even Ailyn could possibly know what happened to us and why I left. So don't judge me."

Mirta's face was set in a snarl. "You never made any attempt to contact them."

"You want to know what my life was like?"

"Yeah, it must have been tough building that fortune."

"My dad was killed in front of me when I was thirteen. I was on the run for three years. I married Sintas at sixteen because I thought I could make my life right by doing what normal people did, but I was *wrong*. I tried to be a Journeyman Protector but I killed a superior officer and I was jailed and exiled from Concord Dawn. And that was the end of trying to be a regular man. After that, I settled on being Boba Fett, because *I just didn't know how to do anything else.*"

Mirta looked at him as if she was debating whether to put a couple of bolts in his head or try a chest shot. He didn't want her sympathy. He wanted her to understand why he would have made Sintas and Ailyn a lot more miserable by coming back to them after his sentence than by leaving.

And he'd killed an officer who had once been his mentor,

his friend. They hadn't really needed to exile him. He'd wanted to get as far from his pain as he could.

But why did he want Mirta to understand at all? She was just a stranger he'd met a few weeks ago. *She's nothing to me. Maybe she isn't even my own flesh and blood, just a chancer trying to make a few credits out of me.*

There was one way of settling this once and for all. He took out his datapad and accessed his accounts. "Got a bank?"

"Why do you want to know?"

"You put the first round into Sal-Solo. Take the million credits and get lost."

Her face was a mask of contempt. "You know what you can do with your credits."

She was family all right. He knew it at a gut level, anyway. "Got any brothers or sisters?"

"No. And no kids, either."

He never thought to ask that. "You're too young anyway."

"I was married. We marry young, don't we?"

Oh, how we repeat history. I don't need this trouble. I've got enough of my own.

Fett didn't ask why she wasn't married any longer. Her sour manner might have had something to do with that. But he'd started to respect her; and she was his granddaughter. She was all the family he had.

No, you need her to find the clone, and she knows what happened to Sintas . . .

He was playing games with himself, justifying his sentimentality with bogus pragmatism. He could find the clone on his own. He didn't need to know what happened to his wife. No, he was driven by the same craving that had made his father ask Dooku for a cloned son as part of his fee for being the progenitor of the clone army: he badly wanted *family*. It would have been simpler to find a wife and settle down, but Boba Fett was no more capable of that than his father had been.

"So we're going to fight over a corpse."

"You just want to win," said Mirta. "Doesn't matter *what* you win."

Fett couldn't even be angry with her. He leaned against *Slave I*'s hull and gazed up at the sky through his helmet's macrobinocular visor, waiting for the *Millennium Falcon* to appear as a speck in the sky and drop onto the landing strip. Mirta waited beside him—but not *with* him. He could almost feel the invisible wall she had placed between them.

It was a long half hour.

The *Falcon* swept across the strip and then looped back to land fifty meters away. Fett straightened up and went to meet her, Mirta at his heels.

Leia Solo was first off the ship and walked toward him as if barring his way. "I'm truly sorry about this, Fett. You, too, Mirta."

Fett walked past her and climbed the open ramp into the cargo hold. Han was maneuvering a repulsor gurney into the main bay, and he glanced over his shoulder at the two of them.

"Are you going to put us back on your hit list?" Han asked. "If you're thinking of going after Jacen, he's too tough a quarry, even for you."

Fett shook his head in slow, measured contempt. "I don't have to punish anyone, Solo. Your son orders his own sister to fire on civilians and then suspends her from duty when she refuses. No, I think I'll leave you to your happy family. I've got more pressing business."

He watched Han look at Leia, and Leia look at Han, and knew that he'd dropped a thermal detonator on them.

So they didn't know.

Fierfek, that's my daughter in that body bag.

The silence was that heavy moment before a thunder-

storm, pressing down on all of them. Leia—yes, his prede-
cessor Fenn Shysa had been very sweet on Leia, way back
before she married the space bum—made a helpless gesture
toward the hatch.

"I can get someone to arrange a funeral for you, Fett."

"No," he said. "She's mine." *Time for a gesture.* "She's
ours."

"Okay." Leia's voice was low and careful. "Take it easy."

"I want to see her body."

"I don't think that's a good idea."

"Princess Leia, I said *I want to see my daughter's body.*"

Mirta took hold of his arm. *Is that for her comfort or
mine?* Fett was once again glad of his helmet, because he
didn't want Han Solo to see his grief. His voice gave nothing away.

"And I want to see my mother," said Mirta.

Leia stepped back, but Han hovered. Fett couldn't stop
his voice hardening. "Leave us for a few minutes, Solo."

"Fett—"

"I said *leave us.*"

Han looked embarrassed and Leia steered him toward
the hatch. Fett and Mirta were now alone in the cargo bay
anteroom with the trolley.

They both hesitated and made a move for it at the same
time. Fett stood back for Mirta, and she eased open the
cover, eyes fixed and staring.

It was only the slight jerk of her chin that told him she
was shocked. He stood beside her and saw a stranger. Ailyn
Vel's face was bruised and cut but surprisingly peaceful: she
wore a Kiffar tattoo, three black lines from her left brow to
cheekbone, like her mother Sintas had done. Her dark hair
was heavily streaked with gray.

That's my little girl.

He tried very hard to feel that the body of a middle-aged
woman he didn't recognize was the child he had once held.

They said that your kids never stopped being your babies, however old they were, but Fett couldn't make that connection.

But I want to. I want to feel that.

You missed her whole life. Everything. Did she ever call me Dada? No, I don't recall that she did.

Mirta leaned over, placed the heart-of-fire around her mother's neck, and laid her cheek against hers. Then she straightened up and stood back, as if to give him space to take his leave of Ailyn as well. And that was hard. He hesitated, because he could feel another memory, one that he hadn't suppressed and didn't want to, crowding in on him. He was in a dusty arena on Geonosis sixty years before, picking up his father's helmet.

Jedi always take everything from me.

Fett would have to remove his helmet to kiss her goodbye and he wasn't ready for that, not here. He tidied Ailyn's hair with gloved fingers and was about to close the body bag when the urge not to lose the heart-of-fire overcame him. It was all he had of a happier time. He unfastened it and found Mirta staring at him, grim and unblinking. She wanted it to rest with Ailyn's body.

There was a solution.

Hearts-of-fire had a grain, a crystalline structure that created lines of weakness that jewelers used to cleave the stones into smaller, workable pieces. Fett set the small disc on its edge and took out his blaster. A couple of hard cracks with the stock split the stone down the cleavage line, and it fell into two slices. Fett eased one piece off the leather thong and handed it to Mirta before placing the remains of the necklace around Ailyn's neck again.

He'd handled a lot of dead bodies. If you were a bounty hunter, it went with the job. It was only when he fumbled fastening the leather cord at the back of the neck and had to remove his gloves that he actually *touched* Ailyn.

Her hair was coarser than he'd imagined. Her skin was icy silk.

And that was the point at which he truly knew that he had lost his only child. He had never been there for her, and that was a pain he knew would *never* fade, not like his memory of Sintas. His father had been there for him. But he'd failed to live up to him in the most important way of all: by being as good a father as Jango Fett.

"Let's go," said Mirta. "We're taking her home."

It had suddenly become *we*. "Where's home? Not Taris."

"Mandalore."

"I don't actually have a property there now."

"Time you got one, then."

Boba Fett and Mirta returned to *Slave I* and laid Ailyn Vel in the refrigerated hold that had been designed for prisoners whose warrant had included the word *dead*. It didn't feel right, but it was the only practical solution for the journey back to Mandalore.

Whoever that Kad'ika was, he had a point. Sometimes you really needed somewhere to call home *forever*. Fett made his way back up through *Slave I*'s central hatch and settled in the pilot's seat. Mirta, still silent, slipped into the copilot's position.

"Beviin says we Mandalorians rarely bury our dead," said Fett. "But I never was much of a Mandalorian."

"Mama was Kiffar."

Okay. "What do you want to do, then?"

Mirta's eyes brimmed. "I don't know right now."

Fett lifted off his helmet. "We'll head back to Mandalore. By way of Geonosis, because that's where I buried my dad. Family needs keeping together."

It was the longest conversation about anything other than business that he'd had with *anyone* since he was a kid. It was personal, agonizingly so, and the effort hurt. He finally let the tears run down his face in silence.

Mirta cried beside him, occasionally gulping for air. It was all very quiet and embarrassed, as if neither was willing to admit they could weep, but the truth was that they both could, and hard.

They were family now. It was the worst possible way to forge a bond. But it *was* a bond, even if there was no affection, and for the first time in his life it was one that Boba Fett would try to approach as a father himself, not as a man constantly living in the past in search of one who would never return.

chapter twenty-three

He will strengthen himself through sacrifice.
He will ruin those who deny justice.
He will immortalize his love.
                              —Prophecy of the Sith,
                              foretold in tassel artifact

LUMIYA'S SAFE HOUSE, GALACTIC CITY.

Jacen had the dream again, the one where he found himself staring at a weapon in his hands and sobbing.

The dream had taken a number of forms in the last few days. In the first, he held his lightsaber; in those that followed, he held a Yuuzhan Vong amphistaff, or a blaster, or a lightwhip. In one, he even held a weapon he didn't recognize at all.

The recurrence bothered him enough to seek Lumiya's advice. He stood at the doorway of her apartment block and looked up into the Coruscant sky to see if he could detect any light from the window. She was there, he knew.

Luke knew, too. He just didn't know *where* she was, how very close. An airspeeder could cover the distance from the Skywalkers' apartment to the safe house in under an hour. But did it matter? Events were moving faster than his uncle would ever believe. They were almost moving too fast for Jacen to comprehend, and he let himself be carried with them, trusting the Force.

Inside the apartment, Lumiya sat meditating, her face veiled again. There was no Force illusion this time; the apartment looked like any other rented apartment with basic furniture and taupe carpet, a strangely mundane setting for such pivotal events.

In her hands Lumiya held the tassels whose knots and threads were a language, a prophecy, an arcane instruction book of what Jacen had to do to achieve full Sith knowledge and power. On the low table in front of her was a candle, burning steadily and occasionally guttering in a draft.

"I have dreams," he said. "Dreams of weapons that I've used."

"And they distress you," said Lumiya.

"All I recall is that I'm looking at a weapon in my hand and feeling enormous grief."

"It might just be a dream and not a vision."

"The weapon is different each time."

"Perhaps just a dream, then."

He hoped so. Even Jedi had dreams like normal people, fed by the day's events and fueled by stresses and strains and unresolved conflicts. If he was having bad dreams, no doctor would be surprised. In a short time he had learned to do things . . . no, he had *instigated* things that he would never have thought he was capable of doing. When he looked at the shock and revulsion on the faces of those close to him—his father, his mother, even Ben—he could stand back and see reflected in their eyes how much he had changed.

"I find myself pursuing the memory of my grandfather with increasing frequency."

Lumiya fondled the strands of the tassels and ran the knots between her thumb and forefinger. She seemed to be reading them.

"You depend on location to flow-walk in time," she said. "So you can only see what happened to Lord Vader on Coruscant."

"Is that your way of telling me I need to find out more elsewhere?"

"No, I'm saying that if you look for vindication in the past, it will be at best *selective*."

"I feel I'm reliving parts of Anakin Skywalker's life. I'd be crazy if I didn't try to learn from that."

"But you already know that your path differs. He was seduced into errors. You won't be."

"All right, let me ask again. What more do I need to learn to fulfill my destiny?"

Lumiya slowly extended her arm and held out the tassels she had been running between her fingers. He reached out and took them. They felt suddenly red-hot, and he tossed them a little in the air out of pure animal instinct, as if he had grabbed a hot breadstick from an oven. When the threads fell back into his hand they were cold.

"*This* is your final trial, Jacen. You've sacrificed a great deal—the approval of all those who meant most to you. You've taken extreme measures to deal with those who deny justice. Now you must consider the third prophecy."

He cradled the knotted tassel in his cupped palms. *He will immortalize his love.* He'd turned that phrase over in his mind a thousand times. What did it mean? Total duty to the galaxy, and no time for family? Building eternal peace at his own personal cost?

He didn't know.

"It means, Jacen, that sacrificing your own feelings and reputation isn't enough."

Jacen had forced himself over the edge of what he had thought of as decency. He'd done the dirty work, the necessary work, the work that no other Jedi would, because they were too concerned about the vanity of their own reputations and the cleanliness of their own hands, to take on the burdens they placed so willingly on ordinary people.

I did my own dirty work. I faced what Grandfather faced—but I did it for the galaxy, not for my own selfish love of a woman.

Motive mattered. Some philosophers said it didn't, but in the end motive was all there was to distinguish between good and evil.

"What, then?"

"You have to kill what you love."

Jacen didn't quite take in the meaning of that at first. Then panic gripped him.

Tenel Ka. Allana. How did Lumiya know? How *could* she know? He'd been so careful. He hardly dared even touch them in the Force because he risked alerting Lumiya to their very existence. Every visit he sneaked in was fraught with danger, but he'd been careful, as careful as only he could be.

Jacen concentrated hard and projected a sense of bewilderment to mask the dread and fear churning his stomach, and it took almost all his strength. He picked up the candle from the table and stared into its flame as if distracted by it, using it to focus his control. "You'll have to explain that."

"I can't teach you any more skills. You now have to pass through the final barrier and do what no ordinary man can—kill someone whose death will cause terrible suffering to those who love them, someone close to you."

"Who?"

"I can't tell you, because I don't know."

"Someone I love?"

"Do you love someone?"

"I allow myself to love many people." *Careful ... careful. You're on the knife-edge.* "How will I know who to kill?"

"It'll become clear when the time is right. You'll *know*."

"And why is it the ultimate test?"

"Because taking the life of an innocent is always harder even than taking your own, if you're sincere. This is the ultimate test of selflessness—whether you're ready to face unending emotional pain, true agony, to gain the power to create peace and order for billions of total strangers. *That* is the sacrifice. To be vilified by others, by people you know and care for, and for your personal sacrifice to be totally unknown to those billions you save, to do your duty as a Sith. To do your duty for the good of the galaxy." She stood so close to him that her breath made the candle's flame flicker. "It's easy to be a clean-cut hero slaying monsters. There's always a little bit of vanity in it. There can be no room for vanity or pride in being despised."

It was true, and it was horrible. Courage often needed an audience. True selfless courage, by definition, took place in darkness, unseen.

Jacen held his hand in the flame. He held it there longer than he had ever done before, until he smelled his own flesh charring, and Lumiya reached out and jerked his arm away. He wasn't sure if he was testing his ability to transcend pain or beginning his own punishment.

He thought of his grandfather, killing simply for Padmé's life. Whoever Jacen had to kill as the price of being able to wield the ultimate defensive weapon of Sith order, he would know his motives were totally divorced from his own narrow wants and needs . . . like Tenel Ka and his Allana.

Oh no. Oh no.

Lumiya took his hand and turned it over to examine the seared palm.

"Now . . . imagine that will be nothing compared to what you'll feel when you confront the ultimate challenge."

He wanted a peaceful, orderly galaxy. He wanted it that way not only because it was right, and necessary, but because he had a daughter and he wanted her future to be free of the fighting and fear he had known all his life. He'd never known peace. He wanted better than that for Allana, and, yes, he wanted that for Tenel Ka, too. He wanted happiness for those he loved.

He *wanted*. He *loved*. And *that* was what had brought down Grandfather.

"The ultimate challenge," Lumiya said again, her voice oddly soft and mournful.

Suddenly Jacen could see his challenge, and the prospect terrified him. He would have to kill those he most loved. He would have to kill Tenel Ka and his precious daughter, his Allana. The fact that even the thought of it was tearing out his heart was the terrible proof that it had to be so.

And still he could hardly bear to think it. The Yuuzhan Vong thought they knew all there was to know about inflicting pain, but they were beginners compared with this.

How could he even *think* it? Jacen put his right hand to his face and touched it, as if it weren't his own. He felt as if he were standing over by the far wall, watching himself die by degrees.

Is it me? Is it really my burden?

Yes, Grandfather.

It's me.

Jacen accepted the burden in its entirety, and his heart—irrelevant, fragile, expendable—broke.

SLAVE I, EN ROUTE TO GEONOSIS.

So they sat in the cargo hold of *Slave I*—Boba Fett, Mirta Gev, and a corpse. And Fett wasn't sure what to say next.

"I never *was* of any use to you, was I?" Mirta said.

"Does that matter?"

"Will I ever get to know you enough to trust you?"

"I could ask the same question."

"You're not what I expected."

"Yeah."

"And you're all I've got."

There were two ways of saying that, and one was to say it like it was a last resort. And that was the way she said it.

Fett wondered if his illness was affecting his mind. He

heard himself say the words, going through the motions of being a normal human being. "Want to hunt with me?"

Mirta looked at him with dark, pained eyes that were an awful lot older than they had been when he'd met her just weeks earlier.

"What's the catch?"

"I'm dying."

"What?"

"Yes. Boba Fett really is on the way out."

"You're playing one of those mind games of yours."

"I'm dying and I need to find some Kaminoan medical data if I stand a chance of surviving. Your clone with the gray gloves might be the path to it."

She seemed to teeter on that knife-edge between wanting to believe him and a lifetime of mistrust and loathing. "Why are you telling me this?"

"Because I'm not what *I* expected, either."

"What about fighting for Corellia?"

"You heard the boys. They're not interested in mercenary work when there's real soldiering to be done. I'm *Mand'alor*, and I want to know what this Kad'ika has to say for himself if he thinks he's taking my job."

"Oh, you heard about Kad'ika, then."

"You're the *Mando'a* speaker. You tell me."

"Never seen him. Hearing plenty, though. What's the matter? Think he's after your *kyr'bes*?"

The crown: the mythosaur skull. *Mand'alor* wasn't a title he'd ever wanted. But Beviin's retort had stung in ways he hadn't thought possible. *No heir, no clan, no sense of duty. You're not Mandalorian. You just wear the armor.* Fett wanted to leave behind more than credits and a trail of bodies. In the end, every being in the galaxy wanted to mean something to somebody—even just one individual.

See, Dad, I know now why you wanted me so badly.

Mirta was stroking the heart-of-fire discreetly as it sat in the hollow at the base of her throat. "Okay," she said. "Okay, *Ba'buir*. Count me in."

"*Ba'buir?*"

"It means 'grandfather,' " she said quietly.

"I don't speak Mandalorian. Thanks to you, I can swear in it a little."

"Your father—Great-Granddad—never even took you through the *verd'goten?*"

"What's that?"

"The warrior trial. When you become an adult at thirteen."

"Does six decades of war and bounty hunting qualify me?"

"You're *dar'manda* without your culture. You don't have a soul."

She was probably right. "Let's go find your clone. And recover my father."

"What about my mama's ship?"

"I'll get Beviin to collect it. You'd be amazed what that man can find."

"Even that clone."

"Yeah. Maybe even that clone."

Fett eased into the cockpit of *Slave I* and set course for Geonosis for the first time since he was thirteen. Mirta, subdued, waited for his gesture to sit up front. He'd teach her to pilot if his time held out.

The galaxy would say that the Mandalorians had finally given up. Staying out of a galactic war was unthinkable; *Mando'ade* had always fought. Well, there was such a thing as a strategic withdrawal, and this was one. It was time for Mandalore to put its own house in order, and if he could grab that time and defeat his illness, he'd do it. If he didn't . . . then maybe this Kad'ika would do it instead.

Either way, Boba Fett was going to let the Jedi and Han Solo fight their little war without his intervention this time.

Because he had more pressing business.

Because Jacen Solo was becoming a pale imitation of his grandfather, Lord Vader, and would take on more than he had ever bargained for.

And because Fett had a granddaughter now.

Family—and Mandalore—came first.

Good night, Dad. We're going home.

Read on for a sneak preview of Troy Denning's

TEMPEST

The third novel in the epic new *Star Wars* series,
featuring the heroes of the New Jedi Order

The object of her desire was walking down the opposite
side of the skylane, moving along a pedwalk so choked with
vines and yorik coral that even the zap gangs traveled single-
file. He was two levels below and ten meters ahead, and he
kept stopping to study door membranes and peer into the
windows of coral-crusted buildings. Then he would just
stand there in the gloom, alone and empty-handed, as though
no Jedi need fear the dangers of the undercity . . . as though *he*
ruled the twilight depths down where Coruscant changed
to Yuuzhan'tar.

Jacen Solo was as arrogant as ever—and this time, it
would be his undoing.

The angle was perfect, almost *too* perfect. If she struck
now, he would be dead almost as soon as he hit the pedwalk. Even if corpse robbers did not drop the body into the
skylane, the only hint of what had killed him would be a
tiny barb in his neck and a trace of venom in his nervous
system. Nobody would know that his death had been an
execution . . . not even Jacen.

But Alema Rar needed them to know. She needed to see
the shock of recognition in Jacen's eyes when he collapsed,

to feel his fear burning in the Force as his heart cramped into an unbeating knot. She needed to hold him dying in her arms and suck the last breath from his lips, to hear his father roaring curses and watch his mother wailing in grief.

That last part, Alema needed more than anything.

She had spent years pondering what she could take from Leia Solo that would be the equal of everything Leia had taken from her. An instep and five toes? That would be a fair trade for the half a foot Leia had cut off on Tenupe. And the Princess's eyes and ears would do for the lekku she had severed aboard *Admiral Ackbar*. But what of the giant spidersloth to which Leia had fed her in the Tenupian jungle? How was Alema to match *that*?

Because this was not about revenge, not about cruelty. It was about *Balance*. The spidersloth had nearly *killed* her, had bitten her almost in half and left her slender dancer's body roped with white scars, an ugly lopsided thing that only a Rodian would desire. Now Alema had to take something equal from Leia, something that would shatter *her* to the core . . . because that's what Jedi *did*. They served the Balance.

And the first thing Alema wanted to take was Jacen, who was moving along the pedwalk toward the corner of an intersecting skylane. She had wanted to take him for a long time, since the day he had returned so mysterious and powerful from his five-year travels to study the Force. And now she would have him—perhaps not in the way she had once desired, but she *would* have him.

Eager to keep her prey in sight, Alema hurried back toward the nearest pedestrian bridge. It was fifty meters away, but she could not risk Force-leaping across the skylane after Jacen rounded the corner. This region was teeming with Ferals, the half-wild survivors of the Yuuzhan Vong invasion who continued to live a primitive existence deep in the undercity. If they saw Alema do something that remarkable, Jacen would sense their shock.

As Alema drew near the bridge, a faint nettling came to the stump of her amputated lekku. She stopped and slipped as far into the shadows as the coral would allow, then stood motionless, listening to the Ferals murmur behind their door membranes. When no danger appeared, she extended her Force-awareness a few meters and felt a pair of nervous presences behind her.

Alema turned to find the sunken-eyed faces of two young humans smirking up from the floor. They were hiding along the back of the pedwalk, in a shadowy stairwell so ringed with yorik coral that she had not noticed it. When they realized she was looking at them, the boys snickered and started to slip back down the stairwell.

Alema caught them in the Force, then pulled the pair back into view. With thin brows and small, round-ended noses, they were clearly brothers. She raised her lip in a twisted half smile, enjoying the sense of power that rushed through her veins as their shock changed to fear.

"And what did you two have planned for us?" Alema always referred to herself in the plural. It was a habit she had acquired when she became a Killik Joiner, and one that she had no interest in losing. Using the singular would mean admitting that her nest was gone—that Jacen and Luke and the rest of the Jedi had destroyed Gorog—and that was not true, not while Alema still lived. "Robbery? Murder? Ravagery?"

The brothers shook their heads and started to open their mouths, but were clearly too repulsed by her deformities to speak.

"You're staring." Alema Force-pinned them against the wall. "That's rude."

"Put us down!" the largest ordered. With a lean face and a shadowy line of mustache fuzz on his upper lip, he was probably a year or two into human adolescence. "We didn't mean nothing. It's just . . ."

His gaze slid from Alema's face toward the lekku stump hanging behind her shoulder, then quickly began to drop. Alema had traded her provocative attire for more traditional Jedi garb, but even those shape-concealing robes were not enough to hide her disfigurements—the lopsided twist of her body, and the way one atrophied arm hung at her side. As the boy's gaze fell, she sensed in the Force his growing revulsion—actually experienced the disgust he felt when he looked at her.

"It's just *what*?" Alema demanded. In her anger, she was pressing both boys against the wall so hard they began to wheeze. "Go ahead. Tell us."

It was the younger brother who answered. "It's just . . ." He nodded at the lightsaber hanging from her belt. "You're a Jedi!"

Alema smiled coldly. "Aren't you clever? Pretending you've never seen a Jedi Knight before." She glanced ten meters down the pedwalk, to where a knobby-scaled radank had backed a screeching Falleen into a tangle of slashvines, then looked back to the boy. "But we have the Force. We *know* what you were looking at."

Allowing the older brother to fall free, she pointed down the pedwalk and Force-hurled his younger sibling into the slashvines next to the Falleen. The startled radank reared back, front feet raised and claws unsheathed, then extended its thin proboscis and began to sniff the new prey. The boy whimpered and called for help.

Alema looked back to the older one, who was already trying to inch his way toward his brother, and waved him on.

"Go." She gave a cruel little laugh. "After the radank is finished with you, you'll know how *we* feel."

The boy's eyes flashed with fear, but he pulled a shiv of

sharpened duiasteel from his sleeve and raced down the pedwalk toward his brother. Alema turned toward the bridge and, as the snarl and shriek of combat erupted behind her, allowed herself a small smile of satisfaction. The boys had mocked her disfigurement, and now they would be disfigured themselves. The Balance had been preserved.

Alema continued up the pedwalk, then started across the bridge. Her stump began to nettle again, and she wondered if someone was watching her. Jacen had seemed to be alone when he left his apartment but—as commander of the Galatic Alliance Guard—he would know to expect assassins. Maybe his young apprentice, Ben Skywalker, had followed a few moments later to watch is back.

Alema gently extended her Force-awareness into the shadows behind her, searching for that flicker of pure bright power that always betrayed the Force presence of earnest young Jedi Knights. She felt nothing and decided that maybe the cause of her uneasiness was a raucous zap gang ahead, which had claimed the middle of the bridge for their own. They were taking turns trying to push a frightened Gamorrean female over the safety rail, but as Alema approached, they spread across the bridge and leered at her twisted form. They were all young human males, all wearing white tabards over various pieces of plastoid armor.

"What do you think you are?" the leader asked, eyeing Alema's black robes. He was a large youth with a three-day growth of beard and a badly swollen cheek. "Some kind of Jedi?"

"We have no time for your games," Alema replied coolly. "Go back and play with your Gamorrean." Alema made a shooing motion with the backs of her fingers, at the same time touching his mind through the Force. "You might have more fun if you let *her* do the pushing."

Swollen cheek frowned, then turned to his companions. "She doesn't have time for us." He started after the Gamorrean, who was lumbering toward the far end of the bridge as fast as her thick legs could take her. "Get her! We'll try something new this time!"

The zap gang spun as one and raced away. Alema followed, catching up as they surrounded the Gamorrean and began to argue about who would be shoved into the safety rail first. Alema slipped past and smiled to herself. *Balance.*

At the other end of the bridge, Jacen was nowhere to be seen. He had either rounded the corner of the building or entered a doorway while Alema was dealing with the city's riff-raff. She drew her lightsaber and advanced up the pedwalk, half expecting to feel the emitter nozzle of a lightsaber pressing into her ribs just before Jacen activated the blade.

The most dangerous thing Alema met was a foraging skrat pack, which skittered away into a tangle of slashvines almost as soon as she saw it. The only other oddity was the sporadic stream of Ferals disappearing through a door membrane near the corner of the building. They were of many species—Bith, Bothan, Ho'Din—and they were all bearing the carcasses of dead animals, including hawk-bats, granite slugs, a few scaly yanskacs. Once, there was even a Chevin clutching what looked like a dead Ewok in its huge claw. They were probably just Ferals returning home with the day's hunt, but as Alema passed in front of the doorway, she kept her lightsaber at the ready.

No one leapt out to attack her, but she sensed a pair of Force presences on the other side of the membrane. Alema did not bother to investigate; had it been Jacen lurking behind the door, she would have sensed nothing at all. Instead, she exchanged her lightsaber for a short blowgun and armed it with a small cone-dart from a sealed container in her utility belt. She had eight more such darts—one for each of the Solos and the Skywalkers, plus two extras—all fashioned from the stinger and venom sac of a deadly Tenupian wasber.

The poison was fairly quick—at least on man-size creatures—but more important, it was certain. It co-opted the white blood cells sent to fight infection, turning them into tiny toxin-producing factories. Within moments of being struck, all of the victim's organs would fall under attack, and within moments of *that,* his vital systems would start to fail. Jacen would live long enough for Alema to reveal herself; he would probably die even before he realized that his Jedi neutralizing techniques could not save him.

Alema raised the blowgun to her lips and stepped around the corner, her body already purring with the sweet tingle of murder.

But Jacen seemed determined to disappoint her. The pedwalk was empty and dark, and there was not a sentient in sight. Thinking Jacen had lured her into a trap after all, Alema whirled back around the corner, her lungs filled with the air that would send the lethal dart shooting into her ambusher.

There was no ambush. That pedwalk was empty as well, and the only danger Alema sensed was the same faint tingle she had been feeling since before crossing the bridge. Could Jacen Solo be *hiding* from her?

Alema's anger welled up inside. It was those boys. They had made her hurt them, and Jacen had always been so sensitive to such things. She cursed the brothers for making her lose control. Her plan had just grown more complicated, and that meant the pair would have to pay—but later. Right now, she needed to go after Jacen. The poison on her dart would lose its effectiveness in less than an hour.

Alema returned to the door she had just passed, the one all the Ferals had been entering with their carcasses. Dark and ringed by a thick crust of yorik coral, it looked more like a cavern mouth than a doorway. She pressed a nerve bundle set into the doorjamb, and the membrane pulled aside. Standing opposite her was a brawny Nikto with a scaly green face and a ring of small horns encircling his eyes. He kept one hand on the pocket of his soiled jerkin, obviously holding a blaster, and Alema could sense two more guards behind him, hiding on either side of the door.

He studied her for an instant, then rasped, "Wrrrong doorrr, lady. Nothing inside to interest *you*."

Alema started to reach for the guard in the Force, but stopped when her danger sense grew so strong that her remaining lekku began to tingle as well. She pointed her blowgun at the Nikto's feet and—using a Force suggestion to ensure he would obey—commanded, "Wait."

The expression in the Nikto's eyes changed from threatening to surprised to obedient, and Alema extended her Force awareness in all directions.

To her astonishment, she brushed a cold presence—something dark and bitter—back up the pedwalk near the bridge. But when she turned to look in that direction, all she saw was the zap gang cheering the Gamorrean on as she belly-bounced their leader into the safety railing.

And the presence did not belong to any of the zappers. It was much too strong in the Force, too focused . . . then the darkness vanished, and the danger tingle in her lekku subsided as quickly as it had come.

Alema continued to study the pedwalk for a few moments more, trying to digest what she had felt. Someone was definitely stalking her, but it could hardly be Jacen. Even had he been careless enough to let her detect him—and he wouldn't have been—the Jacen she remembered was anything but bitter: solemn and brooding, certainly, but also devoted and sincere.

So who *was* stalking her? Not Ben. He was too young to be so bitter. And not Jaina. Her temperament was too fiery to feel that cold. Besides, the presence had felt dark . . . and it made no sense for a dark-sider to be watching Jacen's back. It had to be something else.

Another possibility dawned on her: Maybe *Alema* was not the one being followed. Maybe it was *Jacen*.

Could someone be trying to steal her kill?

Alema turned back to the Nikto, gesturing past him with her blowgun. "Did Jacen Solo go in there?"

"Jacen Solo?" The Nikto shook his head. "Don't know any Solos."

"Come now." Alema used the Force to draw the Nikto out onto the pedwalk. "The news holos reach even down here, and every third report contains his image. The commander of the Galactic Alliance Guard? The savior of Coruscant?"

"Why would someone like that come here?" The Nikto tried to sound uncertain, but Alema could sense his lie in the subtle tremor of his Force presence. "There's nothing inside but housing—"

"You dare lie to *me*?" Alema used the Force to raise her crippled arm, then grabbed him by the throat. "To a *Jedi*?"

Still calling on the Force, she lifted him off his feet and squeezed until she heard the happy crackle of crushed cartilage. The Nikto's mouth fell open and a terrible gurgle came from his throat. Alema continued to hold him aloft until his eyes rolled back and his feet began kick; only when she sensed the other two guards stepping into the doorway did she drop the Nikto on the balcony and turn to find a pair of tentacle-faced Quarren bringing old E-11 blaster rifles to bear.

Alema waved her blowgun, using the Force to turn their weapons aside, then touched their minds with hers to search out the doubt she knew would be foremost in their thoughts— the fear that they would not be able to stop her from entering, that *they* would be the ones who died.

"You do not *need* to die." Alema spoke in a Force whisper

so soft and compelling, it sounded like a thought. "You do not *need* to stop anyone."

The guards relaxed. Alema stepped over the dying Nikto and went through the doorway. "No one is coming through the door," she purred.

As Alema passed between the Quarren, she noticed that one of them had only three face-tentacles. Their beady eyes began to focus on her, and their old E-11 blaster rifles started to swing back toward her.

"You do not *need* to die." Alema tapped the muzzles of their weapons aside. "You do not *need* to see me."

Their eyes grew unfocused again, and they turned their attention back to the door. Once Alema was safely inside, she faced the two Quarren.

"You know me well," she said, continuing to speak in her Force whisper. "We have been talking for several minutes."

The Quarren shifted their stances, opening a place for Alema, and turned their heads slightly toward her.

Now Alema spoke in her normal voice. "Where do you suppose *he* was going?"

Three Tentacle turned to face her. "Who? Solo?"

Alema nodded.

"Where do you *think* he was going?" Three Tentacle retorted. "To see It, of course."

"*It?*" Alema had spent enough of her early life wallowing in the underbelly of the galaxy to know that illicit enterprises were often referred to only in vague terms. Did Jacen have a secret vice—an addiction he was hiding, or a compulsion he had picked up in captivity and been unable to shake? She looked back to the Quarren and spoke in her Force whisper again. "What are we talking about? Spice dens? Death games?"

Now the second Quarren turned toward her, his tentacles straightening in his species' equivalent of a frown. "Is that supposed to be a joke? He's here for the same reason everyone else is. To see It. The friend."

"The friend—of course."

Alema knew the kind of "friends" males kept hidden in places like this . . . the kind they would dare visit only in the anonymous depths of an undercity. Jacen's time with the Yuuzhan Vong had left him more bent than even she had realized. She pointed her blowgun out the door, gesturing at the fallen Nikto, then spoke in her Force whisper again.

"Your companion was attacked by an intruder," she said. "You *saw* the intruder kill him, and soon the intruder will want to come inside."

"To kill It?" the second Quarren gasped.

"Yes, to kill It," Alema agreed. "You must stop the intruder from entering."

Three Tentacle pressed a nerve bundle, closing the door, then both Quarren pointed their blaster rifles at the heart of the membrane.

"Good," Alema said.

Alema turned away from the door, confident the two Quarren had already forgotten her. During her time with the Killiks, the queen of her nest—a Dark Jedi named Lomi Plo—had helped her develop a slippery presence in the Force. Now, as soon as Alema vanished from someone's sight, she also vanished from memory.

Alema left the vestibule and entered a warren of winding, tunnel-like passages lit by the bioluminescent lichen typical of Yuuzhan Vong–converted buildings. She selected the largest, most heavily trodden corridor and started forward at a brisk pace. She had to work fast if she wanted to be the one who killed Jacen; whoever was behind her would not be delayed for long by the Quarren.

The air quickly grew hot and dank, and puffs of what smelled like ammonia and sulfur started to roll up the passage. Alema wrinkled her nose and began to wonder just what kind of pleasure den this was. No spice she had ever used was so harsh; if the odor grew any stronger, it would be enough to quell a rancor in rut.

She had just reached a short side passage when the distant shriek of blaster rifles sang down the corridor—the vestibule guards firing on her mysterious stalker. Alema peered down the side passage and saw that it opened into something vaguely reminiscent of a Kala'uun joy cave: a central chamber surrounded by a number of privacy cells. Was that where she would find Jacen and his *friend*?

A strange chorus of *snap-hiss*es erupted from the entry vestibule, and the blasterfire ceased as suddenly as it had begun. By the sound of it, whoever was following Alema was using some sort of strange lightsaber technology—and using it well. The Quarren had bought Alema even less time than she had expected.

But which way had Jacen gone—into the joy cave, or deeper into the building? Searching for him in the Force would do no good—indeed, would probably prove disastrous. Even if he wasn't concealing his own presence, he would feel her looking for him, and Alema could not best Jacen Solo in a straight duel—not with one half-useless arm and one clumsy half foot.

Fortunately, Alema knew males, and males—especially important males who pursued their secret passions in low places—did not like to wait for their pleasure.

She went down the side passage and was surprised to find no panderer there to greet her, nor any spice dealers, nor any glitter girls waiting for new clients. There was not even a beverage center, only a fountain gurgling in the center of the room and a refresher tucked away into a rear alcove. The doors to most of the privacy cells were open, revealing small dens containing beds, nesting basins, or simple raised pallets.

But a handful of the cells were closed, and Alema could

sense beings in them all. She went to the first and, holding her blowgun ready to shoot, pressed the nerve bundle beside the door. The membrane retracted to reveal a pair of Jenet curled up on large floor cushions, their limbs pulled in tight and their snouts tucked close to their legs. Neither opened an eye, even when Alema grunted in disbelief.

There were no spice pipes in the cell, no aphrodisiacs, not even an empty ale mug. They were sleeping—just sleeping.

Alema moved on, opening two more doors. She found a lone Duros behind one and a trio of Chadra-Fan behind the other—all *sleeping*. Apparently, she had stumbled into some sort of staff dormitory. She cursed under her breath. What kind of pleasure den had the staff quarters in front?

Alema started back toward the main corridor and glimpsed her pursuer's shadow on the far wall. She ducked out of sight and made sure that her Force presence was damped down, then peered around the corner and watched as a thin woman in a scarlet robe came down the corridor.

The woman was middle-aged, with red hair and a thin nose, and she kept the lower half of her face concealed behind a black scarf. In one hand, she held a coil of strands—leather and gem-studded metal—attached to what looked like the hilt of a lightsaber.

Alema was so shocked that she almost let her feelings spill into the Force. At the Jedi academy on Yavin 4, she had studied the story of an Imperial agent named Shira Brie: how Brie had attempted to discredit Luke in the eyes of his fellow pilots, only to be shot down and nearly killed; how Darth Vader had rehabilitated her, turning her into as much machine as he was, then training her in the ways of the Sith; how she had constructed her lightwhip and returned to trouble Luke Skywalker time after time in her new identity as Lumiya, Dark Lady of the Sith.

Could it be that Lumiya had returned one more time?

Alema saw no room to doubt. The woman was the right age and appearance, she concealed her lower face beneath the same dark scarf that Lumiya wore to hide her scarred jawline, and she carried a lightwhip—a weapon unique to the era of modern Jedi.

And she was hunting Jacen Solo.

Alema drew back around the corner, her thoughts whirling as she struggled to sort through the implications. She knew from the histories she had studied that Lumiya hated the Skywalkers and the Solos almost as much as Alema herself did, so it seemed likely their goals were the same—to destroy the Solo-Skywalker clan. But Alema could not permit Lumiya to steal her kills. If the Balance was to be served, Alema had to destroy the prey herself.

She filled her lungs with air, then raised the blowgun to her lips and rolled around the corner to attack.

The corridor was empty.

She rolled back around the corner, expecting Lumiya to attack from the cover of a Force blur or drop off the ceiling at any instant.

When nothing happened, Alema stood and stepped away from the door. Still, Lumiya did not appear. Alema expanded her Force-awareness, searching for the Sith's dark presence.

Nothing.

Alema cautiously peered around the corner again. When no attack came, she studied the walls, ceiling, and floor carefully, searching for any odd shadows or blurred areas where Lumiya might be hiding. When there was still no attack, she advanced up the short side passage to the main corridor and did the same thing.

Lumiya was gone, vanished as quickly as she had appeared.

Alema grew cold and empty inside, and she began to wonder if she had really seen Lumiya at all. Perhaps it had been a Force-vision . . . or perhaps her fever had returned.

Once, near the end of her first year marooned in the Tenupian jungle, she had spent days exploring the Massassi temples on Yavin 4 with her dead sister, Numa—only to find herself stranded high on a Tenupian mountain when the fever finally broke.

But another explanation seemed just as likely: Lumiya had continued after Jacen.

Alema started down the corridor at a run, growing more anxious with each step that Lumiya would beat her to the kill, no longer taking the time to move quietly, barely paying attention to which way she was going, just moving deeper into the building, deeper into the heat and the dankness and that horrid smell of ammonia and sulfur.

Twice, she ran headlong into surprised Ferals, and twice she had to kill them for attempting to lie to her before finally pointing the true way to It. Another time, she heard a large group of armored Ferals clattering up a ramp she was descending. She pressed herself against the wall between two patches of glow-lichen, then drew a Force shadow over herself and watched impatiently as they rushed past to search out the intruder.

Finally, the ammonia-and-sulfur smell grew almost overpowering, and Alema began to hear strange gurglings and splashes. She emerged onto a narrow mezzanine balcony and found herself gazing across a huge well of yellow fog. It looked nothing like the pleasure den she had been expecting, but she stepped out of the passage and crossed the balcony without hesitation. In typical Yuuzhan Vong fashion, there was no railing to keep pedestrians safe. The yorik coral simply ended twenty meters above a vast pool of steaming slime.

A constant supply of bubbles was rising from the depths of the pool, scattering the surface with frequent flashes of light as they dissolved into scarlet and yellow glimmers. The surrounding walls were mottled with patches of bioluminescent lichen, barely visible through the thick fog. Higher up several tiers of balconies curved away on both sides and vanished into the steam. Scattered along the balcony edges were the shadowy silhouettes of Ferals, usually in the process of tossing animal carcasses—or even lifeless bipeds—into the pool below. The splashes were always followed by a short gurgle, as though the bodies were too heavy to float on slime for more than an instant.

Alema furrowed her brow, trying to decide exactly what she was looking at. In Coruscant's savage undercity—especially the part that was still Yuuzhan'tar—dead animals were invariably devoured by Ferals or other scavengers long before the meat spoiled. So it seemed unlikely the pool was some sort of garbage pit. Instead, the Ferals had to be feeding something—something that Jacen was interested in, as well.

Alema was about to back away when a voice murmured up through the fog. It was impossible to make out what it was saying over the gurgling of the pool, but Alema did not care. She recognized that voice—its dark timbre, its careful rhythms, and—unmistakably—its patronizing inflections.

Jacen.

Alema focused all her attention on that voice, trying to pinpoint its source. The fog and the pool worked against her, muffling Jacen's words and drowning them out with gurgles. But eventually she grew attuned enough that she shut out everything else and began to understand what he was saying.

". . . let me worry about Reh'mwa and the Bothans." Jacen sounded irritated. "Leaving the Well was foolish. I can't protect you here."

The only response Alema heard was a long liquid purl, but Jacen responded as though he had been spoken to.

"That's ridiculous. I'd *know* if I had been followed. Not even Bothan assassins are that good."

Ever so carefully, Alema used the Force to clear the fog

between herself and Jacen. She was running the risk that Jacen would feel her drawing on the Force, but she would have only one shot, and she needed to see her target. Besides, Jacen was likely too preoccupied with his conversation to notice such a subtle disturbance.

After another long purl, Jacen's voice grew concerned. "*Inside* the building? You're sure?"

There was a short gurgle.

"Of course I'd care," Jacen replied testily. He snapped his lightsaber off his belt. "You're the Guard's most valuable asset. Without you, we couldn't track a *tenth* of the terrorist cells we do."

The fog cleared, and Alema was astonished to see Jacen addressing a fleshy black monstrosity that had come up from the slime. The thing was so large, she could not even tell how much of it she was seeing. Its eye had a pupil the size of a Sullustan's head, its tentacles were as big around as Alema herself, and—like everything in this part of the undercity—its appearance was distinctly Yuuzhan Vong.

The creature blinked . . . and thrashed its tentacles across the surface.

"I *can't* ban Bothans from the planet," Jacen replied. "That would push Bothawui straight into Corellia's camp."

Alema began to suspect what this creature was. While Jacen had been held captive by the Yuuzhan Vong, he had supposedly struck up a friendship with the World Brain, a sort of genetic master controller that the invaders had created to oversee the remaking of Coruscant. Before escaping, Jacen had persuaded it to thwart its masters' efforts, to cooperate only partially in their efforts to reshape Coruscant. Later, during the final days of the war, he had convinced his "friend" to switch sides and help the Galactic Alliance retake the planet. Now he was using it to spy on Corellian terrorists.

Clever boy.

Alema raised the blowgun to her lips and, using the Force to hide the dart, expelled her breath.

The dart had just left the blowgun when, somewhere above Alema and just to her right, a throaty female voice called out, "Jacen!"

Jacen spun, igniting his lightsaber as he turned. But the dart was tiny, swift, and still hidden in the Force, and Alema realized with a bolt of satisfaction that his blade was not rising to block. Even better, he was turning in her direction.

Then Jacen cried out and flew backward, as though hurled by an invisible hand, and the dart flashed past, eliciting a liquid roar of pain as it disappeared into the enormous eye of the World Brain.

Alema was astonished, dismayed, angry—but she was not stunned. She had been in too many death fights to let herself be paralyzed by *any* surprise. She pivoted toward the voice that had alerted Jacen.

Five meters across the Well's edge—and one balcony up—stood the fog-blurred silhouette of a thin woman in a robe. Her arm was still extended toward the slime pool, leaving no doubt that she had been the one who Force-hurled Jacen to safety.

Lumiya.

As Alema backed away from the balcony's edge, Lumiya pointed toward her. "There, Jacen!"

Alema turned to run, but the fog suddenly flashed blue, and a tremendous crack sounded from behind her. In the next moment she found herself sliding across the floor, snakes of Force lightning dancing across her anguished body until she finally passed from her attacker's line of sight.

Alema did not understand what had just happened—Had Lumiya really *warned* Jacen? Had he been the one who hurled the Force lightning at her?—but there was no time to figure it out. She forced her cramped muscles to drag her into the nearest corridor, then rose to a knee and drew a Force shadow over herself. She reached into her pocket for another dart . . . and that was when she realized the Force lightning had made her drop her blowgun.

Jacen alit on the edge of the balcony, so obscured by yellow fog that he was barely more than a silhouette. But he was burning with a rage that Alema had not thought possible for him, an anger so fierce that it warmed the Force like fire. He ignited his lightsaber, casting a green reflection that made his eyes burn with murderous intent. His gaze fell on the blowgun, and he started forward.

An ear-piercing screech rang out from the Well of the World Brain, then a dozen black tentacles rose out of the fog. They began to thrash about wildly, gashing themselves on the balcony and spraying the walls with black blood. Jacen's eyes darkened to the color of black holes, and he started forward, and his gaze shifted to the corridor where Alema was hiding.

Though Alema knew she lacked the power to kill Jacen with one attack—and that she would not have time for two—she opened herself to the Force, preparing to blast Jacen with lightning.

Then a second silhouette—this one a slender woman with a veiled face—dropped out of the fog, landing on the edge of the balcony and dancing past the thrashing tentacles as only someone trained in Force acrobatics could.

Alema extended her hand. Lumiya was *not* going to steal her kill.

But instead of attacking Jacen, Lumiya merely caught him by the arm and spun him toward the thrashing tentacles.

"Jacen, those are convulsions," she said. "We have to slow the poison *now,* or your spy is dead."

Alema's jaw dropped. Lumiya's tone was one of command . . . a Master to a student.

"But the assassin—"

"Would you rather have vengeance, or preserve an intelligence asset?"

"This isn't about vengeance." Jacen looked toward the corridor where Alema was hiding. "It's about justice. We can't let the assassin—"

"The assassin is only the tool," Lumiya interrupted again. "It's the hand wielding her we need to stop. It's Reh'mwa and his lieutenants."

Jacen continued to stare at Alema's corridor, his fury and desire to kill pouring into the Force.

Lumiya released Jacen's arm, pulling her hand away in disgust. "I can see it was a mistake to pick you. Go on." She waved him toward Alema's hiding place. "You are a servant to your emotions, not a master to them."

"This has nothing to do with my emotions."

"It has *everything* to do with your emotions," Lumiya countered. "You're angry because your friend was hurt, and now you can think of nothing but bringing the attacker to justice. You're hopeless."

Lumiya's last comment seemed to sting Jacen. He continued to glare into the corridor for a moment, then glanced away long enough to summon her blowgun.

"Tell your masters we're coming," he said, pointing the blowgun in Alema's general direction. "This won't go unanswered."

Jacen turned away, then he and Lumiya danced past the thrashing tentacles of the World Brain and dropped into the fog. Even after they were gone, Alema remained in hiding, too shocked to move.

Jacen Solo, apprenticing with a Sith.

Had the galaxy gone mad?

STAR WARS™

LEGACY OF THE FORCE

Read each book in the series!

Star Wars: New Jedi Order: Dark Journey

Elaine Cunnigham

The dazzling Star Wars space adventure continues in this latest instalment from *The New Jedi Order* series.

Following intense personal loss, Jaina Solo descends to the dark sode, determined to take her revenge on the Yuuzhan Vong. In the process, she learns something new about how to fight the alien invaders, but she must also remember that revenge is not the way of the Jedi – even when it seems the only way to fight the enemy.

arrow books

Star Wars: New Jedi Order: Dark Tide Onslaught

Michael Stackpole

Twenty-one years after the destruction of Darth Vader and the Emperor, the Star Wars galaxy has been hit by a threat more deadly than anything that has gone before.

Now, in a climate of mistrust – especially of the Jedi – Leia cannot convince the New Republic that the threat may not be over, even as the next wave of alien warships are entering the galaxy . . . It is up to Leia, Luke and the Solo kids – Jedi Knights all – to defend the Outer Rim planets from invasion!

arrow books

Star Wars: New Jedi Order: Star By Star

Troy Denning

Written by *New York Times* bestselling author Troy Denning, *Star By Star* is the thrilling heart of darkness of the *New Jedi Order*. This is a must-read for every fan of *Star Wars* fiction and the *New Jedi Order* series in particular!

It is a dark time for the New Republic. The Yuuzhan Vong, despite some recent losses, continue to advance into the Core, and continue their relentless hunt for the Jedi. Now, in a desperate act of courage, Anakin Solo leads a Jedi strike force into the heart of Yuuzhan Vong territory, where he hopes to destroy a major Vong anti-Jedi weapon. There, with his brother and sister at his side, he will come face to face with his destiny – as the New Republic, still fighting the good fight, will come face to face with theirs . . .

arrow books